Finding Harmony

LINDSEY CATANZARO

SR
Stillwater
River

First Stillwater River Publications Edition

ISBN-10: 1-946-30030-6
ISBN-13: 978-1-946-30030-0

1 2 3 4 5 6 7 8 9 10
Written by Lindsey Catanzaro
Cover design by Dawn M. Porter
Published by Stillwater River Publications, Glocester, RI, USA.

Dedication

Thank you to my family for all of your support and encouragement.
I couldn't have done it without you. A special thanks to my Granni,
for listening and guiding me through this experience.
This book is dedicated to all of you.

Finding Harmony

Part I

Dissonance

1918

Germany
The Pianist

To put it in musical terms, my life was an ongoing train of a chromatic scale.

"Go on, go on! Don't stop unless you see a rest on the staff." Those words were repeated to me over and over, starting when I was nine years old, right before I played my first concert. They were engraved into my head. Though they did not encourage me as one would think. They bound my fingers to the keys.

At first, I wanted to be famous. What child wouldn't? The attention, the people, the swarms of reporters. Interviewers lined up at my feet to question me, or to ask me to play for different events. My older sister, Lieselotte, loved it. She got to dress up and be seen by the crowds, smiling and laughing dramatically. She basked in the glory of my fame, and I let her. Being the only sunflower in a field was not always fun.

My younger brother, Otto, however, was the opposite. As I got older, I realized just how neglected he had become. My parents paid little attention to him. Their main focus was to get me onstage. Always. Wherever we went, it always seemed as if my mother was trying to show me off to everyone. Like a prize or a medal that she didn't know how she won. Though I wasn't aware of this when I was younger. I thought myself ordinary.

Looking at me, I was an average German boy with dark hair and dark eyes. I was scrawny. I did not look like a prodigy. And frankly, I did not act like one, either. But, seat me at a piano, and my fingers seemed to sprout wings. My brain aged far beyond human comprehension in the few seconds of silence as my fingers hovered above the keys. Those seconds of silence gave me my power. I was born with the ability to play, something no one—not even I—could ever grasp.

Going onstage started to become my daily routine. Before bed, I'd often go back and recall the moment when I stepped out from behind the curtains. Those few seconds of transition, from a foolish child to a master pianist. People would clap at the sight of me. I would smile and wave to the audience, feeling jittery and excited, running about with bursts of adrenaline. That didn't last long, though. I was yelled at afterwards on how I was not being professional enough. So, when I went onstage from that point on, I would look straight ahead, not smiling. I only stared at the piano that sat and awaited me. Every time, out of the corner of my eye, I would catch the quick wave of my brother's hand. His enthralled face lifted my spirits because he actually enjoyed my music. I wished I had simply waved back.

Everyone else seemed to envy me. They saw me as a word. They saw me as an age. But my brother didn't. He simply saw me as his older brother. And what do you do when you see someone you know? Well, if they are far away from you, you just wave. That's all you can do. I couldn't have been farther away from Otto, even as he sat watching me in the front row.

At fifteen, I could play almost any piece that was put in front of me. Not only could I play, but I could feel every note, every vibration. I was my own metronome. Even the piano shook when I played. I did not realize that the shaking was from fear. I had heard a quote describing how a piano reflects its player's true feelings, but I never made the connection. I was quiet, obedient, and disciplined, unlike most of the other teenagers I encountered. Papa made me sit down and practice until my hands were numb. He drilled me over and over in my Opa's name. "Don't stop unless you see a rest on the staff," he'd repeat. He'd hover over my shoulder, yelling out every time my finger even slipped the slightest. I had given up arguing. No one in my family had a job anymore. I was the one who brought in the money and the publicity. They all leaned on me, without even realizing. But it didn't bother me. Because at this point in time, I had truly *enjoyed* playing.

♪ ♪ ♪

A few days after my twentieth birthday, I was scheduled to play in Munich, which was a surprise, because usually I played out of the country. But it was right where I lived. I was extremely glad because I wasn't fond of going on boats after the tragic sinking of the *Titanic*. We arrived early, as usual, so I could get a feel of the piano. As I played, I stared out at the empty seats, knowing that in a short hour, each one would occupy an eager person.

"Alright, you're on in two minutes, Leo," my mutti told me as we gathered backstage. She sat next to me and rubbed my shoulder quickly. My hands were folded to keep them from trembling. My leg bounced without my control. Even my heart raced, which never used to happen to me when I was younger. The older I got, the more nervous and anxious I became. Trying to break the habit was useless.

"Good luck, Leo!" My sister patted my slicked-back hair. She was in a frilly-looking frock. A dark shade coated her lips from the new lipstick she had bought. Mutti despised it. She didn't like the newer fashions. I found it hard to believe that Lieselotte was twenty-two. She looked much older. My whole family surrounded me, looking at me like my anxiety was a show. I was silent, hoping to gain confidence and power if I focused.

"You make sure you perfect that arpeggio, you hear? You know the drill. The faster you go, the more you'll trip up. You always rush it. Take it just a notch slower. And on measure two hundred four—"

"I can't do this," I heard myself say.

"Aw, don't be such a sore sport, Leo. You say that *every time*." My sister sighed, throwing her head back dramatically. She had no idea how hard it was. All she had to do was sit and look pretty backstage. I bit my lip when I realized I was about to blurt that out.

"Go on," Papa said sternly. "Just remember what I taught you." His dark eyes reflected mine. But they did not see me. They saw only a student. A student who was drilled so hard because of immediate relation.

I looked at Otto. He stood off to the side, leaning against a wall, observing our conversation. He looked like me when I was younger, except he had bright eyes and glasses. He was tall and lanky, and he grew like a weed shooting toward the sun. At age sixteen, he was taller than me. He would have made a fine footman in England. Papa always told him that. But he did not require work because I was the provider in our family.

He nodded at me, hoping to encourage me. However, that day, something snapped inside me.

"I can't do this." My hands were sweaty. Playing with sweaty hands never went well. My fingertips would linger the slightest on every key, as if they were stuck. I stared down at my lap, not daring to see my papa's reaction. "I'm not—"

"Come with me," Papa spoke softly. I never got to finish. His voice was like the hissing of a snake. So quiet. So toxic. One bite, and the poison would infect the victim instantly.

I followed him to the staircase, awaiting my fate. Once you walked up the stairs, and the curtain opened, you were practically on the stage. We stood uneasily right at the bottom.

"You listen to me." He was right in my face, almost snarling. "You've got Lord only knows how many people waiting to hear you play out there." He jabbed his finger in the direction of the stage. "You don't just say 'I can't.' This is your life; this is our life. Now you get your wimpy ass out there and do what you love to do. This is how our family gets by, Leonardo. By you. You remember that." His voice sent shivers up my spine. I was familiar with that face. Yes, I saw it all too often. That look of authority. I was never good enough. Opa would have never treated me like this.

"Go," he demanded.

I carefully walked by him, like one footstep would throw him into an uproar of rage. Up the stairs I went. Each one I climbed felt steeper, like climbing a mountain. Sweat beaded my forehead. I had never been this nervous before. I reached the top and took a deep breath. I could not do it. Something seemed to be locked up inside me, and I couldn't find the key no matter where I looked.

"Leonardo," Papa called. His voice was cold, like always. It never seemed to thaw; not from love, not from kindness, not from anything.

I turned and faced him. "Straighten up, boy," he demanded. "You go out there with the posture of a soldier, am I clear? Or that will be our next lesson. Put your head up. Put your heart into it."

"Yes, sir," I replied. His words meant nothing to me now. They were just added to the collection of insults. I was unbreakable on the outside; a diamond. So hard that only another diamond could make a mark. His words could not penetrate my skin. I heard them all too often to actually take them to heart.

The moment I stepped out from behind the curtain, the audience went silent. My head was held up, but my heart had fallen. How could I put my heart into a performance when it was sinking deeper and deeper away from the surface? I felt hundreds upon hundreds of pairs of eyes calculating my every move as I walked over to the piano. The stage went dim, and the spotlight followed me. It made me slightly edgy. I still didn't quite trust electricity.

The piano was a beautiful ebony Steinway. I had played it a few times before, so it was familiar to me. The top was open, ready for the sound to explode out of it. The sight was comforting.

All I heard was the clicking of my own shoes. I stood in front of the piano and bowed. Claps and whistles echoed through the hall. My family had taken their seats right up front. My insides were tight, so tight that I felt like I was slowly snapping, like a rubber band. Nerves got the best of me as I stood wide-eyed in front of everyone, unable to move. There were a few muffled laughs. I smiled meekly. Quickly, I tried to recover, sitting down on the piano bench and trying to act as if nothing happened.

I sat up perfectly straight, like my spine had been replaced by a wooden board. I rolled up my sleeves and breathed. My fingers hovered centimeters above the keys but when I tried to play, they continued to hover, as if paralyzed in midair. I could feel everyone on the edges of their seats. I could almost hear their voices in their heads, screaming out in wonder why the pianist wouldn't play. I wondered the same thing. I tried again, but I was still frozen. I couldn't hear the song.

Without knowing what I was doing, I stood up. I had not even played a single note. My breathing became slower. I walked over to the side of the piano, and closed the enormous lid like it was made of fragile glass. I bowed again, and without a word, exited the stage. An uproar of confused voices echoed behind me. The voices sounded like jumbled moans, or the deep song of a whale.

Backstage, Papa came forward as soon as he saw me, completely infuriated. I saw Mutti take my sister and brother out for a smoke, herding them away from a possibly ugly scene. It was then that I began to resent her. She too was afraid. The thought hit me like never before.

"What the hell did you do?" He grabbed a fistful of my suit jacket and scolded me over and over. "Why? Why? That's your thing! You're a pianist, Leonardo! You play the piano! You love playing! All these people came to hear you play! I don't understand you. You are a disappointment. An utter disappointment. A disgrace! What would Opa think?" he blurted out forcefully, unclenching my jacket. He continued to rant, pacing like a caged animal. In reality, *I* was the caged animal.

"I can't play anymore. I'm tired of my life *revolving* around... around a chunk of wood and some ivory! Like the piano is some sort of planet that I just... *orbit* around. It means nothing to me if I don't enjoy it." I looked down as I spoke, letting my words seep in. I knew I shouldn't have opened my mouth. Why did I say that? I instantly wanted to take it back. I could picture Opa's crushed face. He was the one who had realized I had such talent. He took it upon himself to teach me. That is... until he passed away.

"How dare you say that? You play on pianos that have the same value as pearls and diamonds *themselves*! Don't you have any concept of what that means? You ungrateful...." I never heard him finish. In a flash, his hand whipped across my left cheek. I did not move. Not even a flinch. The stinging lasted long after we were taken back home to our estate. My estate. After all, I was the only one who had earned it.

"This war is financially killing many people, Leonardo. You should think about your family and support us as best as you can! You wouldn't want us living on the streets, would you?" His eyes flashed like bolts of lightning. I heard Papa's voice in my head as we drove home.

"No," was all I had said.

♪ ♪ ♪

Still, Mutti and Papa insisted that I attempt to do another concert. Papa did not insist. Insist is the incorrect word. He *demanded*, without question. After all, I already had one booked in America that was coming up. I feared for my life because of the boat we would have to take. There was nothing I could do. I dreaded it. I began to realize that they only wanted me to play for their own selfish benefits. Mutti liked to boast. Papa liked the money. Lieselotte liked the attention. That's what they wanted this whole time. They did not give a damn about who I was. They just focused on what I did and what they could get out of it. My life had struck a minor chord. A sad, dreadful, minor chord, which rattled my tear ducts.

I remembered pulling Otto aside one night, after dinner later that year. Everyone was depressed from Germany having surrendered. Everyone except Otto. It took a lot to break his spirits.

"Karl, can you excuse us quickly? I want to talk to my brother for a moment," I said to Otto's friend. I had to make sure no one was around.

"One moment, Karl. Before you go." Otto sat forward on his chair and adjusted his glasses. "I don't suppose you have a cigarette on you. I had my last one this morning."

"It's your lucky day. I happen to have a full tin of them." He walked over to where Otto sat and gingerly unlatched it, revealing a cloned lineup of cigarettes.

"Great. Thanks." Otto plucked one out and lit it. A halo of smoke escaped his lips. "Leo, you should have one. It helps the stress," he suggested as Karl left us. He tapped the side of it with his finger and let out another breath of smoke.

"No, I will be fine without that God-awful smell clinging to my clothes," I responded, folding and unfolding my hands. With a deep breath, I launched into a speech.

"I know this is quite sudden, but I need you to listen." I paused, trying to configure words in my head. How could I tell him? I figured the best way was to be quick and blunt. I took a breath. "I am quitting being a performer—"

"What? Brother, what nonsense are you even speaking of?" He almost laughed. "You cannot just *quit*—"

"Yes, I can. I'm doing more than that."

At first, it was as if he was waiting for me to crack the punchline of a joke. He didn't know how to take it. The confusion seeped away. Otto stared at me in horror, like he had just been informed that the sky he saw his whole life was not actually blue. Though, everything always looked the same to me. His cigarette hung limply between his lips.

"I'm leaving early tomorrow morning to go to England. Mutti always said she liked it there when she was growing up. Remember? She said she enjoyed the frequent rain. So that is where I will be and that is where I intend to stay." Every word I said punched him. His eyebrows furrowed deeply and he looked at the floor.

"How? How are you going to get there, and why the hell *England?* You're a *traitor!* It doesn't matter that it rains all the time and they have the best tea! We just ended the war with them! You're completely insane! And… and why… I don't understand, Leo. Maybe it *is* possible to quit being a pianist. But you are not *just* a pianist. You're a prodigy! You were born that way and to quit and… give up that gift you were given is like giving up *yourself,*" he argued, pressing his point forth.

"That's right. I intend to make a new person out of myself. I am going to take a boat to England. Piano is not a part of me anymore. I will work as a servant or some type of laborer like every other man in the world. And I will live in a small village or town, not in a big estate like we do now."

"Boat?" he stuttered, baffled by the thought. "Leo, you *hate* boats!" He stood up, making gestures as he talked. "You despise the waves because you get seasick and—"

"Looks like I'll have to learn to enjoy it," I simply replied. Our eyes met, though he didn't recognize me anymore. His clear eyes were now clouded and foggy, unable to see the full picture. Silence wound around us like an inaudible current of wind. The ticking of the grandfather clock made me shiver. Like a metronome, it kept the beat of each passing second and reminded me how trapped I was.

Tick.

Tick.

Tick.

"What about the rest of us? Mutti, Papa, me…?" Otto gulped. His eyes scanned the room. For the first time, he did not take every little detail and intricate design for granted. He absorbed his surroundings like a sponge. I could read his face like a piece of sheet music. The house he thought he would get married and die in, would no longer be his to live in. And it was my fault. My one act of selfishness would ruin the lives of my whole family. But it was my turn now. I was sick of being the crutch. I was tired of being on the losing side.

I reached into the pocket of my dinner jacket and pulled out two envelopes I had prepared. Otto sat back down across from me, casting more smoke into the air like a train that couldn't come to a stop.

"This is for everyone. Mainly you, Mutti, and Papa, because Lieselotte has her own home. But if she needs, this is hers too." I handed him the envelope. He clutched it in his hand, hearing the many coins clinking inside. "Mutti and Papa will have to find a new house. That will be a big help to them when the time comes," I assured him.

"I still can't believe this. Leo, you're making a big mistake. You are literally throwing every piece of your past life away like garbage. And with the Spanish flu and the end of the war...."

"It wasn't *my* life, Otto. I had thought it was when I was younger, but it's not." I took a breath and passed him the second envelope. "This one is for you. Save it or buy something for yourself. You might find yourself missing something when you no longer live here."

He took it slowly, staring at the crispy pale paper. "I'll try to save it. Maybe I can finally go on a trip to Greece if I save up enough. But what I'll be missing I cannot buy back. We'll all be missing something we can't buy back." He eyed me seriously.

"Go take a girl to the fair or something, then." I managed to smile a slight bit.

Otto's grin looked painful. "Speaking of girls, does Annelise know of this?"

"No. No one knows of it but you. And it will stay that way until I leave tomorrow morning," I enforced, sitting back against the sofa. I was putting all my trust in my brother who I scarcely seemed to know. "When I get settled somewhere, I'll write to you."

"That doesn't sound like the right thing to do. You'll leave Mutti and Papa in shock and Annelise with a broken heart. How could you leave her hanging like that? It seems quite cruel after you have been together for two years. You know, her mother and father really wanted you two to marry. You got along very well, if I may say. I liked her a lot." His eyes searched my face for some soft spot, but found none.

"Otto, I *mean* it. You *can't* tell her. It will make her more upset if you do. It will make her feel as if... as if she wasn't good enough. I know too well how her mind operates, and none of this was her fault anyway. If it was probable, I would bring her with me. But trying to travel together as an unmarried couple is highly looked down upon, and I wouldn't want to ruin her chances or her reputation."

"You care in the coldest ways," he responded sadly, putting the cigarette to his lips once more.

To that, I could not respond. After a moment, he spoke again.

"What should I tell Mutti and Papa tomorrow?" He seemed hopeful, like I'd have a lengthy message of farewells, sending all my love.

I took it into consideration, looking up at the ceiling in thought. "Tell them that I am no longer afraid of boats."

The next morning, I faced my fear. And I waved to Otto as I drove to the harbor.

England

The Violinist

My tears skidded down my cheeks like crystals, dousing the fire on my daughter's skin as I gripped her feeble hand. My life lessons of control and self-dignity vanished like water vapor into thin air. I did not care who saw me. Not even my maid. My daughter's life was being stolen away in front of my eyes at only a year old. Her blonde curls were flattened from the days she spent with her head on a pillow. This was her third day of being completely bedridden from the Spanish flu. Her eyes were only half-open, like a crescent moon, and her cheeks were flushed. Crusted blood was at the base of her nose from all the times her nose had bled. She looked so peaceful. So oblivious. It seemed impossible to believe there was a battle going on inside her frail body. Sometimes she would try to mumble or cry, but it was no good. She was now half-delirious.

I stared up at the celling in agony and utter helplessness. Someone had to save her. God would come through. He wouldn't let my beautiful girl die. How could he? I was in complete denial.

"Ruby, my darling, I'm right here," I whispered, caressing her small hand. "Momma and Poppa are here," I assured. The doctor crouched beside me, dabbing a damp cloth on her forehead. My husband sat on the other side of the bed, seemingly staring into a bottomless void. I watched him release a tense breath. He looked over at me and then to Doctor Morris. Doctor Morris caught his eye.

"Mr. and Mrs. Bolton, I have to ask that you leave little Ruby in peace. I apologize ever so deeply, but this illness can spread very quickly." His small eyes sank as he spoke. He was a small round man with a curled mustache and glasses. He was a friend of my uncle.

"Doctor Morris," I almost yelled with the amount of despair inside me, "how dare you tell me to *leave* my—my *dying* daughter when she needs me—" The shaking worsened as I spoke. I crossed my ankles and attempted to contain myself, biting my tongue and twisting my hands in my lap. "I apologize. I—"

"Stell," my husband Roy said, lifting his eyes away from Ruby. I did not want to listen to him. Now was not the time for the calm and consoling talks I knew him for.

"Roy, I beg of you, do not—I repeat—do *not*," I started, lips trembling and tears racing each other down my face. I never got to finish because he interrupted again.

"Estella." The crack in his voice silenced me, like the desperate call of a crying songbird. I forced myself to look at his face. His chiseled jaw was stiff and the color of his eyes that I adored so much had vanished into blankness.

"What?" I asked. His eyes wandered to the ground and he stood up uneasily. "I daresay! Tell me my darling!" Without being aware, my grip tightened on Ruby's cold hand. I stared hard at him, a frown etched onto my salty face.

"I can't—I can't be here anymore. This... is overwhelming. My heart is in pieces." He placed a finger on each of his eyes, attempting to keep himself together. His voice was thick. "Forgive me, but I must go." He walked out, head hung in grief. His eyes were glossy; I could tell even as he looked down at the carpet. A shadow of depression followed him as he left. Then, the realization hit me.

I tilted my head and gazed at Ruby's body. The life in my eyes died. That's all that was left to her. Just an empty body, a mere shell. No breath or soul to fill up its insides anymore. My voice caught in my throat, and I let out a sound I didn't know existed. A shrill, wailing sound that only death can bring forth. I covered my mouth with my hand, but no good was done. My child. My only child, was gone.

My teeth rattled my skull as I trembled and let out a painful sob. I felt like two different people: one who dared to scream and make a scene, and one who wanted to be crushed into nothingness. I hardly had a purpose now. I was a mother no more. My maid, Della, rushed over to me and held my shoulders. I didn't even care that she was pretending to give her condolences. I knew she wasn't truly fond of me. She had just needed a job. That did not matter now, of course. I greedily took all the comfort I could get. Her caring enough to pretend was good enough for me.

Part II

Polyphony

1919

England

The Violinist

Two months later in January, our lives changed once more due to the flu. My older brother Charlie arrived at my little cottage at ten o'clock at night, with a ghastly face. The late December snow covered his hat and rested on his shoulders. His arrival was a complete surprise to me, unless Roy had asked him to come. Though he did not mention anything of Roy as he entered. He took off his hat and held it at his side.

"Good evening, Estella, sorry to interrupt. I hate to be bothersome. I know you weren't expecting *me*. And never mind at this hour."

"Charlie, don't make me laugh." I closed the door behind him. That in itself was a joke. I couldn't remember the last time I laughed. I was very perplexed by his sudden appearance. Lately, he had been distant from the family. "I am never busy. There's nothing for you to interrupt except maybe sleep. But I don't sleep often." I gestured to an armchair and we sat across from each other. "Would you care for something to eat? Or some tea? Should I ask Della to light a fire?"

"Oh, no. That's quite alright. I just… have some news." He gulped and fidgeted. "Very important news indeed."

"Estella, who in the name of God is here at this hour?" Suddenly, I could hear Roy's footsteps coming nearer, pounding like an elephant's down the stairway. Now, he stood in the entryway of the living room in his maroon robe. His blonde hair was disheveled from sleep and his eyes were heavy and dark around the edges, resembling mine. "Oh goodness. Excuse my apparel, Mr. Breaker. I did not expect you. Of course, you are welcome here at *any* hour if you wish," he backtracked, yawning and standing up straighter. "Is there anything I can do for you?"

"I'm afraid I'm just here to speak to Estella, but I appreciate it. You also forget that you do not always have to call me Mr. Breaker. We *are* brothers-in-law, you know." Charlie put on his best smile, and gave Roy a respectful nod. I could see the pain behind his lips. The amount of muscle work that it actually took for Charlie to smile was equivalent to a boy trying to lift a horse.

"I know, I know. 'Tis pure habit I suppose." He took a big breath, shifting his weight to one foot. "Well, I shall leave you to it then. Until next time, my good fellow." Roy nodded back at him and disappeared down the hallway and up the stairs without even looking my way. He hadn't even bothered to say goodnight. I hadn't expected him to. Lately, my stomach knotted every time I laid eyes on him.

Charlie waited a few seconds to make sure Roy was out of earshot, and then continued. He leaned forward, resting his elbows on his knees, sorting his many thoughts.

"You know my good friend, Lord Hampton, surely?" he inquired, looking up from his hands and searching my face for recognition. I knew the name most definitely. In fact, I recalled meeting the man quite a few times and even going to his wedding long ago. He was fifteen years older than Charlie.

"Why, yes. I most certainly do." I furrowed my eyebrows, attempting to see where this was going.

"Of course… what a stupid question." He shook his head, as if trying to clear his mind. "This is what you may not recall. The woman he married died during childbirth long ago, but the child lived. A son called Joseph. To be correct, *Master* Joseph because he would inherit the estate one day. Anyway, I felt it was my duty to check on him because Lord Hampton was drafted into the war, so…."

"Oh, so *that* is why you never came to dinner. I invited you a countless amount of times. You claimed you were never around."

"Yes, precisely. If Momma or Poppa ever found out I was taking care of him, I fear I would have been chided until the day I die. Lord Hampton had made me Master Joseph's godfather, and when he didn't come back after the war was over, I assumed the worst. In the following weeks, I received a telegram, informing me of the news I had been dreading. It claimed his body had finally been found." He struggled to talk now. "But I never told Master Joseph what had happened to his father. I couldn't find the heart to say it."

"That is very noble of you to take care of the child, if I may say. And I'm so sorry about Lord Hampton. I don't know why you didn't inform me sooner! If you ever want someone to talk to about it, I can help." I took a shaky breath. I tried to continue, but he dismissed my offer with a wave of his hand and changed the subject back to his care of Master Joseph.

"They would have thought otherwise. Claiming it was a job for a nanny, not a grown man of age twenty-five. Truth was, he did in fact have a nanny there to take care of him. But he lived in that enormous estate, without either of his parents. I presume it was lonely. I pitied him and tried to visit often. He was a good lad." Charlie looked at the stone-cold fireplace.

"Was? What do you mean, *was?*" I asked, becoming nervous. I tugged at the faded sweater on my shoulders. He hesitated before responding.

"Today," he began. Seeing my brother resist breaking down was one of the hardest things to watch. He restarted his sentence. "Today, I received an urgent letter from Master Joseph's nanny, saying he was vitally ill and that she couldn't contact a doctor." He reached inside his suit pocket and pulled out the letter. It dated back three days ago. "I went and visited today, as soon as I got the news… but… but it was too late. The nanny was in tears when I walked through the door." Not an ounce of emotion came through his voice. He still seemed to be in shock.

"Oh, Charlie…." I leaned forward and reached for his hand, but he pulled away.

"Estella, you are good to me but I do not want your pity. That is not my point of coming here at this time of night."

"Then do tell, but I pray you it is not more bad news." My eyes wanted to give in to sleep, but my brain was rather active, considering the time.

"It is rather... shocking news. 'Tis only bad if you are seemingly fond of your home." He spoke in the form of a puzzle, pushing back all of his sadness.

"I am fond of my home, of course. I adore it. But I do not understand your riddles, Charlie."

"Then allow me to enlighten you." He folded his hands, voice trembling. "Lord Hampton's estate, or should I say Hampton Court Castle, and his fortune was willed to Master Joseph. All of it, every last pound. The castle, the land, everything." He sat back in the chair and waited for me to nod to go on. "And, as you know, Master Joseph... has deceased as well, so he does not inherit any of it." His eyes cast to the floor, just thinking of it. I easily related. A day never went by where a shadow of grief didn't get tangled up in my pathway.

"Yes," I breathed, still not comprehending. I recalled seeing Master Joseph when he was young. Just once when he was perhaps five years old. Unfortunately, his face had long faded from my mind. It was hard to believe that he too was gone. Another innocent child consumed.

"Master Joseph was Lord Hampton's only heir," Charlie continued. "He was an only child, as was Lord Hampton himself. They were not a big family, as you can presume, so Lord Hampton's will was not very grand. Master Joseph, obviously was the first name written on the will to inherit Hampton Court Castle, but there was one below it, for... *precautions*... for lack of better term. Lord Hampton was not a fool of a man when it came to his finances."

I was not yet lost, only hopelessly wondering why he was going through Lord Hampton's family history with me at ten-thirty at night. My eyes wandered to the worn wood on the armrest of my chair. Surely it would give an unlucky someone a splinter.

"Estella." Charlie lifted my chin with his two fingers. Our eyes were locked now. His black hair had grown from the last time I saw him. Up close, his thick eyebrows were shades lighter than his hair. Even though his features strongly resembled our Poppa, his eyes supposedly resembled our grandmomma's who had passed on. A light, airy blue color with flecks of yellow. "Estella, I beg you. Please listen."

That got my attention. He put his hand back down at his side and took a deep breath. "That name was mine."

My mind crashed and my mouth hung ajar in shock. This had to be a prank was my first thought. A low and cruel joke. I could not come up with the words to express myself.

"What? I—"

"I am Lord Breaker of Hampton Court Castle," he stated and continued on before I could muster a word. "Due to the immense number of rooms and ample amount of space that no man of our social class could even dream of, I would like to invite my family to stay there with me. Meaning you, Roy, Momma, Poppa, the twins, Grandpoppa, and even some of our cousins. I could not bear to live alone in such a grand castle of a home."

My mind was still too disarrayed to think clearly. Evidently, the idea was simply absurd. My entire family living in Hampton Court? Just the thought made me question reality.

"Well then, Lord Breaker…." I stuttered, wide-eyed as a doe. "Then you best be finding yourself a wife!" I exclaimed, feeling as if I was soaring above the clouds. He had actually laughed at my comment. We all knew that Charlie was very… selective… when it came to a mistress. Momma had been trying to get him married for years. His pathetic excuse of a laugh was engraved in my head. A mere chuckle if I were to be generous.

It amazed me that through his grief and doubt, he could find happiness in the most foolish of things. But even so, knowing he was emotionally alright was enough to make me go to sleep smiling for the next couple days. Now, I had no reason to dream. Soon, I would be living one.

♪ ♪ ♪

Today was the last day in my home. It looked rather bare and empty, as trees are during winter. Charlie had already moved into Hampton Court and had been living there for almost two months now, getting to know the servants and maids. He had written me a letter with all the details, inviting Roy and me to move in on the fourth of June, which indeed was today's date. Just three days after my twentieth birthday. He wrote that he would be sending a chauffeur to our cottage to pick us up, as well as our suitcases and bags. It was quite thrilling. I had never been driven by a chauffeur.

Della was also accompanying us, for my brother was kind enough to offer her a job there among the sixteen other servants, so she would not lose her position. Sometimes I found it hard to imagine that Della had emotion, but when I gave her the news, she couldn't have seemed more honored.

"This is exquisite. Never in my life could I have imagined going to live among the first class," Roy exclaimed, placing his hat on his head. I was surprised to hear him speak so openly. The air was brisk, making the trees surrounding our home sway and whisper. I could only imagine the secrets they knew. Roy handed the chauffeur his last suitcase, which was strapped to the back of the car. Then, the chauffeur opened the door for me. It was an unexpected gesture I would have to learn to get used to.

"Roy, you are mistaken, darling. We won't be living among the first class, we will *be* the first class," I corrected him.

"Very true. I stand corrected, which makes this process even more of a child's fantasy. Grand dinners, formal clothing, enormous rooms, and servants waiting on us hand and foot. I think I can quit my job," he concluded happily, sitting in the car beside me. Della got in the car behind ours.

"I suppose so." It was the first real conversation we had since Ruby's death. It seemed to sever our bond. I still wore mourning clothes: a black bombazine dress trimmed with crepe, and a pillbox hat. My spirits weren't completely shot down, but it sincerely depended on the day. Often, I found myself searching for a purpose. No longer did I have a child to look after, or to teach, or sing to sleep. When I dreamed, the only color I saw was red. A brilliant sparkling red that mortal eyes dare not imagine. The official mourning color was black, but specifically to me, it was red. Always red.

"Estella? Estella, are you even listening to me? Ugh, never mind then." Roy's deep voice brought me back from the prison of my head. He turned his whole body away from me, staring out the window, and exulting his disapproval.

"What? Why, yes. I am, really," I assured, making an effort to pay attention and turning to face him.

He tilted his head down at me, seeming doubtful. The blonde stubble on his face looked golden when the sun shone on his skin through the window. Ruby's hair had been the same color. He rested his head back against the luxurious seat, and grumbled something to himself. "Then allow me to repeat myself for the *third* time." His raised his voice ever so slightly, rattling the windows.

"I was simply wondering if you remembered to pack my extra suit. It was in the closet to the left in our room. The light brown plaid one? It was sort of tucked under the shelf."

I took a moment to respond. "I... I don't think I did. I packed the blue one for you, though." I felt bad for my forgetfulness.

"Can't I rely on you for *anything*?" He sighed bitterly, refusing to look at me.

"I beg your pardon!" His comment had made me completely flustered. I couldn't have heard right. "Well then, Mr. Bolton, I do reckon you should pack your own bags! Doing something for yourself couldn't hurt!" I retaliated.

"I do not appreciate your tone with me, Stell. Watch your tongue, I daresay. You are home *all day* while I work. You don't have much of an argument." His voice was completely stiff.

The car shook from going over a bump in the road. I couldn't believe what was coming out of his mouth. "I do, in fact. Do you so easily forget who cooks for you and keeps our rooms tidy?"

"No, I remember quite well that it is *Della*," he replied shortly, turning his nose up at me.

"Not at all. Della could not cook to *your* standards, so I did the cooking. And may I refresh your memory that you didn't let Della into our room because you felt it was invading your privacy. Della may have cleaned a couple of rooms, but she did not do *all* of the work in our home. She did not shop, nor cook, nor clean your room. That was me."

"And I suppose that takes up what... maybe three hours of your day?" He laughed rudely. "What do you do the other nine hours? Estella, I honestly can't believe you are actually arguing with me about this. I never thought you childish until now." He stared at my face authoritatively, making me want to shrink. My lips parted, not knowing what to say. All of our conversations turned to arguments.

"At least I occupy myself in the other nine hours without a glass of whiskey in my hand." I said it in a bare whisper, staring out straight ahead.

"That is a lie. I am not a drunk, Stell. Malicious of you to even think such a thing. You have no argument, so you are turning to lies to do your dirty work." Unfortunately for him, I was not the fool of a wife he thought me to be. When I cleaned, I often found some peculiar things. For the rest of the ride, we sat in cunning silence, listening to the hum of the engine.

♪ ♪ ♪

At five forty-five, a little over an hour later, we arrived in Herefordshire at Hampton Court Castle. My eyes had never seen any building of such a monstrosity this close. Ancient oak trees loomed beside the castle, only enhancing its size. Their shadows swayed on the sides of the building.

The grand doors were opened by valet and footman, and Charlie emerged, followed by a few of his servants and staff. I hardly recognized him in the expensive waistcoat and dinner jacket he wore. The cuffs of his coat were a stunning white color, as if they themselves had been purified by the Lord. Even his posture had improved since I had last laid eyes on him. He strode with such dignity and honor.

One of the footmen opened the car door for me. He stood rigid, head held high with one hand behind his back. He was decently young, perhaps seventeen, if not younger. The image of a statue was all I could imagine in my head as I stepped out of the car, his human figure trapped in a body of stone.

"Thank you," I said to him, making a point to turn my head and make eye contact.

He did not utter a single word; in fact, he barely blinked.

I could not figure out what was going inside his head. Did he think he was unworthy of speaking to me? Me, an absolute nobody? Or was it on the contrary?

"Oh, Estella, I'm so pleased you're here. Welcome!" Charlie rushed over to me, kissing me on the cheek. I was surprised to see him in this mood. "Momma and Poppa arrived here two days ago. They can't wait to see you and hear what you think." His servants swarmed around the two cars like a lineup of army men, immediately taking all of our belongings inside.

"Wonderful." I smiled widely, attempting to conceal my anger that Roy had brought up in me. I so badly wanted to enjoy my first day in my new home. Charlie didn't give it a second glance. He was genuinely pleased that I appeared content.

"Bentley, take Mrs. Bolton to the library," he ordered. A middle-aged valet with red hair appeared beside me at Charlie's command. Like before, this valet wouldn't look at me, either. He was rather tall and broad with freckles dotting his cheeks. A very handsome man with a compressed personality. Two controversial traits.

"And Roy, my good fellow. You as well. How was your trip? Smooth ride I presume?" Charlie headed over to Roy and they both shook hands firmly. Seeing the two of them in the same vicinity made me realize how Charlie towered over Roy.

"Wonderful ride, indeed. I am so honored to be invited here, really. This is very generous of you," Roy admitted. "This house is truly a dream." He stared up at it in awe.

"Why thank you. It was… *difficult* moving in at first, but I have gotten used to it. And the food is spectacular! We'll have to go hunting sometime soon, eh?" I could imagine how difficult the move was. To inhabit the house that a friend never came back to, and where a boy died in one of the rooms.

"Well, I cannot wait. This will take a bit of getting used to, for sure. *And*, it looks like I *will* be calling you Mr. Breaker after all. Actually, Mister is the wrong address. You are now *Lord* Breaker!" He joked dryly, though his head was not in it.

"Ah, nonsense! Just Charlie, you know that." He gripped his shoulder in a brotherly manner and they continued to reminisce.

The valet named Bentley held the door open for me. I reached out and brushed the side of the house with my fingertips as I walked through the door. It was real. All of it. Deep in my mind, I had thought that if I had tried to touch it, the stone would disintegrate as things do in dreams.

My head automatically tilted upwards as I entered. Bentley appeared beside me, waiting to lead the way.

My eyes didn't know where to look first. Never had I seen the complex designs that I saw here. From the stencil work on the arched celling, to the miniscule patterns woven on the rug I stood upon. The Hamptons surely had to have taken great pride in their décor. I felt as if I was at a museum, not a home. And *especially* not *my* home.

The curtains were so thick they could have been used as quilts to cover the beds. They were elegantly draped and pulled to the side of each window like hair framing a young woman's face. The chandelier above my head had too many candles on it to count without losing track. Hundreds of tiny crystals dangled from it. Even the grandfather clock in the corner had to be hand carved, no doubt. Wooden roses and vines wove up to its face. The walls were made of thick wooden panels. All of the colors matched exquisitely.

I was the statue now, unable to tear my eyes from the lavish sight.

"Right this way, Mrs. Bolton," Bentley directed. He gestured down the hall, palm up with his hand outstretched. I followed, completely absorbed in my surroundings.

"It's beautiful, isn't it?" I gushed aloud.

"Indeed so. The men in my family have been here for three generations. My father is the Butler."

"That's intriguing. Three generations. I must say, I am impressed." As we walked down the hall, I marveled at the paintings that completely covered the walls. They were so big I felt as if I could walk into the scene and proportionally fit in. A footman walked by us, brisk and swift on his feet.

"Bentley, don't go boring Mrs. Bolton about your life. There are other things to worry about. More *important* things. Don't waste her precious time." He gave Bentley an unwelcoming glance, furrowing his eyebrows. Creases appeared in his forehead like folded paper. "Mrs." He nodded his head and gave me an all too charming smile.

As quick as he encountered us, he brushed right by us, adjusting his short hair back into position. He was on his way to fetch more suitcases.

"Oh Duncan, of *course* there are more important things. *I* should be advising *you* not to waste *your time.*" Bentley shot him a sly, satisfactory glance that made Duncan's face flush red. He quickened his pace and turned out of sight with the steps of a wind-up toy.

"My sincerest apologies, Mrs. I hope I did not make you uncomfortable or unwelcome."

"Oh, not at all. Everyone quarrels once in a while." Bentley did not reply, and I soon got the impression that it occurred much more often than once in a while. He opened a thick spruce door for me, allowing me into the library. I expected him to follow me inside, but he left, unnoticed by anyone except me.

Momma and Poppa stood abruptly and came over to me.

"Sweetie, how are you, dear?" Momma reached for my hand and squeezed it gently. "Do come sit with us."

"I'm doing just fine. This house is making me speechless. I can't find words to describe it, honestly. It's... so much to take in," I replied happily, sitting between them. The sofa was incredibly soft; I thought I would surely sink into it like quicksand.

"It is." Poppa tapped his cane and carefully picked up his cup of tea in his shaky hands. Slowly, he lifted it to his pale lips and took a sip. His hair was a snowy white color, making his skin seem paler than it was in reality. I had the same ghostly skin. I could easily look at my hand and spot my blue veins.

Momma continued to chatter in my ear as everyone joined us in the library. Every wall was lined with bookshelves that touched the ceiling. There were probably enough words in this one room to make a dictionary for each person in England. Some of the shelves were dustier, but it was a glorious sight. I, one who did not particularly like to read, actually had the urge to pick up a book, even though my reading skills were limited. The feeling was so cozy, it made me feel fuzzy inside.

Charlie came in last, accompanied by my other siblings, Flora, and her younger twin, Claude. They were only twenty-one seconds apart. They were exact duplicates of each other excluding three things. One was obviously the gender difference. The second thing was that Flora's hair was longer, which was expected. And last but not least was that Claude had two different eye colors. It was very odd, but as a child, I had been envious of it. One eye was blue, a much darker blue than Charlie's, and the other eye was a stunning, rich, earthy green like mine.

"Claude! Flora!" I nearly jumped up from the sofa. I hadn't seen Claude since he had gone to America. After serving in the war, he had decided to go and "adventure," as he described it. He and Flora were both twenty-three, three years older than I.

I kissed Flora on the cheek, asking her a million questions about the tailoring business that she was trying to start.

"It's going pretty well. A friend of mine, Theresa, offered to help. Now I have three employees. The service is a little slow, but they work so hard. It's about time a woman can run a business on her own." She lifted her chin proudly. She seemed well, bubbly like usual and full of energy. Then she greeted Momma and Poppa, striking up a conversation about an article she had read in the newspaper. Her mind was all over the board, but she was such a pleasant person to be around.

Claude made his way over to me. His shoulders slumped and his eyes were sunken.

"Hello, Estella." He stood in front of me tiredly. His shyness even persevered with his own family members.

"Claude, how are you? I can't wait to hear about America! You never wrote to me!" I nudged him, kissing his cheek as well.

"There wasn't much to write about, I fear. I still like it here, in England." He nodded slightly, as if he was assuring himself. "That's all I get is a kiss?" he asked timidly, forming a smile.

"You're such a teddy bear, brother. So unusual for an Englishman like yourself. Should I be fetching you some honey?" I rolled my eyes teasingly at him and gave him the hug he so discreetly asked for. He held me with the one good arm he had. Something about his mood shattered my heart.

I wondered if Claude's mind was in its right state. As children, he had been my best friend. With his nonstop energy like Flora, he had never ceased annoying me. Yet with that same energy, he had always brought a smile to my face. After serving in the war, that happiness seemed to have hidden away somewhere in him. With the loss of his right arm, he seemed to have lost something else. I yearned for the happy older brother I once knew.

It took a lot for me to hold myself together at that moment. Claude let me go, and I watched his eyes dart across to the different bookshelves. He didn't know what else to say.

"Sorry to interrupt everyone, but dinner is ready," Charlie announced.

"Wonderful," Momma exclaimed, clasping her hands together. We followed Charlie down the hall to the dining room, passing by many other breathtaking rooms.

The dining room was a very long and narrow room. Every chair was perfectly aligned with the next, and the silverware gleamed like polished jewels. I could see my reflection in the spoons. The wood floor under my feet stretched out in a herringbone pattern.

I pulled my chair out and was about to take my seat when a footman hurried over.

"Allow me, Mrs."

"Oh. That's very kind of you. Thank you," I replied, flattered. He pushed my chair in for me once I was sitting. Other footmen scurried around the table to seat Momma and Flora. Roy sat across from me, now striking up conversation with Claude who seemed disinterested in whatever he was saying. He occasionally nodded, but that was all. The room was filled with excitement and chatter.

"Charlie, are we expecting others?" Flora suddenly asked. I followed her gaze to the empty chairs to my right.

"Yes, in fact. But I was forewarned they'd be late." As if on cue, the butler approached Charlie and whispered something. He was an older man, but he walked with pep. His hair was full of color for his age.

"Claude! Claude Breaker, put your napkin on your lap already!" Momma nudged Claude roughly to get his attention like he was still an incompetent child. She glared at him. "Have more respect for your brother's new home!" She hissed to him unhappily. I didn't know which conversation to listen to. I felt so out of place.

"Act like a gentleman," Poppa reinforced. Claude sighed and placed his napkin on his lap. I could picture him more as a farmer or mechanic than a gentleman. Afterward, he disappeared right back into his trance. I wondered what world he was possibly imagining that was better than the one we were in now. Did he not understand that we lived in Hampton Court?

As the first course was being served, Charlie stood. The footmen froze in place and listened to him. The attention they gave to him reminded me of a dog and master. It was unnerving.

"My apologies everyone, but I must go greet our other guests at the door. Excuse me." He placed his napkin on the table and stood.

"Stand," Poppa harshly whispered to everyone. We all gave him a confused look. Why were we to stand? But at the same time, we obeyed.

"Poppa, why did you say that?" Flora asked in a low voice when Charlie was out of sight. We all sat down simultaneously. Once again, the footmen pushed our chairs in for us. I took a sip of wine, eager to hear the answer.

"It's respect," he responded sternly. Flora didn't ask any other questions. Our average lives now consisted of rules that we never thought applied.

England
The Pianist

The past seven months, I had worked as a fisherman on a boat called *Driftwood Anchor.* I was part of a crew of eleven people. Well, it *was* eleven people until one person went overboard. I'll never forget that morning. It had only been three weeks ago. The wave had come up out of nowhere and slapped our vessel like we were a toy boat in a bathtub. I had slipped on the deck, grabbing at anything to keep me from falling overboard. My head had smacked into something, but we were all so disorientated that I didn't know what had hit me. All I remembered was waking up on the deck of the boat with people hovering over me several hours later. Our shouts had been drowned out by the sea, and no one had heard Louis screaming for help as he fell in.

We worked for a British seafood company, catching crabs, fish, clams, and oysters. Though it was much easier to catch the clams and oysters. They were less resistant. Our main catch was cod. That was how we earned most of our money.

"Blimey, I thought I'd never see land again. What a sight to behold, aye, Bruno?" Edward turned to me, taking off his hat and scratching his light-colored hair. We bent down to pick up a crate. Everyone on the ship called me Bruno. I officially went by my middle name. Shorter, and safer than having these Englishmen know my last name. We smelled like dead fish and salt, carrying giant ice boxes full of fish.

"Agreed, Ed. It's funny to think that I can actually stand without having to grab onto something or fearing that the floor will start rocking back and forth beneath me." I chuckled a little and placed my crate in front of a table at an outdoor market.

"Oh yes! Truly!" He grunted as he placed his crate down. We headed back to the harbor to pick up another crate, passing by more of our crew.

"Bruno!" Curtis scowled at me. His face was dry with dirt streaks on it. "Hurry up, lad! There's a whole crate of oysters at the hull. Last one there." He jutted his chin in the direction of the boat. "I trust you won't eat 'em. Just bring 'em here." Curtis struggled to carry one crate by himself. He adjusted his arms and walked like an unbalanced spider with only two legs instead of eight.

"I'm on it, sir," I called to him, giving Ed a sly smile. We rushed over to *Driftwood Anchor* and ran over to the hull. Sure enough, one crate was left. One *big* crate.

"Come on. We can't pass this opportunity up. Just look at all these oysters! My mouth is watering at the sight!" Ed exclaimed, sliding open the top and pulling a small knife out of his pocket with his other hand. "What do you say? Eh?"

"I don't know." I hesitated. "Oh alright, but hurry up, will you?" Ed and I had learned to live on oysters during seven months on the ship. The first couple times I had become very sick when I ate them raw, spending many hours vomiting off the side of the ship. But now, I could eat thirty without even the slightest feeling of nausea.

"You got it." He crouched down, dug his hand into the crate, and pulled out six. He gave five to me and picked another four out for himself. "Put a few in your pocket. The smaller ones. We won't have time to eat them all now." He whispered, stuffing three out of his five into his pocket for later. I did the same.

Effortlessly, he pried open both of the oysters I was holding, and then his.

"To the Driftwood Anchor, and to all the mishaps, rainstorms, and dead fish that we encountered. And to dear old Louis who would have loved to share these oysters with us." Ed held up one of his oysters.

"Bravo," I exclaimed, slurping up both oysters. I could taste the sea. "To Louis." I didn't know Louis that well, but I knew he had been the oyster-eating champ.

Edward did the same, tilting his head back and enjoying his last oyster until next season.

"And to being fired," another raspy voice interjected. Ed and I whipped our heads around and spotted Curtis. That same scowl was on his face, and his thick arms were crossed angrily. The scar on his right cheek made him look like Frankenstein with facial hair.

We had nothing to say. My lips parted, but I could find no words. The empty shells of the oysters were in our hands.

"Bring that crate to the market and then leave. Both of you. You're lucky I'm not reporting you to the police for stealing." He raised his voice and glared at us like he glared at the sharks that tried to eat the fish on our lines. "Take these and go." He thrust an envelope at each of us.

"Sir—" Ed began.

"I won't hear of it, Edward. Get off my ship." He pointed to the crate and then into the horizon. "You as well, Bruno."

I hung my head and tossed my oyster shells off the boat, hearing a small splash as each one landed in the murky water below. I tucked the envelope in my pocket. Ed and I heaved up the last crate, and slowly made our way toward the market.

"Get off my ship…." Ed mumbled under his breath, mimicking Curtis as we placed the crate down. "Curtis has got nerve, I'll say that. Who does he think he is? My father is one of the most well-known fishermen in all of England. He can't just tell me to *get off* his ship. He probably bought that bloody ship from my father, anyway! He owns dozens of them!" He wiped his hands on his pants. "And, I know for a *fact* that my father wouldn't name it something completely *foolish* like *Driftwood Anchor*."

"It *is* a controversial name, isn't it?" I paused and really considered it. That's when I noticed that my hair hung a little lower than my jawbone. "When did my hair get so long?" I pondered aloud, taking a strand between my fingers.

"Always happens out on the ocean. You don't realize what you look like. You'll be shocked when you look in the mirror. Sometimes it's frightening. I always am when I get back from fishing." He abandoned his rant for

33

now. "Better get it cut or folks might start addressing you as Miss." He laughed, stepping in front of me with a goofy grin.

"Miss? Miss, where did you get that lovely perfume? I need to be gettin' some for myself." He pitched his voice an octave higher, walking daintily on his toes. He pretended to stroke a boa at his shoulder.

"Oh, why thank you, darlin'. It's called "Dead Fish." So *charmed* you like it."

We both cracked up. Then, rather abruptly, we were quiet.

"I've got to be going now," Ed claimed, looking at the sky. "I cannot *wait* to get this dead fish stench off me." He pulled the collar of his shirt to his nose and sniffed. "Doesn't bother me anymore, but I know the ladies don't find it too appealing. I can't wait to be home." He tugged at his suspenders.

"Me too. I'm afraid this smell will be stuck in my nose if I don't wash up soon. I've got to find another job, too," I sighed.

"My father will get me back on that ship. I know he'll find a way. Serrone is a seaman's name. And I plan to keep it that way." He paused. "I wish you luck, Bruno." He held out his hand.

"For you as well," I replied. We shook hands. "Been a pleasure boating with you."

"Oh, there's no pleasure in boating," he snorted. "Don't fool yourself. Not with the disgusting smell of fish and the sting of salt water. I *can* say, however, that it has been a pleasure *meeting* you." He cracked a smile and withdrew his hand. "If you ever want to go have a drink or go to a pub, let me know. I'll see you around, Bruno."

"I sure hope so. Thanks." With a quick wave, I walked into a small town that I didn't know the name of. All I knew was that I was in the county of Gloucester. All I had with me, was one tiny, soaked, suitcase and my earnings from the months on *Driftwood Anchor*.

♪ ♪ ♪

After walking for a while, I was able to stumble across an Inn. It was a plain, square building with two floors. It was made out of brick with a high roof and windows packed closely together. Outside the building, a young boy stood holding a stack of newspapers. People of the lower class strolled the sidewalks or rode cycles, while the upper class took the backseat as their chauffer drove them.

"Top news stories right here, folks! Rumors from Germany and local sales at the market!" the boy shouted to oncoming people and to people with their car windows open. He was a really short child, with a face full of freckles and a grey cap on his head that was too big for him. I stopped in front of him.

"I'll take one." I handed the boy a coin and he handed me a rolled-up newspaper.

"Good day to you, sir!" he called as I went into the Inn. His accent was very thick, almost as if he was speaking gibberish at top speed instead of English. I nodded my head at him and disappeared inside. Instantly, the smell of cigarettes flooded my lungs. It reminded me of Otto. I hadn't written to him because as soon as I had arrived in England, I had applied to be a fisherman. I was positive I had them all wondering. Well… maybe not *all* of them.

"How can I help you, sir?" A stocky man with a scruffy beard stood behind the counter and greeted me as I came in. I took off my cap.

"Um, I need a room here. Just for a couple of nights."

"Sure, sure, lad. What's the name? Also, how many plan to stay?" He shuffled through some papers and then looked back at me.

"Bruno." There was a slight hesitation. "Bruno Leonhardt. I will be the only one," I stated.

"Leonhardt… sounds so familiar." He paused to think while I cringed on the inside. "Oh! I do recall now. There's a pianist with that last name. I am very into classical music, and he is absolutely incredible. I've never been to a concert, but I have heard some of his playing on a Gramophone. Any relation?" he asked me curiously.

"No. None at all, sir. Afraid I've never heard of him. Leonhardt is a common name in Germany. Sorry to disappoint you, but I'm a fisherman," I lied to him, placing my arms on the front desk. I was surprised how calm and collected I had been. I almost convinced *myself* that I was telling the truth.

"Ahh. So *that* is the smell. You will get rid of that if I give you a room, yes? Your neighbors will not enjoy it at *all*." He eyed me and scrunched up his large nose. Wrinkles gathered on his chin and on the folds of his fore-head. He seemed too young of a man to have them.

"Absolutely. The smell will be gone by morning," I assured him. "I cannot wait to be rid of it myself."

"Ah, yes. Wonderful," he exclaimed. He walked over to a glass cab-inet and extracted a small shiny key with a tag on it. Happily, he exchanged the key for my money. "Your room is on the second floor. Number thirty-eight."

"Thank you," I replied, heading toward a carpeted staircase. It creaked as I walked up, making me wonder just how sturdy it was. At the top, I turned left, following an arrow on a sign. "Thirty-five, thirty-six, thirty-seven, thirty-eight," I mumbled quietly, trying out my counting in English. The language wasn't a problem since Mutti and Opa had taught me. But often I confused the numbers.

My room door was an exact replica of every other door in the hall. A sanded wooden slab with a single brass handle. I inserted the key and heard the click as the door opened. The room seemed fit for a king compared to the close quarters on *Driftwood Anchor*. To any person, it would have seemed a normal-size room, but as I stared at the clean bed and the dry floor, I couldn't help but be grateful. I didn't have to worry about rats trying to steal my food, or falling out of bed in the night due to a violent wave.

A smile spread across my face and I collapsed on the bed. The oys-ters in my pocket rattled against each other's shells. I had almost forgotten I had them if it wasn't for the stench. My stomach grumbled as if on cue. But that would have to wait. First, a bath.

I had forgotten what fresh water felt like. Not only fresh water, but *warm* water. Back in Germany, we had the choices of dozens of soaps and shampoos. Now, I was thankful to have just one. My hair was thick with suds, and bubbles floated around me. It was wonderful. I lost track of time as I sat there with my eyes closed. My body felt weightless. Like gravity had given up trying to pull me down.

When I eventually decided to get out, I found my skin completely rid of salt. Each finger was pruned like a raisin and my hair was no longer sticky. But best of all, the odor of dead fish had been washed away, down the drain with the dirty water of my past.

After putting on a clean set of clothes to sleep in, I emptied both pockets of my clothes and placed the oysters on the table. In my suitcase, at the very bottom, was my pocket knife. Like Ed had taught me, I pried each shell open, twisting the knife. Eagerly, I ate them, remembering all the moments on board where we had oyster-eating contests. Typically, I had been first to lose. Some of those guys could eat fifty or sixty in one sitting. I was *certainly* not as good as that.

When I ate the last one, I felt something hit my back tooth. Quickly, I spit it out. Swallowing a piece of sharp shell could do damage going through a person's intestines. But it wasn't a piece of shell. What I spit into my hand was a pearl. It was almost a perfect sphere. From afar, it looked flawless. Its light color shimmered when I held it up.

"Blimey," I whispered aloud. It was my favorite exclamatory word from the English language. Over and over I rolled it between my first finger and thumb, not believing it. I wondered if the other crew members had ever almost swallowed a pearl. I thought of Ed. With his dense personality and love for raw oysters, he probably had a vault of them in his stomach without the slightest clue. Half of the time, he didn't chew before he swallowed.

That evening, I went to sleep with not a single worry. Without even a sliver of fear. I only wished I had claimed my life sooner.

♪ ♪ ♪

The next two days, I busied myself reading through the newspaper in the *Help Wanted* section and going to the barber down the street. I had never been to a public barber shop. In Germany, the barber always came to our estate. It was nicer than I had thought, though; there were hair clippings all over the floor. The barber had cut my hair so the front part fell just barely over my eyebrows. Then, with a tooth comb and some water, he slicked it back like I usually had it. One shorter strand came loose and curled at my temple.

As I looked in the mirror, I was glad to find myself looking like me again. The long shaggy hair had not suited me at all. And the facial hair had made me look ten years older, which was not appealing. Now that it was gone, I was back to being twenty-one.

"If I may, do you have any idea how far Herefordshire is from here?" I had asked the barber when he was done. The newspaper was outstretched in my lap. The only problem was, I was not great at reading English.

"Herefordshire, you say? Hmm. If you take the train, it is not too far at all. Maybe forty or forty-five kilometers away." He scratched his chin. "You should know that, my fellow: basic geography," he replied in a deep voice, dusting off the loose pieces of hair from my neck with a towel.

"Yes, I should. I had forgotten. Thank you," I responded with a curt nod. In truth, I had never heard of the place. But the ad looked promising. It read: Ambitious, respectful man required at Hampton Court, Herefordshire. Located in the village of Hope under Dinmore. Must be flexible with hours and must be willing to work hard. No previous experience in service required. Training included.

In service? More than a year ago, I would have thought the idea foolish. Impossible, even. Me, in service. But now, it was almost exciting. I, who used to be the master of an estate, would now be a servant. A complete role reversal. Something about it was so ironic it made me want to laugh out loud.

The next day, I dressed my best and slicked back my hair with water and a brand-new comb. I packed my one suitcase, and with my lucky pearl in my pocket, boarded a train heading northwest to Herefordshire.

"Here you are." The cab driver turned around to look at me. His arm was draped around the top of the seat.

"This… this is it? Blimey," I breathed. I craned my head upwards to see the tips of the roof of the house. House was the wrong word. This was a castle. Much bigger than my estate had been.

"Yes, indeed. I hear new folks moved in. Something happened to the Hamptons. Their family owned this place for generations, and now, the heir died. I don't mean to scare ya, but I'm almost positive he died of the Spanish flu. You watch yourself," he explained gravely. Under his hat, his eyes fell unsurely on the castle.

"Oh… uh, thank you," I replied nervously. I handed him his money and got out of the car onto a dirt driveway. He left in a hurry, kicking up dirt with his tires as the car bounced back out to the main road.

The pungent smell of flowers rushed into my nose. There must have been thousands of them, and yet, I did not find the view stunning. They were all bland. The bricks were smoothed from years and years of withstanding rain and wind, and the grass was cut perfectly even. Like each blade had been cut using a ruler to measure. Untamed vines wound up parts of the enormous walls. A pond shimmered to my left in the glare of the sunlight where cattails and giant oak trees cast disoriented shadows on the surface of the water.

Taking a deep breath, I walked up to the door and rang the doorbell. I heard it echo all through the home like a gong. I shifted from side to side and tightened my grip on my suitcase. After a minute, the door opened.

"M'lord, with all due respect, it is my job to answer the door," I heard a voice insist in a gritted whisper.

"Ah, nonsense Lemont, I was just passing by. It wasn't a bother at all." Two men came into view. One was tall with sharp eyes and a square face. I did not even need to compare their clothing to know that he was the lord of the house. The other man I immediately identified as the butler. His eyebrows were so thin that they seemed to not be there at all, and his chest was puffed out with the family's pride as he stood there.

"And who might you be?" he asked. He was judging my every move and breath, not even bothering to say hello. I cut right to the point.

"I'm Bruno, and I came here to apply for the job mentioned in the advertisement." I held up my crumpled newspaper. It was hard to keep my gaze on them. They stood so much higher than me on the steps.

"You're a brave one, seeing we didn't list *exactly* what the service requirements are." He paused, waiting for me to react. "You must address me as 'Mr. Lemont,'" the butler stated, looking at me like a bug he wanted to squish under his perfectly-polished shoes.

"Yes, Mr. Lemont." I tried it out to make him satisfied.

"Why don't you come in, Bruno? You are the second person to respond to this position. It is a unique one, I assure you. I, am Lord Charlie Breaker." Lord Breaker opened the door wider and gestured for me to follow.

"Pardon me, M'lord, but servants are required to use the back entrance...." the butler began.

"No need, Lemont. I will be interviewing him myself. I also remind you that he is not a servant *yet*, is he? For now, he is a guest. My guest." I followed him inside, feeling nostalgic about my old home. Already, I could tell that Lord Breaker was... different. I'd have made the servant go through the back entrance. It was foolish of me not to think to find the back door myself. My thoughts were clouded by nerves.

The butler closed the door stiffly and trailed behind us. From his twisted expression, he did not like being reprimanded. But even so, I admired his ability to refrain himself.

"Please inform Miss Everett that I require tea in the library. Mr. Bruno will have some as well. Thank you, Lemont." Charlie dismissed him and led me through thick spruce doors. My estate in Germany certainly did not contain as many details as this house did. Other than that, I was used to the familiar surroundings. I did not feel like a child drooling at the windows of a candy shop.

I did not sit down until asked. On the other side of the room, a young woman sat with a little girl on her lap. Her daughter, I guessed. The girl was in a full pout position. Her arms were crossed and her lips were puckered in a frown as the woman held her like a doll.

"Cousin Flora, I don't want to read!" she wailed. Her bangs fell in her face. I had guessed wrong. They were cousins with a huge age gap. The woman looked to be my age, and the girl had to be six or seven.

"It's fun! You have to learn to read, Cleo, if you want to be a smart girl!" The women picked up the girl and placed her on the floor. "I had to teach myself to read when I was little."

Cleo, the little girl, grumbled unhappily. "I *am* smart! I know three plus two equals five!" she squealed, holding up five fingers. "Can we go see Cousin Estella now? Pleeeaaaasseee. She has a present for me." Cleo spun around and clapped her hands together excitedly, staring at the ceiling. A smile lit up her face as she imagined what it was. She reminded me of a star as she spun in her puffy yellow dress: small, but so bright your eye couldn't pass by it.

"How about I teach you 'Twinkle Twinkle Little Star' on the piano?" Flora suggested, patting Cleo's silky hair. Cleo didn't even take it into consideration.

My heart skipped a beat. It was like the woman, Flora, had read my mind. Then, I realized she had mentioned the piano. I shrank inside. Why did it seem to follow me? I wanted to leave my past behind.

"Mummy already taught me that one," Cleo claimed, and I snapped back into the present. She eyed Lord Breaker and me shyly, realizing we were sitting in the room. She was certainly a stubborn girl. Despite her size, she could stand her own ground. Unfortunately, stubbornness went hand and hand with disobedience.

"Oh, *alright*. But I don't know where Estella is at the moment. We shall try to find her, like hide and seek," Flora finally gave in. "Let's go. Hold my hand, darling." I watched as Cleo reached up and took Flora's hand. I couldn't help but stare in my lap at my own empty hand. A pang of guilt slapped me.

"Flora, I believe Estella is taking a walk in the garden, if you were wondering," Lord Breaker called as they exited, craning his neck to project his voice past the closing door. Then, he turned to me. "Sorry for the interruption. But let's get started, shall we?"

"Indeed, M'lord," I agreed eagerly.

The position he was offering was to be a landscaper early in the day, and then a valet. An odd combination. It was a sort of half and half thing. If I were to take the position, Lord Breaker had explained that I was to tend to the garden and shrubs beginning at four in the morning until eight. Then, I had to eat, clean myself up, and get dressed into the uniform for a valet. By nine o'clock, I would have to go dress Lord Breaker's brother, Claude. After that, I would have to polish shoes downstairs with some of the other valets and maids and tend to other small things until dinner, where I would lay out Claude's dinner clothing and dress him once more.

"So, Mr. Bruno. What are your skills and qualifications? Do you have a good source of references?" Lord Breaker sipped his tea and I did the same.

"No… M'lord. I'm afraid I don't if I am honest. I've been oversea for quite some time. My previous employment was as a fisherman on a boat called *Driftwood Anchor*. I'm good at using a fishing net, and working in undependable conditions. Those are pretty much my only skills," I admitted, still holding my cup of tea.

"Then why did you come to apply? Let's put it this way. If I were to put you up against another man who had interest in the same job, why should I choose you?" He raised his eyebrows and met my eyes. He was indeed a clever man who knew how to get what he wanted. It surprised me how comfortable he seemed, despite the fact that he and his family were considered to be "new money." He had a good handle on things.

"I am used to these surroundings, M'lord. And I'm a very fast learner. I know how these houses operate and what it takes to keep them going. In fact, I have a deep respect for them. I'd say you should choose me because in a unique way, I do have lots of experience taking care of a house like this," I confidently stated, placing my tea on the table in front of us.

"How can you know if your only previous job was as a fisherman?" he asked, narrowing his eyes in confusion.

"Because before I became a fisherman, I owned an estate myself."

"My goodness! What? And now you're here, applying to be in service? How hard that must be. The war did many people in. It is so unfortunate." He looked at me differently now, with more respect. It was irritating. Just because he knew I had previously owned an estate, he felt the need to treat me better. I was still the average fellow applying for his job.

"On the contrary, M'lord. It was not what I enjoyed. Running it takes a lot of organization, cooperation, and patience, which unfortunately began to run thin. The people in my family are all so... *different.* We could never agree, and I found myself doing most of the work which I'm sure you know is a tough thing when running a house of this size. So I had to start anew. After all, I am only twenty-one. I have other paths to choose from," I said. He seemed taken aback by my words.

"Mr. Bruno, what I'm getting from you, is that you *gave up* your estate? That it was not because of the war at all?" He asked as if he couldn't have possibly heard right. Some people's life goals were to own an estate, or be one of the wealthy first-class families. Yet I did not think about it this way.

I paused, giving myself time to think about it in that way. "Yes, Your Lordship. I guess I did. For the better of my family and for the better of myself. My family doesn't see it that way, though. I'm sure they all think me selfish. We all needed a fresh start," I concluded. It was true. I had mainly moved for myself, but I was sure it was making them better people. To know the feeling of hard work and to live in a small town like every other person. I hoped it would humble them. Because for a fact, I knew it was something we had all lacked and yet needed.

"Pardon my saying this, but your whole situation is rather odd. It does not seem your place to tell the rest of your family when *they* need a fresh start, but I guess this doesn't concern me. 'Tis simply my opinion." Lord Breaker placed three sugar cubes into his tea and stirred with a tiny spoon.

"Maybe, M'lord. But you do not know the whole story. You would have done the same as me. But you seem like an intelligent man, so you probably would have done it sooner," I replied, discretely overstepping my boundaries. I knew that higher-ranking people didn't like to be told what they should do or what they would have done.

He tilted his head to the side, trying to understand. "If you do insist. Your personal matters are yours and only yours." He paused, crossing his legs and taking a deep breath. "Anyway, back to the job. In the advertisement, I wrote that no previous experience was needed. And we are in dire need of a suitable person for this position. So," he paused, "if you are willing to be trained, it is yours. But it is not easy, mind you."

"Really?" I could feel my eyes light up. "I mean… thank you, M'lord." I contained myself, finishing up my tea. "I can start whenever necessary." My tight grip on my suitcase loosened.

"How about tomorrow morning? You may sleep here if you like, and get your belongings placed in one of the rooms. I'll have Bentley show you the servants' quarters."

"That would be fine, M'lord."

"Splendid." Lord Breaker turned to Duncan, who stood absently near a huge window on the far side of the room. "Duncan, tell Bentley that I require him to show Mr. Bruno around. He needs to be taught his duties, for as of tomorrow, he is part of our staff." A smile appeared on Lord Breaker's face.

"Yes, certainly, M'lord." With a hop in his step, Duncan left the room.

Lord Breaker stood. Quickly, I did the same. Then, he seemed to remember something.

"Mr. Bruno. I must forewarn you about one thing." He paused, tilting his head and biting his lip. "I feel… it is my *obligation*." The way he said obligation made it seem as if he had to be very careful about how he decided to word his sentence. He gave me a rather odd look and gestured for me to take a seat again. I sank into the cushion.

"My brother, Claude, served in the war." He stopped for a moment, thinking hard. "During this time, he unfortunately lost his right arm. All I say to you is that he is very sensitive about it. Do not ask him about it, and do not stare, of course. He is a quiet, passive man. So don't feel shunned if he doesn't speak to you. He is… trying to cope with himself." Lord Breaker's smile had vanished. He looked genuinely disturbed by the thought of his brother's sadness. "Be patient, this is all I ask. I will introduce you to him tonight after dinner."

"Yes, of course, M'lord." I immediately felt sorry for him.

The doors swung open and a man appeared. Even though he was tall, his shoes made him look like a clown. They were enormous. He had deep set eyes and small, round ears like a mouse. Freckles covered every inch of his exposed skin, even his hands.

"You asked for me, M'lord?" he questioned politely.

"Yes. This is Mr. Bruno…." his eyes darted to my face.

"L—Leonhardt," I filled in.

"Ah, yes. Mr. Bruno Leonhardt, the new valet and landscaper. I would like you to ask Lemont to assign him a room. And I would like you to show him how his duties must be performed and what he must do. He will be starting tomorrow. After you are done, ask one of the gardeners to give him a few lessons," Lord Breaker informed.

"Yes, M'lord," Bentley replied, not moving an inch.

"Thank you. Mr. Bruno, follow Bentley please. Nice meeting you." He made sure to catch my eye. Like he truly wanted me to take it to heart.

"Thank you, M'lord. You as well." I stood and walked over to Bentley, who led me out the door.

"So, you made the cut," he said when we were far enough away from the library. "Hmph. That was fast. Although, His Lordship can be a bit of a softie." Bentley had a quick pace. We passed through a hallway and into a little door off to the side. He opened it and an overflow of aromas almost made me sneeze. Herbs and spices made my mouth water as we walked down a flight of spiral stairs.

"I was surprised too, actually. I've never been a valet *or* landscaper before."

"What?" Bentley stopped mid-step. I almost tripped over his big feet and went sprawling down the stairs with my suitcase. It would have been *completely* embarrassing.

"Odd, isn't it? I know all about being in service, but I've never actually *done* it—" I tried to explain, but he cut me off.

"I pray you are joking with me, Mr. Bruno. *Please* say it isn't true." He pinched the bridge of his nose with his fingers. He had this horrified look on his speckled face, practically begging for me to admit I was joking. His voice shook. I did not understand what his distress was all about. I was here to learn, like everyone else once had to.

"I'm afraid I'm being completely honest." I said it like a question. Like being honest was a bad thing. "The advertisement said no previous—"

"Well then, champ, you've got a bloody hell of a lot of work to do!" he exclaimed, throwing his hands up. His upstairs and downstairs personalities couldn't have differed more.

♪ ♪ ♪

At the bottom of the long stairwell, we turned right and into the kitchen. Pots and pans were settled on the stove, and a kettle was screaming like a little baby. The walls were lined with cooking equipment. In the center of the room, there was one cluttered table with floured dough ready to be baked into fresh bread. Whisks, spatulas, and ladles were scattered around. Three women rushed about. Their aprons were stained with who knew what.

"Miss Everett! Turn the water off already!" one of them shouted to the other. I couldn't tell which one. They were like hummingbirds, only stopping for seconds before taking off to do something else. They were a constant blur as they moved.

"You do it! I have to get this bloody kettle! It's been going off for five minutes and I can't stand to hear it any longer or my eardrums will pop," Miss Everett shouted over the kettle that she wrenched off the stove.

"Ladies, ladies, calm down. You've still got seven minutes until luncheon," a familiar voice chimed in. In all the commotion, I didn't even notice Duncan standing off to the side. He was leaning on the wall. In front of him, an empty silver tray balanced on the corner of the table. Its handles resembled twisted silver rope.

"*You* try being in this kitchen for a day, eh, Duncan?" The voice was sharp with a crystalline clarity that could be heard acres away. "Make yourself useful, will you? Take this up." The shortest of the three, Mrs. Hardwick, placed half a dozen china cups onto a tray and poured steaming hot tea onto each cup. Duncan watched with the same amazement as I did. Not a single drop was spilled. I was astonished how delicate she could be, even though she was bustling about like she was on a rampage.

"A day? I'm here *every day*! I *live* in the midst of all this racket!" Duncan turned on his heels, holding the tray at a perfect ninety-degree bend from his elbows.

"Oh, you watch your cheek, young man. I don't want to hear your backtalk." Another woman appeared through the doorway with a scowl on her face.

"Yes. Miss G." He paused and then headed toward the door. "Outta the way! Hot stuff! Hot stuff!" He nearly ran over Bentley and me as he dashed through the doorway. Bentley glared at his back as he marched up the stairs.

"Have any of you seen Mr. Lemont?" Bentley stepped in the kitchen and motioned for me to follow. I felt sure that one of them would trample me as they swarmed around the table.

"He took up the appetizers already, Mr. Bentley. Can I help?" The young girl actually looked up from her work. She had a narrow face with hollow cheeks. Her eyes were almost completely round, resembling the size of cherries. It wasn't hard to guess that she was the apprentice cook. She was the youngest.

"No. But I would like to introduce Mr. Leonhardt while I've got your attention. He's going to be Mr. Claude Breaker's valet and a part-time land-scaper."

"What? How do you say his last name? Londar? Lerndot?" Miss Everett pounded more dough and looked up at me between each time she stretched it back out. "What kind of last name it that? Mouthful, isn't it?"

"You can call me Mr. Bruno or just Bruno if it makes it easier." I trampled nervously over my own words like I was tripping down stairs. I couldn't have them become too aware of my last name.

"Sounds good to me." The cherry-eyed girl agreed as she whisked something in a huge bowl. "I'm Pauline."

"You're also slacking. Get whisking, hun!" Mrs. Hardwick enforced.

"Yes, Mrs. Hardwick," Pauline replied, kicking in the pace. Her lips tightened as she concentrated.

"You're pushing her too hard. She's still a young girl. And a pretty one, if I may add." Another footman I hadn't seen before entered. His clothes duplicated those of Duncan. He had a flamboyant personality, enough to make Pauline look up from her work and blush. He looked to be a few years younger than me. But then again, looks can be deceiving.

"Wayne, stop distracting me." Pauline laughed, catching his eye just before she went back to whisking.

"I second that request." Mrs. Hardwick handed him a full tray and shooed him upstairs. "Second footmen…." she grumbled to herself, dusting off her hands on her apron.

"Come on, I'll talk to Mr. Lemont later about your room. You've got a lot to learn." Bentley looked toward me and we left the kitchen without any of the cooks noticing.

England
The Violinist

Everything in the house seemed livelier with the arrival of our cousins. Their young energy brought forth a new mood, a new sense of wonder and adventure. Everything wasn't as *monotonous* as usual. Poppa's brother, my Uncle Ted, was many years younger than he, so when he finally got married and had children, there was a big age difference between his children and us. The oldest was seven and the youngest was four. They danced around our feet as we waited outside.

"Stand by me, will you? I'm a bit nervous," Charlie whispered to me.

I gave him a big smile. "Lord Breaker, I don't ever recall seeing you this nervous before. You don't need me. It isn't *all* bad. You should be more excited." I nudged his arm and nodded in the direction of the car driving toward us. The gatemen shut the gate and resumed their places. As the car neared, I could see Charlie tense up.

"I know. I *am* excited, but I know Momma will completely embarrass me, I know it. Her—" he hesitated— "*perfectionism* will ruin everything."

I agreed, but I didn't admit it out loud. He had to harbor *some* hope… even if it was unrealistic. The car pulled up right in front of us. A couple of suitcases were strapped to the top. The chauffeur jumped out of the car to open the back door.

"Cleo, Bonnie, come along. Move out of the way." My aunt scooped up Bonnie, the youngest, and the nurse took Cleo by the hand. Bonnie wore a tiny hat that must have been the size of my fist. It looked adorable on top of her red curls. Arthur, their older brother, stood by his momma's side, not uttering a word. His reckless attitude was suppressed for the moment.

Charlie strode over to the car and held his arm out to the woman emerging. I was eager to see Charlie's special friend. Lately, he couldn't stop talking about her. Apparently, he had met her in town when her horse's shoe came loose. He had stopped to help her and they had become closely acquainted.

"May, wonderful to see you," Charlie exclaimed. She reached out her hand and steadied herself by holding his elbow. She did not wear gloves like the rest of us. She also didn't wear fancy hats like we did. She wore a casual light blue cloche, the color of a hydrangea flower. For me, it was a smack in the face. A reality check. I used to have a hat like that. A black one with a pin attached to the side.

"You, too! I love this car, and the chauffeur is so pleasant. Oh, I'm so impressed!" She embraced Charlie happily. Judging from his face, he had not expected that at all. His cheeks were red like ripe tomatoes. "I'd say your house is beautiful, but I'm sure you hear that from everyone."

"I must say, that is true. But it means more coming from you."

May grinned like a giddy child. Charlie led her over to us and began to introduce her. She was extremely tall for a woman. She was just shy of Charlie's height. Her short chestnut hair framed her face and made her eyes pop. More than half of her body had to be her legs. They were so long and elegant, I couldn't help feel a pang of jealously. She smelled like lilacs.

I quickly glanced in Momma's direction, making a point not to turn my head. She pursed her lips tightly, shifting her weight from her heels to the balls of her feet. I so wished I could tell what she was thinking. Her hair was tied up in a crown, giving the impression that we all should have lined up and kissed her ring. It had to be intimidating for May. But as she approached Momma, I saw no fear. Not even the slightest hesitation. She greeted Momma with warmth, but the warmth was not mutual. I wanted to shake Momma to her senses.

May and Charlie went into the house first. The rest of us followed like a flock of geese in arrow formation. I could tell that even the staff were curious about May. Their eyes shifted and their heads turned as she and Charlie passed by. Their mouths emitted no words, but their heads burst with thoughts. I could almost see them, their questions drifting up toward the sky, unanswered.

"Bruno, get up, or I will have to drag you back inside by your ear," I heard Lemont demand a little ways behind me.

"Mr. Lemont, I can't. I have to find it. I—"

"Now! How dare you tell me what you can and cannot do? You scrub the dishes with the scullery maid if I ask! Or you sweep the rooftops! Am I clear? We don't play games here. Maybe that's something you weren't *accustomed* to in Germany."

"Mr. Lemont, give me a minute, *please....*"

"No, we are running behind already." Lemont stood firm like a tree in a storm, though it was his own storm he created. I came to notice how he liked to demonstrate his authority whenever possible. Which, at the moment, I was finding quite rude. The servants had to listen to him, but they certainly weren't to be treated as pets.

"Excuse me," I muttered, squeezing back through the doorway against the flow of oncoming staff. Instantly, they froze and let me pass like I had put them under a spell with my words. I spotted Lemont hovering over someone in the staff whom he addressed as Mr. Bruno. The name was familiar. Then I remembered. This was Claude's new valet. He had arrived a week ago.

"Lemont, surely you needn't be so harsh. He *is* new." I kind of felt bad. I couldn't imagine it was easy being a servant. But the thought had never crossed my mind until now. The man was crouched down, staring at the dirt like a magical bean stalk was about to appear.

"Yes, Mrs. Bolton, with all due respect, he is. But he is resistant and disagreeable like the horrid country he comes from. He is from Germany, and I am just trying to teach him," Lemont assured, straightening his back. His forehead gleamed in the warm sun. "You see," he continued, "Bruno seems to have... a knack for procrastinating *procrastination*. In other words, *avoiding* his duties."

German? I could not find myself to welcome this man after I learned this. Especially for Claude's sake. I pitied him no more; my empathy had completely evaporated in the sun. Lemont was probably right about him.

"Bruno, I daresay that you need to follow immediate commands, just like everyone else. And you must *especially* respect Lemont's commands. Please move along now," I enforced, taking Lemont's side.

"Thank you, Mrs." Lemont nodded respectfully at me.

I watched as the man stood. Still his eyes were glued to the ground. Then, suddenly, they snapped up to my face. They did not waver, or drift nervously like the other servants'. In time, they would. They were the color of black tea. Bitter, until you added a little honey. And indeed, like the tea, if you looked close enough, golden flecks in his eyes were visible.

"*Auch der höchste Berg ist unter dem gleichen Himmel wie der tiefste See,*" he said bitterly. I had no idea what any of it meant, but I could sense the sadness in his voice. And yet, even with that sadness, he had such confidence in his words.

"If you wish to speak, speak English. We *are* in *England*, Mr. Bruno." Lemont glared at him.

Without another word, he reluctantly followed Lemont and the last of the staff through the door. I was the only one left standing outside. How badly I wished I knew what he said. It was probably an insult of some sort. What had he been looking for? I glanced around to see if anyone was watching me. Then, I began to search.

I felt like a hawk, circling around the same spot where Bruno had been. In a few short seconds, my eye caught a shine. I bent down and picked up a tiny round object. It was a beautiful pearl. Its colors were stunning: a combination of creamy white and peach. My mouth nearly dropped. This had to be what he was looking for. But then again… why would he have it? It was not like he would wear it as a piece of jewelry; he was a man. My thoughts began to run wild. What if he stole it? It was certainly a decent-sized pearl that would be very valuable. What if he planned to sell it on the black market, or on the streets? Hastily, I curled it into the palm of my hand and rushed inside. Maybe it had been stolen from one of *my* jewelry pieces.

I rummaged through my jewelry box, but found every piece intact. Later on, I went into Flora's room and searched through her jewelry, too. But still I found that nothing was missing. It boggled my mind.

"Oh, Mrs. Bolton, there you are."

I was just coming out of Flora's room when Sarah, one of the maids, stopped me. "Hello, Sarah." I hadn't expected her. She was a short, sort of pudgy woman. Her thin hair slipped out of her bun slowly like a woven basket that was coming apart.

"Lord Breaker was looking for you. He seems to want you to accompany him and Miss Farefield on a tour of the gardens."

"Oh, thank you. I shall be right down."

She scuttled away, carrying laundry and a pair of gloves that needed to be resewn on the seam. They all walked like something was chasing them. One glance, and I'd see her, and the next, she was gone. Constantly on the go.

I hurried down the stairs and found Charlie and May in the sitting room. They had just finished their tea. Cleo was poking at the piano keys. Her eyes shone every time the hammer struck the string. She could play little bits of "Mary Had a Little Lamb," but it was quite sloppy. The sound really rattled my insides. How long had it been since I'd played my violin?

"Ah, there you are, Estella. Would you accompany us in the garden? You know much more about it than I, and May is very eager to see it."

Just then, Roy came barging in. "Stell, there's a little bit of an *issue...* with Arthur, and I can't find your aunt. Can you give me a hand?" Roy leaned on the doorframe, eyes wide and unsure. It made my heart flip giddily that he even bothered to consult me. His lips were slightly parted and the golden stubble on his face was gone.

"Oh, of course—" I began. But I stopped. Charlie's eyes burned on my face. He had asked first. "Of course," I started again, "but... but I'll have to help you later. I'm going with Charlie to give May a tour. I'm sorry, darling." His shoulders drooped as the words came out.

"I suppose I'll have to ask Flora, then. Hmph. Never mind." He refused to look at me now. The hardness in his voice echoed in my ears as I listened to him walk away. Charlie stood with a smile, not missing a beat. So dense at the worst times.

"Well, let's begin!" He announced.

My eyes met his, though they were gleaming with lies. A fake smile tore across my lips.

England

The Pianist

"**W**hy? Why are you here again? I told you a hundred times already that I don't need a valet!" I dreaded being in Claude's presence. Every day, he said the same thing. And every day, I tried to convince him that I was solely here to do my duty.

"My brother thinks I'm physically unable to dress myself. That's it. *That* is why he hired you without my consult, isn't it? He didn't want to *offend* me. So he did it behind my back." He was sitting at his desk, complaining as always. Every time I entered the room, I found him at his desk. He certainly wasn't very social. Lord Breaker had been right about him being quiet... but passive? I disagreed.

"Mr. Breaker, I do believe it was on the contrary. He thinks highly of you, so he wanted you to have the best service living here." I laid out his clothes on the bed. I had worked hard on brushing all the lint off. There was not a speck of dust or dirt on the fabric.

"Oh, spare me the pain of calling me Mr. Breaker. Claude is my name. You probably don't even respect me, either. You think me a joke. Admit it. A man with one arm? You probably laugh at me."

"I do not, sir."

"Claude. Call me Claude. Say it now." He whipped around in his chair. I had never seen such a naturally serious face. I have to admit, it did frighten me a little. But as Mrs. Bolton so *rudely* told me, I have to obey my given commands.

"Okay, Claude. I'm sorry. But I can promise I have respect for you. I'd like to think I respect all people who deserve it. Sometimes it's tough to decide," I admitted, placing his newly-polished shoes at the foot of the bed. This was the first civil conversation that didn't consist of the sentence "Get out."

"That I'd have to agree with." He turned himself back around in his chair and hunched over a piece of paper. It was awkward just standing there. I couldn't tell if he was going to dinner or not. If he was, he'd have to get dressed quickly. I cleared my throat.

"Claude, is there anything else I can do for you, or should I leave you be?"

"Well, it is actually *my choice* when to have you dismissed, Bruno, so you shouldn't ask. May I call you that? Yes, I think that is fine, actually. Like friends. I don't have too many of those." He never waited for me to even answer. He rambled on. Between his words I could hear scratching. It seemed like he was writing. Was he recording our conversations? The disturbing thought crossed my mind and lingered uncomfortably.

"Bruno is fine, si—Claude," I corrected myself, shaking the cobwebs out of my head. The friend thing seemed like a stretch. He apparently thought having me as a friend meant yelling at me to get out and to mind my own business. Even with this information, I pitied him. He seemed lonely.

"One last question, sir. Claude." I hesitated. He stopped writing and turned his ear in my direction, waiting.

"Well, go on then! I can't wait until Christmas."

"Oh, um, I was just wondering if you will be attending dinner to-night."

"No." His response was very quick and firm, like an accent in musical terms. "And especially not in this choice of clothing. Bruno, I say you learn to color-coordinate before you come see me again. I'd look like a clown in this… costume. Yes, *costume. That* is how *pathetic* it is." The scratching resumed. A light, wobbly, uneven rhythm like dulled skates scraping on ice.

I felt like a puppet. My mouth opened many times to say something, but no words came out. There was nothing wrong with this outfit. I did not understand. He was too picky for my liking. It angered me that I had worked so hard to prepare and brush the whole thing, and he wouldn't even wear it anyway.

"Alright. I'll work on that." I swallowed what I would have liked to say and stood curtly, waiting to be dismissed.

"You can go now." I draped his clothing neatly on my arm and picked up the shoes. I could see my face in the polish. A brown-haired man with pinched eyes and a potato shaped head because of the disfigured reflection. What if everyone looked at me the way I saw myself in the shoe? I began to understand where Claude was coming from. We are all someone's joke.

I quietly headed out the door, head up, shoulders back, and each footstep in time with the next like Mr. Lemont had demonstrated.

"Bruno," Claude called.

I poked my head back in the room. He was still facing down at his desk. "Yes?"

"People never realize they have two arms until one is gone. One is dominant, and does everything, while the other just hangs back," he randomly blurted out. I didn't know how to respond. What was that supposed to mean?

"I guess you're right. But we have two for a reason," I answered stupidly. I really had nothing else to say. But it was true. The slow scratching resumed, and I left the room in wonder. How could this man have so many personalities? He was philosophical, yet tempered, and secluded, all at the same time.

Afterward, I joined everyone downstairs in the servants' quarters for dinner that Pauline had made. Her official title was the apprentice cook, but everything she made was delicious. I found it hard to believe that the meals served upstairs were better. In my opinion, she had to be as good as Mrs. Hardwick.

"Have you seen the new dress Miss Flora Breaker was wearing? My goodness. It was so beautiful." Sarah's eyes glistened at the thought. "I wish I could own a dress like that."

"Have I seen it? Well yes, girl. You can't miss it. That would have never been accepted back in my day! Showing your ankles? That was forbidden in my time," Miss G explained with disapproval. She was the housekeeper, a rather haggard, tired woman at first glance. But she still got around very well. A woman full of spunk. None of us could pronounce her name correctly, so we all resorted to calling her Miss G, which she approved of. By far, she was the oldest here among the servants.

"I think it's lovely," Another one of the maids agreed. I had forgotten her name.

"That's enough now. Let's not spend our dinner *gossiping* about the family's fashion. I'll have to see an end to this conversation," Lemont stated. He looked down the table at each of our faces, daring someone to continue. No one did. His words were ours.

"Mr. Bruno, how is it tending to the garden? I must say, the hedges are so perfectly trimmed I thought they were fake! I was walking in the garden early this morning because I couldn't sleep, and I felt like I was in a magic garden in some sort of fairytale. Like a fairy might pop out of a flower and waltz around with a butterfly," Miss G complimented.

"It's a really tough job. Makes my back sore. Especially when I have to weed the beds like yesterday. But overall, I can't complain too much." I made sure to swallow before I spoke.

"Oh, I can imagine. Good thing your skin isn't *too* fair, or you would be completely red by now," she teased. "You've at least got *some* color."

I grinned. "True to that." I was the only one left at the table afterward. The ladies' maids had gone up to undress their ladies and get them ready for bed. I did not need to, for Claude still insisted he did not need me. Instead, I opened my notebook and began to write.

"Whatcha doing?" I nearly jumped. Pauline placed her hands on the table and looked over my shoulder. "Are you writing in code? What *is* that, Mr. Bruno?" She squinted, trying to decipher a key or pattern. I couldn't believe my ears.

"It's music, Pauline. You've never seen a music note or staff before?"

"Afraid not. So that's how music is written? How peculiar." She laughed, pulling out a chair next to me. "I've been an understudy cook all my life. I don't know how to read *English*, never mind *music*."

The thought boggled my mind. I couldn't imagine not knowing how to read music. It was by far my dominant language.

"That's… that's so strange. Where have you been all your life?" I joked around, closing the book. I needed to be near a piano to configure the chords together. It would be much easier with a visual.

"I've been living in grand houses like these. They're a trap, I'm telling ya. They look so stunning on the outside—alluring even." She looked out over the table, in a different world. A world where she sat with everyone and ate a meal she didn't have to cook. A life where her plate was full and rich, with zeal and possibility. "Until you see how it operates on the inside. We all have a piece on our shoulder, here downstairs. No time for personal achievements. We all depend on each other like pillars holding up a building." She slid my notebook in front of her and ran her finger across the leather binding. "You're lucky you have this. I've never had anything of my own."

"We'll have to fix that, then, eh?" I assured her.

"Mr. Bruno, that's sweet of you, but don't trouble yourself with me. I'm not worth it." With a wistful sigh, she stood up, pushing her chair back in. "But thank you for even offering." Her cherry eyes were glossy, like a fresh rain had layered them in a thick mist. She wasn't much taller than me when I was sitting, and for the first time, I noticed that she was too thin. Even her cap didn't fit quite right on her head.

She reached out and stroked my hair just once. Once was enough to make a striking impression. It joggled something in my mind, and all of a sudden I was picturing Lieselotte. She'd always pat my head right before a performance. It was then that I acquired my first friend at the Hampton Court.

England

The Violinist

I spent my days avoiding Roy, and it sickened me to admit that to myself. It was hard for us to put on an act in front of the others. We felt like distant friends, only saying "good morning" or "good evening." It was then that I started to dress in normal clothing again. I had to abandon my mourning clothes, though, at the same time, I wished to wear them for the rest of my life as tribute to Ruby. I didn't want her to think I had forgotten, or gotten over her. Because that would never happen. And yet, I wanted to attempt to restore myself. I knew that's what she'd have wanted of me.

I occupied myself by having tea with my mother. Charlie was busy with Miss Farefield, and Flora was constantly going out. Claude stayed in his room most days, so that did not help. Sometimes, Momma and I would go out in the town with Lemont. Other times, we'd chat aimlessly for hours on end. I'd go a whole day without laying an eye on Roy until nighttime. And even then, he was usually asleep by the time I got into bed. But tonight, he was wide awake.

"Estella." The room was dim and I was almost asleep when I heard him whisper from his side of the bed. Slowly, I pulled one eye open after another. I was curled on the right side, all the way to the edge of the bed with one arm dangling down the side.

"Mmm?" I responded.

"You are going to hate me for this." His voice was low. I heard him shift onto his back.

"I don't think I could *hate* you. Only dislike you an awful lot," I joked foolishly. But now he had made my mind wander. He had pulled a string, and I was all too curious to know what it was connected to. Especially coming from him.

"Estella, I'm serious," he sighed. He seemed at a loss for words and his desperate tone surprised me.

"Yes, yes. I apologize." I paused considerably. "What is it?" I turned to the other side and faced him. I could faintly see the silhouette of his head on the puffy pillow. Looking at his silhouette, he could have been any man without the light to differentiate his features.

"Do you think about Ruby a lot?"

"That's a stupid question, Roy. Of course! I don't think there's a time where she is ever fully off my mind. And I don't want that to happen anyway. I want to think of her all the time and enjoy the memories she gave me," I enforced, propping myself up on my elbows. I could feel my hair fall over my shoulders. He hesitated. The sheets rose and fell with each breath.

"I just… it's so hard. One of the servants— I forget her name— has three children that come by quite often. They are her nieces, actually. Sometimes I'll see them wandering the house or playing hide and seek. They don't make any noise. I'll even see them out in the garden a couple days a week, but it's like they're afraid to touch anything. Anyway, that isn't my point. I look at them and feel so… slighted. And having your cousins over doesn't make matters any better. Ruby brought such joy with her. And… and I selfishly wish I had that joy given back to me. And to you as well." He sighed. "I'm not a father anymore, and that was the best job in the world."

I was taken aback by every word. In fact, I didn't know he spoke in such length anymore.

"Estella? Ugh. I am so truly sorry. I knew I'd offend you. This was too soon." He backpedaled and rubbed his forehead with his hand after I didn't respond.

"It's not… *offending*." I found my voice and slowly began to piece my words together. "I— I know what you're saying. I can't say I haven't thought about it, either. But… this is too soon, as much as I would like to say yes. I just need to think. Of course I would like another child, but...." I trailed off, failing to come up with an answer.

"But? What is that supposed to mean? Stella, I seriously don't understand you. We both just admitted raising Ruby made us happy. We could have another chance. Think about it," he pleaded. I could feel his hand on my cheek.

"Roy, we argue every other day. We don't understand each other too well, do we? I want to spend more time with you because I feel like I don't even know you anymore. How could we have another child when we don't even get along ourselves?" I pushed his hand back down.

"You speak of nonsense. You are my wife, and whether or not you think it, I do love you. I don't think this is as bad as you say it is. We have our moments, but we always make up," he argued, turning to face me. I didn't need to see in the dark to know the exact facial expression he was making.

"Is love not speaking to me for days? Is love ignoring or avoiding? Is it being unable to meet the other person's eyes while talking? Is it ashamed? I guess I don't like your version of love. But what of me? I don't know myself."

"Do you love me? Do you love me in whatever version you have?" he simply asked.

I could not answer. Only bite my tongue. I could hear the dark around me. Its creepy, uncomfortable silence made an aura around us. It quietly strangled me. Finally, a tiny voice emerged. "I'm trying to."

"I think it's best if you leave. Come back when you've decided," was his next, and last comment. He turned on his side, back to me, refusing to believe it.

Without responding, I slid out of the bed. I grabbed my book off the nightstand, and padded out on bare feet. Now, I knew sleep would never come to me. Halfheartedly, I made myself go to the library. Rather than sitting and wallowing, I forced myself to read under the lamp.

♪ ♪ ♪

The library was connected to the sitting room by a gap on the far side of the room near the shorter bookcases. Reluctantly, I placed my book back in its bookcase, breaking my own promise of finishing it. It was too uninteresting. I let my fingers skid along each spine until I came to the last shelf just before the entrance to the sitting room.

That's when I heard it.

One, resonating note, echoing through the two rooms. It gave my heart a jumpstart. It was almost one in the morning. Who was up at this hour? Well, besides me. It couldn't have been Cleo or Arthur, for they would be fast asleep by now. The noise had genuinely startled me.

Again, another note was tapped. For some reason, it felt eerie. The sound vibrated through each bone in my body. Someone had their foot on the sustaining pedal, to make the sound last. Ever so slowly, I peered through the entryway. I placed my arms on the wall in front of me to balance myself as I craned my neck. Across the room, I spotted a shadow on the piano bench.

Two notes were hit at the same time now. A staccato sound. Short, sweet, and to the point. Then the figure stopped for a moment and leaned toward the piano. I could hear a fast scratching noise, like a little mouse running through the walls. The scratching stopped rather abruptly, and I watched as the figure placed a book on the floor.

For a while, the person sat there. I did the same, not knowing whether to ask them to leave or to ask them to play. But I didn't have to make that decision. Without notice, sound burst through the stillness of the air. It was like the eruption of an ancient volcano combined with the speed and agility of a lightning strike.

Never in my life had I witnessed anyone play an instrument like this. This was not someone just playing an instrument. No. This was someone who made themselves *part* of the instrument. Who swayed like a pendulum with the beat, and who jolted in place when slamming the keys. It was as if every sound was ricocheted from the piano to the person and vice versa, and couldn't escape. It could only reflect and bounce off both. I was absolutely stunned.

Without thinking, I crept into the sitting room ever so softly. I could have stomped in like a stampede of bulls, but I was convinced that the person wouldn't have noticed. Whoever it was, was in a different world. Some sort of trance.

I made my way between the sofa and a few chairs, past the fireplace, and to the far end of the room. The piano was only a few yards in front of me. As I had thought, the person was oblivious to me. It was a man, but not someone I recognized. He wore a plain white shirt and pants with suspenders. It could have been any commoner or servant, especially since I could only see him from the back. Even so, I was afraid to breathe. I didn't want to distract him.

Slowly, I put one foot forward, balancing on the balls of my feet and easing down onto both feet once more. I felt like some sort of predator, approaching an innocent animal in tall grass. The only difference was, I did not want to strike. I just wanted to watch.

Now I was at an angle where I could see over his shoulders. His hands were a blur. They reminded me of little water bugs that skidded effortlessly on the surface of the water. Water Striders. Yes, that was what they were called. So smooth and fast that in the blink of an eye, his fingers could go from one end of the piano to the other.

I don't know how long I stood there, watching the piano stretch its wings. I never knew the true sound until he brought it out. My comprehension of music was now beyond the limits of the mind. Those mother of pearl keys were not just for decoration. They pleased the eye with such astonishment, enough to make one's eyelashes curl up at the sight. But they pleased the ear even more. I hadn't realized that the song ended. By then, it was too late. He was standing up when it dawned on me that I should have left earlier. I was caught, one way or another.

He bent down and retrieved the book. When he noticed me, he almost tripped on the legs of the bench.

"My God! Why the hell do I always have an audience?" He slammed the book on the top of the piano as he braced his forehead with his hand. His eyes were squeezed shut irritably. "How long were you standing there?" His voice had started out as a yell, but it was softer now. Less frightening.

I was astounded. Then, I caught my voice. "You don't have to be so harsh about it! I was admiring—"

"Mrs. Bolton?" His voice was barely audible. "That's you, isn't it?"

"Yes?" I still couldn't tell who it was. The voice sounded familiar, but I was struck dumb.

"Oh God. Mrs., I'm so, so sorry. Please, I didn't mean to address you like that. I'm sorry. I'm going now." His voice was shaky. It had to be one of the servants.

"Turn on one of the lights. Do not go just yet."

Hesitation, then footsteps. "Yes, Mrs." The lamp closest to the piano was turned on. The person held his fingers on the switch with his back to me. It was as if he needed to take one more precious moment before he faced me. He was like a bat, paralyzed in the light.

"Bruno." I could tell from the back of his head that it was him. Though my eyes told me it was him, my brain failed to acknowledge it. How was it that *he* had just played the piano like that? The *valet*? The nasty German? It was impossible. He was—I couldn't come up with the word. Ordinary, perhaps. I was completely baffled. I stood patiently, waiting for him to turn around, with my hands folded neatly in front of me.

"Yes, Mrs.?" he responded shyly.

"You can turn around now. It is polite to speak to someone face to face, you know." I could feel my insides soften like melting margarine. Pieces of my hatred fell away.

"Yes, you're right, Mrs. Bolton. I apologize." He took one last second, and then turned around. His eyes wandered to the floor. "And... I'm sorry about what I said earlier. I should appreciate an audience if it is you. I'm sorry if I seemed ungrateful about it."

Oddly, that didn't matter to me. At that moment, the image of him being a servant did not exist in my mind. It was unfathomable. I approached him with only one question on my mind. "How did you do that?"

He seemed taken aback. Certainly he hadn't expected me to have an interest. He probably thought I was going to scream at him until the world's end.

He paused, going through the dictionary of words stored in his head. "Willingly. I think that'd be the correct word," was his simple answer. An unexpected smile crossed his face. The kind of smile that is unforgettable. The kind that can't be reimagined in one's mind as an image; only as an action. The kind that can be looked back upon.

"Well, yes, that is kind of obvious." I frowned, not understanding. "I just never would have thought...."

"You're not upset with me?" he asked like a small child. Like I had the power to spank him or send him to bed without dinner.

"I ought to be." I paused, letting the panic sink into him for a moment. "Charlie would be outraged if he knew a servant was playing on his piano at one o'clock in the morning, mind you. But then again, I'm here *listening* to you play at one o'clock in the morning, also. So I am just as guilty." I pressed my lips together in a tiny smile, feeling a little respect for Bruno. I still despised the Germans, but I appreciated musicians. So it was a tough split.

"That's true, Mrs." He held his book tight to his side. "I won't do it again. I promise." His eyes stared steadily into mine. I knew he wanted so badly for me to accept it. From his face, I knew he was trying to bribe me not to tell Charlie. Little to his knowledge, I hadn't planned on it anyway. But I let him think what he wanted.

"You promise? Why? That's quite awful with talent like that," I replied. He looked extremely confused.

"Awful... Mrs.? How?" he stuttered.

"You're the best piano player I've ever seen—"

"You watched *that* closely?

"Well... yes!" Now I felt like the shy one. My face heated up.

We both stood there, unable to extract the correct words from our minds.

"Thank you, then, Mrs. Bolton."

"You're welcome," I managed without tripping up.

"I should probably go now. I need to be getting some sleep. I have an early morning tomorrow."

"Yes, of course. I should be, too." I looked up at him, thinking about the pearl. I would ask about it later. He waited to be dismissed.

"Goodnight, Mr. Bruno. You may leave now." His face softened as I said this, and his body relaxed.

"Goodnight." I could feel his eyes on me as he turned off the lamp. He brushed past me to the doorway and disappeared, concealed by the cloak of darkness. Suddenly, a question burst into my head. I shuffled over to the door and poked my head into the open hall.

"Mr. Bruno!" I yelled in a hoarse whisper. I hoped my voice would carry down the hall, bouncing off the high ceilings.

"Yes?" I half expected him to not answer. There was no going back now.

"What time is the concert tomorrow?" I could hear our voices echoing. I felt slightly odd asking him, but it was worth it. God had smiled down on me. Mr. Bruno was my chance. Maybe, just maybe, he would be my key. My driving force to music again. My connection with my violin. The hope grew inside me. My voice had completely echoed out when he responded.

"Same time."

England
The Pianist

All I could ask myself was *why?* Why had I gotten myself into this? I did not want *her* as my audience. I did not want anyone as my audience. I didn't want an audience in general. All my life people watched me play, and all I wanted was to be alone with the piano. I only wanted to play that once, anyway. It had felt good to pour my thoughts out onto the keys. But now, I felt obliged to be the entertainer once more, and play for someone. Couldn't anyone understand that I only wanted to play for myself? No, apparently not. That would be selfish, wouldn't it?

Tonight I was to meet Mrs. Bolton, but I didn't want to. I couldn't figure out why I had said I would. Spur of the moment, I guess. I shouldn't have said it. I sighed unhappily and climbed the stairs. Making sure no one was around, I quietly made my way to the sitting room. Mrs. Bolton was already there.

"Close that door behind you," she said as I came in. She didn't even look up. Something was in her lap. I did as she instructed and clutched my notebook to my side.

"Are you taking me prisoner, Mrs.?" I joked. I tried to conceal my tiredness by amplifying my happiness. It was not a bad tactic; it just drained my energy. Every one of the doors were closed.

"No. But say the word and it won't be a problem," she shot back at me, giving me a testing glance. Her eyes were shiny, even in the dim light.

"It's so we don't wake anyone up. You have to admit, it would be awkward if someone else came in here, wouldn't it?"

"We? What do you mean by *we?*" Already she was making me uneasy.

She glided over to me and held up a violin. Her hair was loose and wavy, unlike during the day. Her whole face glowed with some sort of calmness that she didn't normally have. It was quite the transformation. Everything about her demeanor had changed.

"You play?" I asked in wonder. I had already made up my mind that she couldn't have been very good. She wasn't the type.

"I do, but I think I'm very rusty. Momma convinced me a while ago that being a musician was not the proper occupation for a young girl, so I gave up on it for a while. But I still remember a decent amount." She held the violin up to her chin and smiled.

Who was this person? For the first time I realized how young she really was. Maybe she did present herself using fancy vocabulary, and maybe she did wear clothes beyond her age. But she was still a girl. It was so odd that it hit me. I felt like I was being introduced to a whole different person than the girl I knew during the day. The little porcelain doll that walked on glass each counting hour had completely disappeared. Once she had been a peasant girl. I had to remember this. But the whole family played it up so well, I often forgot.

"Well, why don't you play for me? If that isn't rude to ask...." I trailed off, realizing what I said. It was not right to ask something of her. I was the servant, not her. I could not ask her of things. That was overstepping my place. I had to remember I was not supposed to be an equal.

"Really?" For some reason, she was thrilled. Her face was layered with excitement. But underneath, I could still sense that she opposed my every being. "I can try and see what I recall." She plucked the bow from her case and went over to the side of the piano. She hadn't noticed the off comment like I had. I was interested to see what she could play. For some reason, I couldn't see her playing the violin as a hobby. She didn't seem like the type of person to have a hobby, unless you count sipping tea and chattering aimlessly. Like most girls, I just assumed she liked to dress up and gossip.

"I am... a little nervous." She was about to play when she put the bow down at her side. "You can sit, you know. You don't have to stand there."

"Oh, thank you, Mrs." I gratefully sat down on the sofa, watching.

"May I see if it is in tune first?"

"Please. I can't stand anything out of tune."

At this, she seemed only more pressured. "I'll just give it a try." She paused considerably and then rambled, like a new driver, slamming the brakes on each word and then rushing forward recklessly. "I don't know too many songs. I mostly make my own songs as I go. I can't read sheet music that well."

"Then make something up if you want, Mrs."

"Yes, I do suppose I could." She didn't seem convinced as she stood there. Her arms were tense. She tapped the bridge of the violin lightly, though she was not conscious of it. "It's just that... you're very good. And even though I'm not playing piano, I'm still a slight bit... *intimidated*," she admitted.

"By me?" I laughed, walking over to her. "Let me fix that for you, Mrs., may I?" I held out my hand. Hesitantly, she placed the violin in my palm and handed me the bow. I had never held a violin before. It was surprisingly light. The smell of the wood brought my imagination into a long overgrown forest, one with thriving trees and humid air that carried the natural perfume of flowers.

"Like this, right?" I balanced the violin on my left arm and tucked it snugly under my chin. It was not at all comfortable. She nodded, staring wide eyed at it like it was a newborn baby that I would drop at any second.

"Hold the bow like this." She took it from me and placed her fingers delicately on one side. I mentally snapped an image of it and tried to remember as I fumbled to get the same position. My fingers did not want to cooperate. They were all scrunched up and in each other's way like tangled tree roots.

"Here I go." I took a breath. The friction from the bow on the strings created a pitiful screeching noise. It was like the violin was being strangled. Even she cringed, wincing as I slid the bow across the second string, and then the third and fourth.

"See?" I couldn't help but chuckle as I handed it back to her. "Nothing to be intimidated by. I am absolutely, one hundred and ten percent *terrible*. Mrs., you can admit it."

"I don't have a problem admitting it," she grinned slyly. "I am only kidding with you, Bruno. But, please stay with the piano instead." She took a breath. "I'm still intimidated, but that's only because I will never quite be able to make the screech that you just did. Quite incredible, I'll give you that." She laughed.

"Thank you," I replied. I could see the confidence blooming inside her as she stood next to the piano. She blinked slowly, and began to play.

Each wrong note added to the song, like it couldn't develop without there being fumbles. Keeping inside the key signature was not always the greatest idea in my opinion. It was good to switch keys to give the song some depth and mystery. And that's what she did. I didn't know if she did it purposely, but it still sounded extraordinary, especially to me, who could only make the sound of a distressed cat come from the instrument. She was not too bad at all. I was not afraid to admit that I had been wrong. The Celtic tune bounced happily through the air.

"Argh, I messed up on the ending." She swung the violin down at her side and I clapped a couple of times. "Oh, please, Bruno. If you only knew the mistakes I made." She tilted her head to the side and gave me a disapproving glance, but I couldn't take it seriously.

The thing was, I did. It was not hard to pick them out. But I still enjoyed it. Papa would not have. He crept into my mind the way a nightmare does. You don't realize you're having one until it is too late and you're stuck in it. I could see myself sitting at the piano at my house, with him hovering over me. I could almost smell the smoke on his clothes, even in my imagination. He'd point to the measures and tap his finger on the side of the piano in time with the metronome. It was the tempo of the piece. He'd drill it into my mind until my heart itself seemed to adjust to the beat.

Tap.

Tap.

Tap.

Opa had never done such things.

"It's your turn now," she exclaimed eagerly, sitting on the piano bench. It was like sparks lived on her skin. She was so full of energy.

"Oh, alright. But you might have to move because it's harder to play with someone else on the bench, Mrs." She looked up at me as I came over to the piano. The keys were iridescent, giving off different shades of light which drew my eye to them.

"Excuse you, sir, but it's not *polite* to ask a lady to move." I knew she was toying with me. She folded her arms, waiting to be readdressed.

"Oh, my apologies, madam, but would you please remove yourself from this bench? Is that better?" I raised my eyebrows, keeping up with the act. An honest smile spread across my face without my permission. I smothered it quickly. I did not like her.

"Very well. Since you asked so *kindly*." She stood to the side of the piano while I adjusted the distance of the bench. Particular things like the position and angle affected my playing ability. It was bizarre. Taking a breath, I erupted into a song: Beethoven's "Moonlight Sonata," movement three. By far my favorite out of all of them. The technical level was decent, and the speed only encouraged me. I did not even see her in my peripheral view anymore. I was too focused on the sound. Closing my eyes was the best part, because it was like nothing else existed. Just noise. Most of my world consisted of just sound anyway. With everything so dull, sound was the only way for me to escape and to see something else. It was a way to go deeper into my head and bring out undiscovered sights.

I opened my eyes without realizing, losing grip on my inside world. I could still hear the sound, but I couldn't connect with it. It was just... there. Like a cherub in a church. It was something that was expected. Just another angel.

My eyes lingered on Mrs. Bolton's face. She was perplexed. Spellbound. Hypnotized. And I couldn't understand why. I was three minutes to the end when I abruptly stopped. Instantly, the spell was broken. Her eyes shifted in their sockets to me instead of the piano.

"Was that the end? It couldn't have been...." she pondered aloud.

"No, I'm afraid it wasn't, Mrs. I... need to be going." This was wrong. Realization flushed my mind, causing a catastrophic breakout of thoughts to rattle inside my skull. This was wrong, I repeated to myself again. I was sitting, playing the piano at two o'clock in the morning for a married woman who should have been asleep and not even bothering to realize I existed. If this ever reached anyone, we were doomed. Actually, better put, *she* would be doomed. People had no better thoughts than to guess that something was going on. And they couldn't have been more wrong. My hatred settled in once more. It jarred me back to life.

"Going already?" she sighed, but her spirits weren't down for long. "When will you play again?" It was difficult to put out the light in her eyes. It was now a bit more tempting to say yes, but I refused. She was certainly good at concealing her hatred.

"Mrs. Bolton, excuse me for speaking so freely, but I won't be." I watched her face twist like she was looking at an illusion and couldn't figure out how it was being done. "This isn't right." I swallowed, configuring my words. "What would your family think? Being down here with a servant in the early morning?" I knew that would get her. She would leave me alone now.

"Why does it have to come to that? I don't care what they think because it is irrelevant in this particular circumstance. I just wanted to hear you play. And I thought that maybe... we could become friends." The words came out of her mouth like they hurt to say. "That's all, Mr. Bruno. I... honestly didn't think of it like that." Her innocent mind shattered.

"Well, it can't go on like this. I'm sure you have people lined up wanting to make your acquaintance, Mrs. Bolton. You certainly seem like a well-liked person." I didn't show it, but my brain nearly froze when I heard her words. Friends? *Friends?* She had to be mocking me. It almost made me choke.

"Ha. I'm sure there is a line all right. A line of beggars and self-indulging, over-pleasing *rats.*" She turned her head from me, looking like she had swallowed something sour. There was that dingy personality I knew her for.

She crossed her arms defiantly. "Oh, they just want a piece of our money. That's all. There aren't too many truthful individuals out there anymore. They live in a fog. A fog they surround themselves with to shield their flaws and uphold their own oversized image of themselves. I don't want any part of that." She scrunched up her nose, hitting random keys on the upper register of the piano with one finger.

"That's quite a generalization, Mrs. You can never be too sure. Not all people are puppets. Sometimes I think we fail to see that their strings don't exist, which is wrong. Some stand on their own and are good people," I explained, hoping for her to see. She paused and narrowed her eyes, thinking. Maybe it had sunk in.

"What *is* this?" She picked up my notebook and curiously opened it. I changed my mind. Maybe it *didn't* sink in. At first, she skimmed through the pages. I reached out to take it from her, but she stepped back. Gradually, her pace slowed until she gave each page a thorough look over. She studied it, but gained nothing from it.

"I need that back." I stood and plucked it from her grasp. It wasn't her right or her business to pry.

"I was just *looking*. I wasn't going to throw it in the fireplace, Mr. Bruno. Honestly. No need to be flustered."

"I wasn't flustered, Mrs.," I replied stiffly, tightening my jaw.

"That was an awful lot of sheet music in that small book. And, they all have your name on them." She glided over to the sofa and sat down, not ready to leave.

"Yes. They do," I confirmed.

"I see, Leonardo. Quite interesting that you go by your middle name, may I say. All of your sheet music has Leonardo Bruno Leonhardt written on it." She stated, testing my response. I did not give her the satisfaction. She was not stupid. She knew something was odd.

"Yes. I prefer my middle name," I enforced, turning my body on the bench to face the sofa. She was lying on her back, happily gazing at the ceiling like she was stargazing on a warm spring night.

"Alright, Bruno. Well, I prefer my *first* name." We were both quiet. I watched as she continued to stare. I couldn't determine her personality. She reminded me of her brother. One moment, I felt as if her hatred of me went to the moon and back, and the next, she was asking to be called by her first name. "Alright, Estella." She did not even seem to hear what I said. I had expected her to reprimand me for not saying Mrs. Maybe she did really mean it. "So, does this mean were friends now?" I prodded.

"Hmmm." A smile played on her lips. "I suppose it does, Bruno. No more elaborate sentences. Just normal conversations. It's actually nice to be like the common person again. I kind of miss that part of me, though I know it's there. Just bear with me."

"If I must," I sighed, throwing up my hands. Inside, I could feel myself relax, no longer concerned about how to address her anymore. I never understood the rules about how to address people. She could think what she wanted about this friend business, but I was certainly not keen on it.

"Well, since we're friends… I was wondering something."

I waited warily for her to continue.

"Well, you see, I have this song that I learned years ago. I remember most of it by heart, but I have a problem. There's supposed to be a piano accompaniment. You know, to get the full effect of the piece," she rambled. "And—"

"And you wanted me to learn it." I filled in her sentence dryly. Completely disappointing. Of course. How come I didn't see this coming? She wanted to use me this whole time. These rich English snobs… I couldn't trust any of them. The voice in my head shouted *I told you so.*

"Yes."

"No, sorry." I was quick to reply. "I only play for myself."

"But what's the point in that? You've got such talent! Why not put it to use?"

"Because I don't want to. I don't play that much, anyway. And even if I did, how would I learn it? I couldn't just come up here in broad daylight and jump on the piano. Your family would have a fit. Those keys themselves are probably worth more than my life."

"Oh, don't say such *stupid* things! Please? I would find a way. It would mean a great deal to me," she insisted. She sat up and leaned forward, locking eyes.

"No."

Silence wavered between us.

"What if I paid you?" she suggested. Her determination was irritating.

"Your brother already does that."

"In a different type of currency, I mean." She paused. "How about with this?" She reached her hand into a small compartment in the violin case and pulled out a tiny sphere. The little bit of light in the room made it shine. A pearl. She delicately balanced it between her two fingers.

My mouth dropped. It looked like the one I had lost in the front yard of the estate. "Where did you get that?" I hurried over to her and reached out for it. She curled her fingers around it protectively.

"I found it after Lemont led everyone inside. It was sitting there on the ground. Does it look familiar?" She searched my face carefully. I couldn't tell what she was looking for.

76

"Yes! I know it's hard to believe, but it fell out of my pocket," I rambled. "Well, actually… I had been holding it in my hand as Miss Farefield got out of her motorcar. Sometimes I don't realize I'm even doing it. Sort of a habit, you know? Anyway, it slipped from my grip and I couldn't find it. I was positive I had lost it for good." Still, I couldn't believe that she found it. I held my hand out in front of her, expecting her to give it back, but her iron grip on it wouldn't loosen. The excitement from my voice dwindled away.

"How about we make a deal? You know, like real adults do." She stared up at me, and then continued to talk before I could respond. Her eyes were alluring and convincing, like the flute of a snake charmer. "I will give this pearl back to you, if you will learn that song. It's only about four pages—"

I had stopped listening. So *that* is the life of a modern gentry's family? To make bargains and deals to further themselves? The pearl was rightfully mine anyway! I could feel the anger burning in my stomach.

"Keep the pearl, then," I hissed. I knew she wouldn't appreciate its value anyway. She probably had many pearls.

"What? But—"

She would not get to me. I would not be her puppet. My voice changed abruptly. I was surprised to find myself speaking with such a searing calmness. "Goodnight, Mrs. Bolton." I grabbed my notebook from the piano bench and headed out the door.

Suddenly, I felt a tug on my arm. "You've certainly got some nerve for a German in this household!" She pushed the pearl into my hand and quickly stalked past me. Her wavy hair swished along behind her as she walked, swinging her violin case at her side. I stared at my palm, unable to grasp why she had given it back. Then, I snapped my head up, watching her disappear up the grand stairway.

"And you, for a lady in this household," I retorted. She faced me from the banister up above for just a few seconds. A surprising laugh emitted from her lips. Quickly, she covered her mouth, stifling it.

"Looks like my first-class dresses can't conceal a third-class heart. Good observation, Mr. Bruno."

♪ ♪ ♪

I dusted my hands off and stood with a great effort. My spine was unfamiliar with the feeling of being upright after crouching down to yank weeds and spread fresh soil. The sky was gloomy and it had started to rain, making soft plinking noises as it hit the roaring water in the fountain not far from me.

"Aye, Bruno! You aren't done yet! Just a wee bit more. If you don't remove those weeds before the rain, their roots will cement 'em into the ground. Get a move on now."

"But Quin, I have to go in and change! If Mr. Breaker requires my service—"

"See, lad. You said *if.* Don't you worry. I'll inform the butler that you will be a tad late. Alamar will lend you a hand."

"But—"

"Go on then! Hurry up before it starts to downpour!" He wiped his sweaty face with a rag he kept tucked in his belt loop.

"Alright! Alright!" I huffed as I knelt down on my hands and knees. I heard Alamar's footsteps stop next to me as he, too, knelt down. Our pants became soaked where our knees touched the wet soil. He was much more skilled and experienced than I was. He could identify plants quickly, and knew just how much to water the different flowers. I assumed he had been working in the landscaping or gardening industry for a while. I could only assume this because he didn't speak English.

It was odd working next to a man who could hear, and yet not understand. He probably thought the same of me. He had very dark skin and a thin layer of hair on his head that looked like carpet. The palms of his hands were a lighter shade. He worked tirelessly, using up every second to achieve exactly what Quin had instructed, which, in the bigger picture, was what the Breakers instructed. Often, he and a few other men would work on the wisteria tunnel, making sure the flowers didn't get too long. Once in a while, he'd also work on the maze, due to his precision when trimming. The less experienced people would work in the sunken garden. People like myself.

When I looked at him, I noticed he had stopped weeding. He was perched like a bird, stretching his neck to look at something. Then, he tapped my arm and pointed.

"What?" I asked, trying to pinpoint his gaze.

He stood up, wiped the rain from his eyes, and walked on the stone path a few yards ahead of me. His feet hung on the edge of the wall. In front of him, where he stooped, was the canal of water. The water surrounded a gazebo that was only accessible by going over a tiny wooden bridge, like you'd see in a watercolor painting.

"Oh, if it's a rabbit I'll kill it. They eat all of our plants. Such pointless animals." I followed quickly, but I didn't see a rabbit. He stood at the edge of the canal and pointed. The water level in the canals the past few days had been extremely low. But with the rain, they were gradually starting to fill up again.

"The water's rising," I said out loud. "Finally. I thought these canals would run dry." I leaned forward and watched as each individual drop splattered into the water, making tiny bubbles. They only lasted seconds before another drop would shatter the tiny domes. The process was in a never-ending cycle. As quick as a drop came, the next would crush it.

I barely had time to realize what had happened. Water rushed up my nose and filled my mouth. Quickly, my feet found ground. I opened my eyes to find myself standing in the canal. The water only went up to my waist, but my whole body was soaking wet. Alamar stood on the edge of the wall, slapping his thigh with his hand as the air rang with his obnoxious laughter.

"Hey! Alamar!" I frowned at him, squeezing the water from the bottom of my shirt. He continued to laugh, a full belly laugh filled with mockery. "Why'd you do that?" I splashed him with a wave of water. He disappeared from my view, and the sound of his laughter died off.

I sighed and stared up at the puffy clouds. It was actually nice to let loose for a minute. So, I let out a laugh myself, and held my nose as I went underwater. When I came up, I pulled myself out by grabbing onto the wall above me and climbing back up. Quin was probably wondering where I was. I left a trail of droplets as I made my way back to my assigned flowerbed. Alamar was nowhere to be seen. I couldn't believe I had fallen for that. Quite literally, actually.

I was just about finished when a shadow covered my back. I turned and looked up to find an umbrella covering me. Then, it moved. I spotted the owner.

"Estella?" I stuttered. "What are you doing out here in a rainstorm?"

"Don't look *that* surprised, Bruno. I was gathering some flowers to arrange in a vase for dinner. It's my little cousin's birthday." She bent down and plucked a few flowers next to me, trying to hold her umbrella at the same time.

"Uhh, you shouldn't do that, Mrs. There could be poison ivy. I haven't finished weeding yet. And isn't that a job for a maid?"

"Oh, that's alright. I enjoy it. And don't worry, there's no poison ivy. Poison ivy has a little bit of red on the leaves. That's how you can tell. I don't see any here." She was fully occupied, picking the best blooms. I found it odd that she was even up at this time. It had to be eight o'clock in the morning. I thought that most of the Breaker family woke up at nine or even ten o'clock.

"Red, right? I've heard of that before." Although I knew of it, it confused me. I reached over her and pulled out a patch of dandelions.

"Do me a favor and hold my umbrella, please." She thrust it toward me expectantly. "Sarah just did my hair and I wouldn't want the rain to make a mess of it. It will only be for a few moments," she added.

Obediently, I held it over her head, watching as the rain trickled down the sides. A few moments evolved into a while, as she stopped to consider each shape and scent before she picked a flower. I grumbled to myself that I was going to be late to attend to Claude. Finally, I made up my mind to close the umbrella.

"What are you doing? I need that!" she whined, attempting to cover her head with her free hand.

"Well, the rain is actually more fun without an umbrella," I stated in a matter-of-fact way.

"Fun? I don't see the fun in it. Please, put my umbrella back up and I'll be done momentarily. I promise. Only a few more violets." She reached out and picked four to the right of me.

"Aw, come on. Are you too pretty to be out in the rain, Estella? No one is going to notice that a *strand* of your hair is out of place. Plants don't judge, you know," I mocked her.

"Don't you flatter me," she warned. "And yes, I'm very aware that plants don't judge, but people *do*." She glanced at me from the side for only a quick second. "I like the rain. It's just that I didn't want to ruin Sarah's hard work. But I suppose it's too late for that now, thanks to *you*." She blinked the rain from her eyes and touched her damp hair. "What do you say we go to the wisteria tunnel? I could use some of those flowers in my arrangement, but I doubt I'm tall enough to reach them."

Before I had time to consider an answer, she was already on her way, running past the maze to the tunnel. I picked up the umbrella, scraping the soil off the handle.

"Hey! Wait! You forgot your umbrella." I took off after her, waving it in my hand to shake the water off. Really, I shouldn't have cared. In fact, I should have buried it as a prank.

"Oh, that's quite alright! It's more fun *without* an umbrella!" she called back to me as she ran. We both stopped at the entrance. A small wooden bench was inside, but the wood was soaked and almost all rotted. "Stunning, isn't it?" she breathed.

"I know. I had never seen anything like it before I came here. But at the same time, it seems dreary. Like, the flowers are slowly falling down as they grow. Can't you see it?" I asked.

She hesitated, and then a puff of laughter came from her throat. "No, I don't see it. They look rather cheerful to me. Such brilliant shades of purple. It's impossible to think they're sad when they have colors like that."

We watched as the water dripped off the petals and collided with the ground.

"Well, come on. I'll give you a hand, but I have to go in a few minutes," I explained, reaching up and pulling one of the flowers down. The drops of water from the leaves fell on my face. I snorted and wiped my cheeks roughly with my sleeve.

"Alright. Oh, how about this one over here?" She walked toward the center and pointed up.

"What? This one?" I held the flower between my fingers.

"No, the one next to it." I turned my head, flashing stern lips and half-closed eyes that glimmered with impatience. I had a feeling she was exercising her pestering talent. "Yes, there you go," she exclaimed happily as I handed it to her. "Just one more and that should be good."

"This one looks nice over here." I headed over to the side of the bench and retrieved the last flower.

"Oh, good eye, I must say. Perfect." She bunched all the flowers she collected into her left hand. "Well, thank you very much, Bruno. I appreciate it. We're supposed to have some of Arthur's friends over later on for a celebration and *this* shall be the centerpiece," she proclaimed. "The only thing is, I know he won't really appreciate it like I do. And even more troubling is that I have to get him a gift, but I'm not sure what."

"What does he like?"

"That's the problem… I'm not really sure. I feel terrible about it. If it were for Cleo or Bonnie I could get them a doll or a dress or even a necklace. But for a young boy? I'm not really sure."

"How about candy? I don't know a kid in the world who'd deny candy. And not just kids. All people in general. I don't know a person who doesn't like chocolate, including myself," I pointed out. It had been a while since I'd had even a *piece* of chocolate. When the war was going on, finding chocolate was like finding gold.

"Maybe… it's just not… personal. I don't know. I'll figure it out. Maybe I'll head into town this afternoon with Roy and find a toy store or something among the sort. If I remember correctly, I think there's a rather big shop called Winfred's that sells toys and puzzles and games." We headed out of the tunnel into the rain. Just when my clothes had begun to dry, they became drenched again.

"The name sounds familiar, but I don't think I've ever been there."

"Bruno! You're slacking on the job, my boy! I informed the butler you'd be a tad late, not gone altogether!" I heard Quin's scratchy voice over the rain and turned around. I spotted him standing under a tree, clipping off the dead limbs.

"I'm sorry, Quin. I—"

"Oh, it's my fault, sir. I apologize. I borrowed Mr. Bruno to assist me," Estella interrupted.

"Good golly. I'm ever so sorry, Mrs. Bolton. I did not realize that was you. That's quite alright, then. I'm sure Bruno was happy to help. Weren't you?" I could feel his glare under his painted smile.

"Yes… of course," I replied.

"Well, hurry along then, Bruno. You must make up your lost time."

"Yes Quin, but… I was going to escort Mrs. Bolton inside. I'm holding her umbrella for her." I gestured to the closed umbrella in my hand.

"You're not very good at your job then. The point is to have the umbrella *open*, boy! Go on then! It's raining cats and dogs out here! Quickly!" he enforced crossly.

"Oh. Yes." I fumbled with the umbrella and finally got it to open. Quickly, I held it over Estella's head and we resumed walking. Once we were far enough away from Quin, she started to talk.

"You're pretty good at acting," she said, not looking at me. "But I do appreciate you helping me out."

"You mean by holding the umbrella? It's not like it's a bother."

"No, I mean by walking me back." She hopped up the front steps and jiggled the doorknob, but it was locked, so she rang the doorbell and waited. I closed the umbrella and handed it back to her.

"I... well, I have to go. Sorry. I'm already late. Good day to you, Estella."

"And to you, Mr. Bruno."

England

The Violinist

"Aunt Desiree." Charlie approached my aunt cautiously. She was having a laughing fit, splurging out random syllables that somehow were supposed to sound like words. Her eyes fluttered rapidly like the wings of a butterfly as her shrill laughter filled the room.

"Aunt Desiree! Arthur is trying to speak to you!" he whispered between gritted teeth.

"Ah? Oh, Arthur, my sweet boy. What? Did you see… did you see your new cap?" She attempted to sit up and spilled her sherry on her skirt. "Oh, what a shame," she mumbled. Her disoriented eyes swooped around the room, trying to identify Arthur.

"Mum, look! Cousin Charlie got me a toy soldier!" He held it up in front of Desiree's face. She grabbed at it twice and missed before she took it in her unsteady hand.

"My, my! How… how wongerfhul, my darling."

"Arthur, you must get to bed. Mummy is becoming giddy and tired. Come on. Your sisters are already sleeping." Uncle Ted finally found some common sense and took Arthur to bed. "Hope you enjoyed getting to stay up a little later."

Arthur thanked all of us and grinned widely as he left the room with his father. We could still hear him chattering away as they left our view.

"Claude, you never got him anything, did you?" I turned to him with disappointment. He seemed sleepy as he sat on the sofa next to me. His eyes drooped, but his mood was unusually happy.

"Well… not exactly. I told him that the train you got him was from both of us," he admitted.

"You what? Claude! That's horrible. You did not put one ounce of effort or care into our little cousin's birthday and you should be *ashamed*." I stared him down, but he was not at all intimidated or sympathetic.

"Shhh. Keep your voice down or Aunt Desiree will hear you." He glanced at her quickly. She had found our card deck and was playing a game of solitaire with herself. But her cards became all jumbled and she quickly quit.

"Aunt Desiree? Hmph. More like Aunt *Disarray*. She made a complete joke of Arthur's big day. I hope he never remembers this or he'll feel terrible when he gets older. Like she doesn't get drunk enough already." I lowered my voice to a whisper. Charlie was having a chat with Flora on the other end of the room. Claude cracked a big smile.

"Aunt Disarray? Stella, I must say, that was pretty good."

"It was not meant to be funny."

"But it is."

"You just don't understand."

"Maybe I don't. But I suppose it's not vital." He paused. "On a different subject, I must go upstairs now and change. I'm about ready for bed." He rubbed his eyes and stood.

"You're like a child. You go to bed so early." I shook my head and rolled my eyes.

"It's not a bad thing. Plus, it will probably be another half hour anyway before I actually get to sleep. My valet is clueless. Just about every night, he lays out mismatched nightclothes. Then I have to call him back up and have him find a matching pair. He's a piece of work, you know. I'm better off on my own," he grumbled.

"Mismatched?" I laughed. "Oh, surely it isn't the end of the world, Claude."

"It's an embarrassment! Yesterday, he gave me a pair of mismatched socks. If I didn't correct him every day, I'd be fit to join the circus with my attire. Ugh." He placed his glass down and left the room. Lemont opened the door for him.

It was funny picturing Bruno giving Claude mismatched clothes. He seemed to be the sort of person who never wanted to mess up. A sort of drive for precision. It was easy to assume that by the way he played the piano. I remembered watching his nose slightly scrunch up if his finger slipped. Maybe he just needed more training. But it did seem like common knowledge to match white socks with white, brown with brown and green with green.

"Lemmmmont? Do fill my glass for me, please." Aunt Desiree held her glass up in the air. But it slipped out of her grasp and fell straight to the floor. The glass bits buried themselves in the carpet.

"Oopsie. Ohh, deary. I'm so sorry." She giggled while Lemont rushed over to pick up the bigger chunks of glass.

"Auntie, come on. We're going upstairs." No emotion came out of my voice. It was hard and bossy. I strode to where she was sitting, forcefully made her stand, and led her out of the room like she was a convicted criminal. I was sure she had no idea what was actually going on around her.

♪ ♪ ♪

"How about we take a boat? I've heard that America is the greatest. We could go there for a while. What do you say?" Roy wiped his mouth with his napkin and looked over at me eagerly. We were back on talking terms, and he had made it up to me by taking me to a concert. We both had agreed we were being too pushy with each other. The orchestra was supposed to start momentarily.

"Hmmm… America? I'm not quite sure. Claude said it wasn't that grand of a place. He said he liked it better here," I recalled. I looked out over the balcony where we were sitting as all the instrumentalists took their seats. My heart rose in my chest.

"Well, your brother is a… unique type of person, Stell. You know, I don't think he enjoys boisterous parties, or champagne, or even dancing. America seems like it wouldn't suit him that well, so don't always take his word for it."

"You're probably right," I agreed. "But as unbelievable as it may seem, we *are* related. You must remember that."

The lights dimmed and a conductor with long coattails appeared at the front of the stage. He bowed, then turned his back toward the audience with his arms high in the air.

"Ooh! It's starting!" I smiled giddily, not taking my eyes off the violin section. I imagined another seat in the first row. In it sat me in an all-black dress with my violin at my chin.

They all sat with perfect posture as the conductor's hands hovered in the air. Then, all at once, they began to play. I never understood why conductors waved their arms. It didn't make any sense. It was as if the man was a bird and he was about to take off. I envied his position.

"So, there is a boat leaving a month from now. I've heard it's very big and gallant with plenty of room on deck. There will be many things to do. Perhaps a theatre, and a—" he rambled on and on. As much as I tried to listen, my ears were drawn to the sounds of the instruments rather than his enthusiastic voice.

"How about it, Stell? Eh?" I felt his hand grasp mine. It was warm and comforting, bringing my mind back to when I first met him.

"Hmm…." I mumbled and faced him. He looked so hopeful. "I promise I'll think about it." I straightened his bow tie and grinned with just my lips. But I couldn't focus on it then. The music filled every nook and cranny in my mind.

The next day started off ordinary, but it didn't last long. Once Lemont delivered the newspaper to my mother, everything fell apart.

"Claude! Claude! Lemont, go get Claude this instant! Or tell one of the valets! I don't care if he's still asleep," she fumed, as her silverware clanked on the plate in front of her. She refused to eat another bite.

"Yes, madame," he responded, unfazed by her sudden shouts.

"Momma, what happened? What's the matter?" I leaned over to have a peek at the paper while eating my breakfast. She yanked it from my prying eyes. "Just read this! I cannot even fathom…." She roughly handed off the paper to Poppa. His eyes grew wide as he absorbed every word. It was killing me now. What did the newspaper have to do with Claude?

"We are now a complete laughing stock! How can one even believe this is true?" Momma continued to say.

"Aw. What's the fuss? Claude is a free man. He can make his own choices. Hey, and maybe it's all just gossip," Uncle Ted chimed in as he spread peach marmalade on his toast.

"Maybe it is not. Darling, give Claude a chance to explain when he arrives," Poppa reacted calmly. He always did. He was a man of few words, but they never went to waste. "Charlie? Did you know about this?" The paper was passed to him.

"No! Of course I didn't! If—" Just then, Claude was announced as he came into the dining room. Everyone went silent.

"Would you care for the morning paper?" Momma's eyes flashed. She didn't give Claude time to answer as she opened it and placed it right in front of his seat. He was barely dressed and his hair was untidy. From the corner of my eye, I saw Duncan tighten the stupid grin that was displayed on his face.

Claude slowly sat down and immediately recognized his face staring back at him. He scanned all of our faces, weighing our thoughts.

"Read it," Momma insisted coldly. "Out loud."

"But Mother, it's—"

"Go on, then!" She didn't back down.

His lips parted, but he knew it was useless. Everyone was waiting on him. Silently, he pled for someone to interrupt, or switch the subject, but only blank faces reflected back at him. He cleared his throat.

"Claude Breaker, the younger brother to Lord Charlie Breaker, was seen last Saturday at a nightclub. Accompanying him was a young woman with the name Venus Achebe. The two were exceedingly happy, as Miss Achebe convinced Mr. Breaker to dance (pictured left)." Claude took a breath and continued. His throat tightened. "Miss—"

"That's quite enough. I don't think I can bear to hear any more babbling. It's just the papers trying to make a big deal of nothing. Claude, do what you must. I have to go. Roy? Come on, now. Do excuse us," Uncle Ted interrupted. The two of them always seemed to be on some sort of secret mission lately. Claude shot him a grateful look.

Roy came over to me and kissed the top of my head, then they both left. I turned my attention back to Claude.

"It is true. The papers only exaggerate. Honestly, Mother, it wasn't what it seemed. If you'll allow me to explain—"

"I don't understand. Momma, why are you so against this? He just wanted to have a little fun. It isn't the end of the world you know, being spotted at a nightclub," I exclaimed.

"No, but it isn't right either, Estella! Especially for our kind of people! Not in these… *circumstances*. You keep out of this, anyway. It is not your issue," Mother argued. I looked over at Duncan and Lemont. They were surely getting an earful. It made me uneasy. We were supposed to trust the servants, and vice versa, but even *they* could use the tiniest amounts of information against Charlie at any point they wished. I knew that. Trusting their mouths was the most absolute test in loyalty, and it wasn't even a part of their job.

"Actually, Estella, you're right. It isn't that *huge* of a disaster. But you haven't got the full story. Mother is so… *objected* to this whole thing because Miss Achebe is *black*. That is all it is, simply." He confronted her with such bluntness that the whole room went speechless. He slid the newspaper over to me and jabbed his finger in the direction of the photograph. Mother fumbled recklessly with her words.

"You! I… oh, Claude! You have to *watch yourself*! You can't be doing these things! They're nothing but trouble for our kind of people! And think about your brother, for goodness sake! You cannot go off *ruining* our last name when Charlie is in this position. The papers poked enough fun at this family when we first moved in! We do *not* need this extra nonsense." Mother was nearly screeching now, like a great horned owl. I always thought of her like that. A woman with knowledge, but of the wrong sorts. And a woman who wouldn't hesitate to swoop down on her prey, silent until she had them in her talons.

"There you go again with that idiotic line! *Our* kind of people. We are the same kind of people! You, Mother, are just a plain ordinary person like the rest of us! In fact, there's only one person in this room who has a legitimate reason to be different, and that is Charlie! He gave us the clothes on our backs and let us live here. He actually *inherited* his status. *You* are just where his extra charity goes!"

"Don't you *dare* speak for me, Claude. That's not t—" Charlie stood up from his seat, snarling defensively. His jaw was clenched and bolted. His menacing gaze made Claude turn cold.

"Shut up! Shush, all of you!" Flora, who had been trying so hard to ignore what was going on, had finally broken. "Claude, leave this instant! Do it! Go! You're making everyone upset! The only time we see you is when you are causing some kind of problem. Stop putting words in people's mouths and stop trying to constantly get attention!"

Claude stood stiffly near the doorway, lips white from restraint. He glared daggers at his twin, and stormed off like a piece of molten rock that had just shot out of a volcano: searing, burning, and seeming to fall endlessly until crashing into the dirt. I took a shaky breath and looked toward Momma. She was poking at the remnants of her meal. Her hands trembled as she held her fork.

Lemont cleared his throat. "More coffee, madame?" He looked at Momma pointedly. We were appreciative of his attempts to replenish the atmosphere with lightness, but unfortunately, he failed.

"No. It's too bitter. Tell the cook to learn how to make a cup of coffee." She waved him away and finished eating as if nothing had happened.

England

The Pianist

Loud footsteps grew nearer and nearer until the door was yanked open. It was the last person I had expected to see: Mr. Claude Breaker. I had thought he was eating breakfast.

"I'm sorry, Claude. I didn't expect you here. I was just returning your shoes that I polished," I explained, as I set them down. He slammed the door and huffed loudly. I noticed that the curtains weren't even drawn open yet. His whole room was cast with shadows, and the bed didn't even look slept in.

"Yes, whatever. Continue on then. Don't let me be a bother to you." He made a beeline for his desk and had barely sat down when I heard the scratching of his pen.

I watched him for a moment. He wrote awfully slow, making big circles with his hand. It looked so unnatural—so uncomfortable to have a brain that moved much faster than his hand. Nevertheless, I continued on, making a mental checklist in my head.

"Sir—I mean, Claude, would you like me to bring this jacket to a tailor? A button is missing so they will all have to be replaced, I'm guessing." I held up the jacket.

"Bruno, you keep interrupting my train of thought. Yes, yes, do whatever." He didn't even look up. I could have been stealing his jacket for all he knew. "Buttons are the least of my concerns at the moment." He grabbed at his hair stressfully and then picked up his pen again.

"Oh. I'm sorry," I said. I had never seen him like this. He seemed… crushed. That's when I made up my mind. "Claude? I don't mean to be a pest but I have a question."

He sighed irritably. "You are one anyway. What do you want?"

"I… was going to ask if you wanted me to write for you, you know… like a secretary. I don't know if it would be of any help, but I'd be glad to try." There was no taking it back now. The scratching stopped dead.

"You know, I really *hate* people like yourself," he glowered. Immediately, a surge of defensiveness came around me. My lips twitched from holding back words. I wanted to lash out at him, but he continued to speak. He actually turned in his chair to look at me. "I hate that you are so willing to help me, even though I'm a rotten, *lazy* fool. It easily makes me want to defy every ounce of help you have to offer. I want to be an independent man like everyone else. But you make me want to accept your help, too. That's what makes me despise you even more." He paused. "You don't understand. As much as I would appreciate the favor, I'm a forever condemned one-armed man who has to learn to write on his own, despite how grudgingly slow and damn awful it is."

It was some speech. At first, it stung, but after a moment, I was surprised to find myself at ease. "I understand that. Not the hating me part, of course, but the wanting to be independent. If you'll allow me to say so… independence does not have to go hand in hand with loneliness. Just a tiny word of advice."

"It's impossible to confuse the two, Bruno. Between them, there is a fine line. I don't need the advice. And who ever said I am lonely? Hmm? You are dismissed." The scratching resumed, and I stoically backed out.

♪ ♪ ♪

"Now where's that last piece of cake?" Duncan complained. "Mrs. Hardwick? Mrs. Hardwick, I told you, I don't see it. Someone had to have eaten it… unless a rodent somehow wedged itself in our cupboard." Duncan opened all the cabinet doors.

"Oh, you stupid boy. Let me check. You've got the vision of a mole." Mrs. Hardwick shuffled over to where Duncan was standing. Dinner was almost ready. Plates of steaming food rested on the tablecloth, making my mouth water. She peeked inside the cupboard.

"Well, good gracious! I don't see it!"

"I bet you'd like to take that comment back now, wouldn't you, Mrs. Hardwick? And anyway, I don't see the problem with a mole's vision," Duncan defended. He leaned against the wall and crossed his arms.

"The problem is that they haven't got no vision! Hope you've learned your fact for the day! Now go put out these cherry tarts instead. I know they're Mr. Lemont's favorite. Good thing I made extra." She passed Duncan a platter with them neatly stacked on top of each other. Her voice was all scratchy. "Oh, Mr. Bruno. You're just in time. Dinner is all set and ready," she exclaimed when she realized I was there. We both made our way to the table where everyone else was already sitting and waiting patiently.

"May God look down upon us and bless this meal we are receiving. Amen," Mr. Lemont prayed. We all opened our eyes and began to pass around dishes.

"Wayne, did you eat my last piece of cake? I was saving it, you know." Mrs. Hardwick was already making assumptions. Her eyebrows joined in a scowl when she met Wayne's eyes.

"I did *not*, Mrs. Hardwick. Why you accusing me? How could you even ask me such a thing?" he said. I could never tell if he was just being overly dramatic.

"I was just *wondering*. You never know around here… especially with you, Wayne. You are the one with the sweet tooth. And pass me the sauce, will you?"

I quietly chewed my piece of pork and reluctantly moved on to the potatoes. I had never really liked potatoes. During the war, we were forced to portion all of our foods, and unfortunately, that's where I began to despise the taste. They were so common that I easily got sick of them.

"Wayne, do you want the rest of these? I'm full." I gestured to the lonely pile of roasted potatoes sitting on my plate.

"Oh, yes please! You bet I do!" He grabbed the plate and scarfed them down.

"Bruno! There are people starving around the world! You eat whatever you're given, you hear? Wayne gets enough." Mr. Lemont shot me his usual glare from the head of the table. It seemed as if every day his hair was getting thinner. Probably stress related. I tried to picture myself at his age, but couldn't. It seemed impossible.

"Yes, Mr. Lemont," I responded politely.

"Hmph. You're probably full from eating my last piece of cake." Mrs. Hardwick looked away from me, trying to get me to admit something I didn't do.

"I didn't do it! I didn't even know you still had a piece left," I argued. She was certainly making a big deal of nothing, in my opinion.

"Then we have a dishonest thief somewhere in this house. That's my conclusion," she insisted with a surplus of stubbornness.

Duncan leaned over to me and whispered, "Don't worry. The batty old woman probably ate it herself, and then I reckon she forgot." We both laughed.

"I can believe it." I side-glanced her, laughing in my head.

After dinner, Pauline pulled me aside. "Bruno, come on! Just give me a hand? They had a few extra guests upstairs, and these dishes kept piling up! Just look at them all. Mrs. Hardwick won't ever know if you did. And with Miss Everett visiting her mother...." She gestured to a heap of food-stained dishes in the scullery.

"I can't, I already said. I'm going out for a smoke with Bentley." My feet and back ached from this morning. I rolled my shoulders and felt my body begin to relax.

"You smoke? Oh, that's not true at all. You're just kidding around with me."

"I just might start if you keep trying to recruit me as your little kitchen maid," I retorted. "Hurry up! Someone's coming!" I turned the other way and headed toward the back door.

"You're just trying to trick me so you can go off and enjoy your free time." She narrowed her bulging eyes into slits. "I'm not a little child, Bruno. Your *stupid* tricks can't fool—"

"Pauline? Who on earth are you jabbering to? Do you know how many dishes and glasses you have to wash? If you slack off one more—" I closed the door just in time, so I wouldn't have to listen in on Mrs. Hard-wick's daily lecture.

"What are you chuckling about?" Bentley spoke, pulling his cigarette away from his mouth. I sat next to him on the picnic table, just outside the door. He looked over at me just as smoke came out of his nose.

"Nothing really. Just Pauline." She reminded me so much of my sis-ter when she had been younger, it made my heart ache. "As strange as it is to say, I think I'm feeling homesick for the first time. I thought I'd never say I miss my sister, but here I am doing so. And my younger brother, too. Now, it just seems so far away. Like a whole different life."

"Sorry to say, lad, but I'm afraid I don't know the feeling. I've been in service practically my whole life." He paused, thinking and tossing the re-mains of the cigarette on the ground. "I, um, have heard that you're not from around here."

"I know you know, Bentley." I glanced at him, trying to read his thoughts. At first, I was leery, but I made my declaration anyway. "Yes, I'm German." I sighed deeply. "I get a lot of hate from admitting that here. And for that matter, in Germany, too. My brother Otto thinks I'm a traitor be-cause I migrated to the winning side of the war."

"It's hard to say if there really was a winning or losing side. Both sides lost so many people, it was just horrible. Like all hell was let loose. I don't think I'd call you a traitor though. To be quite frank, I wouldn't even know you were from Germany if I hadn't heard it going around in the serv-ants' hall when you first came. You don't have that mean accent that I always imagined. And you've certainly matched the English accent pretty well." He stared at the cracked cobblestone, poking at blades of grass growing through with his shoes.

"That's only because my mother is English."

The door creaked behind us.

"Ohhhh. Hope I'm not interrupting a man-to-man talk. Golly, look at that moon, eh? Looks completely made of gold." Wayne casually strode over and took up the other side of the bench. He kicked up his feet and sighed, taking off his jacket. "If only I could have a piece."

"Hey, put your feet down. You aren't the king, y'know." Bentley glared at him. "You could have a bit more *respect*."

"I may not be the king, but I'm not *your servant,* either. Calm yourself already. I'm not committing a crime." Reluctantly, Wayne obeyed, but not without a few grunts of annoyance. Seconds ticked by, and then Bentley started talking again. I wished he hadn't brought it back up.

"Anyway, Bruno. I was thinking, why don't you write to them? Your siblings, I mean. Then, maybe, just *maybe*, you can get some time off and go see them. I could try to slip some hints to my father." He wiggled his eyebrows, scheming up a plan.

"Hey! I want some time off! You never offered to do that for me, Bentley. Although I may be younger, I've got seniority!" Wayne complained. We both ignored him and continued.

"You see, that's the hard part. They were in the middle of moving when I left, so I don't know where they live now." Truth was, I did know how to contact them. But to do that, I would have to contact the middle person. The person who would know where they went. And that person was Annelise. I couldn't face her. Even the harmless words in my letter would shatter her. I had to give her more time.

"Blimey. That's rough, Bruno. I'm sorry. Maybe they'll send you a letter when they get completely settled in. Don't give up hope just yet." He tried to encourage me, but it only made me feel worse about myself. I had abandoned them. Every day, I went back and forth, wondering if what I did was truly right. Germany was in ruin and I left them in that ruin. It sent goosebumps up my arms and shivers curling around my spine. If only they knew where I was. Then maybe, they could get a letter to me. But only *I* could tell them where I was. Because no one else had the slightest idea.

"I'm going in. I'm feeling quite excluded, thanks to you gentlemen." Wayne stood and clapped his hands on the wooden table. "I think I'd rather watch a pendulum swing than be out here with you folks. It's more interesting." He sauntered inside with his typical attitude.

"Funny how that kid can wait on people all day, and still, that's all he cares about is himself." Bentley shook his head. "He'll never make it to be a butler, and I'll laugh when he thinks he will."

The next morning, I refused to get up. I went over the consequences in an endless cycle of telling myself "I can" and "I can't." Every time, I'd roll over again and put my face in my pillow. My back was still aching from crouching down for hours. I plain out didn't want to do my job. It made me feel guilty. No one else complained but me. Me, who had been here the least amount of time, has had more complaints than the amount of hair on Mr. Lemont's head. I was just dozing back off when an unpleasant rapping on my door jerked me to my senses.

"Bruno? Are you in there? Your door is still closed!" I couldn't identify the voice. It was such a low whisper, but it sounded like Duncan.

"Yeah… I'm um… not feeling too great." I mumbled. It wasn't *really* a lie. My back *did* hurt. "Just tell Alamar to tell Quin—"

"You don't sound too sick to me. Come on, get up. We all have issues." The pound of his footsteps grew farther and farther away. It was odd that he was up at this hour. With all the willpower I could muster, I dragged myself out of my cot and got dressed. I placed my cap on my head, although I knew it would only increase my body heat. At least it would protect my face from the scalding sun.

After a good couple of minutes of solid reprimands from Quin, I got down on my knees and started to break up the soil. Apparently, Mrs. Hardwick and His Lordship had some sort of agreement that we should have a small vegetable garden. Our versions of small were not the same. The vegetable garden was to be mostly out of sight so it didn't take away from the presentation of the flowers in the backyard. So, a whole new area needed to be cleared out. The saplings, the roots, the ferns, and even a few bigger trees that we'd have to take an ax to. I dreaded every moment.

As I worked, a tune kept playing in my head. I so badly wanted to run inside and write it down before I lost it, but it was too late. By the time I was finished, it was completely cleared from my mind. Hastily, I washed up and changed clothes, mumbling a tired greeting to anyone who passed by me on the stairs.

"Sarah! Where are you? Sarah, Mrs. Bolton is ringing!" Miss G spun wildly in circles. Her eyes landed on Sarah. She was guzzling down the last of her apple juice.

"Yes, Miss G. I've got it." In a tizzy, she turned the corner and hustled up the stairs.

"Fix your dress! You can't go up looking like *that*. You didn't iron it this morning," Miss G called up from the bottom of the stairs. "For someone who is a lady's maid, you cannot even iron your *own* clothes to look presentable!"

"It's okay, it's okay." Sarah's voice dwindled away, along with her stomping. Personally, I couldn't find anything wrong with it.

"You may say so. But I certainly do *not*. The moment you return, you must iron it." She touched the top of her head, making sure her hair was in place. Then, she continued on, finding someone else to pester. Every morning was like this. Miss G would check that all of the preparation work was done. It included things like dusting, polishing, tidying the rooms, fluffing the pillows, and making the beds.

"There's some leftover breakfast over there on the table. Sorry, we couldn't wait for you. They kept you out there later than usual, huh?" Pauline tilted her head in the direction of the table and hurried by with a few plates cradled in her arms.

"Yes. We're making a vegetable garden. It has a certain deadline because some vegetables only grow during certain seasons."

"What?" She peeped her head out of the scullery.

I repeated my sentence.

"Oh, yes. But that ought to be nice! Some fresh vegetables to have with dinner. I'm sure they'll taste better because they'll be home-grown."

"Maybe. I'm not too sure," I replied halfheartedly. "It's probably an old folk tale." One of the bells rang in the other room. "That's probably His Lordship. But I haven't seen Bentley around." My eyes wandered around.

"I'll check." Pauline shot out of the scullery and into the dining room. Her hands were dripping with soapy water. With her shoulder, she nudged a loose piece of hair from her face.

"It's Mr. Claude Breaker!" she called.

"Really?"

"Yes!"

"Looks like I better get moving."

"Wash your hands at least! You've still got dirt on them."

"No I don't—"

"Under your nails, I mean. It looks all black! To be honest with ya, it's none too attractive. So I suggest you wash them. Just go in the scullery." I could hear clanking glasses as she plucked them from the table.

"Ugh. Okay. But don't get *too* used to ordering me around. I know you enjoy it," I warned. The room was tiny with a big tub of dried silverware off to the side. The plates Pauline had brought in were sitting in soapy water. I pulled the sink knob and water rushed out. The bell rang again.

"Hurry up, Mr. Bruno," she sang. Now, she was just teasing me smugly. She came in carrying seven glasses intertwined in her fingers. I scrubbed the soap into my hands and dried them on a towel she gave me. She took my hands in hers. "Wonderful! Now you look quite presentable."

I uneasily pulled my hands away. "If you say so." I turned away from her and strode up the stairs.

I knocked on Claude's room door and waited.

"Come in," he called.

"Good morning, Claude," I greeted stiffly. It seemed so unusual for me to be here. He had never rung for me in the morning before. In fact, he never rang for me in general. Out of habit, I would go up to his room around six o'clock to see if he wanted to change for dinner, but that was typically it.

"Hello there, Bruno. I'm going to go down for breakfast, but I was wondering if you might post this letter for me." He stood from his desk and held out a tiny envelope. I was caught by surprise. His hatred for me wasn't as prominent today.

"Of course. Mr. Lemont is actually heading to the post office this afternoon, so I'll give it to—"

"No. I need you to take it yourself. That's the point. I don't want anyone else prying into my business. I'm losing people on my side daily, because of the crude gossip in the papers. Funny, how some people would rather side with ink than blood." He grimaced at this thought.

"Oh, I see," I gulped.

"Have you been reading the paper?" he asked. I knew I'd disappoint him if I said yes, but it was the truth. I didn't read the papers for the gossip, though it was impossible not to come across that page. I mainly read the news to hone my reading skills.

"Yes, I do. Mr. Lemont hands it off to us once he is done," I confessed. "But don't worry. I don't believe a word of it. They're just trying to humiliate your family because you're new to this type of position in society. That's my opinion."

"Is it, now?" he inquired.

I nodded.

"Well, Bruno. What if I told you it was true?"

"I... don't know. What if I was struck down by lightning?" I cracked an unsure smile. His face softened, and a smile almost appeared. It was like a rainbow that had thought to be seen at one fast glance, but gone the next, making one wonder if it was truly there in the first place.

"Then I'm sure many people would be very upset, like in my case currently."

I took a moment to comprehend. "You are saying... that it is true?"

"Take a look for yourself." He eyed the letter. I stared at him, making sure he meant it, and then I carefully turned it over. In a light scribble was the name Venus Achebe, the same name of the girl who had been pictured in the paper dancing with Claude.

"To Miss Venus Achebe," I stammered aloud, trying to pronounce the last name the best I could muster. So it was true.

"That's right," he casually confirmed. He went to his desk and began to sort through his papers. Usually, it was a neat and tidy desk. In fact, the room itself always seemed to be unnaturally clean. The maids must have enjoyed tidying Claude's room, because there wasn't much to tidy. It must have only taken them minutes.

"What do you think? Since you're the only person who hasn't practically exploded since the news."

"My opinion doesn't matter."

"It matters if I say it does. So?"

"I think that if you are fond of her, then... then no one else should scold you for it." It took strength for me to say it because I, myself, was uneasy about interracial marriages. I didn't find them bad, just so *unusual*. I explained this to him. "I mean... it is strange... I'll admit that, but...."

"But she has no money," he finished.

"No, that's not what I was going to say at all. I cannot judge that because I'm a servant myself."

"My mother despises her because she's Negro. But she'd despise her even more if she knew how I actually came to meet her. It's this enormous ordeal that I shouldn't have gotten myself into. Sometimes I envy Estella. She's the youngest, and the only one married successfully out of the four of us. She... she even had a daughter. Ruby." His voice grew quiet. The papers were in one giant heap now. He searched through them one by one, as if they had a certain order.

Estella had a daughter? The thought struck me numb. I would have never guessed. The way I looked at her seemed to alter instantly. She always seemed so young and *free*, I guess would be the word. I actually found myself admiring it after the shock settled in. When I realized this, my thoughts rotted. How could I admire someone who hated me deep inside? I changed the subject back to Claude. "How did you meet her then?"

"That's an awful nosy question," he concluded. I was about to apologize, when I realized he was just joking with me in a dry way. He began to explain. "Usually, on Fridays and Saturdays, I go to a soup kitchen to volunteer there. The volunteers are mainly women, but I felt the need to help out, too. Many of the men who come in are war veterans, and I feel that it's my duty to help them. So I've been learning about making different kinds of soup. Then, when we're finished, we line up stacks and stacks of bowls and open the doors. Usually, there's an enormous crowd of people out there. Men, women, and too many children. They all rush through the doors, yelling at each other and pushing and shoving like uncivilized savages, all for one bowl of soup. It's as if they have no dignity left." He shook his head sadly.

"So, Venus Achebe was a volunteer with you? At the soup kitchen?" I asked.

"No. She was not."

The thought came crashing down on me. "She was one of the people who came in for soup," I realized, stupefied by his words.

"That's right. She came in, wearing torn clothes and shoes with holes in them. But she was absolutely striking, even under that. Over time we just started to talk. I don't really know how. And I got to be really fond of her. But… it's not mutual," he sighed.

"Not mutual? It certainly looked like it in that photograph," I recalled.

"Yes, I suppose she is good at putting on a show."

I furrowed my eyebrows. I didn't understand. "Claude, I'm not sure—"

"It won't ever work out. It's simply a favor, since I can't do much else for her. That's all."

He was such a mysterious person. A favor? Was she trying to use him because of his social status? I couldn't quite grasp what the favor was.

103

But, I did know that as much as it was helping her, it was undoubtedly destroying him.

"I don't know what you mean, but I'm sure it can't be that bad. She must like you if she agrees to go out with you. That seems pretty clear to me."

"One can never be too sure. Clear lenses may ensure vividness, but not an accurate perspective." He opened the drawer and placed the stack of papers inside.

"Will that be all?" I asked.

"Yes, yes I think so. Remember to post that letter with the utmost discretion. Oh, and I will be dining out tonight. Tell Mrs. Hardwick for me. And Bruno, I'm trusting you not to utter a single word about any of this. Not one. Not to the other servants, and especially not to anyone in my family or outside it."

"Yes. You do not have to worry about that." I tucked the letter in my pocket.

"Good. Thank you."

I left the room and greeted Miss Flora Breaker as she glided up the stairs. I felt as if I was hired for merely being a friend, not a valet. Every day, Claude hated me less and less. It actually made me feel better to know that I was starting to be accepted. Both he *and* his sister's hatred was being displayed less. Whether or not they still harbored it deep inside themselves was something I was determined to find out.

England

The Violinist

"Sarah, I truly don't know why I even bought this. It feels… so unnatural." I touched my hands to my hips. The dress swayed with my movement.

"What ever do you mean, Mrs. Bolton? I think it looks *gorgeous*. The color suits you perfectly, and your sister did such a fine job hemming it, may I say. It certainly saved me from doing a tough job. So may God bless her." We both stared at my dress in the looking glass. No doubt, it was beautiful… but it was too unusual. It was a navy blue flapper dress, with beaded fringe. It was made finely of chiffon, and had a zipper on the left side.

"I don't know… I think I'll wear one of my old ones," I declared, gazing at it like it was something foreign.

"Oh, but Mrs., that's the newest style coming out! I'm sure everyone will be wearing one."

"Perhaps. Then it shall be everyone but me. Get me my pink silk, please."

"If you do insist." She rummaged through my closet and pulled it out.

"Ah, yes. Perfect." I beamed as soon as I laid eyes on it. The small train formed a pleated overpanel at the back, and the pink color was so faint that it would easily catch the eye in contrast to the other dresses. Sarah assisted me out of the flapper dress, and tightened my corset before I put on the other one. "I feel so much better," I exclaimed, watching myself smile in the reflection.

"And you still look wonderful, Mrs. Now, what would you like to wear with it? Oh, how about this necklace?"

I took a seat in front of my vanity and watched as her nimble fingers carefully worked the clasp. Just then, there was a knock on the door.

"Who is it?" I asked as I touched the necklace.

"Me of course." The door clicked as Roy came in. He looked sharp in his new evening suit. His eyes were bold and full of life. They swept across the dressing room. My heart did a flip.

"Are you modeling now? There are dresses everywhere! My my, you are so *particular*."

"Suppose I am?" I raised my eyebrows in a challenge. "But I finally decided on this dress. Not the necklace though. Sarah," I looked into the mirror at her. "Can you find me a slightly simpler piece?"

"Of course, Mrs." She took the little key on my vanity and opened my jewelry box. "Hmm, how about this one? I know you like silver." She placed it gingerly around my neck.

"That's still too much. But I'm afraid it will have to do if I really do not possess anything simpler." I sighed and ran my finger over it. "Thank you very much, Sarah. That shall be all."

"You're welcome, Mrs." She hung up the other dresses that I had declined and exited swiftly.

I stood up and faced Roy. "You certainly look charming," I complimented with a playful smile.

"Not compared to you. Though, I must say, the dark blue one fits you more so. I've always thought that since the day you bought it and tried it on at your sister's shop." Both of his hands rested just above my elbows as he pulled me in closer.

"Maybe, but I don't see it. I like this one much more. Especially since we will be spending most of the night out in the garden. It just seems more suitable."

"Yes, *suitable*." He repeated the word. Both of our noses were touching. I closed my eyes and was still, taking in the seconds before the spark. His thumb grazed my cheek over and over, and I could feel him lean in. His lips were hard against mine, like he was searching to withdraw something within me that I did not have. But I did not want to pull away. It was on the contrary.

"Did you ever think about the boat? The boat we could take to America?" His voice was so soft and gentle, barely audible, like a summer breeze.

My eyes fluttered to his. "Yes, and I think that we should stay here and get used to it. We cannot run away to a new place and think that it will change our morals and thoughts. Because it won't. Perhaps temporarily, but not permanently, for certain."

"Are you sure that's your final decision?" The light in his eyes had dulled like old silver.

"Yes. I'm sorry, Roy."

"It's alright. Maybe we can decide on somewhere else. But for now, let's go eat dinner." He cradled my hand between the crook of his elbow and forearm as we left the room.

Many people showed for dinner. Some were friends of friends. The night was clear and warm, perfect for an outdoor event. Makeshift chairs and tables were taken and set up outside in the garden where people chatted and laughed until the tip of the sun was the only sliver of light left to be seen.

"Goodbye, Grandpoppa." Flora stood up from her chair beside mine and kissed the top of his head. He was a small man with age spots and a perfect pointed nose. He stumbled about, but never fell. His feet were stronger than his legs.

"Oh, goodbye, my darling. You take care." He was missing a bottom tooth. When we were little, he always made up a grand, heroic story of how he lost it. We could have listened to him for hours. Even now, none of us knew the real story. But I was content with the version that he had given it up when he was young as collateral to save a duchess.

"Are you sure you don't want to stay here with us? Charlie invited you many of times and he made it seem like you evaded the question." Flora placed her arm around his back and proceeded to walk with him to the house. Their footsteps were small and uneven like a rocker with chipped wood. I placed my drink down and went after them.

"Grandpoppa, Flora's right! You should come here! Isn't it lonely living in your home by yourself?" I interjected. Flora gave me a grateful look. She worried about him all the time. They had a special connection ever since

Flora was young. He used to take her places all the time when he was more mobile.

He mumbled to himself a bit, ticking his head to and fro. "No, no. I like it there. I cannot leave."

"But… what if something were to happen to you? I know we could hire a nurse or—" she rambled on. Flora spoke loudly whenever talking to him. He was hard of hearing.

"Flora, you're a good girl. But I like my home. I don't mind being alone. Don't become a pest to me now. You know you are too good for that. Too good for that."

She cast her eyes to the ground, concealing her disappointment. "Yes, Grandpoppa."

"Don't worry about him. He's got high spirits for a short man." I lowered my voice so only she could hear.

"Estella, you don't understand. We should really be forcing him to live here at this point. What could he possibly do in that old house besides sleep? Answer me that." She gripped his arm tighter as he wobbled up a small incline.

"He could… read a book? Or learn to knit?" I suggested, shrugging my shoulders. It was definitely not the answer she wanted to hear.

"Oh, posh. I'm trying to be serious about this! He could fall and break his hip and no one would know until days later! Is that what you want for him?" she snapped.

"No! Of course not! All I'm saying is that you must respect his choice, and better yet, accept his words. He says he's not lonely. You have no other option than to believe what he says."

"That's what you think. I have to talk to Poppa about this later. Surely he will know a way to bring him to his senses." Flora was determined, but I found it pointless. We both bid him off, and I went to go find my friend Victoria.

"There you are!" I spotted her passing her hat around to two other women who marveled at it. She was a middle-class person whom I had become friends with the past four years. Her fiancé sat to her left. He was a jolly man with eyelashes longer than any female's, and a cleft chin. My mind ran blank when it came to his name though, so in my head, I referred to him as Chippy. Chippy, because his bucked smile reminded me of a beaver's.

"You magically reappeared, I see. We were wondering where you went. I was just showing off my new hat that I bought from the little corner shop in the village." She held it out to me and I touched the feathers on it. "By golly, are they expensive, though! This will have to last me at *least* a year or two before I can save up to buy another one!"

My insides cringed. She hadn't stopped talking about that *daft* hat since she had arrived. Normally, I could find the patience. But tonight was testing my limits. People who pretended to have the world spin in their palms irritated me. Victoria only acted like this in front of others, just to impress. *I* was well aware of that, but they seemed not to have any clue.

"Yes. It's lovely," I replied blankly. She met my eyes and received my unpleasant message that hushed her up. Besides her need to impress, she was a great person. No one had to pry it out of me to admit it. I strived to be like her. She was so involved with the community, charities and various boards. Her life seemed so full and plentiful.

Lemont made his way over and offered another cocktail to Chippy, who politely refused. They began to chatter lightly about politics. At first, I listened in, giving my input. After all, everything was flipped inside out because of the war.

In time, I could feel my eyes trailing off.

In the distance, I was surprised to find Mr. Bruno in footman's livery. He probably had a quick training lesson so he could be of use during the party. I watched him stand there. His foot tapped slowly in the grass, like he had a gramophone in his head. Or, even better, a piano. Something just swelled over me. I really wanted to talk to him.

He shifted the weight of the tray from hand to hand, but it was barely noticeable. The rest of his body was completely firm and confident, despite the fact that he was doing a job he'd never done before.

"Excuse me, but I'm going to get another drink," I announced.

"Are you now? Daring for such a young lady. You're a tough one! Go for it." Chippy poked at me encouragingly. Both he and Victoria were just about ten years older than me. But I never felt the age gap.

"You leave Stella alone. She's twenty now, and can make up her own mind." Victoria nudged him, trying to monitor his comments. "You're such an American, it's painful." I left them, listening as their jokes slowly died out.

"Bruno."

"Yes? Oh, good evening, Mrs. Bolton." He turned and stopped tapping his foot. "You should have called me over. I could have brought you another drink," he said, holding out a full glass.

"No, no. I only drank half of my last one. It was quite head-splitting. I just came over to get away from Victoria rambling on about her hat. I needed a good excuse."

"Victoria?" he asked.

"Yes, the woman over there in the sort of green-colored frock? She has the fancy feathered hat and she's sitting next to—" I explained as he peered past me.

"Oh. I see her now."

"Yes. That's her." I paused, not knowing what else to talk about, but it didn't faze him.

"So is the drink really that bad? It looks so refreshing." He stared at his tray.

"To me at least. It's more toxic looking. Bright green and pink. Try some if you want."

"I couldn't do that. Mr. Lemont would probably drop kick me," he laughed.

"No. That's *impossible*," I insisted, grinning at his laugh. "Go on."

His eyes shifted from side to side. "Alright. But only because I actually want to try it. Just a sip. I'm going to have to give it to you afterward, though. Just pretend you're drinking it."

"Of course. Every so often I'll water the lawn with it when no one is looking."

"Perfect." He turned his back to the nearest group of loungers and took a sip. At first, his face puckered like he had eaten something sour. He gave the glass to me and forced himself to swallow. Unexpectedly, the face he had conjured turned back to normal again.

"Well?" I asked curiously.

"It's sour at first... but it's not that bad. I thought you might have been trying to poison me," he jeered. "There's a little hint of sweetness in it, enough for me to manage not to spit it out."

"Yes. I suppose it will take some getting used to. Lord Breaker loves it, and I cannot imagine how. He must have something wrong with his taste buds. I'll have to convince him to serve something different at our next garden party."

"You can try. That is, if we have another one before the season is over."

"Probably not, then. The next party might be a Christmas one." Victoria and Chippy approached us. Chippy lumbered about rather slowly next to her.

"Estella, I'm afraid we have to leave. My fiancé isn't feeling too grand, and we wouldn't like to cast a shadow on this lovely party. We've seen enough flowers and butterflies to last us until next summer, I'm afraid." Victoria thanked me and squeezed my hand.

"You needn't mind that. I'm sorry to hear the news. Hope you have a good trip back." I patted Chippy's shoulder and told him to get some rest.

"I'm sure of it. And tell your footman there that Mrs. Wernor requires another drink. She's under that white tent there." She gave a quick wave, and they both left the premises. Before she was out of sight, she plucked a flower and tucked it behind her ear.

I went to relay Mrs. Wernor's request to Bruno, but he had heard it himself, and had started for the tent. Later on, when everyone had left, I approached him again. He was folding up chairs and bringing them back into the house, along with the other footmen and Mr. Lemont. They had more energy than I could even imagine. Their puffy breaths could be heard as they marched back and forth.

"Ah, there you are," I exclaimed. He had his back to me as he leaned the chairs up against one of the old trees. Bentley came over and took a couple, one tucked tightly under each arm. He yawned as he walked, watching the moon rise in the sky. He saw me pass by, and quickly covered his yawn.

"Here I am," Bruno said aloud. "Do you have another drink that you require my opinion?"

"No. Not that I can think of. It seems like you could use help," I commented, observing the many pieces of furniture still left.

"I probably could, but not from you or your family. Mr. Lemont would boil over if he knew anyone in this family so much as lifted a duster. He's very specific with all of our duties, and the duties upstairs, too." He pulled a table out from beneath the tent. "Mr. Lemont says, 'A person cannot perform in a play wearing two costumes at once.'"

"Hmm. What if that person has two different parts, though?"

"Even so, you can't wear a dragon costume and a dog costume and say you are just a dragon. On that I do agree with him."

"My, my. You've got an answer for everything." I raised my eyebrows inquisitively.

"Me? Have you heard yourself, Mrs.?" he asked with a hint of spice. Another footman approached. It was as if he had appeared from the shadows of the trees. I couldn't remember his name.

"Here, Wayne. Take some of these. I'll get the table with Bentley when he comes back." Bruno handed off a few chairs to the tired-looking footman. He took them limply in his gloved hands and grumbled.

"Where's Duncan in all this, eh? He's the *first footman* after all. He should be getting his back end out here to do some work!" he spat bitterly.

"Really? Is that how you're going to speak in front of Mrs. Bolton, Wayne?"

"Oh, good. You're here, Mrs." He turned and faced me directly. "I'm sorry if I'm acting terrible, but it's just not fair in all of this. I don't understand why I wasn't moved up from second footman before. I started off as a pantry boy in this house when the late Lord Hampton lived here, and I've been nothing but a good servant. I feel as if I've been slighted. Especially—"

"Wayne—" Bruno shot him a dirty look that he was overstepping his boundaries.

"*Especially* when His Lordship had an ad in the paper for a valet. Duncan wanted to stay first footman, so the valet job should have belonged to me. Mr. Bruno, here, should be the second footman." He stood with his chin held high, refusing to be told otherwise.

I didn't know whether to scold him or applaud him for his daring pronouncement. "To tell you the truth, this really isn't a matter I am allowed to handle. His Lordship is the one to be spoken to if you feel that way, Wayne. It is Wayne, right?"

"Yes, Mrs."

"But, mind you, he isn't as lenient with mannerism as I am. You better figure out your words. The *correct* and *respectful* words," I assessed sternly. He seemed to understand what I meant without me having to fully reprimand him. His lips were taut like he was holding back an avalanche of words behind them.

"I suppose I could try, Mrs."

"Good. I'm glad to hear it." He tilted his head respectfully at me and rushed back to the house with the two chairs thumping against his sides.

"He has certainly got nerve. I sort of envy it," Bruno admitted, watching him disappear into the house.

"Me, too."

"So, have you been playing the violin lately?" he asked quite randomly. He had stopped what he was doing, just to have a normal conversation. The moonlight shone on his left cheek, making his face two-toned. I found my eyes lingering on him.

"I played a bit yesterday." I clasped my hands in front of me. "But not much. I can't seem to come up with a new tune. I feel as if I play the same song over and over with a different rhythm. It gets rather dreary."

"I'd think so." He paused, listening to the crickets embedded in the grass. "I... I have an idea. An odd one, but an idea nevertheless."

"Go on."

"I want to be your music instructor... if you're not afraid of Germans anymore," he stated simply with a hint of a smile. As he said this, I could feel my lips go slack. A look of concern crossed my face, making my eyebrows scrunch in and my eyes grow wider. "I write sheet music and that sort of thing," he continued. "If I could get you to learn how to read music, you would be fit for an orchestra, I know it."

I stopped to consider. My thoughts and emotions swayed back and forth with his words like the swinging of a pendulum. Ever so slightly, my vivid revulsion against him had started to trickle away.

"And what if I don't wish to be in an orchestra? Have you thought of that? What if I simply want to play for myself?" I asked, stealing the line that he had once told me. He was not impressed.

"But you don't play for yourself. Because if you did, you would be content as your own audience, listening to the same tune." He had such a way with explaining things so I could never get around them. I hated to admit that what he had said made sense.

"I don't think I have any other option than to accept with your wit."

"That's what I hoped." He grabbed two more chairs and grinned widely. I certainly hadn't expected to hear that. "I'll switch my day off to tomorrow afternoon," he continued. "Meet me in front of the monument in the village at one o'clock."

"W—What do you mean? Why are we to meet there? I cannot simply show up at random, Bruno. I might already have plans or…."

"Or?" he repeated, staring at me expectantly.

I moved my mouth to form words, hearing no sound escape from my lips. It was silent stutter. The sound of crickets filled the air between us with their soft screeching. I gave up with a defeated groan.

"Do I bring my violin?" My voice couldn't have sounded more un-enthusiastic.

"No, no. Bring nothing for now. Just *please* show up." He headed toward the house before I could muster another word. His plan was absurd. But, I was interested to see how it would unfold. Gradually, I found myself becoming more and more attached to him. This thought didn't last long be-fore the pendulum swung to the other side once again, because the instant I realized the controversy in my mind, an uproar of disgust crowded in my chest and a war broke out in my brain. Me, enjoying the company of… *him*? A *German*? It was hysterical. No.

England

The Pianist

"You want this afternoon off? Hmph. Very demanding you are, Mr. Bruno. Sorry to inform you, but *I* manage your schedule, not *you*." Mr. Lemont gave me a sharp stare-down. Sharp, like the knives and forks that he had finished polishing. He was now sorting through the wines, taking careful note of each one missing and recording it in the booklet that he kept in his desk. His pantry was a cramped little room, with keyholes attached to anything with a small door or drawer. The room was a mystery in itself. Mr. Lemont had more keys than the King had horses.

"Please, Mr. Lemont. I would really appreciate it—"

"Begging will get you nowhere. Better you leave as a dignified man, and accept my terms." He didn't look up from his seemingly noble task. He picked up a bottle of wine, inspecting the label.

"It will only be for an hour! And I'll even skip my afternoon off next week. Mr. Breaker's clothes are all set for today, and Sarah helped me mend the rip in his dinner jacket. My duties are done as of now," I insisted.

"You may leave me be now, Mr. Bruno. You will have your day off two days from now, as usual. That will be all." His tone of voice drove me out of the room. There was no argument now. He had always despised me, for no good reason. I knew I would let Mrs. Bolton down. My insides tightened at the thought of her standing at the monument, waiting. This was her test. Now I'd find out what she really thought of me.

I sat quietly at the table, staring out into nowhere. My elbow rested on my notebook. It was then that I made up my mind. I would have to write to Annelise. Carefully, I ripped a page from my notebook. One page turned into two, and then three. My hand didn't stop.

"Unusual to find you here." Pauline pulled out a chair across from me.

"I might say the same for you," I replied, still scribbling away.

"Ohhh. Are you writing to a lover?" She smirked, leaning over the table to have a look. I shielded my letter with my arm and frowned.

"No. And anyway, what's it to you?" I shot back. She looked disappointed, as she lowered herself back into her chair.

"What? It doesn't hurt to *ask*. I was just *wondering*. It seems strange that a person like you don't have a *special someone*."

"What do you mean?" Now she had gotten me curious. "Not everyone has, wants, or needs a *special someone*." I mimicked her voice.

"I don't know… you haven't got anyone in mind, hmm?" Her eyes hungrily searched for an answer. My eyes stayed blank. I gave her nothing to work with.

"No. If you really must know, I'm writing to a friend. You're awfully impertinent."

"Oh, Mr. Bruno. Don't give me that. You know I'm just a bit curious. That's all. Nothing interesting goes on in this house." She sighed and rested her cheek in the palm of her hand. "I better get going now. Mrs. Hardwick is probably wondering why it took me so long to use the lav." She left with a skip in her step.

I was about to reread my letter from the beginning when Sarah popped her head in. She looked cross, like she had woken up on the wrong side of the bed.

"Have you seen Pauline?" she inquired. Her eyes examined the room.

"She went back into the kitchen. At least, that's where she's *supposed* to be."

"Well I cannot find her," she huffed. "Hear this. I went to clean our room this morning, and all I came across was her junk. She's got piles of little trinkets in boxes, taking up all the space on the closet shelves. I'm tired of

asking her to move it. She forbids me to touch her belongings, and yet, re-
fuses to move them from my space." It was like the end of the world, the
way she spoke of the issue.

"Make a bargain with her, I don't know. Split the room up so each
of you has a spot where you can keep all of your stuff." The solution seemed
pretty simple, though it pained me to even be involved in this petty argument.
It was almost as if girls liked to quarrel, just so they could gossip about it to
others.

"That's the system we have *now*, and it's failing *miserably*. She doesn't
abide to it. She thinks she owns *everything*." Sarah placed her hands on her
hips and marched off in search of her roommate.

For some reason, I found myself holding my breath as I read my
letter. It was my last resort. I hoped Annelise and her family still lived in the
same house. And I hoped the war hadn't done them in. It frightened me that
just about every element in this situation relied purely on hope. Hope, the
backstabber of a friend.

I folded it up hastily, and tucked it in an envelope. Thoughts began
to scurry through my head. What if she didn't respond? What if she downright didn't *want* to respond? Could she possibly weigh that against my need
to get in touch with my family? She had to relay the message and my address
to them. She just had to. I knew I would have no other option without her. I
smoothed the flap of the envelope and had just gotten up when I heard a
thunder of footsteps coming from the stairs.

"We're back! We're back!" Two thrilled faces appeared in the doorway with goofy grins and sparkly eyes. Cleo and Arthur.

"Back from where?" I asked.

"From Ireland of course, Mr. Bruno!"

"Yes! From Ireland!" Cleo echoed her older brother.

"Oh, stop copying me," he grunted at Cleo, who smiled innocently.
"Mum told me we should come down and say hello."

"Well that's nice of both of you. Mrs. Hardwick and Pauline are
probably in the kitchen if you want to see them. So, what did you do in Ireland?"

"Dad went on a hunting trip, and he showed me how to shoot! But
he says I'm too little to do it by meself. You don't think so, do you, Mr.

Bruno? I'm eight now! I'm not a little boy." He rambled on and on, without a care in the world. He spoke with random bursts of energy.

"Oh no. Not at all. Eight is pretty old. You'd better be careful you don't start to get wrinkles and a mustache. Next thing you know, you'll be needing a walking stick!"

"Noooo. I'm not *that* old," he laughed, throwing his arms out. "Not like Mr. Lemont!"

"You'd better be careful who you say that to! I was only messing with you, anyway. But your dad is right. Don't worry *too* much. You'll soon be a very tall, grown-up boy."

"I cannot wait. Mr. Bruno, do you think if I stretch my arms way up, that I can grow faster? I think I could! Maybe I can be as tall as you!" he said excitedly, giving it a try. Cleo clapped her hands in delight.

"I wanna try too!" she squealed, mirroring her brother carefully. She rocked up onto her toes.

"Miss Cleo, I'll show you the real trick." I swooped her up and slung her over my shoulder. Her feet dangled on my back, while I held her steady on her stomach against my shoulder.

She let out a cry. "I'm going to fall!" Her eyes filled with shaky tears.

"No, you aren't. See?" I held her hand and curled my other arm around her. Her lip quivered, but she didn't cry. I slowly walked her around the room.

"Look, you're like a bird!" I exclaimed, reading her face from the corner of my eye. A shy smile crossed her face, and her tears were absorbed back into her eyes.

"Tweet. Tweet," she piped in her little voice, chipping away at her shyness.

"Mr. Bruno! What in God's name are you doing with that child! Put her down!" I hadn't noticed Miss G looming in the corner. Her arms were folded as she stared disapprovingly at the situation. She wore the same shoes that she wore every day. As many times as Mr. Lemont suggested it, she refused to give them up, even though the back of the heel was worn. She said they reminded her of her younger days in service.

"I'm sorry, Miss G," I stuttered. I turned to Cleo. "Hold on, I'm going to put you down." I lowered her gingerly to the ground. Her face was twisted to a pout.

"Again! Again! Again!" She reached her arms up toward me, opening and closing her hands.

"I thought you were afraid!" I chuckled. "You're a brave one after all."

"Pleeeaaassseee," she whined as her squeaky voice cracked. She tilted her head up to display her disappointment.

"Sorry, Cleo. Another time maybe." I side-glanced at Miss G, testing her reaction. "I've got to go do some work. You'd better go greet everyone before they think you've snubbed them!"

"Hurry up, Cleo! Mr. Bruno's right! Maybe Mrs. Hardwick will have some cookies for us!" Arthur grabbed Cleo's arm, and they ran into the kitchen with sugar on their minds.

"You be careful with that girl. She can be a witch. It's not hard to believe with her mother the way she is," Miss G grumbled to me.

"Cleo? I don't think she is. She's always sort of shy. She's also a bit *demanding*, but other than that—"

"Oh, just wait until she's older. I feel bad for the poor thing." She left the room. Miss Everett took her place, shuffling into the room with her hands over her eyes. Two suitcases dangled off her arms, and Duncan entered behind her, carrying a third.

I was about to question it, but Duncan shot me a glance of "Don't ask." His face was grim and wild-eyed.

"I can't believe it. After all these years of service. *Good* service. And this is what I get in return. Oh, how I wish Lord Hampton could see this. God rest his soul. These stupid young folks don't appreciate hard work." Miss Everett had returned from visiting her mother who had been ill. Thankfully, her mother had recovered. Now, Miss Everett looked completely distraught. Her eyes were red and puffy as she dabbed her tears.

What happened? I mouthed to Duncan. He shook his head and led her out the door. Immediately, I thought of her mother. Had she died suddenly? Maybe she was still ill. It was just so abrupt. After minutes went by, Duncan came back through the door by himself.

"The poor woman. I do sort of feel bad," he grimaced.

"What do you mean? Is it her mother?"

"No. Nothing of the sort, in fact. She got the sack." My eyes grew wide. I tried to think up a reason, but nothing came to me. She always seemed such a diligent worker. Duncan continued on. "Apparently, the family upstairs told her that they were gradually cutting back on staff. They didn't feel the need to have her with Mrs. Hardwick as the head cook and Pauline as the apprentice and kitchen maid. They gave her a month's wages and all, but still. It's rough."

"That's terrible. After being loyal for so many years. Should we be worried?" I asked nervously.

"Nah. You're still pretty new here, so you've got nothing to worry about. As for me, I figure that they need at least one footman, and I'm the first. So, if anyone else were to be cut, it would be Wayne, not me. I wouldn't mind it anyway. He's nothing but a sniggering storyteller."

"To be frank, I don't really know Wayne that well, so I couldn't say. Bentley thinks the same as you. He's constantly telling me how Wayne isn't 'service material.'"

"By no means do I like Bentley either, but at least we can agree on *something*. He's got some common sense under all those freckles." He smirked at his own comment. From the kitchen, Mrs. Hardwick shouted his name.

"The afternoon tea is probably ready. I best be hurrying or she'll bite my head off." He put a kick in his step and pulled on his gloves. He was the type of person that constantly was on time. He had a regimented schedule throughout his day. Even stranger to me was that he didn't appear to mind it.

♪ ♪ ♪

Two days later, Alamar approached me while I was trimming one of the hedges. It looked as if it would rain. The clouds were extremely dark for an early morning. The rays of the sun were barely visible. He got my attention by tapping on my shoulder.

"What is it, Alamar? If you're trying to play one of your nasty jokes on me, don't bother. I'm not in the mood." I wiped the sweat from my forehead and gave him an unwelcoming stare. His face reflected the same one that he always wore. Completely blank and unreadable.

He pointed toward the wisteria tunnel. In my head, I groaned. This was exactly how it went last time. He had pointed to something, I had followed, and then he had proceeded to push me into a water canal.

"I don't care what's over there. I just want to be done with this task already. My eyelids feel like they have dumbbells attached to them," I muttered, getting back to work. But he wouldn't leave me alone. He was insistent, like a fruit fly buzzing near airing wine. Finally, I gave in.

"What is the matter with you? I don't understand. You'd better have a legitimate reason for bringing me here," I threatened as we entered the wisteria tunnel. Of course, he didn't answer, and I hadn't expected him to. Whatever language he spoke, Quin did, too. I felt like the odd one out.

He led me over to the rotted looking bench and waved his hand in that general direction. Roughly, he skimmed his hand over the damp wood and pulled it away with a flinch. He probably had gotten a splinter, I guessed.

"Did you get a piece of wood stuck in your hand?"

He held his hand out and pinched a small spot between his thumb and first finger. I squinted and could faintly see the splinter embedded in his skin. He tried to pry it out, with no use, and then decided to ignore it. He brought my attention to a small pile of wooden planks off to the side. They were very thin, but the abundant amount made up for it.

Once more, he pointed to the bench, and then to the pile of wood. Right beside the pile of wood was a thicker, carved piece. When I looked closer, I realized that there were actually *two* carved pieces, and that they were identical to each other. Alamar bent down, and set them vertically on the ground, with one held steadily in each hand. Then, he tilted his head in the direction of the long thin planks. Finally, I figured out what he was saying.

He was making another bench. It made sense, of course; the other one was old and rotted and covered in moss. I thought it was an ingenious idea.

"You want me to help you make another bench! I got it now," I exclaimed while looking at the legs he had carved. They were shaped very well, with immaculate precision. It surprised me. I would have never thought Alamar liked carving. Or, maybe he didn't. My thought was altered. Maybe, he was just forced to do it, and wanted some help.

"I'm useless when it comes to measurements and shaping, but I might be able to help you out." I picked up a hammer from the soft grass.

Alamar grabbed a tiny handful of nails. In a solid hour, we had half of the bench done. I laid the thin planks side by side, attached to both legs. The next day, we would have to sand the wood and probably coat it with something to make it look nice.

Quin approached us and told us we were done. At first, he looked frightened at the sight of our new bench, but then a smile crossed his face.

"Very well done, lads! Very kind of ya to think of that. I'm sure His Lordship will be pleased." He repeated the same thing in a different language, to which Alamar responded. The two started a lengthy conversation while I handed Alamar the extra nails. I nodded respectfully to Quin, and headed back inside.

Just as I was finishing breakfast, Claude rang. It was becoming a daily thing now. I pushed my hair back. It was still damp from a washing.

"Off you go, Mr. Bruno!" Miss G shooed me away and went to talk to Della. Della was a housemaid, along with Sarah, though Sarah served as a lady's maid, too. No one had spoken of Miss Everett since her departure. It seemed to be a hushed thing. Whenever one of the younger servants brought it up, the adults would veer the conversation in a different direction. No one knew exactly why.

"Open the window, will you? This room is like a chamber in a volcano," were Claude's first words to me when I entered. His hair was sticking to his forehead and his skin glimmered.

I hurried to the window and pulled it open, letting the stale air from outside waver in. There wasn't much of a breeze at all, to his disappointment. His window overlooked the front yard and the driveway. He rolled up his sleeves.

"It looks like it will rain today. Maybe even a downpour," I stated, hanging his trousers on his desk chair. There was not a single crinkle in them. Then, I moved on to arranging his waistcoat and jacket on the bed.

"Good. I do hope so. It will make riding a little more thrilling than it is. My sister is making me go later today, so I shall need my riding gear."

"Estella?"

"Yes. And just because you may address me by my first name, doesn't mean you can address her like that. She actually *deserves* the respect...." he cast his eyes down, "much more than I."

"I apologize for that." I could hear my conscience yelling at me. "Mrs. Bolton."

"Correct."

I bit my tongue, and then stopped. He gave me an odd look.

"You seem... *distressed*," he inquired.

"I just feel... " I began self-consciously. "No, never mind."

"I insist. Go on," he prompted.

I tried to pull the words out carefully. "Are you sure you should go riding when—"

"Nonsense. I am capable. Don't think that for a moment." He had full confidence in himself.

"But—"

"No. I'm sorry, Bruno, but I will not hear of it."

"I'm not trying to say you are incapable. Not at all, in fact." I cut myself off there. There was an eerie moment of silence, then he spoke up.

"May I say, well done with the clothing coordination today. You seem to be improving." He switched the subject entirely.

"Thank you. I'm trying." I had never thought I'd hear that.

"Good. Now if you will, go run a bath for me. I don't care if it's as cold as the Arctic Ocean. In fact, I will prefer it." He almost smiled. Almost. I couldn't help wondering if he had heard from Miss Venus Achebe lately. Yesterday, he had gone to the soup kitchen again, but he mentioned nothing of it.

"Alright. I will have your riding gear ready by one o'clock. Will that be fine?"

"No, no. How about noon? Twelve o'clock. The sooner I can leave, the sooner I can return, you see?"

"Oh. I see. Yes, then twelve o'clock." I didn't understand why he kept himself separate from everyone. I would have gladly exchanged places with him to go riding.

"Good." He shrugged on his robe and headed through the door to the dressing room that was attached to his bedroom.

After I was done assisting him, I went back downstairs to work on my next task: riding clothes. I had found some in his closet and had to iron them out. Then, I was to find a suitable hat for the occasion. This was something I was not sure about. Perhaps a derby hat? Or maybe, just simply, a helmet? I had to ask Bentley. Many things in this job were still unfamiliar to me.

I stood outside with Claude and Mrs. Bolton. She was already on her horse, trotting in circles to get used to him. The veil from her black straw hat cast patterns of shadows over her eyes.

"Come on, Bret. Don't get feisty with me now." She patted the horse's mane and pulled the reins back. He came to a rusty halt, shaking his head and prancing in place. His hooves clunked on the ground in a rhythmic pattern.

I handed Claude his top hat and clasped my hands behind my back. He wedged his boot into the stirrup, gripping the reins with one arm. It took him a couple of tries, but he managed to push himself up on his horse and swing his leg over. It would have been easier if he accepted help, but he never wanted assistance.

"Thank you, Bruno. We'll be back for dinner, I'm sure. Especially with the scent of rain in the air." He adjusted his hat and nudged his horse next to Estella's.

"Of course, sir. I'll inform Mrs. Hardwick and I'll have dry clothes ready for you when you get back." I looked up at him.

"Good. We'll be off then." He poked the tips of his shoes into the horse's side. Estella did the same. She glanced at me quickly, turning her head before gaining speed. Her eyes were latched onto mine, just for a few moments. As quickly as she did, she turned back to Claude. Bret, her horse, obeyed her command and started at a slow trot. The two slowly grew out of sight.

England

The Violinist

"Stop it. You're going too fast for your own good."

"You forced me on this ride; you can't expect me to waddle along lamely. That's not any fun." I eyed my brother sharply as he said this. I didn't know if I wanted to call him brave or stupid. He'd always loved horses from when he was a kid. His childhood friend had been the son of a farmer, and they had always attended to the livestock.

"It's beneficial for your health. You're constantly cooped up in your own room. It's rather uncomforting to think of such a thing. And I am well aware that you don't like shopping. This was the only thing I could think of."

"It's not uncomforting for me. Is it impossible to believe that I *enjoy* it?" he retorted, picking up the pace.

"Not *entirely*... but mostly."

"You're becoming like Mother. You buzz around and don't leave anyone to be." I hated to admit that the comment stung like a wasp. I would have to wait for my body to reject the stinger embedded into my skin.

I flicked the reins and my horse caught up to Claude. We were now at a speedy trot. I bit my lip, focusing my eyes on the shops up ahead. "Well, it is not just pure instinct, you know." Thoughts of Ruby stirred in my mind.

He was quiet, afraid to say any more. He hadn't known Ruby too well, since she was so young. But he knew enough to fall silent. I missed her so much. So much that I sometimes prayed to her at the side of my bed. I was not an outwardly religious person, besides attending church. But her death made me confident that there was somewhere waiting for her, for all good people. Some glorious kingdom, because where else would a sweet, innocent baby go?

We stopped by Flora's shop. It was not very busy when we first entered. I said a quick hello, while Claude stooped like a shadow in the background. Flora had insisted that she and he would not be on good terms unless he put the family back together. Everyone had taken sides since his little rendezvous with Venus, about which he refused to give any information. It made me so upset. Before our new position, we all so easily got along. Greed sold pieces of our selflessness with every purchase made.

A sudden burst of rain came down on us as we headed back. It was bound to happen anyway. The horses easily blinked it out of their big eyes, while we constantly squinted.

"Almost back! I'll beat you there!" Claude gave me a challenging stare.

"No! Don't even—"

He jabbed his shoes into the horse's side and he took off, full throttle. His hat was scrunched under his armpit. It would have flown off his head otherwise.

"Claude! Don't be *stupid*!" I screamed out. "Go on, Bret! Hurry along! You've got the speed!" I leaned forward, blinking the rain rapidly from my vision. Bret transitioned into a full canter, while I kept a steady eye on Claude up ahead. He was a better rider than I. He always had been.

Our home was in view now. Bret was catching up, but not as easily as I thought he would have. Merrick, Claude's horse, was much bigger, but could canter like he was Bret's size. My whole body was rocking and jolting with every step he took.

"Slow down already! You don't know what you're getting into!" I called. Claude didn't answer. Even if he had, I wouldn't have heard. Now, we were just about side by side. Bret was going along more smoothly now. I could hear his streams of breath even over the rain and the stomp of his hooves.

"Course I do!" He looked in my direction for a split second, and then back to the terrain ahead of him. We were nearing the beginning of the driveway now, and he wasn't slowing. He was also leaned forward, limiting the rain and wind friction. His knuckles were white from gripping the reins with the one arm he had. Drops of rain collided with our faces.

Abruptly, he pulled back. Merrick jolted to a halt, throwing his head back and shaking it in irritation. I slowed Bret to a stop, and let him walk it off.

"You're absolutely *insane*, Claude! I don't know what got into you. You always have to find a way to be... *difficult*, don't you? Or to make others around you skeptical, or worrisome. Do you enjoy it?" I was off my horse in seconds, handing the reins to Bruno, who was awaiting our return. I stormed up to Claude as he was dismounting.

"Why must you act like a know-it-all?" he replied. "It was just some fun."

I erupted. "You have to have *limits*! Damn it, Claude! You've only got one arm, for heaven's sake! You could fall off and be killed in an instant. Do you not understand the... the precautions you must take? Or what we would do if something happened to you?"

"I'd imagine you'd be feeling awfully sorry, that everyone would, in fact. Sorry for treating me so badly, and sorry for judging me for things that are *ridiculous*." His feet touched the ground softly, and he wiped his face with his hand. "I was hoping we'd have a nice time, you and I. But I was wrong. You're just another person who has ears merely for *decoration*." He handed his hat to Bruno and disappeared through the doors.

Tears of frustration made clumps out of the scenery around me. I turned my back toward the door and stroked Bret's mane, while resting my head on the base of his neck. Was it so awful to want someone to understand? My brother dug his own holes. No doubt, he felt sorry for himself, but then he would have to go and counter it by acting relentless and stubborn. I had tried to force myself to stay neutral, but his thoughtless actions made me want to side with Momma more and more.

"Mrs. Bolton—"

"No one is around, Bruno. No need for formalities," I breathed quietly, stripping my voice from the strain so he wouldn't know. Like the flip of a switch, his personality changed.

"Estella, I'm sorry about all of this. I tried to tell him to cancel or take it easy, but... you know."

"Yes," I sniffled. "Unfortunately, I do." I made sure my eyes were dry before I faced him, though the rain probably concealed it. It was lightening up. "The thing is, I did want him to ride. I don't want him to be limited *all* the time. I just wish so *badly* that he would *simplify* things. He's not the same anymore."

"It's easy to say that as an onlooker. You can't always worry about him, though. You're his younger sister. It's about time that he look after *you*, eh?"

"I suppose." I reflected his smile, but mine was small, and worried, and unsure. "You'd better get these two back. They're probably hungry." I patted Bret one last time.

"Yes. While you're here, I... I wanted to explain about the other day. I feel terrible that I told you to meet me and I wasn't there. I promise I didn't abandon you," he said firmly. I was leery of this at first. "Mr. Lemont wouldn't switch my day off. I know that sounds like an excuse. Here I was, teasing *you* about not showing up, and *I* didn't. It's quite ironic," he laughed, nervously scratching his head.

"I don't blame you. It gave me another chance to think about your idea, anyway."

"What do you mean?" His face was stiff in wonder.

"It was a nice offer, but I will have to decline. The idea is just absurd. I'm seeing what Claude's little act of defiance did to my family, and it's making me rethink. I know you're not too familiar with my mother, but you know enough about how she acts, just by seeing her. How would you think she would feel if she knew I was taking up music again? She was the one who convinced me to abandon it when I was young, in the first place. Not to mention that I would be taking music lessons from a German? She might as well faint," I sighed.

"That's not true! I'm not just a crummy valet from Germany!" His defensiveness shocked me. He regained himself, and calmed down. "Why do people have a singular image about *everyone*?"

"Then what are you? Because if you'd like her to think otherwise, Bruno, then you've got a lot of convincing to do." I waited for an answer, but received none. He went quiet for a moment, thinking what to say.

"It's not about what she thinks. Right now, it's about what *you* think. Why do something wrong for someone else's approval when you can do something right?

"When I can do it right for that same someone's *disapproval*, you mean?" I edited his sentence.

"You know what I'm trying to say."

"I know, but I refuse to understand it. I don't mean to be rude, but I would much more like to have mother's approval than yours. It pains me to say that, because—because I *admire* you, Bruno." I clenched my teeth as the words strained between them. "But you cannot expect me to upset her more after my brother's stunts."

"I do not understand why it is such a big thing, though. So what, if you decide to take up music? The world isn't ending. In these giant houses, it seems like the littlest brick out of place can make the whole thing crumble. Am I right?" he inquired, gazing up at it and identifying each individual brick.

"Yes. I think you are, to be frankly honest. And that's one thing I miss about my old life. My individuality. Now that a lot of my family lives here, we're constantly sticking our noses in everyone else's business."

"Then break yourself from the habit. Try something new to bring your individuality back," he insisted once more.

"What makes you so sure about all this?"

"Because I did it. I'm here, in another country, trying something new. My Opa always said trying is succeeding, because taking the first step is the only one necessary. But of course, it was in German."

I hesitated, narrowing my eyes in thought. "That doesn't make much sense."

He shrugged, tapping his fingers on the side of his leg. "But I agree with him. The way I see it, as you take your first step, your stride widens and widens, but your foot never touches the ground. If it did, there would be no point to anything because we'd all be perfect at everything. We'd succeed in one bound. One step. The greatest achievement is the decision to take the step. Overall, it basically means that just purely *trying* can get us infinitely further, but nothing is ever complete, and no one is the master of anything."

It took me a few moments to actually register what he had said. It was all so confusing and jumbled, but I had gotten the gist of it. "Rather depressing, if you ask me. Your Opa must have had a creative mind to think humans could float." I pursed my lips, attempting to say it seriously.

His eyes sunk. Disappointment exalted from his face. It was then I realized that he wanted me to understand his way, just like I wanted Claude to understand mine. I was being that irritating, stubborn fool, like my brother was to me. My lips eased up, and I searched for words to correct the situation.

"Bruno, I apologize. I'm being rash." I could feel my expression soften up. "I didn't mean that. It's not right of me to dislike what I do not get. I just... don't know about this whole thing. My life has been very mixed up."

"So your definite answer is no to the lessons?" he asked.

I took my time, watching the water ripple in the pond nearby. "I'll give it a try. But just *once*." I gave in, eyeing him seriously.

"Good. That's better." His spirits lightened up. "We'll meet up every Monday, starting today. Don't bring your violin at first, until I teach you how to read music."

It was bound to be boring without my violin, but I agreed. The first few lessons took place in the village. Mr. Bruno brought his book of sheet music and explained to me the different notes. Slowly, it was coming back to me. E,G,B,D,F, and F,A,C,E for the treble clef. He'd point to random notes on the page and ask me to name them.

Usually, I'd get them wrong and have to go and name each line out loud until I came across that particular note. I couldn't understand how a pianist could read two separate staves at once. It boggled my mind. Most of his songs had staves stacked on top of staves, though he told me to only pay attention to the violin part. Once I was sufficient enough with my reading, he told me to start bringing my violin.

♪ ♪ ♪

It was almost winter. Leaves gathered on the tops of the grass, shading it from the sun. I was setting up my violin in the sitting room when a knock came on the door.

"Estellla? Can I come in for a moment? I want to get my book that I left on the table." It was Flora. Bruno and I locked eyes. I hustled to the door and stood in front of it, just in case she tried to open it. Bruno froze where he was on the piano bench.

I cleared my throat. "Uhh… no. I'm practicing and I don't want any interruption. I'll get it for you. Which one is it?"

"I don't know. I forget the title," she huffed impatiently. "It's this little orange book with gold letters."

Silently, I motioned to Bruno, pointing to the table she meant. Four books were spread out on it. He got up swiftly, and went over to it, grabbing the book closest to him.

I shook my head fervently. *Orange*, I mouthed to him. He switched it out and picked up another book, but it was a dark brown color. *That's not orange!* I mouthed. The words would have come out as a snarl if I had really said them. He shrugged his shoulders, confused. *Guard the door.* I pointed to him and then to where I was standing. We switched spots.

"Estella, I know it's there. Just let me get it. You're being so strange." My sister's voice became clearer as the door swung open.

"N—" I began, but I was too late. I spun around, book in hand, and saw her standing in the doorway. Inches to her left, stood Bruno, flat against the wall. The only thing that separated them was the spruce door. Neither of them could see the other. Bruno could only hear her voice. He looked like he was painted on the wall.

"I thought you had got lost. Golly," she mocked.

"I didn't. Now stop interrupting me. Here." I rushed through my words and met her at the doorway, driving her out.

"Hmph. Have it your way then," she articulated sharply, turning her head up as she left. I closed the door instantly after her. Bruno just looked at me, blinking. We both didn't move until at least thirty seconds went by.

"That was all too close," he grimaced, shaking his head. He let out a breath and the tension was released from his body.

"I told you it was the orange book! You just about grabbed every one *but* the orange one. She wouldn't have come in if you had got it right the first time. Did you not learn your colors as a child or something?"

"No. I—I think I know them." He made his way back to the piano. It was meant to be a joke, but now, he had me curious. It made me hesitant.

"What makes you so *unsure*?" I asked.

"Mr. Breaker always makes comments about how I never can seem to match things. It's irritating, because I never understand what he means by it. But now, there are more and more instances where I'm confused about people mentioning certain colors." He cut himself short. "I cannot explain it, really." He gently pressed the piano keys, looking troubled. "It sounds completely stupid, I know."

"Oh, you don't mind my brother. He's picky, that's all." I dismissed his concern as nothing.

"Is it?" he asked.

"Yes!" I replied confidently. "Don't get all worried. Look." I held up the brown book and the murky green one. "What colors are these?"

He licked his lips, concentrating on each one. The grandfather clock clicked in the far side of the room, counting each second he failed to come up with a word.

"Stop messing with me," I laughed. "I know you know, Bruno."

"But I don't." His voice was desperate and strained. "I can't see a difference. Are you tricking me?" He fidgeted, tapping his fingers restlessly on his knee. He rapidly blinked his eyes, clearing them from fog that didn't exist.

"Why would I trick you? I'm not *that* cruel."

"I don't know," he responded blandly, clearly not convinced. I watched him carefully. He focused on the piano now, hitting more random keys and making them sprout into arpeggios. He had taught me what arpeggios were. I was proud I remembered it. His deep-set eyes zeroed in on the exact center of each key.

"Anyway, what is today's exciting lesson on, hmm?" I put the books back and stood by the bench.

"Here, you sit." He abruptly stood and let me have the bench seat. "More chords today and then I'll write out some sheet music for you to try on violin. We'll see how fast you can read each note *and* remember each value." He leaned over my shoulder and struck three notes at the same time. "We'll start easy."

I looked at each key, reciting the alphabet in my head. He hit the notes A, C sharp, and E.

"Umm... umm. I know this one!" I snapped my fingers and it clicked. "A major?" I was hesitant about the major part. He had started teaching me minors, and I always got the two mixed up.

"Excellent." Over and over he switched. He said that I was doing decently well, which made me glad. But I couldn't wait to pick up my violin and try it. When he gave me the okay, I tucked my violin under my chin and began to play what he had written in his notebook.

"Not bad, not bad," he exclaimed when I finished, leaning against the piano. My insides were cringing. I felt as though I wasn't any good. Trying to transfer the notes from the page to my fingers was delayed.

"I agree. I'm a bit slow, still." It was disappointing. In my head, I pictured myself doing so much better, but my progress was so subtle that I almost found it nonexistent.

"You'll get faster the more you do it." As he talked, he struck random chords. I guessed he had no idea what he was doing, because he wasn't even looking at the piano. Even so, it sounded quite nice. "Try this." He hit a C chord and instructed me to play a C at the same time.

"Oh! That's so intriguing how they match up. So is that how composers do it?" I asked, putting my bow down at my side.

"Yes, but it's a lot more complicated than that. For now, we'll just focus on this. So next lesson, I'll test you some more. But keep playing your violin. Your sight-reading skills and your actual playing skills need to be balanced."

"Yes, then I shall continue to work on it. Thank you." He didn't seem to want to move from the bench. He was sinking into his own world, sitting there.

"Why don't you play something? I know you want to," I blurted out.

He snapped out of his trance. His eyes ascended to my face, processing my sentence. "But... what if someone hears it? What if they come in?"

"They won't. Everyone in my family is out but my sister and Claude. Momma and Poppa are out to dine, and my little cousins are with the nanny."

"Well... I... wouldn't know what to play."

I gave him a smug, disapproving glance. "I'm sure that's not true."

"What? I don't...." He attempted to say once more, but it was too late. I had broken him and saw right through it. He was itching to play. It was obvious. The slightest grin made cracks in his staid face.

"I knew it! Go on then, stop making a dupe of me."

"You are a nuisance." He let his words linger in the air before continuing. "But if you really insist." He took a moment to think, then placed his hands in a ready position. His fingers moved slowly, merely pushing each key down rather than striking it.

"This piece is my favorite," I heard him say over the low notes. It was slow and gloomy in the beginning, the sort of song played to drag out feelings of deep sadness. I could picture empty streets and a sky covered with clouds. But like many classical songs, it didn't last long. The notes doubled and tripled their speeds. His right hand sprang into action, leaving me goggling in shock over his shoulder. It was played with such ease, like it was a second sense.

His body was in synchronization with each pitch, absorbing the emotion and releasing it. His eyes grew narrow, like he was at the picture palace and witnessing an argument in a film. It was so impossible to understand. I so badly wished to see the story in his head that he was hearing. The scene was almost frightening. There was a certain transformation that happened to him that I couldn't quite describe.

I continued to watch intently, whilst hundreds of thoughts spun like a record in my head. My ears couldn't believe that this quiet, humble instrument was speaking. Screaming, and throwing a tantrum, in fact. Abruptly, the tune changed like the calming of a storm. Such sweet resolution filled the air. And then the battle started up again. It might as well have been two separate pianos and pianists battling it out with each other. So fast like the wings of a hummingbird. It was awing. I didn't know what to say when he let the last note resonate.

"I wish he could have seen that one," Bruno mumbled, more to himself. He rested his chin on his hand.

"W—what?" I stuttered, puzzled.

He seemed to be in some sort of pain by the way he squeezed his eyes shut. Even his breathing was slow. After such a burst of sound, I'd half-expected him to be jittery with adrenaline, but it had the opposite effect, like it had drained him of everything.

"What are you talking about? Do you not know what you just did? You're slouching there in your own world after a mighty performance, as if what you just did was nothing." It was all so baffling. "Like it was something as simple as lifting a fork to your mouth. Bruno!" I laughed in disbelief. "That was incredible!" I could feel my eyes brighten with delight. "You... you're like a prodigy."

"But... oh, never mind." He seemed highly disturbed by the thought. A look of anger slapped itself on his face like a mask and he started to play the song all over from the very beginning. I hadn't even had a chance to ask what it was called. I stood there, like I was intruding as he played it, two, and three times, only pausing the slightest to let the last note ring. He did not slow down, even during the third time he played it. That was when he stopped for good. He placed his hands on his lap as the corners of his lips dripped downward.

I watched as he reached up to play the song again. "Stop it. I don't know what is the matter with you, but you need to stop." I threw my arms out at my sides. "Why are you so *angry*?" I picked up his hand and placed it back on his lap, gingerly. His face was blank while his insides seemed to go rogue. "I don't understand."

He didn't speak. He was deep inside his head, though he couldn't hide the upset expressions on the surface.

"Bruno, you're frightening me now. Are you ill?"

"I'm okay," he claimed with a searing calmness. He rubbed his eyes, blinked multiple times, and stood up.

"Sit down, please. Just so you're not in this state when you go back downstairs," I insisted, watching his every move. The bitter coffee color in his eyes was stale. He listened, taking a seat on the sofa and leaning back.

I tried to ask him questions, but he was reluctant to answer any.

"Why do you play when it just makes you mad?" I finally asked, figuring it wasn't too unreasonable. "No one is *perfect*." At first, he answered with his typical "I do not know." But he seemed to be considering it more than I noticed.

"Sometimes, anger is the driving force. I always thought... that was wrong when I was told that. But, I'm realizing it has some truth to it, no matter how... *absurd* it sounds." He drummed his fingers on the arm of the sofa and I came and sat beside him.

"I do think it's absurd. Who would ever say that? Anger is a horrid, brute force that only drives horrid, brute things." I watched as he looked at the piano. His long eyelashes were prominent when looking at him from the side. A light, almost unnoticeable cluster of freckles gathered under his eyes.

"Then hear this. One day when I'm feeling incredibly happy, ask me to play that piece, "Fantasie Impromptu," and listen for how different it will sound. Only when I'm truly connected with the emotion of the piece can I play it well. That's why I'm a petty excuse of a pianist."

"Then... what are you so angry about? That is... I'm assuming it was anger."

His voice cracked as he spoke. "Myself, my papa, and my Opa." He stopped talking, sinking into thought. He resurfaced again. "I don't know why I'm saying this. You probably think I'm insane. But there's nothing I can do about it. I feel so helpless here, with the distance of an ocean between my past and present."

"I can help if you explain—"

"I don't want to. There's not much to explain."

I failed to come up with anything to say. So I responded with a slight nod.

"Anyway, I'm sorry for spoiling your lesson. I didn't mean to make you upset. Sometimes I don't know what comes over me." He braced his forehead with his hand and stood. "I really have to be going now."

"Right," I replied, swallowing thoughts. It was like he had a dark cloud over his head, and only when there was a storm was it noticeable. Never before had I seen the anger that drove him forward. It gave me an unsettling feeling how he harbored it like it was a piece of him he couldn't lose. I walked out first, carrying my violin and my case as I did every time. I checked the halls and then gestured for him to come.

We both glanced at each other and then went in separate directions, pretending the other didn't exist. It had to be this way.

England

The Pianist

"**M**r. Bruno, I believe this is addressed to you. Oh, and there is also one for Mr. Breaker." Mr. Lemont passed out a few letters to the people sitting around me. It was just before lunch time.

"The mail is late. His Lordship will not be pleased. Wayne, go on and press the paper." Duncan pushed the paper toward Wayne while Mrs. Hardwick cautioned Bentley on how he almost elbowed over his cup of tea.

I could not believe she had written back. Just by the penmanship, I knew. I tore open the letter, afraid as much as I was excited. The writing was smooth and curling from one word to the other. It didn't even start with Dear Leonardo. It jumped right into the body of the letter, which took up most of the front of the page.

"Anything concerning, Mr. Bruno? Your face has been stuck to that paper." Miss G sat near the head of the table and leaned forward.

"Nothing much, Miss G," I replied, still reading. There it was. The address of my parents.

I do not know whether to write ten pages of why I am so happy you are alright, or to write one condensed page of all the insults I can muster up. I rather would not like to write to you, but I feel an obligation, though I do not know how nor why. I despise you for not telling me that you were to leave. You will be happy to know Otto betrayed you, and told me that you were leaving to England just a day after your departure. To my knowledge, I found that he was indeed disobeying your every command by doing so. I thought it the right thing to do. Do you know how many times I've wondered if you are even living, Leo? My God. If you only had an ounce of the compassion I have. Maybe then you would have thought twice of leaving, or perhaps even offered for me to accompany you. But, to my knowledge, you do not possess much of this trait.

In Germany, we are all in a tizzy. There were uprisings. Even worse than before. Kaiser Wilhelm II abdicated as German Emperor, and our chancellor Max Von Baden resigned! We have signed a treaty now, but it is hated among most. People were being slaughtered, Leo, like animals. It was so horrible. I feared for my own life, I admit it. My father still resents the government, saying it is weak and two-faced. But don't say anything to anyone about it all. We have limited everything…money, food, soldiers. We are dug deep in debt and living in poverty. I don't know what my father is going to do with the farm because we are failing to gain money from it. The local children sometimes steal our vegetables anyway. I'm sorry I wrote all that. I don't mean to worry you----actually, scratch that thought. I do mean to, with every intent. I wrote your parents' address on the back. I have no idea of the whereabouts of your brother and sister, I'm sorry. However, I hope they are well, and not for your own selfish sake, but for <u>theirs</u>.

Annelise----

It made me feel like a horrid person. To even think that not long ago, I had planned to marry her. Of course, I remembered being attracted to her, but now, I felt as if I didn't have a clear image of her face. How much I was in her debt now. I didn't know how to repay her. As much as I pitied her, I realized I had escaped just in time. Then guilt swooped down on me and I thought of my family, and all of the suffering people who did nothing wrong but want choices.

"Now, Mr. Bruno. You best go and give this to Mr. Breaker. I will not have any more of this *sulking* around." Mr. Lemont made it clear, handing me the other letter.

"I was not sulking, Mr. Lemont. And I don't mean to speak out of turn, but is that not your job?"

He shot me a look as if I had spit on him. "Pardon you, Mr. Bruno, but I decide who does what and when. It would certainly not be appropriate to have me, the butler, intrude into Mr. Breaker's room to deliver a letter. You are his valet, and you will do so now." He turned from me and left before letting me say another word. I learned to close my lips and move on with it.

I made my way through the kitchen and up the stairs, arriving in the main hall. The house seemed quiet without little Cleo and Arthur running and playing. The curtains were like blocks of cement carved next to the windows. They no longer swayed with encouragement of a warm breeze. Even the intricate stencil work slowly mutated to scribbles before my eyes.

"Good afternoon, Bruno!" As I traveled up the stairs to Claude's room, I caught Mrs. Bolton coming down. Her face was flushed at the cheeks and her hair was pulled back, the same style she always had. More and more women were cutting their hair short and walking around in flapper dresses, but not Estella. She gleamed with happiness.

"And to you, Mrs."

"Don't tell the other servants yet, but I overheard His Lordship talking with my father about having a ball! Isn't that exciting? By no means do I enjoy dancing, but it will rid the gloom from this house, don't you agree?"

I cleared my throat. "I do."

She peeped her head around, stepping down another step so she was just taller than me. Her lips were level with my nose so I tilted my head up as we spoke. She had a fringed shawl curled around her shoulders.

"Why don't you come for a walk with me?" she suddenly asked, "or we could go riding or—"

"You've got a lot of time on your hands," I teased her. "You should be using it to practice." It was strange…I could not look at her and feel the same repulsion that had been so prominent when I had first met her.

"Indeed I do, but I have other plans."

"As much as I'd like to *honor* you with my presence, I have to deliver this letter to Mr. Breaker and then probably go back downstairs for lunch." Giving her music lessons had gradually softened her. She no longer dwelled on where I came from, or the fact that she had disliked me before.

"Look, Bruno." She paused. Her eyes drifted upwards at the painting hanging above me. "I know it was your idea that everything is… sort of kept *hushed*… you know?" She clasped and unclasped her hands. "But I am tired of it. I may have a friend, may I not? At first when you started to give me lessons we agreed to keep it quiet because my family would find it odd that I was spending so much time with a servant. But I find myself caring less because," she stuttered slightly, "what I mean to say, is that you teach me a lot. And if they are going to judge me for your presence, then so be it." Her stubbornness was shining through.

I couldn't believe my ears. I admired her for saying all of this, but it was not the real reason I didn't want the family upstairs to connect me with the piano. "But, not too long ago, you said you didn't want to upset your mother any more after Mr. Breaker's stunt."

"That is true. But I've been really putting thought into it." She took a breath. "Frankly, they can't have too much of an objection. It's not like I'm unmarried, or have hundreds of sneaky suitors after my huge fortune." At this she laughed and rolled her eyes. "My sister goes off to Belgravia Square all the time with her friends when she is not busy with her business. They do not seem to mind that," she thought aloud, pressing her lips together.

"Yes, but they might be of better social status. Maybe that is why they don't mind her being seen with them," I countered. I spoke quickly, just wanting to deliver my letter before Mr. Lemont came up and caught me stalling.

"Perhaps. But it's not like you are *unrespectable* in any way."

"Estella, I'm a *musician*. Most people don't consider that anything to be proud of."

"No, you are a respectable valet who has a superior talent with music." She tilted her head up, like she was the queen making a declaration. "You're not in a gaudy band that travels around, and you don't sing like a dreadful howling dog, or—"

"To be fair, you don't know that." I raised my eyebrows and rested my hand on the banister.

"Then I'll just have to find out."

"I play the piano for a reason. The only way you'll find that out is by pure force." I chuckled, but I was absolutely determined that she never find out.

"Oh, that is *unfair.*" She scowled.

"I must be going to deliver this letter now. Excuse me."

I stepped to the side and she mirrored my movement, blocking my way. So we were playing this game. She seemed all too happy with herself and with a sneaky smile, met my challenging stare.

"You're such a child," I ridiculed, unable to take her seriously.

"Well, I would not consider twenty to be *old*, would you?"

"Not old at all. Although...." I looked inquisitively at her face, squinting my eyes. They did not waver. I could feel my smile slowly vanishing, as the corners of my lips were no longer turned up. My eyes were concentrated on her face, like she was a sculpture.

"What? What are you looking at?" She seemed a bit uneasy—even frazzled. "Bruno?" She tightened up, pulling away.

"I think...." I dragged out my sentence, making her seem worried. "Ahhh, just as I thought!" My voice grew grave. "A sun spot." I touched my thumb right below her cheek bone, smirked, and then dashed up the stairs, making it to the top even before she turned around. She touched her hand to her cheek.

"So funny, Mr. Bruno. So cleverly *funny*," her voice deadpanned as her eyes became slits. Irritation eased across her face like marmalade on toast.

"If you'll excuse me, Mrs. Bolton." I gave her a bold, cheeky grin and continued on to Mr. Breaker's room. I greeted him and he ranted about a couple of dreadful plans he had for the day. They were really not *bad*, but the man seemed to want to do nothing except hibernate in his room. His fingertips were always stained with ink, and the sides of his hands were no better. I had to admit, the thought of what he wrote sparked my curiosity, though I was hesitant to ask him.

I was not there for long. In ten minutes I was striding quickly down the hall again, turning to go down the staircase. My stomach grumbled repeatedly. For some reason, I felt as if I was always hungry. My foot had just touched the top step to begin my journey down when Estella appeared next to me as if she had waved a wand and popped out of thin air.

"You actually made me jump. I was not at all expecting you," I stuttered. This time, she was wearing a hat and thick coat.

"Good. Then I feel accomplished."

An answer for everything, I thought to myself as we neared the bottom.

"So, what do you say to that walk? You never gave me a proper reply."

"You already know what my answer is."

"Oh, indeed! Then let's go. How about—" She led me out the door before I could even say no.

"I can't be here. I don't have time off," I insisted, stopping on the front lawn near the pond. "And anyway, you seem cold," I remarked observantly.

She swatted at the cattails with her hand, watching them bob back up as she walked around the outskirts of the pond.

"Not especially, no." She held her hat down as the breeze almost pulled it from her head. "You can just say that you were tidying Mr. Breaker's room. I'll ask him myself to go along with it if Lemont questions you. But I don't think he will. He will assume you are with Mr. Breaker." She paused. "And before you say so yourself, yes, I have an answer for everything." She faced me and laughed.

"I— I guess I cannot argue with that." A surge of excitement came over me. It was like having a miniature adventure. I hadn't felt so... *free* in a while. It was exhilarating. My feet never left the floor on the weekdays. "Where to?"

"We can walk the riding path in the woods if you like. It's cleared out very well, thanks to you and the rest of the landscapers. You know, the one past the stables and the maze with the topiary?" Leaves crunched under her feet as she came over to me. She waved her hand in the general direction we were going.

"I have not been there, surprisingly enough. Usually I only work in the garden. But that sounds fine," I agreed happily.

"Wonderful." We hurried past the stables after Estella paid a short visit to Bret, her horse. He seemed happy to see her, though I was never really great at reading horses. They were moody, frightened creatures with dark pearls for eyes.

There was no one in the garden area, as we strode by. We debated which one of us could get through the maze faster. I had been in it dozens of times, clipping and trimming hedges, so I claimed I could. But she thought otherwise, saying she'd given many of her brother's guests tours and made it through without fault. We crossed over an open area of grass and then swerved over to the woodland area.

"Just look at all these leaves! To think that they will go from bright lemon to brown is sort of sad. It's practically *snowing* leaves!"

"That's probably the most *ridiculous* phrase I've ever heard," I mocked as I snatched one out of midair. My other hand was in my pocket, gripping my pearl without being conscious of it.

"Well, I am no poet, Bruno." She walked slightly ahead, turning her head to glance back at me. "You forget, I am not a Renaissance man such as *yourself*." She pressed her lips together.

"I think you think too highly of me. You haven't seen me try to paint. I'm quite awful, if I do say so myself. Certainly a Renaissance man would know how to paint well." I admired the trees up above me, picturing an enormous paintbrush swabbing the limbs in place.

"I'm sure with a little guidance you would be excellent at it. One time you must let me show you. We could go to the white cliffs of Dover or London and set up easels there. Oh! I know! We could go to Castle Comb!" she exclaimed, grabbing my arm. I was taken by surprise. All of my nerves clustered into the one spot under my skin where her hand rested.

"Castle Comb?" I asked.

"Why, yes. Sometimes I forget you are not from here." This, I was astonished at. Her view of me always seemed to be 'The German.'

"Castle Comb is this little village. It's not at all modern, or flashy like the streets of London. But something about the place is so tranquil. It's such a genuine, pretty place. It would be ideal for painting. I've always wanted to go back," she sighed happily, as if she was picturing herself already there.

"Go back? Oh, I thought you had not been there before." I looked up at the sky. Leaves spiraled down, just grazing my hair.

"No, I have been there countless times. When I was younger, I used to visit my friend Janet there. She lived in the village during the summer with her granny and grandfather. They were such sweet people. Well, her grandfather was rather overprotective and careful, which could become difficult at times... but I always enjoyed myself there." There was a fork in the path and she turned right.

"It sounds very nice."

"It was."

"Do you still keep in touch with Janet?"

"No," she said bitterly. There was obviously some sort of backstory by her tone of voice. She hesitated, cutting her own breath short. Before I asked, she jumped into an explanation.

"Janet was a good friend of mine. Most of the time I was jealous of her when I was younger because she had everything a girl could dream of. It sounds stupid to me now, that I was envious of her dolls and hats and shoes. She was always much prettier than I, too. But in the end, she became envious of me. And I feel so horrible about it. I never meant to make her jealous."

"So because of this, she's upset with you? It seems very wrong to me. Just because you moved into a castle doesn't mean she should act so terribly towards you. She should be happy that you're so fortunate and—"

"Bruno, I'm afraid I gave you the wrong impression. She's not jealous of my house. In fact, she doesn't know I even reside here." Her eyes wandered to the ground. "She is jealous because... because Roy married *me*."

"Oh." I went quiet. "I see it is a much... *different* situation than I imagined." It was odd. I had never heard her refer to Roy as her husband. I rarely saw the two of them together. Often, I failed to imagine Estella as someone's wife. I looked at her from the side as we walked. Smooth skin of only one light tone, shiny eyes with bold pupils and soft lips. Something burned inside my chest; something warm and yet suffocating. I smiled without realizing.

"What? What are you smiling at?" She giggled curiously. She liked to pry at my mind. Whenever I played the piano she would give me the same look: laughable, yet hinted with interest.

"Just the snowstorm of leaves that you enlightened me about." I met her eyes for a split second and then looked straight ahead. I could feel her wondering eyes on my face. Out of my peripheral vision, she shook her head, suppressing a row of beautiful teeth the shade of fresh paper. "You're a liar, Mr. Bruno."

The pathway led in a circle, and came out at the back of the house. She had been right, it was wide and clear. The only downfall was that one had to watch each step taken. After all, horses did go up and down the trails often, and no one would want to step in something *unpleasant.*

"Well, that wasn't bad at all. It didn't take too long, so there will be less suspicion." I stared down at my pocket watch. "Though I probably missed lunch." My stomach's clock was about as accurate as a real one. The tip of my nose was stone cold like my ears.

"I'm sorry, Bruno. Next time, we will plan it better. Also, we can start discussing different lesson times. I'm going to let Lord Breaker know that I am going to be taking music lessons. So the more often I can take them, the better. It all depends on your schedule now."

I didn't answer right away, and she could see the concern washing over me.

"Don't worry."

"I don't want them to think badly of you," I stated. "Especially your mother, as you've said before." I also didn't want them to make the connection of my name and being a famous pianist. The newspapers would be all over me. However, I did not mention this to her.

"It might take time for her to get used to, but she will have to. I like music. I like your lessons. I'll have to explain it to her—probably a hundred times—but nevertheless, I will." She was determined now, unlike before.

"I hope it works out for you. Anyway I've got to go in now, so—"

"No, wait. Don't go through that way. That's foolish. The other servants might see you come in through the back door and wonder. Come through the front door with me and head down the stairs like you had just come from Mr. Breaker's room." She nodded her head toward the front of the house and I followed her there. It made sense.

"This was nice," I admitted fully.

"I knew you'd think so, Mr. Bruno. I'm glad. The dirt and worms didn't repulse a city boy such as yourself?"

"Not a bit. I will let you know about more lessons. Maybe… just maybe I can mention it to Mr. Lemont. Perhaps he would give me a little more time off if he knew I was instructing *you*, a member of this house. After all, he would not want to go against your wishes…." I trailed off, plotting.

Estella grinned from ear to ear. "Of course he wouldn't. That would be a rather *uncomfortable* situation."

"True to that."

We both walked in hastily. She waved with her hand down at her side. I gave her a curt nod, and without a word, hurried through the hall and down the staircase.

England

The Violinist

"Isn't it beautiful out today?" Roy asked. I entered the library and found him sitting there with Uncle Ted. He looked up at me, cutting off his conversation with my uncle.

"Oh, yes, quite nice," I replied, taking a seat.

"I saw you walking earlier. Did you enjoy yourself?" Roy questioned. His piercing eyes were laid steadily on my face. I did not answer for a second, biting my lip. He was being a tease. I didn't want to answer.

"Yes. I did," I responded shortly while smiling charmingly. I had to drag the words from my mouth.

"I'm glad." He returned the same charm, without an ounce of sarcasm in his voice. He resumed talking to Uncle Ted. Both of their faces lit up when they spoke. I did not want to feel left out any longer, so I grabbed a random book from the shelf and began reading, drowning out their lulled, repetitive words. Day by day, my reading was becoming better.

"Estella."

"Hm?" I lowered my book away from my face, turning my head toward Roy. I was lying on my back comfortably with two pillows tucked under my neck to keep me awake. His expression was so... suppressed. I wondered what they could have possibly wanted with me. After all, they never seemed to take an interest in inviting anyone else into their conversations.

147

"Well, it's all quite exciting, really." He couldn't refrain the grin from his face. "But we need your honest opinion, yes?" Before I even agreed, he plowed on, crossing his legs. "Your uncle and I have been trying to come up with some sort of fundraiser that would bring in a good amount of money."

"Money? For what exactly?" I nearly choked on my own words. How could they possibly be greedier? Didn't we have enough? They were mad, completely mad.

"Mmm… that's not the point. We have finally come up with a fundraiser. At first we wanted to host horseback rides here, in the front lawn and through the garden, but we have come up with something else."

"How interesting. And that is…?"

"Boxing!" my uncle exclaimed. He ran his fingers over his mustache. It took me a moment to think this through.

"Boxing? *This* is your plan?" At any rate, I liked the idea of horseback rides much better. Or even hosting a baking contest. The idea of two people standing in a ring willingly trying to knock the other out was quite lurid in my mind. It was not at all a pleasant image.

"Why yes! People love a good fight! It could be hosted in London, and there would be a fee for signup and a fee for watching," my uncle claimed. He wrote something down on a piece of paper next to him. "Surely it would be a profitable night. People would enjoy themselves, and the fundraiser would be a success." He was absolutely determined now, which made my stomach churn.

"It will be called 'Fight for a Cause,'" Roy announced.

"So ironic it's *brilliant!*" Uncle Ted clapped him on the back.

"You mean to say cliché," I corrected. "I do hate to spoil your idea, but who would want to sign up? Do you know of even *one* person?" I closed my book and sat up. Leaves flying by the window snagged my curious eyes.

"Oh, surely. For one, everyone in this family would attend, including the servants. Maybe some of the servants would even be kind enough to *participate*." He turned to Roy who nodded approvingly.

"*I* will participate." The sarcasm was thick in my throat. "With my swiftness I shall take them all!" I cracked a smile, getting up to leave. I was just walking out when I stubbed my toes on the leg of the round, granite card table. I sucked in a sharp breath, muting my pained grunt.

"Yes, my niece. Impeccably *swift*. And the champion belt goes to… the card table!" Both of them sniggered, failing miserably at pretending to have sympathy.

♪ ♪ ♪

Charlie was rushing through the hallway, face buried in a letter. His face was frozen as he beamed joyfully. He walked with extra pep in each step, and energy buzzed about his person.

"Charlie! Just the person I wanted to see. I must ask you—"

"I have the most wonderful news! Miss Farefield has returned from France! She's been gone so long I began to doubt she even existed. I thought maybe she was merely a figure of my imagination. Isn't it excellent?" His rapturous aura was contagious. He grabbed my wrists and spun us around. The walls looked as if they were moving with us.

"Indeed so!" I laughed, dizzy and attempting to regain my balance. I hadn't seen him this happy in a long while. "You are quite fond of her." I rubbed my eyes, halting the blurred images around me.

"I am, I am." He let go, straightening his suit. "I must write to her at once and ask her here."

"Why of course! It would be a good opportunity to ask her to the ball that is coming up."

"Always one step ahead of me, aren't you? Very right you are." Before I got the chance to change the subject, he dashed away to the sitting room. I was left open-mouthed, standing idly in the hall.

♪ ♪ ♪

Days later, I was going into my room to find my hat when I spotted a book sitting in the middle of my bed. It was unusual. Roy never read. Quickly, I abandoned the search and assumed Flora had stolen it for an outing.

"Strange," I whispered to myself, grabbing the book. It looked brand new. A ribbon was tied around it, ending with a single bow set crookedly on the front cover. The binding cracked as I opened it. "The Virtuoso Violinist,"

I read aloud. A small corner of paper fell out, slipping through my fingers and landing in my lap. I flipped it around.

'Just a thought,' I read. The words were tiny and written hastily. 'Most sincere, Leo.' I flipped through the pages and found myself absorbed in it. The door handle clicked, but I did not notice until I heard the breath of another person.

"I didn't expect you here." It was our favorite line to one another. Roy came in timidly like a deer stepping into a large field. He closed the door behind him. We both started to talk at the same time to break the silence, but it became more uncomfortable. "I'm off to go to London to find a building where we can host the boxing match."

"Good luck, then," I said genuinely. As much as *I* hated it, some people obviously did not.

"Thank you." He slid his suitcase out from under the bed, and began to rummage through the drawers. Only now did he seem to be in a rush. He practically threw his clothes in, unfolded and without a bit of care. Though he looked dapper on the outside, he was disheveled. I was convinced a monkey could have done a better job.

"They are all going to be wrinkled when you get there! Let me help you. You hand them to me, and I'll fold." I crawled over to the edge of the bed where the suitcase sat.

"No, no. No need. Charlie *insisted* we bring one of the valets." This sentence rang in my ears. There were only two valets, Bruno and Bentley. I had to figure out who. It was unlikely that they would take Bruno because he wasn't as experienced. But it was just as unlikely that they would take Bentley because he was Charlie's valet.

"Oh, well, you don't need my help then. Bentley will know what to do." I eyed him carefully, trying to read him. But it was like trying to read a book upside-down. Laughable, not to mention completely pointless.

"*That's* his name!" he exclaimed, zipping his suitcase. It bulged out on the top like it was bloated. "Golly, I've been trying to remember it all day. Frankly, it would have been an embarrassment. I knew it began with a B, but that's all. Yes, he will do quite fine." He patted his suitcase contently. It dawned on me that he never smiled. The thought bubbled in my head at random, and yet it seemed a completely necessary observation.

Great, I thought. He could have meant either Bruno or Bentley. I planned to find out who. Roy fixed his blonde hair in front of the mirror and hustled to the door. He had gotten a haircut, and I had overlooked it until now.

"Ugh. We better not miss this train!" he huffed. He scanned the room for anything he might have forgotten. "I'm going now. It shouldn't take too long. Goodbye, Stell." He tipped his hat in my direction and left. The door banged shut. With him, my thoughts flew from my head. The closing of the door smashed all the perfect jigsaw pieces inside me, once so carefully bound together. Now they were missing, chipped and bent. Suddenly, I couldn't see myself, I couldn't see him. But I saw Ruby. I thought for her sake I could make myself a fine wife to such an honorable man. But day after day I walked with such a lie masked over my face. And day after day, he put up with me for my sake. *My sake.* That is what melted the hardened crystals that crusted my heart, to become the soft drops at my eyes.

With those thoughts as an insight, I opened my violin case.

England

The Pianist

"**S**hush already or you'll make me sorry I ever breathed a word!"

"Oh, how little faith you have in me, Wayne. It's rather degrading to a young lady such as myself."

"Just... never mind. Do you want to do it? That's all I'm asking."

I was leaving the pantry when I came to a halt. Pauline and Wayne were talking so closely that their foreheads were almost touching. She had this sly look about her. The stretched lips and pointed cheeks could outdo any fox's. In no way could she ever be discreet. This I was convinced of. If she thought something, it was sure to pass through her lips seconds afterward. As much as they tried to whisper, it turned out to be no better than crows cawing in the early morning.

"'Course, you goon! You'd be surprised with the talent I've got." She tapped the tip of his nose with her finger. "Maybe if you bothered to pay *attention* to me, you would *know*."

My hands were cold, but not from the temperature. Pauline ran back to the kitchen. Bentley had been completely right about Wayne. The nerve of him to even pursue Pauline when he didn't even give her a second glance some days. And to think that he thought *he* should have been the valet. Oh, he'll be a valet, alright. *Pauline's* valet. It put a nasty taste in my mouth.

After dinner, I watched the two of them slink off, while applying more and more pressure on my tongue. It made me uneasy to have the thought wrestling against altruism in my head. I wished Bentley were here because he always knew what to do.

I had finally made up my mind to confront Mr. Lemont, when they unexpectedly returned, easing back into routine, like they were never gone. It was so *strange*. They had only disappeared for two minutes. It took me off guard, so I held my tongue, easing up on the pressure. They didn't seem to interact any differently besides the fact that they were a bit more solemn than usual. In observing this, I kept silent.

Out of nowhere, everyone went rigid at the same time. I spun around, assuming one of the family members had to have entered. Standing in the doorway was Estella. Her searching eyes landed on me like darts that had finally hit their mark.

"Mrs. Bolton. How may we help you?" Lemont asked, straightening up.

"Goodness, I didn't mean to intrude on you all. I've come with a message from Mr. Breaker to Mr. Bruno."

I could feel all eyes on me. I began to scroll through my head. What did I do *now*? Or was it just the opposite? Did I *forget* to do something?

"Of course. You may talk in my pantry if you wish."

"Hmph. That really says something about grumpy Mr. Breaker. He won't even appear to you *personally* to issue a complaint. He sends his sister!" Wayne sniggered in my ear. I ignored him and resisted a strong urge to break his nose. With the utmost control, I led Estella into the pantry.

"You're here!" It was certainly not what I had expected her to say first.

"Yes… of course I'm here," I replied, confused.

"I thought Roy and my uncle took you to London. How happy I am to be wrong." We both sat down, stiffly at first, but then relaxing.

What a genuine surprise, I thought to myself. "What does Mr. Breaker say? I've been going through my routine in my head and I think I did everything." I slid my hands on my lap anxiously. "Unless, of course, he didn't like his clothing or he—"

"He says nothing at all."

"He—he says nothing?" I stuttered. Now I was even more puzzled. She must have seen the pensive look written on my face.

"I came down here to see if you had left. *And* I never got to thank you for the "Virtuoso Violinist" book. So, I will say thank you now." She smiled at me.

"No problem at all. I've been trying to read up about violin, since I'm to be a real music teacher to you now. I was pretty clueless about the violin before, but I'm slowly understanding."

"Wonderful. I'm going to mention the lessons to my mother later tonight. If I can make her sit down long enough to listen, that is," she chuffed unsurely, tilting her head. She looked about like she had never been in this room.

"Hmph. Indeed so." Before I knew what was coming out of my mouth, the question was out. "Would you want to go to Castle Comb on Wednesday?" Of course, I had thought about asking. In my head, it came out at just the right moment. I had pictured it so vividly, but in my imagination, both of our circumstances were different than the current ones. Now, I had probably caused a major issue.

Her face lit up, and then sunk. "But that's three days from now. That's the day of the ball."

"Then... never mind." I tried to backpedal, but it was useless. My face heated up, and there was nothing I could do about it. "I was being stupid. I thought... since you mentioned how you didn't like dancing...."

"I'd love to."

Those three words shut me up. "Really? I'm aware that if it's too cold it would be difficult to paint... but since it doesn't seem windy and it's not snowing, it might be possible. The cold would be the only thing in the way." I watched her reaction, as if I would miss something critical. Oddly enough, there was not the slightest tinge of reluctance when she answered.

"It would *definitely* be possible," she assured shyly, with happiness that she attempted to tie down.

"You don't think... there would be a problem. You know, with—"

"With Roy?" she finished. I closed my mouth. It was such a delicate subject. I had gone from despising her to enjoying her company just a *little* too much. It confused me even more. It was as if I couldn't remember a time when I disliked her.

"No. I will make sure of that. You are simply my music instructor who happens to be a friend. And you aren't native to England, so I'll tell him

155

I wanted to show you around. He's not like that anyway." I found this hard to believe, but I went along with it. "I don't even know if he'll be back for the ball anyway. Who on earth knows how long he'll be in London. He doesn't tell me much."

"If you say so." It twisted me to hear her say that. Part of me wanted her to think the opposite. I wanted to be more than a valet, more than a musician, more than a friend and a pianist. I was tired of my one word labels. The decent part of me respected what she said and compromised with myself that it had to be this way. But the rest of me admired and ached for her with such a steady force that it drove my brain mad. It drove my eyes to her face, my fingers to her neck, and my lips to her lips. Like a carver whittling away at a tree, temptation whittled away at me.

"Leo?"

My head snapped up at my first name.

"Did you get anything I just said?" She laughed it off. "I called your name at least three times." Her eyes smiled like the glowing sliver of a crescent moon.

"Yes. You said it would probably be best to catch a very early train and...."

"And that I would bring the supplies. I was thinking the six o'clock train on Wednesday morning. That way we will have plenty of time to spend the day."

"I'll at *least* need a whole day just to learn how to hold the brush correctly. Anytime I've ever painted something, people just gaped at it like I'd created some... *monster*. Even my parents had done it." I remembered their confused faces when I had finger-painted a tree.

"Well, that's about to change. It will be *so* great that you'll want to send it to them," she stated with too much confidence. If only she was right.

"Let's plan to meet outside at five thirty. I can ask William to drive us."

"William?" she questioned.

"The chauffer," I reminded her. "Now don't forget, okay?"

"Okay. As long as you don't abandon me at the platform," she teased. It hit a soft spot, making me feel bad once again for not meeting her in the village.

I opened the door for her and she left. Wayne suspiciously hurried past when I did. It got my head spinning. Surely someone would have moved him along if they thought he was loitering around the door. This I hoped, more than finding reassurance in it.

I arrived back at the table waiting for Mr. Breaker's bell to ring. Duncan sat beside me, pulling a cigarette out of his pocket and lighting it. He was hovering over a tin, plucking out little round objects from it. They all clinked together when they landed on the table.

"What have you got there?" I asked.

"Coins. I collect them. But it seems I've lost one. I have eight, but I only see seven." He tipped the tin upside-down as a last effort, but it was still just as empty.

"Hmph. Maybe it fell out somewhere. You should go backtrack." I picked up one of his coins and studied it. Nothing about it seemed familiar. It was either very old, or foreign. "What's this one?" The shape was more of a rough circle. It was dull and the edges had little nicks in it. The front and back were so obscured by rust that no words were visible.

"Ehhh… probably nothing. Well, it's probably *worth* nothing, I mean." He took it from me, turning it over in his hands. "Miss G gave me this one yesterday. She said her nephew owns an antique shop. I don't collect them for their worth anyway. I just think they're rather interesting to have."

"Yeah. But it wouldn't hurt for them to have *some* worth. I'm sure at least *one* of them must be some lost treasure from an ancient civilization."

He laughed deep from his throat. "That's ridiculous."

"Yes. Maybe it was a little over the top. But you never know."

He held the open part of the tin level with the table, and slid them in. "Sooo, what were you scolded about today?" He tapped the end of his cigarette on the side of the tin.

"You know… the usual," I replied calmly.

"Aw, come on. No need to be embarrassed. You must know by now that we get a good laugh about how Mr. Breaker is so *particular*. You always get the blame for things. I hate to admit, but it's comical."

"Wayne especially enjoys my misery." I raised my eyebrows, remembering his smug expression when Mrs. Bolton wanted to speak with me.

"He enjoys everyone's. 'Cept his own, of course. To be perfectly honest, I've tried to set up the lad a couple of times. But it's never worked out." His eyes circled around to make sure no one was overhearing. Other than that, he put on this proud expression like he was ridding the house of an insect.

I could feel my lips part in surprise. "Duncan. You what…?"

"Exactly what I said, Bruno. I won't go into the juicy details o' course, but I've tried all too many times." A devious smirk made a crack in his face. Suddenly a flare burned up inside me.

"Duncan, that's rotten. He's a nuisance, no doubt, but you can't want him *exterminated* from this household! He needs a job. Some people are out there starving, or begging on the streets wearing nothing but strips of dirty cloth and rags. They want a job more than anything. You could not want that for Wayne." I could feel my insides ripping at the thought. I was imagining all of the people in Germany. Starving. Crying. Depressed. It was real. They dreamt of having a job like some sort of whimsical tale.

An image flickered across my eyes. It was my family under an awning of a factory that used to be up and running. It was slightly drizzling, and they all sat, unblinking like dolls and staring at the sky. Their eyes were transfixed on clouds that appeared frozen.

Something yanked at my gut. It was this defined feeling of desperation, surfacing and pouring into my veins. Had I left them with enough money? Were they okay? Did they find a house? How are—

"You're *against* me now?" He flashed a warning at me. He placed his arms on the table, nodding over and over. "So this is how it's going to be," he grumbled, rubbing his throat. "He would be fine, you know. He has family. You're exaggerating, Bruno."

"No. I'm not," I shot back. "Just because you haven't seen people live that way, doesn't mean it doesn't exist. It *does*." He wouldn't meet my eyes.

"Phhft. Maybe in *Germany*," he exhaled, rolling the tin on the table. "You're taking this too seriously, anyway. I just… don't like him, alright? If you kn—"

"I knew I smelled smoke! Duncan, you know how this operation works. Go outside with that thing or I'll inform Miss G." Della poked her head in the room with her hand over her nose. I had never really talked to her. She was a quiet, often reserved woman who only said 'yes' and 'no' on occasion.

Duncan disregarded her excess amount of drama, heading toward the back door. He filtered his words carefully, replying with a sharp 'fine.' The back door slammed shut. I couldn't possibly imagine what happened between Duncan and Wayne.

I drummed my fingers on the table, listening to the notes scrolling through my head, blocking out thoughts of my previous conversation. The tune I had been trying to remember came back. With this, I rushed up the many flights of stairs to my room on the top floor. Before getting into bed, I wrote the letters of the notes down.

England

The Violinist

"Yes, I'd like the table to be moved there. Excellent. Thank you, Lemont. Now as for drinks, I cannot make up my mind just yet." I stood next to Charlie in the giant ballroom that I had never been in before. Normally, it was closed off, but today the curtains had been drawn. Beams of light bounced off the shiny wood floor. Just an hour ago, it had been covered with dust, but Sarah and Della saw to removing every speck. The walls in the rectangular room were a creamy yellow tint. A singular chandelier dangled from the coffered ceiling, illuminating sky blue curtains that gave the room its softness.

A smaller girl tended to the fireplace, replacing it with fresh coals. She was easily distracted, glancing behind her to see what the others were up to. Above the fireplace stood a mirror that watched over everyone. I peered at it, observing how Charlie directed the servants beside me.

"M'lord, what shall we do with the nails on the far wall?" Lemont inquired.

"I forgot about those wretched things! It's not too welcoming to see a bunch of nails protruding out of a wall, is it?" He concentrated in thought. Lemont actually laughed, which was astonishing to me. It was an unnatural, tumultuous noise that bounced off the walls.

"I think it would be best to remove them... though... the wall will have to be painted over."

"If you'll excuse my interruption, M'lord." Lemont cleared his throat unsurely, clasping his hands behind his back. "Wayne, the footman… had a suggestion."

"Oh, wonderful. And what might that be?" I bit my lip, unsure if Charlie was being sarcastic or not.

"He mentioned that wreaths could be displayed there. They would fit the room well, and they would *certainly* add some more—what one would call—*holiday spirit*, if I do say so myself."

"Ah, brilliant! Very smart chap he is. You give him my thanks. I will personally go out and pick some wreaths today. Please tell William to be ready in twenty minutes." Charlie nodded approvingly at the whole room and I followed him out.

"Isn't it just marvelous?" He beamed. I had to take fast steps to keep up with him. Sometimes, he threw me in a whirlwind. "You know, sometimes I forget that you and Flora and Momma and everyone weren't here when I initially moved in. Believe it or not, this whole castle was filled with armor and such when I came."

"Armor?" The thought struck me as so peculiar.

"Yes. It was *everywhere*. The walls, the ceilings. That is why those nails were there. There used to be a massive cluster of medieval-type swords hanging on that wall," he explained. As we passed through the hall he stuck his arm out to the side. "All along the left side of this hall used to be statues of knights in armor."

"How peculiar. I would have never known." That era was unfamiliar to me, where knights jousted on horses and people were trapped in dungeons. It was more acceptable as the setting in a novel than imagining that it truly existed.

"It is. See, I do not know too much about this castle other than that it was built in 1434. Obviously, it has been modernized quite a bit, but the base of the architectural design is from the medieval times." He pointed upward at the ceiling. "Such as these."

My eyes drifted upward at some fancy archway beams above us. They crisscrossed over each other like someone who had messed up a knitting pattern. "So what did you do with all the armor? Is it in storage somewhere?"

"I didn't have any use for it. I mean, it was incredible and all, but it made the house feel sort of cold and eerie. So I donated all of it to a museum and did an *immense* amount of redecorating." He breathed out heavily. "It was a lot of work, but it was worth it. It feels like a large house instead of a nostalgic war fortress."

"Well, you did a fine job. But, a house can *always* use a little bit of a *woman's* touch. Don't forget that." I half smiled as both of our minds wandered to the same person. Miss Farefield.

"Oh, stop it," he demanded as his ears glowed crimson. We came across Poppa, moving steadily toward the ballroom at a slow, calming pace. Sometimes he wandered the castle as if he wondered how on earth he got here.

"Poppa! You must go see it. I'll show you. The whole room looks charming," I squealed. "Charlie is on a mission to buy some wreaths." I linked my arm to his and guided him.

"I will be back shortly," Charlie called to us, continuing on. "See, Father? I told you it would be a good idea." He turned his head back, giving us a satisfactory smile.

"There couldn't be a better person at the helm," Poppa affirmed when Charlie's energetic footsteps were inaudible. "I didn't think he was up for the task of taking on this house at first, but here he is, and I am very proud of him."

"I couldn't agree more. He seems right for it. He's personable, witty, respectable—"

"My daughter, how are you?" His words paralyzed my lips. He never interrupted anyone. He always said, "Words are strings to the brain which cannot be cut short," to try to teach us manners. But with four children running around, all near the same age, it was tough. I took a moment to think about it, as I felt he wanted me to.

"I'm pretty well, Poppa." We stood at the entrance of the ballroom, but he didn't even look at it. He looked at me. I wanted to unscramble his thoughts, but they were so subdued that I could not tell what they were in the first place. For once, I wished for him to rant on and on, instead of storing his words in his head like a bank.

"Pardon us." A voice came from behind. Poppa and I slid off to the side while Wayne and Bruno came through holding a wooden ladder. Their arms were awkwardly entangled in the rungs like vines. Bruno caught my eye as they passed.

"Good afternoon, Mrs. Bolton." He nodded to my father and me while adjusting his grip on the ladder. "Mr. Breaker." Both their faces were red with a sheen of sweat from squeezing the ladder up the stairwell.

My father did not return the greeting. He turned his back to the open room and tilted his head toward my ear. "Who is that man?" came his hoarse whisper.

"That's Bruno, Claude's valet. Charlie hired him quite some time ago." I eyed them as they set up the ladder at the far side of the wall. Wayne tested out the rungs, cautiously stepping on the first two and backing off. "Why?"

"His face...."

"What about it?"

"I know I've seen it before," he claimed, narrowing his eyes.

"Well, of course you have! He's up and about the house all the time. You know, Poppa, if you weren't out at the garage so often, you might know. It seems like not even this beautiful home can entice you to stay."

He grumbled, "Perhaps. But just because I am here does not mean I will throw my soul of the working-class man away. Cars are like people, my dearest. They need doctors such as we do." He took in the view of the room. In all his life, I knew he had never imagined this for himself. He pictured dying with oil-stained fingers holding a wrench in one hand, and keys in another.

"Speaking of jobs and working and so forth... I wondered if I might ask your advice."

"The last time you asked me that, you were contemplating how to apologize to Pup for crashing his favorite cycle in the brook."

His words shot me back in time. Pup. The name rung in my head like echoing bells. How Claude had absolutely loathed it. When we were little, we had lived next to a couple who had a monstrous fluffy dog that left trails of slobber wherever it went. I remembered how the fur on his back was a silvery grey color, which often dulled in the spring. When they first got the dog, Flora had instantly pointed out how it had two different-colored eyes, like Claude. It was the only other living creature we had ever seen with the same condition. She went on to believe that our brother was somehow part dog, which was how she came up with the name, Pup. I, being the gullible younger sister, proceeded to follow her lead in calling him that until I was about fourteen years old.

"Poppa, it's nothing like that again," I assured, laughing lightly at the story. "Let us go to the sitting room and I will explain."

♪ ♪ ♪

My desire to be a musician tumbled from behind my lips.

Mother had joined the two of us in the sitting room, perplexed and twisting at my thoughts. Her whole body was tensed as she sat on the corner of her chair.

"*Back* with the violin?" It was like a disapproved marriage. "But Estella, surely you have everything and anything you could dream of. Why are you *making* work for yourself? This is your time to enjoy life, and to relax."

"I think it would be… fun. Not as much of a job as it would be a hobby, Momma." The word hobby repulsed her as if I had cursed. She blinked hard, still persisting.

"Darling, I mean this in the kindest, but sternest way possible." She paused. "You are not cut out for this. Any of it. You are not your sister. Flora is unmarried, and without a child, so she has the time and possibly the skill to manage in this new, modern world. You have never been modern, sweetie. You know that. You are a respectable married woman, and a mother, whether you believe it or not. Once a mother, always a mother. You have already molded your life into a shape. You cannot undo it."

"So you are saying my only job now is to be a mother? That's all that's left to me? To raise a family?" The hope inside me simmered into disbelief. Maybe that was the job of a woman in Momma's generation, but it was surely not for everyone in mine. Of course, it was not a bad thing, but it had crept up on me too soon and bit me, in the end.

"Dearest, your mother is right. What would become of you and Roy if you went off as a traveling musician? You would never see each other. You would be alone in this huge world, wandering. Think about it. I know you can see what I am saying," Poppa added.

I went quiet. In my head, I watched myself walking. At first, I was walking into nothingness. Everything around me was a blinding white. But then, shapes started to appear. Bricks filled the ground under my feet so I made soft thumping sounds when I stepped. My violin case slipped into my hand out of thin air, swishing against my dress. Color rained down into the picture. I could feel laughter, hear color, see sound and all the while, I was surrounded by other people. They walked like I did. And when I looked to my left, I saw a familiar pair of brown eyes looming beside me.

"I cannot see what you are saying, I'm afraid. My vision of it is so glamorous! I would not be alone at all. I'd have a music teacher, of course, and maybe even a tiny audience if I ever become good enough." A sudden feeling of nostalgia hit me. When I was younger, living in the country, my parents had allowed me to do most things by myself. I could walk the half hour from our home to church, or even to my friend's house on the other side of the village. I had been independent. They had let me. When did the conversion happen that required me to be accompanied by someone all the time?

"You are living in a dream world. People do not just go on stage because they are good. They have to be so much more than *good*. They have to be blessed," Momma retaliated. "And mind you, *respectable* people do not run off on the road with a suitcase and wander. At any rate, it would not be far from being a prostitute."

I shrugged off her discouraging speech as nothing, but her words became imprinted into my mind. They rung through my ears, driving me to snap back, but I wouldn't. She was too narrow-minded to understand. I couldn't let her get to me. "Then I will not go on stage. How come it is so hard to believe I want to do it just because I like it? Momma, the war has changed everything. I know you deny it, but women like me have a chance now. A chance in the real world, outside of a kitchen or laundry room. I could have a chance at a career." My eyes wandered from my mute father to my ranting mother, and then back to my father. I needed his input so badly. I knew if he was on my side that I would be able to convince Momma. But until then, I was up against a solid rock wall with no give. His words could make the rock malleable. "Poppa, what do you say?"

Both of us looked toward Poppa, waiting patiently. Momma's hard face softened as she looked at him. I could tell what was about to happen.

Poppa was going to side with Momma and that would be it. Momma seemed overly pleased that she had won.

"Estella, you are young, and still have a long life ahead of you, I know this. In that perspective—" I knew what he was going to say. Disappointment clouded my eyes and ears, making me block out his voice.

"…in no way do I agree that this is right for you, but, I will give you a chance to prove me wrong," he finished.

I blinked, once and then twice. A smile whipped across my face. "Oh, I will, I will!" I nearly jumped up from my chair. "Thank you Poppa. It's not a huge change like you both think. I simply want something to do, something that can be useful to me. Maybe nothing will come of it, but I believe musicians are extremely respectable, whether man or woman."

He nodded as Momma clamped her mouth shut. She couldn't look at my face when hers was so caked with disapproval.

"Momma, don't worry. I won't go and ruin my name. Chances are, I will not become anything at all."

♪ ♪ ♪

The piano had been moved into the ballroom. It was the finishing touch. It was set next to the fireplace with garland spread out on top of it. The scent of pine wafted all throughout the house, making my nose tingle with joy. Leo met me in the ballroom after dinner for my usual lesson, except this time, he didn't have to shy away from anyone. He didn't seem thrilled with the news, but he was happy to be able to teach me. For some reason, he still tried to be discreet, which left me with nagging wonder.

"Why on earth would they move it *there?*" he nearly yelled in exasperation, making me jump. We had just walked into the ballroom when a look of horror crossed his face.

"Leo calm down. It's not going to catch on fire," I chided him as I set up my violin.

"I'm not worried about *that.* The close heat can crack the sound board and warp the wood. You have to be careful with a piano like this." He pressed his hands on the side of it, pushing it away from the heat. A vein popped up near his temple as he heaved it forward. It only moved slightly, but his persistence increased the distance.

"Estella. Estella, Claude's been taken ill. He's got a very high fever." Charlie burst in the room. His face went from anxious, to a scowl, and then ended with a look of shock. "W—what are you doing?" His eyes darted from me who stood with my violin, to Leo who was tapping away at the piano keys. He instantly stopped and stood when he realized Charlie had come in.

"M'lord. I am so—"

"What do you mean?" My words ran right over Leo's. "Claude was fine earlier. How did this happen?"

"Never mind *that*! What is going on *here*? Bruno, you of *all* people should be up there helping my brother. Did you not even go up to dress him? I am completely disappointed and *astounded* at this action. Maybe if you did, we would have found out about his poor condition sooner!" He frowned deeply, and his frown was like a slice in his face. His dark eyebrows were curved in with disgrace.

"M'lord, he never rang the bell for me, so I didn't go up. He doesn't always require my help, so I simply go when he rings. I deeply apologize. I will go now." Bruno was out of the doorway in a flash.

"Charlie, ease up!" I complained when Bruno had gone.

"Ease up? *Ease up*? It's you who I should be really reprimanding!" He came toward me, staring at my violin. "What are you doing? You haven't seen Roy in two or three days and then I come in to see you mingling casually with my servant who, mind you, is also playing on a mother of pearl piano? Estella, I believe in fairness, but not in taking advantage."

"Oh you are so dense! He's teaching me about music," I claimed, matching his tone. The words tossed him back, stopping his thoughts in their tracks. I held up my violin, proving my case.

"*What?*" He almost laughed, as he braced his fingers against his forehead.

"He's an incredible pianist, Charlie. Better than anyone I've ever seen. I'm being honest. I talked it over with Momma and Poppa and they are letting me try it out. I had tried to tell you earlier so a scene like this would have been avoidable, but it didn't work out. But let me announce now that I'm taking a new life path," I concluded, lifting my chin and daring him to challenge me.

"So my servant is teaching you *piano*? News to me." His anger eroded away as he huffed in disbelief. "Never mind that. This whole household is going haywire," he groaned. "I'll have to talk to Bruno. Go up and see Claude."

"Charlie, you don't have to always look out for me. If I hit an iceberg one day, it's not your fault. You can't always preserve the good." I spoke sharply, jabbing at the heart he wore on his sleeve. "Sometimes the man in the crow's nest cannot oversee everything."

♪ ♪ ♪

Everything was a disaster the next day. Claude was shouting things that he wasn't conscious of, while downstairs, people laughed and waltzed giddily. My ears seemed to cry as the combination of fiddles and Claude's frightened voice boomed through my head, colliding and intertwining simultaneously into horrible screeches. Momma dabbed his face with a cool cloth, murmuring to him. Flora and I watched in struck silence, pulling our eyes away when he'd start to shout.

"This is ridiculous, Momma. He needs a doctor. You've been doing this all day. Let me see the cloth." Flora took Momma's place, wringing out the cloth. Flora had barely spoken a sentence to Claude, and now she was practically his nurse. Occasionally he'd open his eyes, but it was as if he couldn't see. Then they would close again.

Momma's eyes widened. She was just as shocked. "The doctor was supposed to be here hours ago. Maybe the snow beat him to it. I don't know what happened!" she snapped. She was overtired and grumpy from posing in the same spot all day.

I tiptoed over to the closed door, pressing my ear against it. Everyone's voices sounded like one endless hum. The rhythmical clicking of the women's heels as they spun around the dance floor, echoed all around. People had to be wondering, where was the rest of the Breaker family? But no person would downright ask. Oh, no. It was gossip material to be used when our backs were turned. Once again, we were failing as everyone expected. After all, we were nothing but new money. An average family tossed into an extraordinary lifestyle.

I nearly fell over as the door opened from the other side. Leo clung tight to a bowl of cold water. The water swayed from one side to the other, but stayed within the rim.

"I apologize, Mrs. Bolton. I did not know you were there." He stumbled backward.

"No, no. 'Tis my fault. Come in." I stepped back and he came forward, replacing the bowl beside Flora with fresh water.

"Thank you," Flora muttered, not taking her eyes off our brother.

"Is there anything else I can do?" Leo asked, grimacing at the sight of Claude.

"Only if you can magically turn yourself into a doctor."

"Flora, that's unkind. Pray, do not be so *rude*," came Momma's shrill voice. She flashed her a warning glance, taking a seat at Claude's desk. "Maybe if he didn't stay in this room all the time, he wouldn't be sick. Some fresh air can work miracles sometimes. Claude is a decent man, but he does not put himself out there. And the few times he has, fate did not take his side. He needs something with which to occupy his boredom. He also needs a wife, but that is beside the point." She sighed sadly, dreaming of the utopia she grasped at with her fingertips.

Claude began to twitch, but Flora calmed him by striking up a one-way conversation. I didn't know what to do. I wasn't being useful, or helpful. I was just standing without purpose.

"What in the Lord's name is this?" Momma held up a stack of papers, tied together with string. She placed them on the desk and began to untie the knot. I was not sure myself, but I was too absorbed in my own thoughts to care about a random pile of papers.

"Please don't touch that." Leo's voice cut through the room. The last word of his sentence got caught in his throat, as he realized what he said.

"Pardon me?" Momma spun around in the chair, glaring knives at Leo. Her eyebrows joined in disbelief and her hands curled around the arms of the chair.

"Mr. Breaker doesn't like his desk being rummaged through. Every day, he informs the maids and he informs me as well."

"Do you *know* who you are talking to? I'm his *mother!* Do you understand that? To think that I am being *commanded* by a servant such as yourself is just… just humiliating and disrespectful," she huffed. "What is your name? I shall be speaking to His Lordship about you."

Leo hesitated. I could tell he hadn't anticipated this. Now, he got to know the real wrath of my mother. I could not come up with something fast enough to stop it.

"Bruno Leonhardt," he answered quietly.

"What?"

"Bruno Leonhardt," he repeated once more, staring at his shoes.

"Well that explains your disrespect! Your kind are all the same. I'm surprised that you are *permitted* in this country, with your tainted *German blood*."

Abruptly, Claude started yelling again. I hurried over to the door, closing it swiftly. Flora pushed his shoulders down, but he did not comply. Bruno rushed over to help her, since her resistance was nothing against Claude. Once they soothed him, Flora resumed her work. She was in her flapper dress, with crimped hair that resembled welded gold. Certainly, she had not expected to find herself here tonight. I pitied her. She enjoyed dancing the most, yet here she was, bound to Claude's side. Just like they were as children.

I had just changed into my evening dress, but I did not expect to make any use of it. I was sure I would be here the whole night.

Momma was still grumbling to herself when Leo approached the door.

"Mrs. Breaker, with all due respect, Germany is not bad. It is *depressed*. I respect it, and in turn, it respects me. Good evening to all." He backed out of the room with radiating confidence, clicking the door shut.

Momma's bottom teeth poked sharply into her upper lip, unable to say what she would have liked. "That man… I cannot wait to inform Charlie about him. He speaks nonsense. His country probably fails to recognize that he even exists, so this *respect* he babbles about is clearly one-sided," she seethed, finally grasping words.

"Momma, you *did* insult his country. What did you presume would happen? That he would let you prance all over it?" I defended. "You would be among the first to rebuke if you heard someone insult the King, or England itself."

"Oh, you mind your mouth! You of all people...." she scoffed, shaking her head. Her whispers captivated my sister and me more than her screeching ever could. "That man's country *st—stole* part of my son." Her voice ripped and trembled like the loose string on a violin. "Do you not *comprehend* that? How could you feel sympathy or want justice for... *those people* when you have a firsthand experience of what their evil minds have done?"

Her words reeled me back and suddenly, I was eight years old, struggling to tie bows at the ends of my braided hair. Charlie was to bring me to school for the first time. It was in the center of the overgrown village we lived in. The schoolhouse was just one room with a lineup of chairs and desks that teetered on uneven legs. I remembered Claude and Flora running far ahead of us, racing each other to the door. But when I would walk in, only two of my siblings were ever there. This happened almost every day. Claude never showed up. He told me he went to Brim's Peak Lake to swim because he didn't care about school. He would meet a couple of older kids, and they would skip it.

One particular day, however, Poppa had walked us to school. Claude had no choice but to go in. That day changed Claude's resentment toward school. The teacher went over to him after class, and said that Claude had such beautiful penmanship that the Americans could have used him to write the United States Constitution. Well, that did it; it was as easy as that. Claude then took an interest in school. Even after Flora, Charlie, and I dropped out a couple of years later, Claude remained. He probably was the most intelligent out of the four of us, not that anyone would ever know due to his reclusive habits.

I was back in the present now, staring at the grown version of the little boy I pictured so distinctly in my head. My eyes glazed the stack of papers on his desk. Broken lines. That's what his penmanship had become. Words lodged in my throat when I tried to answer Momma.

England

The Pianist

I eased downstairs, slinking through the hallway. Guests huddled around and made their way down to the ballroom. The moon had not even begun to set, and I wished it over already. The trip to Castle Comb had not happened at all, due to Claude's condition. Deep resentment boiled up inside me, but I refused to let it boil over. They did not understand. I repeated it to myself over and over to ease the sizzling. The grandfather clock called out, ringing eleven times. Each time my heart fluttered, absorbing the consecutive rings into its pounding pattern. It then merged into my footsteps as I clambered down the stairs.

"Bruno! Bruno? That is you, yes?" I had just stepped into the kitchen of the servants' hall when another pair of footsteps layered my own. They were heavy, quick pounds. I swiveled around and faced His Lordship with a look of utmost confusion. Surely, he was supposed to be entertaining in the ballroom.

"Yes, M'lord, it is."

"Good. It appears that we are short on staff in the ballroom, so I wondered if you may take it upon yourself to serve drinks. You remember how, yes?"

"Yes, M'lord." I cleared my throat uneasily. "I do."

"Splendid. Now please hurry. Take a tray from down here and Duncan will give you half of his so you can offer them."

"I will, M'lord." I crouched down, and pulled open the cabinet. Many trays for different events were stacked upon each other. They clanged together as I picked one out. I had not noticed His Lordship standing beside me until I stood with the tray in my hand.

"You know, Bruno. I wanted to apologize again for how I acted toward you yesterday. I hope our conversation this morning… *cleared* things up a bit."

"It did, M'lord. I would have not done it without your permission, but it was understood by me that Mrs. Bolton had informed you. I didn't know."

Yes, quite alright, now. Anyway, I must be upstairs." He clapped his hands together. "I mustn't keep Miss Farefield waiting." He bounded back up. I was soon to follow, fixing my hair and preparing a smile.

All of the servers had to stay in their assigned zone of the room to assure that everything was as easy and accessible as possible. Occasionally, we would glance at each other, trying to communicate the muted words behind our lips. Other than serving, we idled, watching people dance and eat to their heart's content. I was not in the moment. My mind kept falling back to what Estella's mother had said. Just then, Lemont opened the door. His typically somber face was coated with opposition that seeped its way into people's eyes nearby.

"Miss Achebe," he announced as the door swung closed behind her. I nearly dropped my tray. The people grouped around the door fell silent, while the rest took no notice and continued to spin and listen to the string quartet. Miss Achebe stepped forward timidly, glancing about for one person in the crowd that she would not see tonight. She had an angular face, with bold, dark lips. The ends of her hair looked like springs, bouncing with each step. Not a piece of jewelry could be seen on her, but that didn't matter, because her beaded dress made heads turn by itself.

By now, others began to notice. It was not hard to spot her in a room of blurring paleness. My stomach churned. If Claude were here, he would have doused their unhappy glares easily.

I found His Lordship on the other side of the room. He was leaning against a wall, making small talk with Miss Farefield and a few other folks. He led the party to a table, separating himself from it just before heading to see Mr. Lemont. The two talked discreetly, occasionally glancing over their shoulders. His Lordship had this undeniably exasperated look on his face, like he was about to pull a stupid stunt. They disengaged, and he sauntered over to me.

"Did you know about this? A—About this guest?" His eyes flashed warily, like the flickering flame of a gas lamp.

"No, M'lord," I defended. He paused as I held out my tray for a woman. She took the glass in her gloved hand and left rather hastily, glancing back at His Lordship.

"I cannot believe this. I thought this was a short-time courtship. A temporary thing! Now my brother went off and invited this woman, and he is not *even present!*" He inhaled deeply, trying to determine a solution. He pressed his fingertips to his forehead. I personally could not see how it was so damaging to the family. England seemed to be a harsh, prejudiced place, the way I saw it. It had its wealthiest families begging on their knees of its shores for acceptance.

"If—" His Lordship began.

"Excuse me." Out of all the people in the ballroom, Miss Achebe came and stood before us. "I was told that you are the owner of this estate?" She eyed His Lordship, calculating her words and testing the vibes coming from him. Anyone could tell she was overly analytical and extremely alert, by the way she skimmed each person's face with cautious eyes.

"Yes. That would be me," His Lordship replied coldly.

"Oh. I just—you know—wanted to introduce myself personally."

"Do not worry. I know who you are."

"Indeed? I'm pleasantly surprised," she laughed. She spoke with a manner of authority, even though she must have felt the repulsing glances that people gave to her.

"Charlie…." People parted and Miss Farefield came toward us. "Oh, there you are! I've been wondering where you have been! We never finished talking about—"

"May!" He put a phony smile on his face. "I'd like to introduce you to Miss Venus Achebe. Miss Achebe, this is Miss Farefield."

"Charmed," Miss Achebe curtsied slightly. Miss Farefield was taken aback, but replied with a warm welcome.

"Yes, charmed as well." The two briefly looked at each other with immense curiosity. They were polar opposites in every way, but May did not burn her with an unpleasant stare like everyone else did.

"Care for a drink?" May smiled in an overly happy way, gesturing to me and my tray. She broke the silence like a pick breaking ice. Miss Achebe seemed delighted at the thought.

"I was hoping someone would say that! Yes, indeed." I lowered my tray for her. Her eyes flickered with something strange when she looked at me. Once she had the glass in her hands, she peered at me at least three more times, but no words were exchanged between us.

"So, where is Claude all this time?" She looked about and laughed, though no one shared her mood. "He invited me, and yet he is not present himself. Sly man."

"Excuse you, Miss. My brother is referred to as Mr. Breaker here. If you would kindly obey that," Lord Breaker snapped. He was becoming picky like his mother.

"Oh, yes. Wouldn't want to… *overstep* the *boundaries* when dealing with your strict English rules." Her words were smooth, and she kept a calm, knowing composure. She knew her words prodded at His Lordship.

"Good," he stated, unwavering. "As for Mr. Breaker, he will not be here tonight." Now he had the upper hand, leaving her with an abrupt, nasty conclusion.

"What do you mean? He does live here, correct?" Miss Achebe's calmness around her began to shrivel away like a wilting flower. His Lordship's words brought on more heat.

"Yes."

"Yes?" she repeated, confused. She focused on all of our faces, searching for a clear answer. His Lordship had two choices now. The first was to tell her the truth that Claude was sick. The second could be followed up by infinite stories, but they all ended with her leaving crossly.

"Miss Achebe, would you care to dance with me?" I blurted out suddenly. In the split seconds of silence before her reply, I chided myself. If she said no, it would undoubtedly make the situation worse. She answered with a simple, accented, "Yes." Her smooth voice had returned, and oddly, she was not the least bit thrown by my question.

I placed my tray behind me on an empty card table, not daring to look at His Lordship's face. My insides tightened as Miss Achebe and I walked by them. Neither His Lordship, nor Miss Farefield muttered a word. Their lips froze in shock.

We had been dancing for around five minutes when Miss Achebe started to speak. The quartet had just started to play a waltz. At first, people stared—goggled even—like we were the starring act in a circus. But now, it was as if we blended in completely with the other dancers around us. Occasionally I'd catch the glint of the whites of eyes, but that was all.

"What are you doing?" she asked simply.

"I'm dancing?" I meant to say it as a statement, but it came out as a question. She was probably pondering my dancing ability out loud.

"Yes." She glared at me. "Clearly. The point I am trying to get at is, why are you here? You must know that I didn't just say yes to a random footman when you asked me to dance. You are that German pianist. Leonardo Leonhardt."

I hesitated. "Yes." Sweat beaded up on my forehead. It felt wonderful and horrible to let it out.

"I knew I wasn't losing my mind when I first saw your face!" She giggled.

"Miss Achebe, I want to apologize for Mr. Breaker not being here. He is actually sick in bed right now." I stepped backward, unconsciously loosening my grip on her hand as we turned. I didn't want her to talk about me anymore.

"Hmph. And why should I take it into my interest to believe *you*?"

"I'm his personal valet. I'm posing as a footman for tonight."

"Ha!" She laughed, tilting her head back. "You went from being at the top of the chain to the bottom. How does it feel? Tell me," she hissed, narrowing her huge round eyes into slits.

"First," I let the word linger as my eyes sifted across the ceiling. "You tell *me* how it feels to have gone from the bottom to the top." I gave her a stern stare, making her feel uncomfortable. She backed off the subject, because I knew the answer already. She didn't want to confirm it.

"I should smack you for that comment," she whispered bitterly. "I don't get how you still carry your high and mighty conscience. It's laughable, in all truth. You're a *valet*. You should embrace it and cut being king, for your acting is proving a failure. You've lost your claim to fame, Mr. Leonhardt."

"That is the one thing we have in common, Miss. We play the same part. You should be grateful you were invited here, as I am to work here."

"Of course I am! Do you think every week I get invited to a party like this? The biggest party I get invited to is held in the so—" She cut her words off sharply. The music passed between us, making invisible bubbles around the room that popped in dancers' ears.

"The soup kitchen?"

She nodded, tearing her eyes away from me. And that was when Estella walked in.

♪ ♪ ♪

"Bruno. His Lordship would like to see you in the library." It was two days after the ball. Claude had improved tremendously. They had sent another doctor out because the first one had been held up from the snowstorm. I had been anticipating the moment with Lord Breaker for a long time, though I hadn't expected it to arrive after two whole days had gone by. I pushed out my chair, and headed toward the stairs. I could feel my face heating with nerves.

"Oh, Mr. Bruno. How many times do I have to tell you? Fix that hair of yours. If you can't get that piece to stay, I will gladly cut it. There's no way you are going up like that." Miss G barely had her foot in the room, and she was already calling me out.

"Yes, Miss G." I stopped and fixed it. Pauline came skipping through the room, taking our silverware and plates from lunch.

"Mr. Bruno," she sang, "I hear you are in for some trouble." She waggled her eyebrows, making a joke of it all.

"Pauline, did we ask for your opinion on the subject? No. Now hurry along, and stop messing with Mr. Bruno." Pauline's hollow cheeks flushed red. With one arm, she piled up the plates. She and Wayne smirked at each other as they passed opposite ways through the door. They clasped hands for two seconds, and then went their own ways.

"Ah, Bruno." His Lordship squashed the cigarette he had been smoking in an ashtray to his left. He coughed, and gestured for me to sit. I couldn't decipher his thoughts. Instead, I found myself stuck in a slew of memories; they were quicksand, dragging me under and holding me hostage.

"You probably have a good guess of why you are here, yes?"

"Yes... M'lord."

"Enlighten me." He held his gaze, but he was not trying to be humiliating.

"I... I danced with Miss Venus Achebe, which made a disaster of the whole ball. I was... I was *unaware* of Mr. Breaker's illness, proving me to be undiligent and irresponsible. I could not hold my tongue when Mrs. Breaker insulted my country." As I rambled, I had not noticed that he had slapped a stack of letters on the table between us until he pointed to them.

"So, in all, Bruno, would you agree... if I said that you do not fit into this position? Now, I'm being frank with you, so watch yourself."

I didn't want to say yes. I didn't want to agree. But my actions showed differently, so I had no choice. "Yes, M'lord."

"Can I tell you something?" he asked politely.

"Yes, M'lord."

"Do you remember when I first hired you? I had written in the advertisement that no previous experience was needed. Surely you can recall that." He raised one eyebrow and smoothed the stubble on his face.

"I do." I slid my sweaty palms on my pants.

"I did this for a specific reason. I wanted a person who could learn to adjust to their surroundings, and someone who could adjust to handling my brother. I did not want a valet who would compare everything they had previously been taught to my expectations, or to my way of running this estate. Because I know for a fact that I have plenty of servants downstairs who do this. But I cannot blame them. I could never live up to be half as good as the late Lord Hampton once was. You understand my point?"

"Uh, yes. I think so, M'lord."

"In other words, I wanted to give someone else a chance, and in doing this I wanted that chance reciprocated and given back to me as well. But, I have a problem." He picked up the first letter of the stack. I realized that it had already been opened. The seal was broken, along with all the others.

"'We appreciate your consideration with inviting us'— etcetera," he mumbled, unable to find the right spot. "Oh, here it is." He crossed his legs, and read each word loudly and clearly. "'We would be ever so honored to be invited back. Both my husband and I were absolutely stunned to see Leonardo Leonhardt, and next time, I will be sure to bring some parchment to have him autograph.'" He looked at me, analyzing my face the same way Miss Achebe had. Without another word, he picked up the next letter and continued to read.

"'By golly, you should have told us about that footman of yours! Why wasn't he playing the piano? I absolutely must introduce myself to him, *if* you will be ever so kind to want to invite Lilly and myself back again.'" He unfolded the next one. "'I'm his biggest follower! I adore all of his music, and I've even been to a performance. To think that he works in your house is quite exquisite.'" Charlie paused, grabbing at another. Now he read shorter, broken up sentences:

"'So this is where Mr. Leonhardt has been all this time? It's upsetting! Nothing against you of course, dearest friend. You must be enthralled to have him in your employ.'"

I couldn't come up with what to say. The strong backbone I thought I had was bending with each word he read. I could not get away.

"Bruno, correct me if I am mistaken, but from my understanding and research that I have done in the last day, I have found that you are a well-known pianist? Better put, a very *famous pianist*."

"I used to be, M'lord. That's why I took this job here." Lord Breaker's eyebrows furrowed in bewilderment. He had given me the same look when he had first interviewed me.

"Bruno, that's where I think you are incorrect. You cannot be a servant. It is not right for you. I gave you a chance here, as you did with me as a new estate owner, and as you did with my brother. But after reviewing your conduct and finding out who you really are, I'm afraid I have to give you notice, and advise you into a different job. I'm giving you two weeks and a month's wages to find other employment." He squished the dead cigarette even more into the plate. "I really am sorry, Bruno."

I could feel myself sinking even more. My empty eyes grabbed at my surroundings as disappointment swirled around me. Everything he said after that to console me flew over my head.

A letter was placed in front of my seat before lunch. Mrs. Hardwick was scurrying about, passing mittens and hats to Pauline, Duncan, and Wayne. Duncan swigged the last of his hot cocoa, then tied a scarf around his neck, pulling it up over his mouth as if he was planning to rob a bank. We had been given a day off because the family had gone to London, and Pauline decided that we were all to go sledding. Mrs. Hardwick had not hesitated to suggest that she, herself, stay behind.

"Mr. Bruno, are you coming?" Pauline peeped. I picked up my letter, letting its sealed contents tease me.

"Sure, Pauline. Why not?" I had never been sledding before. Not like this, at least. When we arrived, I noticed how the hills looked as if they scraped the sky. They were bumps on the earth's swollen face. My hat whipped off my head as we sailed down to the bottom, piling as many of us as possible onto one wooden sled and yelling all the way down.

Exactly two weeks later, I sat alone, in the sitting room. His Lordship had let me play the piano one last time. I slid my fingers back and forth over the glimmering keys. Songs wouldn't come to me. Instead, I found myself bracing my arm on the music shelf, resting my head there in shame. Once again, the piano offered me sanction that I did not want, nor deserve. I closed my eyes and listened. I heard the snow melt from the roof, dribbling down the window panes. I heard the birds, ruffling their stiffened wings to take flight under the new sun. I heard the crickets. The crickets with their fiddles playing late into the night of summer, and the leaves, freshly clipped from the trees' limbs, waiting to be compressed by more snow. And round and round it went. The same melody, behind a different setting, because by the time the song was over, I was far away from the house, from the winter, and from that piano.

Part III

Nocturne

1924

England

The Pianist

Three-four time. As soon as I walked through the gates to the carnival, my musical instincts soared. The breeze was strong, making the torches that the clown was juggling flicker rapidly. He jumped from one foot to the other, expertly tossing one of the six he was holding, making it spiral up into the air. The carousel was going around for the thousandth time today. The same old ecstatic tune whirled around it.

"Bruno, whatdya say we grab a drink?" George nudged me, eying the cotton candy enviously.

"I'm not up for one. This medication I take makes my stomach all queasy," I replied. "Probably later."

"You're always a sore sport," he sighed. Did he overlook the bandage on my head too?

"Come on, George. You know that's not *completely* true. You gotta give me some slack," I insisted, gesturing to my arm in its sling. "Let's go play one of those games." I pointed to a couple of small booths lined up.

"I'm the best at the ring toss. Come on, Bruno, I'll go and win you a doll," he laughed.

"I can win myself a doll... even with my bad arm," I bluffed. George and I had become friends years ago. He and I were next door neighbors, though he still lived with his parents. Once and a while, he, his older sister, and I would go out, but those times were rare. Oddly enough, he had just

185

heard of this carnival and invited me to go, though I was probably a substitute for a closer friend of his who couldn't come.

He was about to pay for another three turns when someone started yelling.

"Cricket tournament! Sign up here!" We turned around and a man with a bushy mustache was standing in front of the carousel, waving a paper. He yelled, over and over, and flocks of boys ran toward him, hooting and hollering about who would be captain.

"Oh yeah! Sorry, Bruno, but I can't miss this chance!" He stuffed his money back in his wallet and hurried over, leaving me at the booth. "Come and watch!"

"You going to play, kind sir? You have to play to win!" An older man came toward me, diverting my attention from George and pointing toward the plush animals at his booth. "All you have to do is roll this golf ball, and the prize is yours!"

"Uh, no thank you." I gave him a wave and left. I watched everyone around me, smoking, laughing, and spilling popcorn. A chicken from the petting zoo was running around, pecking at crumbs and sneaking through people's ankles. I didn't want to watch cricket. Even after living in England for five years, the whole concept was foreign. My mind wandered to tomorrow as it overworked itself into a state of panic.

I continued to walk, passing the petting zoo where little kids chased a couple of goats. I could feel this certain… vibration. People occasionally glanced at me as I passed, but it didn't bother me anymore. Then, I heard it, over the mooing of the cow, and the yelling of the vendors. I followed the sound to a somewhat less populated part of the carnival where the grass still stood erect and the air didn't smell of sweets. I could hear them before I spotted them. A quartet. Their music easily overpowered the carnival theme. I joined a small crowd, huddled in front of them while the cello began a solo.

The tone was so rich, sending jolts through my ribcage. My fingers tingled with the sound. Gradually, people dispersed, tossing coins in an open case that I spotted between shoulders. As the crowd died out, the instruments became visible. A viola, two violins, and a cello. The man playing the cello was fantastic. It was a captivating performance. I stood there the whole time as they played Joseph Haydn's Op. 76 No. 2 in D minor. Just when I thought the cellist was good, the first violinist would take over. No one seemed to take as much of an interest in it as I did. I sat down in the grass in front of them, letting them drown out my surroundings. It was such an unusual piece to choose to play near a carnival setting, but maybe that's what made it fascinating.

Toward the end, both violinists really got into it, scrunching their faces in concentration. That's when something caught my eye. Both of them wore hats that casted shadows over their faces, until the sun struck their cheeks. That's when I noticed the difference. One of them had freckles plastered on her cheekbones. Her light hair was just visible tucked under her hat. The other was shorter with dark, wavy hair. But the way she swayed.... The whole piece ended with a quarter note. I clapped, along with other people standing and sitting around me. They all bowed, and when they came up, that's when my thoughts were confirmed.

"Estella," I whispered. I could feel my eyes growing wider as I watched her. My worry snapped like dry twigs. It couldn't have been her. That speed? That precision? "Estella," I called aloud. The women looked up from her sheet music. Her eyes wandered until they tripped onto my face. She stared at me, long and hard, blinking her eyes.

"Leo?" she choked. She didn't know whether to grin or frown. Abruptly, she broke from her group and came over, still clutching her violin and bow in her hands. "My lord, what happened to you?" I didn't get a chance to answer before her arms wrapped around my neck. I could feel her chin on my shoulder, and the side of her violin touching my back. The eyes of people around us burned onto my face.

I didn't want her to let go. My breath caught in my chest. She stepped back, admiring my bandages. It was a vague question, really. I hadn't told her that I had been fired from being Claude's valet years ago. But that was only because I didn't want her to be mad at His Lordship. To her, it must have seemed like I had fallen off the earth.

"I was in a car accident." I found my voice.

"Are you okay? What happened to your arm? It isn't *broken*, is it?" She gave me this look, like she didn't want to believe it. Her eyes were stuck on my sling. Instantly, I knew she was thinking about her brother.

"No, no. It *was* broken, but it is almost better, now. The gash on my head is healed through. I have to keep this on for the stitching."

"Stitching," she muttered, disturbed by the thought. Her trance was soon broken. Mounds of words and questions flashed under her eyes.

"Miss Breaker," the cellist called, waving his bow in the air like a sword. What did he say? His words sounded jumbled. I couldn't focus on anything else.

"I'm ever so sorry." She turned her head toward them, gave me an apologetic look, and hurried back to join.

"Oh, no, I don't mean to interrupt. In fact, I was thinking we could take a short break and you could introduce us to your friend," the cellist said. He rose, leaning his instrument against his chair as the group came over to me.

"Oh, of course, John," she replied eagerly. John was a middle-aged man with a narrow build. He had short, stubby hair, making an impression that he fit the part of a soldier better than that of a cellist. The tips of his fingers were calloused, and he removed his glasses when he wasn't reading music.

"Everyone, I'd like you to meet my friend, Leonardo Leonhardt. Leo, this is John, our cellist, Willy, our *wild* violist, and Isobel, a violinist like myself." She pointed to each person.

"I cannot believe I'm seeing you in the flesh," Willy claimed, shaking his head. "Afraid I don't quite know what to say. So, M—Mr. Leonhardt, how is this carnival treating you?" he stuttered.

"Good to meet you, Willy." I shook his hand, hoping to ease his nerves. "I just got here, but it is pretty good. I came with my friend, George, but he's somewhere either playing cricket, drinking, or stuffing his face with popcorn. I haven't decided which." I cracked a smile.

"Wil, calm yourself, dearest." Isobel placed her hand on his shoulder. She turned to me. Her puzzled look was obvious. "*Who* are you again?" She squinted. She had to be French. Her poise, appearance and accent clearly framed her ethnicity.

"Izzy, he's a pianist. A prodigy pianist from the age of four years old!" John butted in. His tone of voice was the same for each sentence he said. "So strange to see such a man as yourself here in a makeshift carnival, though, take no offense, of course."

"I like places like this. It shows me what I missed out on as a child. So, in being here now, I attempt to make up for it." I spoke lightly of it, but it was all true.

"Hmph. Estella, how come you never mentioned that you knew Mr. Leonhardt?" Willy turned to her, throwing his arms out. "We could have asked him to play with us at some point. It would have been incredible! How'd the both of you become acquainted?" He was still in awe of the whole thing.

Estella studied my face, unsure whether I wanted my backstory to be told. "We met through work," she wound up saying. I was content with that answer.

"Quite impressive. Now, Mr. Leonhardt, I haven't heard about any upcoming tours of yours in *ages*. I wonder if I might ask when the next one will be," Willy continued on.

"Tours? I'm very sorry, Willy, but I don't do tours anymore." I watched his expression sink. "I stopped a while back."

His mouth fell agape. "I'm utterly surprised. I read in a couple of newspapers that you were taking a break, but that you would eventually return. Forgive me, but I find myself *very* disappointed." A frown etched itself into his face. His whole demeanor shifted. His attitude went stale, and his expression hardened. "I thought musicians were more dedicated than that. I know I am." He left the conversation and went over to his viola, leaving Estella, John, and Izzy all baffled at his conduct.

"Uhh... do excuse him." Izzy hesitantly backed out of the conversation also, and went over to Willy.

"Leo, would you care for a walk?" Estella interrupted before anything else was said. John's eyes bounced between us, sensing something.

"Sure," I replied.

"Be back in a half hour! We still have to play!" John shouted as we headed toward the center of the carnival.

England:
The Violinist

I had never thought that a singular person could evoke so many questions. The last time I had seen Leo had been at the ball. It was engraved in my head because I had walked in to find him dancing with Miss Achebe. Now, it was as if he randomly appeared, just as easily as he had disappeared before. He hadn't mentioned a word. In fact, I thought for sure he would have been back in Germany. I glanced at him from the side as we walked, not believing he was really there. A part of me wanted to snub him, for abandoning Claude, for ruining the ball, and for leaving without a single word of goodbye, but the better half of me didn't have that willpower.

"...so, after that, I moved here, to Scarborough, and I've been living here since," he concluded. I only heard half of it.

"Where do you live again?" I asked. My head felt light and airy like freshly popped corn.

"Here, in Scarborough," he repeated, cracking a smile at my oblivion. "I have a little beach house actually not far from here. The fellow that I mentioned earlier, George, is my neighbor. We walked here."

"Oh. How nice," I remarked blandly.

He tilted his head from side to side, clearly not agreeing with it. He rambled on, something that I had not known him to do, previously.

"If you don't mind my asking, when can you take off the sling?" I questioned, finding a pause between his words. It was an ugly, blue cloth that hugged his forearm to his side.

"Mmm… probably a week or two left. In truth, probably more like a week." He wiggled his fingers. "When the accident first happened, I couldn't move any of my fingers on this hand." His expression changed. His lips straightened, taking the eased glint in his eyes and transforming it into something hard; something bogged with worry.

"That's awful," I grimaced, blinking away the gory pictures in my mind. "When did it happen?"

He sighed. "It was about a month ago. It sounds embarrassing when I tell the story, honestly." He ran his hand through his hair, watching it replay in his head as he recounted it to me. "I was driving in Lincolnshire, in a small town called Boston, when I came up to a traffic light at an intersection. A four way intersection. I forget the name of the street, or… maybe I never really knew. That's beside the point, though. I was slowing down in case the light changed. As I kept going toward it, the light stayed the same, so I continued on, naturally. And then, I remember this crunching sound. I couldn't figure out where I was, even though my eyes were open. I hadn't even noticed my forehead was cut open until someone pulled me out of the car and tied a piece of cloth to my head. Another car that had the green light hit the right side of my car." He swallowed. "It happened within moments." He clenched his hand, remembering it all too vividly.

A shiver slithered down my back. "It's odd. No one ever thinks things such as that will happen to them. But you're okay, and that's what matters." Three kids whizzed by us, fighting over a plush bear that the fastest kid waved above his head. The other two were like hunting dogs chasing behind him.

Leo went quiet, stopping to watch the cricket game in the field next to us. He seemed overly alert, as if he was on the search for something. His eyes narrowed every time the ball was hit. People's cheers rang out into the sky as the bowler threw an expert curveball.

"Estella, there's another problem, though. I *know* that my arm will heal. But… for weeks and weeks I find myself dwelling on this accident." He jumped back into his story, picking up toward the end. "The sheriff of that town I had been in asked me to tell him what happened after I woke up at the hospital. So, I told him everything I could remember. But as I told it, he *actually* started to *argue* with me. I told him that the light stayed the same, so I kept going, but he insisted that he had spoken to witnesses who had claimed the contrary. They said I went through the red light."

"He was actually arguing with you? How unkind. After all, you were in the hospital!" I scrunched up my nose in disapproval. I was not familiar with the job of a sheriff, but I was almost positive that it did not involve pestering and squabbling with hospital patients.

"No, but… but he was *convincing* me!" His voice was strained like he was in pain. "Somewhere, inside me, I believed him." He shifted his weight, leaning on the fence that separated the cricket field from the rest of the carnival. We watched a short boy go scrambling after a grounder.

"What do you possibly mean? He was convincing you what? That you went through the light when you specifically told him that you didn't see the light change?" I glanced over at him, trying to read his face. The pieces to his story tossed around in my head.

"Yes. In fact, by the time I was freed from the hospital, he had helped me schedule an appointment with an eye doctor." Leo deliberately wouldn't look at me, taking interest in the flowers in the grass on the other side of the fence. "The nurses at the hospital told me that I probably needed glasses, so they recommended me to a specialist named Doctor Hawthorn. I have an appointment tomorrow at ten fifteen."

"Leo, it's okay," I assured him. I reached out instinctively to touch his shoulder, but then stopped myself. "It's probably just for precaution. Even if you do need glasses, per chance, it cannot be *that* bad. Glasses are quite handsome." I gave him a cheeky grin, hoping to bring the blood back to his cold face. My attempts failed.

"You don't understand! I *know* that I don't need glasses! I know it because I was checked once before when I was a child. My brother, Otto, has them to this day. I can read sheet music perfectly fine, and those notes are smaller than anyone's written alphabet." I could tell he wanted to go on, but he cut himself short, sinking deep into thought. "I'm just—I'm just so afraid," he stumbled. His voice was a loose string, vibrating in an untimely manner that made each word too flat.

"*Afraid?* Of what? The doctor?" I chided lightly.

"I'm afraid I'm going blind." It took him a while before he said anything else. His eyes were glazed to perfection with salt and water.

It was something too complicated for me to imagine. Blind? It was... it was impossible... completely unlikely... *extremely* rare. It could not happen to him. After all, why would it? As much as I told myself, my memory fought against me. I saw Leo and me in the sitting room, scrambling to keep Flora out. He was handing me the wrong books when my sister had specifically asked for the orange one.

"It is the only reasonable conclusion, Estella." He let out a shaky breath, sniffling. "The past month or so, I've walked about, wondering if what I'm seeing is real. I don't trust myself. Or I wonder if I'm missing something. As— as if I was looking at a painting and suddenly, coffee was spilled on it, obscuring a portion. It's keeping me up, making me think I'm crazy, and I'm so afraid to be tested tomorrow because I don't want it to be confirmed."

"Leo, you're not going blind," I whispered meekly.

"You can't say that. You have no idea. Wouldn't it all make sense? I could never put together proper clothing when I was a valet. Surely, you know that. I'm never able to pick a ripe fruit at the market. They always turn out to be hard or near rotted. I remember that one time Bentley asked me to help him with the wine for future training and he yelled at me for mixing two different ones. I don't know what to do. Something is missing. What if there's this big blur in everything I see and I don't even realize it's there?" He was on the verge of breaking down. It was then I noticed the changes in him. The rims of his eyes were dark, his lips were dry and cracked, and his hands trembled, something I had never seen in him before.

"You're getting ahead of yourself. Be calm, for you are not a doctor and have no idea what it could be." I removed the nagging worry from my voice. He couldn't know that I feared for him.

"You don't understand the significance in this! My whole world could go dark, like an eternal sleep and you are here, telling me to relax?" He snapped his fingers. "Like this! Gone. Estella, if you only half knew—" He roughly wiped his eyes with his hand.

"I'm trying to help you before you worry yourself sick! My great aunt had an ulcer because of her stress levels, you know." I felt small next to him, like my words would never reach his ears. They were carried away by the wind, fluttering into the clouds that suppressed them into silence. He tightened his quivering lips. After a moment, I spoke up again.

"What time does your pocket watch read?"

He pulled it out, not even hesitating or squinting as he said, "Four twenty-three."

"I'd best be going. I apologize for leaving you like this, but I wish you luck during your appointment tomorrow. I hope I see you again sometime. Try not to get too worked up." I left him mute. He rooted himself in place.

♪ ♪ ♪

We played for another hour and a half. By now, the crowds of people at the carnival were dying down. The fun was over and many people sat in front of us, relaxing in the soft grass. Another wave would come in later, though, mostly adults. We did not plan to stay for this. At the end of our last piece, a quarter of the individuals in front of us clapped. They scattered as we tucked our instruments away in our cases. The sky was starting its transformation from blue to black, making the sun shoot out slashes of pink and orange in its last effort to remain. But it surrendered, being blocked out by the clouds.

John congratulated our group, as always. He reorganized his sheet music into his folder from shortest to longest pieces. Usually, we played at dinner parties or outdoor gatherings, but John, as our leader, decided we needed to advertise ourselves by playing for free to the public at random events. It was exciting to travel to different cities in England.

"Estella...." Isobel thrust her chin toward a small, twisted ash tree. It was not far ahead, adjacent to the Ring the Bell game that no one had won all day.

"Hm?" I peered up from my stand, loosening the screw to fold it up.

"Is that not your prodigy we met earlier?"

"What pro— oh— you mean Leo." I pinpointed her gaze. "He's probably waiting for his friend, George."

"I highly doubt it," she giggled. "It looks to me as if he's asleep. Either that or he drank a bit too much." She tightened her A string and closed up her case. "I'll see you soon. Sorry, I cannot wait for you fine people. I have to meet my aunt and granny." She kissed my cheek, then went over to John and Willy to do the same.

Willy and I left just minutes after her. "Don't forget, we must be at Summerset Place this Thursday at two o'clock sharp. Bring all music. And please, by the mercy of God, do *not* forget your instrument." John stared at Willy, laughing. He went a separate way, toward his carriage at the bottom of the hill.

I was about to pass by the tree when I realized that Leo's eyes were, in fact, closed. Cautiously, I went over to him. He was in complete peace with his legs stretched out in front of him. His head was back against the tree, while his chest rose and fell softly. It looked as if he needed sleep. I placed my violin case and folder on the ground, and sat beside him. Hopefully, his friend George was coming soon. I didn't want to wake him, but I felt bad leaving him at the same time.

Over an hour passed, and no one was even in my sight. Maybe George couldn't find Leo and decided to go back. After all, they were neighbors. It was intriguing. If I were an artist, I would have attempted to sketch him. But I did not have an artist's eye, so when I looked at his face, my heart flared instead of my pencil. It was then I decided to wake him.

"Leo, come on," I whispered softly, leaning in toward his ear. He didn't budge. "I know you can hear me. Wake up." Not even his eyes shifted. I sighed, rolling my eyes. Something inside me fluttered when I looked at him. He had no idea I was next to him. My mind began to wander. If he really was going blind, every day would be like this. He would always seem as if sleeping, with not a clue of who or what was beside him. Before my eyes got caught up, I whispered to him again, this time shaking his arm.

He jolted awake, widening his eyes like he couldn't absorb his surroundings fast enough. "Wha—Estella?" He blinked, sucking in a big breath of air.

"Hello."

"Um, hello." He sat up, grinning lopsidedly. "What are you doing?" The whites of his eyes were slightly red.

"You fell asleep, and when I was leaving, I saw you here. Hope you don't mind my intrusion."

"No, I don't mind." He picked at the grass and adjusted his sling. "About what time was that?"

"Ohhhh, not too long ago. I felt bad that you were here alone, so I stayed, hoping George would show up."

"He left a long time ago. We met up and his clothes were all dirty from Cricket, so he said he was going back home. He also had a girl following him back, but I don't suppose *that* could have anything to do with it," he sighed sarcastically.

I raised my eyebrows. "*No,* of course *not.*"

He stood, cracking his back. "You should have woken me up. I would have been a bit more, you know, *talkative.*" His hand hovered in front of me and I took it as he pulled me to my feet.

"No, no. It's quite alright," I assured him. He pressed his finger and thumb to his eyes and held them there for a second. We strode past the bell game and through the empty booths. The crowd was slowly transforming from kids to rowdy adults, which was in all sense, equivalent.

He dove into conversation about my violin playing, asking about my new teacher and how often I took lessons. In his eyes, I had improved immensely, which made me satisfied and proud to hear.

"I cannot believe that the whole time you were in service for my brother, I had no idea who you were. I wish you had said something," I told him. "It all made such sense once Charlie told me. The music compositions, the talent you have with the piano; it all added up perfectly. I should have realized it myself."

"Nothing would have differed, though. I meant to keep it that way. I didn't want to be known as the pianist, Leonardo Leonhardt, because it's not who I am."

"I've seen the way you play, though, and I strongly feel you should go back to it. In fact, it is what makes you, you. It's *exactly* who you are."

"That is precisely what I do *not* want to hear." His voice was curt and rough.

"You should go back onstage."

His face twisted as he held back all the words he wanted to say. I could tell my comment ate at him, but that didn't mean I would let my opinion falter. He wasn't given the talent to play so he could go work as an indentured servant or businessman. It was given to him for a reason, to utilize it.

He huffed in irritation, gesturing with his hand wildly as he spoke, as if it would prove to be more convincing. "It's not that *simple*. First of all, above *all* things, it requires my willingness to do it. Second, it requires about seven hours of practice a day. And lastly, I would only go back to it if certain conditions were upheld." We exited the carnival, parting through crowds of oncoming people, and listened as our soft steps evolved into hard clicks on the road. The music died out, along with the tempting smells of sweets.

"*Conditions*," I mimicked. "Who ever heard of such nonsense? You are making excuses for yourself."

"Estella, has it ever occurred to you that I might find other interests than—than being the prophet that everyone else wants me to be? You know, typical things, such as raising a family, or driving cars, or boating, or playing golf, or actually settling down just living life as it comes at me? Rather than spending my days chasing after a life that I am not even sure I want?" He threw his hand out, exasperated and desperate. "You're just like my father! My father, who I chose to move away from. My father who punished and pressured and *pushed*. Guess what he wound up with? *Broken pieces*." He stared at the pebbles on the ground, then kicked at them, sending them scuttling into the road where hooves crushed them.

I couldn't find my voice. My tongue tingled with numbness. Leo had never mentioned his family back in Germany. Often, I had wondered before if he had any. "Broken pieces of what?" I was afraid to look him in the eye. It was not my intent to make him angry, but he told me before that anger was a driving force. It certainly was, but an unpredictable one that brought out the worst in people.

"Of his son."

England

The Pianist

I expected her to say "To hell with you," and turn her cheek toward a better, sunnier direction. She didn't. Maybe she needed a compass. I would have gladly pointed her in the opposite direction. However, she stayed beside me, pressing her lips together and fumbling with the handle of her violin case. Suddenly, she stopped. Beside us was a fancy black car that I remembered from Hampton Court. The windows were pristine, and the tires looked like they hadn't touched dirt before.

"I'm sorry. I truly apologize," she whispered, genuinely distraught. She had to stop pretending that she really knew me. Not often had I seen her this way. Her eyes dulled, and her shoulders drooped. She looked at me as if I was drowning, and she had no way of saving me.

The chauffer got out of the car. I was expecting William, but he had probably moved on as well. The man took Estella's violin case and strapped it to the back of the car, with the roughness of a bear. His movements were sluggish for that of a chauffeur.

"Would you like a ride back to your house?" she asked stiffly, stepping into the car. Her voice was hollow.

"Yes." I squeezed in next to her, emitting a tense breath. "Thank you."

The drive was only about ten minutes, but I felt every second of it. It was mostly made of silence. Estella's voice broke through the gurgling engine.

"Where is your appointment tomorrow?" She continued to stare out the window. Her expression stayed blank like an empty journal. From a glimpse, I could see her reflection; the trees and houses across the street intermingled with it.

"I think it's on Oriental Way. Somewhere in London." I shrugged my shoulders absently. "I wrote it down."

She nodded, taking it in. The car slowed to a stop in front of my little house. George's house was completely dark across the way, as expected. I could smell the salt water as the chauffeur opened my door. The lull of the waves lodged itself back into my memory. Even if I wasn't at the beach, I felt as if I could always hear it. I thanked both of them, hurried down my cobblestone walkway, and collapsed into my house. My brain felt like a clock, keeping itself awake with its constant ticking thoughts. In reality, all those thoughts only made the minute hand move a smidge. As much as I wanted to go to sleep, I was too afraid to close my eyes.

England
The Violinist

By the time I was back home, I was exhausted. Sarah brought me one of the ten fashion magazines from Paris that had come in earlier in the day, but I was too tired to review it. She brushed my hair gingerly, and braided it loosely down my back. We chatted about our day and then she bid me goodnight. I remained at my vanity, staring at myself.

I rose from my chair, closing my eyes. Instinctively, I brought my hands out in front of me. My steps were unsteady and uneven as I crossed my room and felt around for my violin case that rested on my bureau. It took me a few tries to make contact with it. Once I did, I gave myself a new task. I was to walk back to the vanity and pick up my favorite perfume bottle. Nervously, I stumbled back across the room. I thought I had a couple of steps to go when I banged into the vanity. My knee struck it, making the whole thing shake. I ripped open my eyes just in time to see my mirror crash down in front of me, sending shards of glass penetrating through the air like bullets.

My hand flew to my mouth in shock. The door opened without a knock, and Claude poked his sleepy face in. I then realized that something was stinging my hand. The pain was centered in the webbing between my thumb and forefinger.

"What the bloody hell was that?" He was quickly shaken awake when he saw what happened. I was biting my fingers, shamefully bowing my eyes to the floor. "Oh, Estella! You should be asleep. Let me help." His robe was not tied all the way and it swished as he walked, like a cape.

"I—I don't know. I feel awful. I was being stupid. Let me ring for Sarah." I pulled the tassel near the side of my bed. Claude was kneeling on the floor, picking up the larger pieces and placing them carefully on the vanity.

"What were you *doing*? You didn't get hurt, right?" He turned toward me, placing another stack of glass atop the vanity.

"I think I did." My voice cracked. I winced as I looked at the sharp piece in my hand. The blood was draining rapidly from my face and simultaneously oozing gently from the cut.

"You did?" He jumped right up, and sat me down on the bed. I held out my hand while turning my eyes away. "I see now. Yes, you did. It's not a big piece, don't worry. But we need to get it out fast. Alright? Don't look, okay?" He balled up his sleeve and as softly as he could, pressed it to my skin. I did not want to speak.

"Sarah should be up here soon, and then tomorrow, you and Momma can go out and pick another mirror. It will be a fun shopping expedition for you. Of course, the complete opposite for me, but you know that. That's why I don't do those types of things. Maybe you can convince Charlie to let you redo your whole room, in fact. It never seemed to suit you, if you want my opinion." He spoke without purpose, and by the time he finished, the sliver of glass was removed from my hand. I took a big breath, still refusing to look at it or speak. He removed his tie from the loops of his robe and with his one good hand and my one good hand, we tied it tightly over the cut.

Sarah came up and fetched a bucket and a broom. The mess was cleaned up pretty quickly. Claude sat next to me on the edge of my bed until everything was cleaned. Sarah grabbed an actual bandage from the bathroom, and placed it over the cut. It was not deep, thankfully.

"Claude, thank you. I'm glad you at least heard it, or I would have been thrown into a panic," I exclaimed, slowly moving my hand.

"Lucky for you, I wasn't sleeping or daydreaming as I tend to do."

"Yes, lucky for me, indeed." I examined my hand. Sarah left the room with the bucket of all the broken pieces. "I really must be going to bed now. Gosh, what an eventful night. Goodnight, Claude." I kissed his cheek.

He returned the gesture, holding my hand for a second more before leaving. It had been the first time I had talked to him in a couple of days. Though he was starting to improve, his room still proved to be his most favorite spot, from which he did not remove himself unless persuaded.

I climbed into bed and curled up on my side. So that was what it was like to be blind. To stumble about, guessing. I pictured myself walking downstairs with my eyes closed and falling, eating and missing my mouth, missing a door handle as I tried to grasp it, tripping over tree roots on the horse trail. This was what Leo feared. I closed my eyes and as I drifted into sleep, I imagined being surrounded by dark shapes for the rest of my existence. For then, without vision, it would be hard to prove my existence at all. Yes, this was what he feared. I shivered at the thought until sleep rescued me.

England
The Pianist

"**M**r. Leonhardt?"

My head snapped up at my name. A frail women searched the room under her glasses until I stood. My stomach lurched like I was back on *Driftwood Anchor*.

"Yes. That's me."

"Good morning. Be so kind as to follow me." She led me into a small room where I was told to sit at a desk. The desk had a pile of books on the corner. To the left, I observed many differing eye charts. Some had pictures, some had letters, and some had numbers. They started off big at the top, and gradually shrank until they resembled dots.

"Doctor Hawthorn will be right in." She left, closing the door behind her. I fidgeted in my seat, unable to think anything positive. I started to rub my eyes, blinking them fast to rid any blurriness that I might have been seeing. My heart sped up as if I had started a race.

Minutes later, the door creaked open. I expected an old man, perhaps sixty, with a bushel of grey hair on his head, but this man looked almost my age. I estimated around mid-thirties, though I was not *that* old yet. He placed papers on his desk, and began to take out some funny looking appliances. He glanced at the top of his paper.

"Mr. Leonhardt, I presume?"

"Yes."

"Well, that's a good start. Half the time, my secretary gives me the wrong names!" He chuffed. "Last evening, for instance, this older woman came in. She's a regular, actually. She constantly gets her prescription changed. So Mary, you know, the secretary, tells me that Mr. Robenson is in room six, when really, it was *her*! I had no idea, so when I walked in, I said, 'Oh, Mr. Robenson, so good to see you,' and it turns out to be this woman. I felt awful about it. But I cannot blame Mary." He sighed, picked up his pen and took a seat.

I smiled at his story, but didn't say much.

"Mr. Leonhardt, why don't you begin telling me about your vision troubles while I examine your eyes. Say, do you have trouble reading, or distinguishing faces or such? My document here says probable nearsightedness due to a misread traffic light." As he was talking, he took a light and angled it toward my eyes. It wasn't intolerably bright, like I expected.

"I have no trouble reading. English isn't my first language, so sometimes I have to really think about the context of a word, but I don't have trouble deciphering what a word says."

"Hmph. Yes, that sounds accurate, especially if you do have nearsightedness." He took the light away from my eyes. I listened to the scratching of his pen, letting its familiarity calm me.

"What exactly is nearsightedness?" I asked anxiously.

"Don't let the name trip you up. It means that you have difficulty focusing on objects far away. This would explain the problem with the traffic light."

I grimaced, clenching my hand.

"Let me check. How about you tell me the letters on the chart over there? You can name them even though they are English, yes? The alphabet is pretty similar."

"Yes." I replied. He instructed me to stand on the other side of the room and cover one eye with my hand. I remembered Otto doing this test when he was young.

"E, O, S, C, D, R, Y, Z…." I began. Once I couldn't see the letters anymore, I switched eyes and repeated it. Doctor Hawthorn took notes at his desk as I rambled.

"Hmph. Alright, well done. Come over here and sit."

I took a seat and he placed a book in front of me. He reached over the desk and flipped to page eight, where he then underlined a sentence in the middle of the page. "Start reading here," he explained as he sat back. All of the words overwhelmed me.

"Doctor, I'm not the best at reading English—"

"Oh, yes. That was unfair of me. What I meant to do is give you a book in your native language. See, your English accent is so admirable that it almost slipped my mind! What might it be then?" He bent down, pulling five brand new books from the bottom drawer.

"German."

"Oh, good. I thought for a moment you might have said Italian, and then I would have had to go grab the book in the other room." He smiled, spinning the gold ring on his finger. Once again, he flipped to page eight, underlining the first sentence I was to read.

"You read German, Doctor Hawthorn?" I asked, surprised. My nerves subdued for the moment. The only time I ever saw German writing was when Otto sent me a letter. Besides that, I was happy to see familiar words.

"Indeed so. In fact, I'm fluent in four languages. Now, I want you to take your time and read until the bottom of page nine. Pay no attention to me. Although this is not a typical test, it definitely helps confirm or dispense probable vision issues."

I nodded and began. It was not the last test I took. I had to look through odd-shaped lenses, and name tiny images. The doctor seemed outwardly pleased with my results, while I itched with questions.

"What was that image there again?" he asked as I said the name of the last image.

"Um, a circle, I think. Oh, no. It's an orange. Didn't see the little stem there."

"Yes. Good correction." He nodded, but I could sense an uneasiness about him. I pulled my eyes away from the lenses and sat back in the chair. He continued to take notes, shaking his head unsurely.

"Doctor... you don't think there is anything seriously wrong with my vision, right?" I finally had to ask. It gnawed at me during every test I took.

"To be perfectly frank, I can find nothing wrong yet. But it is not *only my* decision. Other doctors have to look this over. As of now, I can say, however, that your results seem perfectly normal."

"Good." I placed my hands on the desk, letting out a breath. Normal. My results were normal. I could feel the weight dropping from my shoulders. The chains that had tied me down turned to rubber and snapped. There was nothing wrong with my vision! I had been right about the traffic light. I was not going blind! My insides were jumping with joy. My heart's droning minor beat switched to a major one. It made my whole body feel rejuvenated.

"However… I'd like to give you one more test." The constant tapping of his foot came to a stop. "I will be right back. I need to get the plates." He left me there, taking his clipboard with him.

When he returned, he had a thin pile of papers with him. "This," he began, "is called the Ishihara test. Now, what I'm going to do is ask you to tell me what number you can decipher between the little dots. Got it? For example." He placed one of the papers in front of me. "If I were to ask, what number is in this one, you would say two." He traced the number with his finger. Once he did this, I could see it. It became more prominent.

"Okay," I replied, eager to get it over with. Estella had been right. I wasn't going blind. But I had been right, too. I knew I did not need glasses. My spirit was soaring above the clouds, and I didn't care if it came down or not.

"You get three seconds to name the number in each plate. There are twenty four in total. Okay? Begin… now."

The first plate he put in front of me, showed nothing on it. "Is this one a trick ques—?"

"That's three seconds." He quickly took that plate away and replaced it. I squinted at the new one, but again, nothing was there. "Time." The doctor switched to a third one. Finally, one that actually had a number.

"Twelve," I said. He nodded and gave me the next one. The next five had nothing. What was the point of this ridiculous test? I tried to tell him nothing was there, but the three seconds passed by too quickly.

"Seven. No… two? Twenty one?" He shook his head no, and went on to the next one. The next fourteen plates had nothing on them, and yet, he still placed them in front of me, expecting an answer. I said nothing. Sometimes, I thought I could see a glimpse of a number, but I was imagining things. No matter how I turned my head, or squinted my eyes, I found nothing there.

"Doctor, what was the point of that?"

He didn't answer at first. He was checking and double-checking what he had written on his chart. I could tell there was something wrong by the way he kept glancing from the plates to the paper he wrote on. "I—I've never seen anything like it," he muttered.

"What, Dr. Hawthorn?"

"It is just to help me analyze what the problem could be. Let me discuss your results with the head doctor, Doctor Koga."

A knock came on the door, and the secretary peered in. "I'm sorry to interrupt. Doctor Hawthorn, may I speak to you a moment?" Her voice was low pitched for a woman. She pushed up her glasses after every sentence.

"Why, of course. A moment, if you will, Mr. Leonhardt." He was out of the room in seconds. I leaned forward, trying to read his notes upside-down. His writing was very messy, and organized in a strange manner like a code. As the door opened, I snapped back to my normal position, hoping he hadn't seen me.

"I am off to discuss this with Doctor Koga now. I'd prefer if you would wait in the waiting room, then I will call you back in here when results have been confirmed. Also, Mary just informed me that your sister has arrived, looking for you. She's in the waiting room now. Whether you would like her to be present for the results is your decision." He ducked out of the room, leaving me completely baffled.

My sister? How had Lieselotte gotten to London? And how on earth had she known I was here, at this time? My head was spinning from stories that failed to fit together. As I walked back to the waiting room, I tried to think of what to say. It had been forever since I had actually seen her face to face. Would she recognize me? Better yet, would I recognize *her*? I had just assembled the perfect sentence when I stepped into the room.

Lieselotte was nowhere. My eyes landed on a more familiar face. I stood in front of her, looking down on a light, rounded hat with a bow on the side. She looked up at me, closing her book.

"I hope everything is okay. Last night, I… I had this sudden realization about how significantly this could change everything you've ever known, and crudely mash it up." She pulled at her white gloves, staring at her lap. "I want to help you, Leo, if I can. I know your family is back in Germany, so I wanted to come and see if there was anything I could do or say or—"

"I cannot believe you are here. How did you know?"

"I *do* pay attention when you talk. In fact, I like listening to you. You mentioned yesterday that your appointment was here, remember?"

"I suppose so." I took a seat beside Estella. Something about her clothing was different. It seemed to make her glow, like she had the brightness of the sun, and yet, I didn't want to pull my eyes away. She had come all the way from Herefordshire, to be with me.

"I don't know what to say besides thank you. You told them that you were my sister, though?"

"Shhh, she giggled. "Doctors are always picky about friends, so I simply told them I was your sister. If I told them I had just seen you for the first time in five years yesterday, they would have *absolutely* thrown me out of here." She grinned slyly.

"Mr. Leonhardt?" Mary called after a while. Estella and I had been talking about the servants, and who still worked at the house, when I heard my name.

"Will you come with me?" I asked her. "I'm so nervous about the results, I probably won't hear what the doctor is saying. I'll need someone to repeat it back to me later." I rubbed my hands on my pants and got up.

"Of course," she replied.

Four people sat at Dr. Hawthorn's desk. Estella, me, Doctor Hawthorn, and someone I guessed to be Dr. Koga.

"Please meet my sister, Estella." I introduced her as we all took our places.

"Pleasure to meet you, Miss Leonhardt." Miss Leonhardt. It was a funny thing to hear. The two doctors introduced themselves, taking her hand. I noticed that she had a bandage around it, which hadn't been there yesterday afternoon.

"Shall we begin?" Doctor Koga asked, spreading out a couple of papers. He spoke with a directness that Doctor Hawthorn definitely did not have. He was a tall Japanese man with hair that matched shades with Estella's. He had small hands, freckles on his nose, and perfectly even teeth.

"Mr. Leonhardt, both myself and my team have never seen results like yours."

England

The Violinist

"Colorblind? What does that term even mean?" Leo's voice shook like a wobbling top. The word froze the blood in my veins.

"Typically, we use the term, color-*deficient*, but in your case, it is correct to use colorblind. Mr. Leonhardt, you cannot see color. From these results it shows that you only perceive shades of grey, with black being the darkest color, and white, being the lightest," Dr. Koga explained.

"How ridiculous. Who cannot see color? I've never heard of this." Leo laughed nervously.

"We have never heard of it quite like this, either. Typically, people have color *deficiency*, which means that they cannot see two or three colors that the average human is supposed to see. But you are a completely different story. I'm going to be honest with you in saying that we do not know a lot about your condition. What makes it so rare is that all the parts in your eyes still work perfectly, you don't appear to have increased light sensitivity, or issues with depth and perception."

"I'm sorry, Doctor. But this isn't possible. How is it that I cannot see color? You cannot see through my eyes, so how would you know? Objects are painted with color, so if I do not see it, it is simply because... because it is left dull." His voice dwindled away. His declaration was unstable, and I could tell he grew more and more unsure.

"But the tests, Mr. Le—"

"Then the tests are wrong! I know color! I was three years old once, too! The sky is blue, grass is green, fire is red, the moon is white," he interrupted, placing his hand on the desk. With each word, his voice grew more desperate.

"Mr. Leonhardt," Doctor Koga tried again. "This is common. You know these things because you memorized them. I hear this a lot among color-deficient people. You memorized that the sky is supposed to be blue, and that grass is supposed to be green. However, you have never seen it for yourself."

"I have! I *know* I have. This is *absurd*."

"You have not." Dr. Koga's voice was as dry as a piece of wood in a fireplace. His composure did not differ, no matter what he or Leo said.

"Then tell me how this happened! How is it that I see differently than everyone else? I've been fine my whole life, and now you say I have this rare disease." His whole body was tensed up like he was testifying in front of court.

"It is not a *disease*." Dr. Koga glared at him harshly for his incorrect term. "Colorblindness is usually a genetic defect. There have been some rare cases where it has been caused by trauma, but the more probable answer is that you were born with it, and just never knew. I have had patients in their seventies who come here and have found out for the first time in their lives that they are color-deficient. By your results, I have narrowed it down. You have a specific type of monochromacy, known as cone monochromacy."

"I cannot believe I see anything differently than anyone else," he insisted stubbornly. "Let me take the tests again."

"Mr. Leonhardt, you trust your sister, yes?" Doctor Hawthorn butted in, pulling a slim stack of papers in front of him.

"Well, yes." Leo glanced at me.

"Then let me show you this. I know it is hard to swallow, but I'm afraid there's no other way to prove it to you." He placed the pile of papers in front of me. He was a very attractive man with snowy white skin and a sweet, calming voice. He was young to be a doctor, which was admirable.

"Miss Leonhardt, I'd like you to read the numbers embedded in these little dots. You have three seconds to call out the number. Mr. Leonhardt, I want you to watch closely. These are the exact plates I gave you."

"Doctor... I'm sorry. I wasn't prepared for a test," I stuttered, staring at the first one.

"No, no. Not to worry. It will not seem like a test to you. Ready, begin." He slid a piece of paper in front of me with a circle on it. The circle was made up of other tiny circles that had usually two to three colors in them.

"Two, thirty-five, twelve, eight, twenty-one, fifty-five, nineteen, twenty-six...." I went on and on. It wasn't like a test at all. The color of the numbers differed from the color of the outer dots, so it was simple to differentiate. When I was done, Doctor Hawthorn nodded contently at me. Leo's face was completely blank. He stared at the papers in horror. His lips were slack. The confidence in his posture was no longer there, so gravity pulled on his hollow eyes and backbone.

"You... you named all of them." He picked up one of the papers, holding it to his face. He tilted it toward the light. I didn't understand. What went wrong with this test? The way he looked at it... there was such hatred in his gaze.

"Why, how many did you name?" I asked innocently. I couldn't take my eyes off him. With each passing moment, he was losing grip on reality. He blinked hard, like he was clearing away imaginary images. It was as if his chair was about to collapse under him, and he was bracing himself for the fall. The men watched both of us closely. Doctor Hawthorn opened his mouth, and then closed it.

"One." He swallowed his fear. "I...I only saw one." His voice went hoarse, and then it was gone altogether. One. Out of the twenty-four. My brain could not wrap itself around his condition. One? I narrowed my eyes in thought.

"How is that possible? I do not understand." I could feel my face sinking in. Thinking of it ruptured my view on the world when I realized that not everyone could see it like I did.

"Miss Leonhardt, picture the color grey," Doctor Hawthorn instructed. "That is how your brother sees everything. In shades of grey." All three of us looked at Leo. He had gone mute. He rested his hand on top of the paper, staring at it as if he were bewitched.

"Is there any cure?" I immediately asked. I was willing to spend any amount of money I had. To think that Leo's world was always dreary and grey made depression swell over me. Imagine not seeing sunsets. Imagine not being able to watch the leaves change color. Imagine living in a world that was always dark, and rainy. I didn't know how he wasn't driven mad by it. "I can have money sent to you at any time if there is a medicine or procedure to cure it," I stated firmly. I felt the determination flood my body.

Leo's trance was broken. He goggled at me in surprise, but his worried frown was still stuck to his face. All of the hope inside me tumbled from my lips, waiting to be picked back up by the assuring doctors.

"I regret to inform you that there is no cure," Dr. Koga stated. The hope I had was left on the floor to step on.

"How is there no cure? You're telling me that there is nothing you can do? He has to live in a dark, dreary world—"

"We are very sorry." Some people were dying of cancer, or malaria, or starving to death. This monochromacy condition was not fatal. It did not cause him pain, or gradually get worse. I couldn't help the grudging feeling, though. It was more than not seeing color. He was missing an essential part of life. A part that everyone else on earth, including myself, took for granted.

♪ ♪ ♪

For the remainder of the time, they went into detail about genetics, trying to be as professional about it as possible. I lost it halfway through with all of their medical terms that blurred together. They spoke of scientific X's and Y's. Leo seemed to understand more than I, but even then, he was not alert.

"At least I know that I'm not going blind. Last night, I didn't sleep a wink. It was terrifying, thinking that I was going to slip away into darkness for the rest of my life." Leo broke the peaceful silence between us as we boarded the train. The woman who sat across from us had two babies that began to wail as the train whistled and rumbled out of the station.

"Yes. That is a relief. But…I have to say, I cannot imagine it. What's it like?" I peered at him curiously. He didn't seem as horrified. He no longer drummed his fingers, or gazed around with jumpy, hollow eyes. The emptiness that surrounded him in the office was being swept away.

"Hmmm." He stared out the window at trees that smudged like watercolor as we picked up speed. "I cannot quite describe it, because I have nothing to compare it against." His voice was unexpectedly calm.

"But, surely you can give an example. Oh, I know. Look at this." I brought my hand to my throat and held out a pendant attached to a long, thin, scaly chain. "I see this little diamond as yellow. A kind of faint yellow. How would you describe it?"

"You see yellow, huh?" He took the little diamond in his palm and studied it. "I'd say it's very shiny. It's got a light coming from it in several directions. Other than that, I'd say it reminds me of an upside down pear, and that it kind of wobbles in its clasp." He let go, and it landed back down at my collar bone.

"Well, it wasn't a *bad* description, but I could say that, too. You just avoided the color part."

"I didn't *avoid* it. I can't say it. I wouldn't know if it's red, yellow, or purple, honestly. I don't know what red or yellow or any other color word actually means anyway."

"So then... you have no idea what you look like? You could stand in front of a mirror and not know if you're a brunette or a blonde?"

"I can tell the difference between that. Blonde it usually lighter. There's this certain brightness to blonde hair. But all the other colors sort of blend together. So, I guess I really don't know what I look like, at least color wise. I've been told I have brown eyes. That's true, right?"

"Yes." I was quick to respond. The pin in my hat had loosened, so I began to readjust it.

"You didn't even look!" He chuckled.

"I don't need to look! I've seen your eyes plenty of times to know." There. It caught in my hair right at the perfect spot.

"Well, what do you look like then?" he asked simply.

"You can see me perfectly fine, Leo."

"You know what I mean."

I sighed, pressing my lips together. "I have green eyes...."

"Describe green," he prodded, staring at me with a perplexed curiosity. I had definitely expected a worse response dealing with the whole matter. But rather than wallowing about it, he was taking an interest. He was almost making it into a game.

"Describe green?" I hesitated, really trying to pull enough words from my head to describe it. "It's a sort of rich, earthy color. The same as the leaves on the trees and the grass. It's wispy and calming." I really stopped to ponder what green entailed. "I think I'd call it a color of connection. A connection from people to nature."

"That's some description. Very good, actually. It certainly puts a vision in my head." He yawned, closing his mouth quickly to cover it.

"Mr. Leonhardt, am I *boring* you?" I folded my hands, pulling at the fingers of my gloves.

"Not a bit. Not a *bit*." He closed his eyes, smiling in bliss with just his lips. "I think I'm beginning to smell green."

"And *I* think you're a crazy man," I stated, matter-of-factly. It didn't wipe the unusual grin off his face. In minutes, he was sleeping. The train ride was not unpleasantly long. His head slipped down in the seat until his cheek pressed against my shoulder.

England

The Pianist

"This surprise has been making me wait all day, Leo. Please, just the *slightest* hint," Estella whined. She bent over and picked up a rock, turning it over and over in her hand.

I sat back in the sand, bracing myself with both arms. The sling was long gone, stuffed somewhere in my closet, never to be seen again.

"Not a chance." I grinned pleasurably, countering her frown. She paced through the sand, passing by her shoes that she so carefully had left on a rock nearby. She never took her eyes off the ocean. I couldn't imagine what she was seeing. I envied her. The waves were gentle at this time, kissing the shores rather than shoving them back.

"I should warn you not to get *too* excited." I could see it coming up. Finally. She had absolutely no idea what it was going to be. She tossed her rock at me, and I snatched it out of the air.

"So you persuaded me to come here by telling me of a mythical *surprise?*" She raised her eyebrows, holding her hand toward me.

"I assure you, it is not mythical." I handed her a shell, which she dropped from her hand.

"Come on. Give the stone back."

"I don't have it!" It was the perfect opportunity to distract her from what was in the water. I opened both hands and held them out in front of her.

"You horrible liar. It's in your pocket."

I reached inside both of my pockets and held out my hands once more. What I held was much lighter than a rock. It gave off a blinding glare, and yet, was no bigger than a button.

"Do not tell me that is the *same pearl*," she murmured in awe. I let her take it. She sat down beside me, pulling at her dress. She no longer was interested in the ocean, or the gulls flying overhead.

"Of course it is. I thought surely you were going to keep it back then. It would have been a shame, really. It's my good luck charm. Every day, I put it in my pocket, hoping for some luck that I don't have."

"It's a miracle you don't lose it more often," she teased. "I must say, it's very beautiful."

"It is. I think pearls are the best gemstones, if you'd call them that. By far, they succeed a diamond."

"Then why are the gemstones in wedding rings always diamond? Hmm?" she asked smartly. Her lips curled up as she awaited an answer. I found myself staring.

"Because people don't think of the meaning behind a pearl. There's a whole list of symbolism behind it, you know? How they're created is pretty incredible."

She placed it back in my palm while I told her the story.

"Pearls are created from irritation. Sand and other particles get inside a clam or oyster and then basically become stuck. So it creates this layer called nacre to protect itself from the unwelcome, foreign substance. And over time, it just builds up, becoming a pearl. The oyster kind of takes it in. It's amazing how a grain of sand can become something like this," I explained, rolling it between my fingers.

"Hmm. It's a sweet story. Maybe you should petition that pearls be the stone of marriage." She laughed to herself, digging her toes into the sand. "How'd you find that one, anyway?"

"I worked on a boat for a little while before I went to work at your brother's house, and on my last day, a friend of mine and I decided to steal a couple of oysters that were supposed to be put in the market."

"You thief!" She scowled.

"I know, it was a dumb idea. But we did it. I put mine in my pocket and ate them for dinner, raw. Then I bit down, and there it was. I was just happy I didn't swallow it," I chuckled.

"You ate them raw? You didn't get sick?" She scrunched up her nose like a shriveling leaf.

"Not after a while. I miss it a little, the boat and everything. It feels as though I've gotten nowhere in my life. I'm only twenty-six, and yet I feel as if I'm wasting away. Do you ever think about that?"

"Not often." She paused, giving me a funny look. Her head cocked slightly to the side, but she did not appear to be confused. Maybe she was simply wondering about what I had said. "You remind me of Claude with your words sometimes. I don't know where on earth it comes from."

Just then, my ears perked. Shouts rang out from the shoreline, and I spotted the boat I had been expecting. Estella turned her attention to it.

"Come on!" I hopped up, pulling her to her feet and making a bee-line toward the rowboat.

"Easy for you to say! These shells hurt my feet. My lord! What is *that* doing here?" She stumbled behind me, wobbling through the sand to avoid broken shells. Her eyes never fell from the little boat. In the distance, a larger one was anchored, swaying side to side like a giddy whale.

Four muscular men stepped out, speaking rapid German and hoisting my delivery from the boat. Their paddles were scattered on the sand at our feet. My ears rang with pleasure, hearing my native language. Remembering my tongue, I responded, directing them to my house.

"A piano!" she exclaimed, bringing her hands to her mouth. We followed the men, and I opened the door for them. They grunted in effort, turning the body of the piano so it fit through the doorway.

"To your right, gentlemen. It can go right in the middle of the room. Yes, thank you," I directed in German. Estella stood next to me. Her eyes had that shininess to them once more.

"This is my piano from Germany. Blimey, it's been through some rough weather," I grimaced. We watched them place it down and attach the legs. The smooth wood was covered in salt and grime, which fell to the floor.

"Sir. This have two legs only. Need another on ship. Apologies, we forget." One of the men spoke up in broken English. He nodded at me and exited.

"What did he say to you?" she peeped curiously.

"They forgot one of the piano legs on the ship. He's bringing it back." We observed them as they wiped the piano down. Dust flew into the air, making Estella sneeze. I hovered over them, waiting for someone to give me the tiny key that unlocked the fallboard. The keys probably hadn't seen the light of day in years.

"Sir, I have the last leg," the man announced in German while I grabbed a towel from the closet at the end of the hall. Estella seemed lost. She stood on the outskirts of the room, watching the chaos unveil.

"Thank you." I began to dust off the lid, not looking up.

"Would you like me to attach it now?" he asked. What did he think I wanted him to do? Use it as a door stopper?

"Of course—" I began, letting my attitude seep into my voice. My whole sentence was cut off before my words could get any further.

The man was thin like a rod. He cradled the piano leg with one arm, and then held it out to me. He had glasses that were streaked with dirt. They slipped down his nose from the perspiration on his face.

Hot water tremored in the bottom half of my eyes. My vision shifted between foggy and clear, like a child playing with a telescope.

"I had to come, I just had to. I know you're a traitor, but I had to know—" His voice was brand new, marked with the battle scars of manhood. He lingered hesitantly, posture muddled with the unknown. His hair had become lighter. It curled almost like the fur of a poodle.

"Otto. I didn't recognize your voice. I'm sorry." My volume diminished away, ashamed. My whole body was in rigid shock. He came forward slowly and put his arms around me. By now, my eyes stung with salt. The very salt that was adding to my inner wounds as each tear clipped the edge of my jaw.

"How is everyone? It's killing me." I steadied my voice, sniffling. We were both speaking in English now, since the other men spoke German. I tightened my grip, and suddenly, I was hugging a little boy. The boy who was forced to adventure out on his own when I practiced. I remembered Mutti telling him to stay outside until I was done. Practicing was never a simple hour. Only now did I wonder where Otto had gone every day.

"Good. Better," he answered, letting go. As gentle as he was, he stood with a profound stiffness. "Leo, I would go months without ever thinking of you. Without ever caring to remember that I had an older brother. And when I ever realized that I was beginning to accept it, it crushed me." He looked away from me. "I *hate* you for leaving me with Papa. Oh it was *hell*, Leo." He clenched his teeth. "If you even had a clue. He was so beside himself for years. That was before I earned enough money to move out."

"Don't start this now," I begged him. My voice suddenly turned cold. My heart pulled heavily on my body as I endured the strain. One of the other men took the leg from Otto and attached it as the finishing touch.

"I have to start, or else I'd find no end. You need to know what's going on there. The inflation is just starting to die down, but I'm out of a job. Papa and Mutti are struggling, selling everything in the house but the walls themselves."

"How could it be? I left them money."

"The inflation! I swear it was like we needed a wheelbarrow of money just to get a loaf of bread. Papa was in the middle of selling this piano when I got your letter."

"He was selling it? You're joking." My eyes went wild. How could he have wanted to sell it? Didn't it mean anything to him? It had been my Opa's piano, and when my family discovered I had a talent, Opa had given it to me and taught me the basics. Now that Opa was gone, it was tough to believe that Papa wanted no part of the piano. Not the sound, the look, or the memory of it.

"No. He had someone coming to the house to look at it."

"Then how did you get it? I don't know what I would've done if he'd sold it." I pondered it aloud, letting it sink in.

Otto took a big breath and looked me dead in the eyes. "The night before the person was coming to look at it, I cut all of the strings inside it. I told Papa that no one would want to buy it because it was too broken for repair, and that none of us had the money to fix it."

"But… there *are* strings in it." I stepped back and peered inside while the shortest of the men began to tune it, tapping the same key over and over that made my eardrums cringe.

"Yes."

"How?" I implored, practically pulling the answers from him.

"Someone, a while ago, left me money that I saved." He stared right past me.

Estella appeared by my side, from the shadows of the wall. She raised her eyebrows at me, allowing space for an introduction.

"Otto, I almost forgot, this is Mrs. Bolton—"

"Miss Breaker, actually," Estella corrected awkwardly, holding out her hand to Otto. He didn't want to take her hand. His resentment of the English and their culture was plainly painted on his face. The sound froze around me, echoing with the remnants of her words. I had never thought to ask about Roy. Vaguely, I recalled Estella's cellist friend calling her 'Miss Breaker,' but only now did it seem to hit me. Suddenly, poof, Roy was erased from her. The name that she upheld was no longer anyone else's, but her own.

"Estella, this is my brother, Otto." My voice returned to me.

"So I can finally put a name to a face," Otto remarked dryly. He clasped his hands behind his back stiffly.

"Otto, let's talk more, later. Why don't you come into the kitchen? You've got to be hungry. I can't cook to save my own life, but I can try." I purposely veered the subject sharply.

"No. I'm surviving just fine off of stale bread and undercooked veg-etables from the ship. It's not far off from what I eat in Germany, anyway. I will not be staying long enough for that," he replied quickly. The few things that I thought I did know about Otto had disintegrated. I could have easily been talking to a stranger.

"That's ridiculous. Why are you acting like this?" I could feel my confusion burning behind my face, merging into my furrowed eyebrows.

"Brother, I came here as a messenger. That is all. I refuse to be a burden, or ask for anything."

"I'm *offering!* Do you have *so* much *dignity* that you'd walk out of here like you're a neighbor I see every day? Do we send apple pies back and forth? Hm? Would you please *sit down* and explain yourself before rushing away?"

"I lost my job as a dentist." He pulled at his suspenders, irritably. "I'm married to Annelise who is with a child we cannot afford. And I wanted to come see you, to make sure you are doing alright. Which you are. So, I must go back to the boat."

I didn't know what to respond to first. Large moments of silence stretched between us until Estella's voice broke through the rising wall of anticipation.

"Leo, I think I'm going to go for a walk on the beach and watch the boat before its departure." She backed out, aiming for the door. "I wish you well, Otto." The door creaked behind her, leaving me to fight my own battle. Otto grunted a farewell and looked to me.

"I'm sorry I didn't tell you about Annelise sooner. We were married a little over a year ago."

"Has she put you up to this? To get answers out of me and to finally figure out where I am?"

"I told you it was my own doing. How could you think that of her?" He folded his arms defensively. "We *all* wonder how you are doing. Do *you* wonder about *us*?"

"Of cour—"

"No, you don't, Leo. It's okay. You've moved on, to move back. I always knew that you were meant to play the piano. Remember? It's a part of who you are. I said that to you years ago, and here you are, going back to it. Now it will be of your will. I'm happy for you," he claimed. His bitterness didn't have me convinced.

I found my eyes drawn to the floor as they began to fog up again. I didn't deserve a single word that he said. "Let me give you money to pay you back for fixing the strings. Please. If you don't want it, give it to Mutti and Papa. I'll pay them the money they wanted for it."

"No. That's alright. We will make it by." He held his hand out. I took it firmly, blinking my eyes rapidly. What had I done? I had left them to allow myself some freedom, and now the cage doors were permanently locked. I couldn't go back, even if I wanted to.

"I will never stop owing you, Otto. I mean it." I grasped his hand firmly.

"Then I shall sit contently in your debt." He turned his back to me, in time for my eyes to let loose the rain. I watched him leave; his image shimmered, shaking from side to side until the next tear fell.

♪ ♪ ♪

"Are you going to try it out already?" The boat was long gone, a speck of pepper in the soup of the ocean. Estella lifted her violin from its case, tweaking the knobs on top to tune it.

"I feel guilty. My brother paid for this whole thing. The shipping, the strings...." I sat on the bench, drumming my fingers on the wood. It ate me up inside, and continued to gnaw, even when there was nothing left.

"Because he cares. I think it's awfully generous of him."

"There comes a point where generosity turns into sacrifice. He cannot be generous if he doesn't have much to begin with!" I dragged my hand down my face, pulling the stress. I stood up, only to pace in front of the window.

"Leo, it's okay! You cannot blame yourself," she insisted forcefully, playing an E scale.

"Of course I can. You don't know the full story behind it."

"I don't need to. Your brother knows enough of it to still appreciate you, and to send you your piano on a *boat* all the way from *Germany*. Doesn't that seem like enough?"

"I don't know anymore," I sniffled, rubbing my eyes with my palms. A wave of warmth came over me. I could feel her cheek against my shoulder blade. Her fingers laced together, resting on my torso. I forced myself to breathe, letting my breath dry my eyes. For a moment, time stopped. I let myself feel the pulse in her fingertips. These pulses instantly brought unknown nerves to life.

"I've got to show you something." Without thought, I placed my hands over hers, tilting my head back. Slowly, I pried her fingers apart and led her over to the piano. On top of it rested my book. "The last couple of days, I've had some notes stuck in my head. I'm not done with this yet, but do you think if I write a copy for you, that you could practice the violin part?"

She took the book from me, flipping through the pages like a doctor examining a patient.

"It's in the key of D flat?" she asked.

"Yes." I took a seat on the bench, stretching out my hand to play the D flat scale so she could visually see the notes.

"I think I could try. You'd have to let me practice it. My sight-reading skills aren't anything spectacular." She laughed at herself as she attempted it.

"What does your part sound like?" She placed the book in front of me and I started from the beginning. Some parts I had to squint, not knowing what notes I had written. They clustered together so tightly that I could easily mistake a spaced note for a lined one.

"That's... that's beautiful. I did pick up on some wrong notes, though. It has this... *wave* quality. The tempo is slow, and then rises for a measure or two, only to let out again. Don't laugh, but that's what comes to my mind." She pointed to the first couple of measures with her bow, dragging it along the first two lines.

"It's not bad. I improvised my part quite a bit. So don't give me *too* much credit."

"I should have guessed that. I don't understand how you do that. It's like... it's like you have a constant supply of notes in your head." She shook her head in disbelief. "Something about your brain is different. I know—"

"Ah, that's stupid." I brushed the idea aside. "You can do it, too. I'll show you."

"I don't—" she began. I looped my arm around her waist and gently tugged her toward me. I sat her on my lap, pushing back on the bench to give her leg room. Her back was right up against my chest, and I could feel each of her breaths. At first, she wasn't sure. She didn't say anything, but she didn't get up, either. I was almost positive she could feel my throbbing heart against her spine.

"It goes like this." I breathed calmly. "Pick a scale, then a chord to go with the key. That's the most basic part of improvising."

"How about G?" she asked. "Actually, no. F."

"Alright." I tilted my head, looking over her shoulder at the keys. Then, I played the scale for her and sprang into a song. I could hear the tune in my head before I hit the notes. She watched closely, not even twitching or fidgeting. I went into deeper explanation, forming chords, which she tried on her own.

"Leo, I can't do that." She shifted, turning her face to the side to catch my eye. "It doesn't come that *naturally* to me."

"No, I'm sure I can—"

"That's okay." She smiled widely at me. "I'd much rather watch you do it. It's like a magician giving away all of his secret tricks. If he does, the trick somehow seems less enthralling than it was before. I don't need to know your tricks," she laughed, putting her arm around my shoulder.

Her nose touched mine. It was shockingly cold, but it didn't faze me. I couldn't stop thinking about green, as I stared through her eyes. Our eyelashes almost brushed. And all of a sudden, I hated the centimeters between us. I leaned in, placing my hand on her cheek, and kissed her. That same hand, once broken, traced her. A shape unlike any other, that burned at the tender touch.

She did not have soft lips as I had imagined all these years. But they were not vicious, or hard. Instead, I found she had a force—a force that I had never thought to be kept inside such a delicate shell. In looking at her, it wasn't visible. In talking to her, it wasn't audible. But I couldn't stop, because of this force.

England

The Violinist

Never had my brain been so empty and yet full of the explicit at the same time. Not an ounce of hesitation consumed him as my feet left the floor. I was shaking in his arms, running my fingers over the back of his neck, which sent goosebumps all the way to his forehead. He had this urgency about him that made me tremble in fear and excitement. For once, I was uncovering something: a raw, compelling part of his personality that only seemed to glow at the piano. It was here, no longer a dim light in the fog.

Vaguely, I thought I heard a door shut. A soft thud, in a cloud of rattling noise that hovered in tense silence. There was nothing to be heard but the spark of his lips on mine. I didn't even know where I was, nor did I care to look until I found myself on my back, and him hovering over me. Those dark eyes. They centered me, giving me something to focus on while the thoughts in my head kicked up a storm.

He smiled. I knew this not because I saw him do it, but because it shot right through him, through his cheekbones and right into his eyes. I skimmed his lips with my thumb, easing my hand over his shoulder and the warm skin on his chest until it dropped at my side. Slowly, I propped myself up on my elbow, eyeing his shirt lying next to us. It was the only piece of clothing there.

"What color is it?" he asked, catching my eye.

"T—the shirt?"

"Yes."

"I'd call it maroon." I steadied my voice, taking a big breath.

"In my terms, I mean." He studied me, as if he could sense some sort of apprehension.

"Maroon is like… a mix of red and brown. Red is usually… a bright, cunning color that can be seen through anything. Brown is more down to earth. It's a color that's so simple, it's actually quite nice. It's subtle and easily overlooked by what surrounds it." My voice was almost nonexistent.

"No wonder I have mixed feelings about that shirt."

"To be frank, I despise the color." I eased back into normal conversation, laughing at the whole thing.

"Yes, I can tell. You certainly wanted to get rid of it quickly," he remark, raising his eyebrows.

"You are *nothing* like an Englishman." I let out a laugh, planting my lips on his. He pressed his hand on my collarbone when I flinched back.

"Leo, I cannot give you what you want." I sat up, staring down at my lap. I folded my hands tightly, feeling awful about encouraging him. The height of the moment had left me as I fell back into reality.

"But you already have." He seemed confused; so blissfully confused. I looked up as he said this, narrowing my eyes. He was being so genuine that it seemed too raw to be real. He couldn't have meant it. And yet, as I stared at him, he could have. That's when my past erupted. He had to know.

"I made a mistake… when I was younger." I swallowed. "A *big* mistake… that resulted in the best event in my life, my daughter, Ruby." At first, it looked as though he wanted to cut me off, but it broke away. He went still, waiting for me to speak.

"A while ago, I told you about my childhood friend Janet. She hated me because Roy chose to marry me instead of her. At first, I thought she was a complete snob to hate me, but she had a right. I look back on it now, and she had and still has an *absolute* right. *She* was the one who was supposed to wind up with him. It was set up that way. They talked a lot, took walks together, and all of that. But I *ruined* it. Roy drew his attention to me whenever I went over."

Leo seemed to be getting it so far. I could see him trying to figure out where it was going. He reached out and took a lock of my hair between his fingers.

"One day… we just got caught up. I was very shallow, and couldn't see past his handsome face. He felt very attracted to me also…." I cleared my throat. "I found out I was with his child about two months later." My voice faded away, but I pulled it back. "I was terrified. I went to him, and he immediately suggested that we get married. So we did. We married before the child was born and before I was big enough for people to notice. He was so noble for taking it all on. I hadn't expected him to. But he sacrificed the whole beginning of his life— his prime years— to be a husband to an undeserving, lustful girl. He did it for the child's sake, and for mine. He cared enough to make sure that my reputation wasn't ruined, and that my child…" I felt my lips quiver. "That my child wasn't a bastard."

He didn't answer for what seemed like months. The story tossed back and forth in his head, and I desperately wanted to know his thoughts.

"I wouldn't ask that of you. We're not married, so it would be wrong of me. That's what you were getting at, right? You wanted to know if—"

"Yes. I— I'm sorry I shoved that whole story on you at once. I… wanted to be clear on your intentions." It was hard to form the words on such an awkward subject. He didn't seem to have as big an issue with it as I did.

"On my intentions?" he inquired. I really didn't want to elaborate.

"Yes, I'm afraid." I let out a huge breath. "Look, I never meant for—"

"It's alright. I understand what you're getting at. It's just a little funny to see you English people spell it out." He patted my arm, cracking a smile. I smacked it away, frowning. But my frown quickly flipped upward. I could feel the intensity of his eyes.

"You should probably head home. It's getting late. I can show you where the nearest station is," he said.

"Are you kicking me out?" I asked.

"Not at all. It was merely a suggestion."

"Good. Because I don't intend to take it," I admitted shyly. At this, he gave me a look of complete surprise.

"Then might I ask, what are *your* intentions?" He raised his eyebrows, sitting at the edge of the bed. I began to observe things in the room now.

Everything was somewhat mismatched, from the stained wood to the curtains. It was not a pretty sight, but one that made me smile and reminded me of him.

"To stay here until the sun comes up tomorrow. When I was younger, we almost never went to the beach. It was too far away, and there was always too much to pack. I've always dreamed of living on a beach."

"Then be my guest." He flopped down on the left side, resting his head against an overstuffed pillow. I crawled on top of him. My cheek rested comfortably on his chest as it rose and fell out of rhythm. I could feel his chin resting on the top of my head. My heart went from racing, to jogging, to walking, and then, it went calm, putting my body in rest mode.

"Leo," I whispered, just before I fell asleep.

"Mmhm?" His throat and chest vibrated with his voice.

"What time is it?" It was getting dark outside. The sand was invisible against the blackening sky, and the waves sounded farther and farther off.

"I don't know. I don't own a clock."

♪ ♪ ♪

"Are you awake?"

I squeezed my eyes shut, but it was too late. "Now I am," I sighed.

"Good. Let's go get breakfast somewhere."

"Are you asking *me*?" I yawned, feeling groggy and still half asleep. Slowly, I pried each eye open.

"Who else would I be asking, Estella? The hermit crab next door? Of course *you*. Come on." He stood up and grunted as I listened to closet doors banging toward the front of the room.

"I can't go out like this. I'm truly a disaster." I rubbed my hands over my eyes, curling up on my side.

"Meet you in the living room in ten minutes," he sang cheerfully, leaving the room with new clothes tucked under his arm. Good. That horrible maroon shirt wouldn't be making another appearance.

I grumbled to myself, rolled off the bed and stood in front of the mirror. That was when I remembered having a dream. I was sitting on a stone wall in the middle of nowhere. For some reason, I recalled the trickle of water. But I never saw the source. It was one of those dreams where you watched yourself, instead of actually being yourself. I saw myself leveling the stones on the wall, picking up rigidly-shaped ones and tossing them aside until I found a smooth one that fit.

It was then that I bent down and reached on the other side of the wall, pulling up a red violin. It was so shiny that I could easily detect a disfigured face in it. The dream had abruptly ended when Leo woke me. It was so odd. Nothing else in the dream had been red.

My hair was knotted, but I managed to make it look decent. Strands hung loose and my bangs were scattered, but it was much better than it had been before. Leo was already dressed and sitting at the piano when I walked into the living room. He was completely focused, playing a couple of phrases before scribbling them down in his book. Even so, he heard me walk in.

"All set?" he asked, turning to me. His book fell from his lap onto the floor. I handed it back to him, and he took it quickly.

"I think so. I'm just going to use the telephone when we get to town."

♪ ♪ ♪

"It's completely preposterous! Nothing was broken or missing other than that! The whole story makes no sense, you see." My mother was in the middle of a rant when I walked into the sitting room. Her friends, Mrs. Donnel and Mrs. Halburry, sipped their tea, wide-eyed and in a trance at Momma's words.

"Oh, my darling. Come have tea with us. I have told you this story, haven't I?" Momma's head snapped up as I came in. She held her hand out, gesturing for me to take a seat. I had always liked Mrs. Donnel. She had an easing aura with a sturdy head on her shoulders. She had a petite face, lightly wrinkled and creased from the sun. Her hair started out grey near her scalp, and faded into the only brown she had left.

"My, my! Miss Estella! I feel like I haven't seen you in ages! I remember when you and Claude used to run around the schoolyard with my sons," she exclaimed, reaching out to kiss my cheek.

"Mathew and Gordon always pulled the ribbons out of my hair," I laughed lightly, picturing it in my mind. "How are they?" I took a seat beside her, trying to recount the names of all of her sons. She had nine, which seemed crazy to me at times. It was even funnier that they all closely resembled each other. Thomas, Adrian, and Wilson had been Claude's best friends growing up. I never forgot the day that Mrs. Donnel found them at Brim's Peak during school hours. She completely reamed them out, along with Claude who immediately put the blame on Wilson.

"They… they are doing quite fine. Adrian, Thomas, and Maurice passed quite a few years ago, in the war. And—"

"Oh, that's awful! My greatest sympathies."

"No, no, dear. Every single one of my sons served in that war, and I'm so proud of them. They died with honor, wearing a pride for their country. I do not grieve it. Instead, I am able to look out across the ocean, then to the land under my feet and think, my boys gave their lives for me to stand on this soil."

I was completely taken back by her powerful words. All of a sudden, I could see differently. I pictured myself standing at the beach, pretending to be her. Three out of nine sons dead. *I* could barely cope with my only daughter's death; never mind losing three sons. It seemed like such a horror to envision.

"They were good boys, Phoebe, fine, good boys." Mrs. Halburry affirmed, squeezing Mrs. Donnel's hand.

"I know, I know. But, enough of me. Back to your story." Mrs. Donnel focused on Momma.

"Indeed," Momma agreed. "Anyway, my father-in-law lives in Gloucester, as I mentioned, and he claims that someone broke into his house and stole a golden compass that he kept hidden in a locked wooden box with memorabilia of his late wife." She turned to me. "Stell, didn't I already tell you the news? It happened a few days ago."

"I'm afraid not, Momma. I must have not been home. That sounds terrible. Who would think to do that to an old man?" I could feel my face tense up. Flora had always wanted to get him out of that house. She claimed it was too big and lonely for him. She was probably seething at the news, yelling "I told you so," to everyone she saw.

"That's *exactly* it. He's an old man, and that's why people do it. There are some wicked individuals in this world. Good thing their income is low, or else it would go straight to their heads and feed their *infested* minds," Momma chided, laughing. She held out her teacup as Lemont refilled it. Their laughs joined hers, while I sat in solemn thought, picturing Otto.

"Anyway, I went over there with my husband, to ask him more about it, but he couldn't answer anything straight. His old age has him cornered. It's such a pity to see. Half the time we were there, he appeared delirious. The poor man didn't know who we were until we told him. It's really ripping my husband apart, seeing him at this stage."

"My cousin's great-aunt went through the same thing. She was a wily, batty women with no wits and no marbles. Shouted in the night, spoke to imaginary people. It was traumatic, even frightening, to be in her presence. You should hear the stories that my cousin has... good gracious." Mrs. Halburry looked as if she might faint at the thought. Her eyes bulged like a horse's eyes, filled with uncertainties with a proneness to being spooked.

"Oh, don't tell me about it. I'm afraid of becoming old myself." My mother shook her head sadly, sitting forward on the chair. "To tell you the truth, we cannot even imagine that anyone broke in. The windows are intact, the door was locked, and everything is in place. How would someone even know to look for the compass in that little box, anyway? My father-in-law is home practically all day, so I see no opportunity for a thief to invade. And yet, he still *insists* on it."

"So what are you thinking then? That he made it up?"

"I fear we have no other option. How can he describe the thief, and yet fail to identify who *I* am? Not only me. He didn't recognize his own son, either! It took lengthy convincing for him to accept that he even *had* a son." She threw her hands up. "He claims that a sailor walked right into his house and took it. He claims the man himself was hairy and had a mop of blonde hair. He also mentioned that he had a scarf on and a bunch of other gibberish. I don't know what to make of it all."

"Is the compass actually missing, though? Or is he making that part up, too?" Mrs. Donnel asked.

"Why, yes! But I fear he has misplaced it, and nothing more. I don't know why he cares about it so much. It doesn't even work. He only likes it because it has some sort of quote engraved on the front."

"Why do we always get caught up in thief problems, Momma?" I butted in, crossing my ankles.

"What do you mean?"

"Remember those two servants we had a while ago? Wayne and... oh... what was her name? Pauline! Yes, that's it. She convinced him to steal food to feed that stray cat? Meanwhile, she had a whole collection of stolen items in her room. We clearly have some sort of bad omen, Momma."

"I have no doubt about that," Momma replied. "It's true what you speak of, darling. Somehow, we always get caught up in these unthinkable situations."

After tea, Mrs. Donnel caught my arm and led me aside.

"Dear, I know I haven't seen you in a while, but I figured I would leave an open invitation to come by whenever. You know, Gordon still mentions your name once in a while. I know you went through a divorce some time ago, but I wanted to inform you. He's widowed, and he's only a few years older than you. But I ever so wish to see him happy. And you as well, of course. I know he thinks about you." She buttoned her coat, tilting her head.

"Oh, that's kind of you, Mrs. Donnel. I would like to see Gordon sometime... but I am involved with someone, actually." It was the first time the words passed through my lips. At first, they were shy to be heard, but as I said them, my confidence bubbled.

"Really? How curious. Your mother told me earlier that you do not have a beau." She gave me a cheeky smile, fluffing her hair. I could feel the blood drain from my face. "Oh, don't you worry, child. You'll have to tell me about this fellow at some time. Hmm?" She hugged me, patting the back of my neck with beautiful, silk gloves. "Goodbye now."

♪ ♪ ♪

"John is going to have my head! Out of all the times for me to be late. Look at that crowd up ahead." I was at a near run, with Leo beside me. He insisted on coming to one of my performances with the quartet.

"My mother made me go with her to pay a visit to my grandpoppa because he lives here, in Gloucester. She said it would work out perfectly, seeing I could make the visit with her, and then walk a kilometer to Westgate Street. It didn't work out like that because my grandpoppa sounds like he's going mad, so she wanted to stay and try to talk with him and have him identify—" I huffed, out of breath, holding my hat to my head. My shoes scraped the pavement, making puddles shatter like glass in front of me.

"Mad? How so?" Leo questioned in disbelief.

"He says that a sailor broke into his house and took a golden compass out of a little locked box that he had. It's thrown me in a complete tizzy. He talks about this sailor like he had a full blown conversation with him, and yet, he fails to recognize me or my mother!" I slid between two people. Cars honked around us, dropping folks off at shops nearby. Horses were tied down, waiting patiently for their owners to return and take them out of the sun.

"Strange. Maybe he—"

"Oh! There's John!" I waved frantically, picking him out amongst the crowd. He motioned for me to hurry. Everyone else was set up. We were going to be standing during this performance. I turned to Leo. "You'll get a good view from Oliver's. We will be performing right in front of there. I've got to hurry! See you there!" I dashed in front of him and crossed the street. A car blared its horn in my direction, making me jump out of my skin, but I kept going. I could hear them warming up on a C scale.

England

The Pianist

The quartet was beginning with scales and simple exercises. I figured I just had enough time to stop at the pub across the street and grab drinks. I couldn't imagine that Estella would get too far without water, especially on such a warm day. I whirled around, jogged to the pub, and pulled open the heavy doors. Smoke filled my lungs. The whole place was dim and cool, chilling the sweat on my forehead. The men closest to me had pipes in their mouths. They laughed heartily as they clicked their glasses together in a toast.

"Excuse me! Sir!" I leaned over the counter and waved at the bartender.

"You in a hurry, mister? What can I do for ya?" The man was extremely short, but his voice boomed over all the rest of them. He reminded me of a leprechaun.

"Two glasses of water. Thanks."

"Water, eh? Okay." He shrugged his shoulders and disappeared.

He came back, shuffling on his stubby legs. "Here you go." I exchanged my money for the glasses.

"Sir, what's this?" I asked dumbly. He gave me two identical glasses. One had cold water, the other looked like it had lemonade with leaves in it. I held them up, giving him a puzzled look.

"You looked like you might need this. Give it a try, pal. It's mint julep. My treat." He was called over by someone else, and left me with an unwanted drink. I started to protest, but decided not to bother, and walked out. As soon as I did, I could hear the quartet up ahead. I walked carefully, balancing both glasses. The mint drink didn't look that bad. Slowly, I took a sip.

"Hey! Watch yourself!" I slammed into someone, spilling both drinks. The ice cubes clattered to the ground, falling all over my shoes. People stepped to the side, rolling their eyes. They must have thought I was drunk.

"It wasn't my fault!" I immediately defended, staring down at my soaked shirt.

"Yeah it—Bruno? Blimey! It *is* you, you clumsy fool! Don't you recognize me?" The man clapped me on the back, grinning. He had light-colored hair and wore a fedora.

"Ed?" I stuttered, mouth open. It was my friend from my time on *Driftwood Anchor.* I never imagined meeting up with him again… and especially not like this.

"So you *do* remember me! How are you? Blimey, you're much more pleasant to be around when you don't stink!" I couldn't believe how much he'd changed. Before, when I had worked with him, he had looked like a scrawny teenager, like I had been. His shoulders had broadened now, and he had even grown a little. His face had thinned, making his chin appear angular. I wondered if I looked different in his eyes.

"Hey, I could say the same for you."

"So what are you doing around here? Where've you been all this time?" he asked. We completely forgot about the drinks. He followed me, keeping up with my pace as I listened for Estella's group to begin.

"I actually live in Scarborough, now. On a beach—"

"Of course you live near a beach! Our crew made the sea a part of ya." His voice was all gravelly.

"Speaking of the sea, tell me that you lived your legacy. Tell me you kept Serrone as a seaman's name after all this time."

"Oh I'm *living* the legacy, my good champ," he gushed, thrusting his hand out toward the horizon. "I've got my own ship, a couple of crew members, and a boatload of oysters. It's going great. I actually don't live too far from here. You should come over! My wife is a great cook, and you can meet Ed junior!"

"Oh, Blimey. There's an Edward *junior*? You *have* been busy, then. I can barely handle one of you." I smirked at him. Just being in his presence brought me back. His enthusiasm was contagious, and I felt like we could have been childhood friends by the way we laughed and talked with each other.

I stopped at the edge of the crowd. People were rooted in place to listen to the quartet. Their heads blocked our view. I didn't mind, though. The sounds made a better impression than the visual. I put my hands in my pockets, soaking up the sun, while Ed shielded his eyes with his hand.

"You like this music?" he asked.

"I love it. It's such a good story," I replied. He gave me a funny look, which made his ears twitch.

"If you're looking for a story, I highly suggest jazz. Now *that* is music to my ears. It's got such a flow."

"Y'know, I've never really listened to jazz," I admitted. For a musician, the new jazz genre was something I had accidentally neglected.

"You're *joking*! Jazz is the music of the soul. Come on, I'll show you. Usually there's a band playing at the bar down the street. They play at two o'clock. Tell you what? I'll even buy you another drink."

"But—"

"I know… you just got *so excited* to see me that you spilled your drink on yourself. I get that a lot. Don't be so star-struck, buddy! You'll embarrass yourself!" he whispered, throwing me a disapproving glance.

"Sure, Ed. Next time I get *that* excited about seeing you, I'll make sure to toss the drink at you, instead," I said.

"Ah, ha. Very funny." He pretended to laugh, but it came out as dry as a sun-toned stone. "Let's go. Let me educate you about nineteen twenty-four."

"I can't. I'm here for my friend. She's the main violinist in this group and I told her I'd come and listen. She's really good," I added, tilting my head in Estella's direction. Ed peered around a group of teenagers, going up on his toes.

"*Her*? Bruno, she looks a little old for you," he winced, biting his bottom lip.

"No, no. The other one."

"Oh, oh, *oh*. Wait, what? She looks too *young* for you!"

"How are you assuming that I'm with one of these girls, anyway? What if you're wrong and it isn't a romantic thing at all?"

"Because that's not how it works. I can tell by the way you're talking about her."

"Who's to say, I'm not married already?" I challenged.

"I didn't see a ring," he replied smoothly.

"Hmph. You're pretty observant." I let out a breath, defeated by him.

"Always have been. It's what makes me a good navigator on the seas." He puffed out his chest, boasting happily. The first song began, leading with Estella. The viola took over then, making the violinists harmonize in the background while the cello kept the beat. They did not have many long songs. Most of them were short and bubbly, which is hard to find in most classical music.

Ed brought me over to the store in front of us, gesturing for me to sit next to him on the curb. An awning draped over our heads, casting a boxed shadow under our feet. Not only was it cooler, but it gave me a better view. The bell on the door jingled as people came and went. It was a sluggish day for most. The air was completely still, and the sun itself seemed to hum carelessly.

I sat and listened, letting my mind take me away. I no longer saw anything around me. Everything I saw was in my own head. The images jumped to life from the sounds. I could see the notes scurrying along the staff, pushing through different key signatures. When I opened my eyes, people walked differently. They no longer strolled along passively, soaking up time. Now, they had energy. Their steps quickened with the beat of the song, which brought the dragging day from being minor to major. It had such a stunning impact, and I pitied those who failed to notice. Their paces almost duplicated those of the people around them.

"Uhh, Bruno. They're finished. I think that girl is looking for you." Ed's voice pulled me back to reality. I hadn't realized that the sound had ceased.

"Estella!" I abruptly stood, shaking my hands to catch her attention. In split seconds, the sky boomed up above, and rain came pouring down. I ran out from under the awning and let the drops wash away the sweat on my face. I tilted my head back, letting it run over my chin and throat. People clustered together, bickering over the little space under the awning.

"There you are! Did you like it?" Estella beamed, wiping her eyes and squinting at me.

"I did enjoy it. Twelve-eighths time isn't your thing, is it?" I jeered.

"Not one bit. I'm horrible with it," she admitted, smiling shyly. She tucked her violin case close to her chest and stepped under the awning.

"You're going to catch a cold, standing there like that. Let's go," she called over the roar of the rain. It battered against the windows and made the grains of wood shiver.

"I'm Ed Serrone. Pleased to meet you, miss." Ed made his way through the little mob and tipped his fedora toward Estella, who had the look of utmost confusion plastered to her face. The wind whipped the rain in all directions, like a swarm of bugs.

"Estella, this is Ed, my old friend from when I used to work on the fishing boat. I happened to bump into him here." I ran my fingers through hair that now molded to my head. My shirt was soaked, dripping inconsistently.

"Oh, in that case, hello, Ed." She instantly eased up, letting out her friendly personality.

"Why don't you both come over to my house?" Ed asked. "Please, just stop by. Bruno, I'd be more than happy to have the both of ya."

I looked to Estella, waiting for her response. She wore a neutral look, as if she didn't mind either way. As I waited for her reaction, I could feel a flare in my chest again. The drops beaded her eyelashes, making glints on her cheeks as if she were made of crystals. Every time I looked at her—

"Thank you, Ed. That's kind of you. I'd be happy to. Leo?" She glanced at me.

I snapped myself back in the moment. "I'm up for it."

"Leo? Did you call him Leo? Is that some sort of a pet name?"

"Heavens, no!" She stepped back, appalled. A scowl seeped into her lips. "It's his first name. Bruno is his middle name," she explained to him, hoisting her case above her head and stepping out into the storm.

"Do you mean to say that I've been calling you the wrong name since I've known you?" The gears in Ed's mind were on fire, making steam build behind his ears. He walked beside us, occasionally leaping over puddles. "Leo, Bruno—whatever the hell your name is—is this true?"

"To an extent. I go by either, really. It's not a big deal," I replied, while Estella muttered about not having an umbrella.

"Yeah, it is! I've been telling people about how this kid got hired to work on a boat and couldn't even down two raw oysters at first, and I've been giving them the wrong name! You're making a liar outta me!"

"Sorry, Ed." I shrugged, squeezing out the bottom of my shirt. The water crackled on the sidewalk like fireworks. In minutes, we arrived at the stoop of Ed's house. It was in a close neighborhood, but the house itself was very large. It was the same light color as the house next to it, and the one next to that. It seemed to be a plaza of cloned houses. There were iron numbers above each door.

"Come on in, everyone." Ed held open the door, bowing dramatically as if we were royalty. "Alice? Alice?" His voice echoed from behind us. We did our best, trying to dry our shoes on the doormat.

"Eddy? Oh thank goodness, I—" She lurched back, almost bonking heads with Estella in the doorway.

"Alice, we have visitors! This is Leo… or Bruno, and Estella," Ed announced. His eyes lingered on her anguished face, then darted to the floor around us.

"I wish you had forewarned me! I could have tidied up a bit! Junior left his toys scattered on the floor—"

"Poppa!" A voice peeped from beyond the walls. Mrs. Serrone immediately attended to it, not bothering to introduce herself. She turned on her heels like first instinct. We followed Ed to the living room, where Mrs. Serrone attempted to throw all of Edward junior's toys into a basket in the corner.

It was a plain house. The walls were mostly bare. An occasional drawing of the ocean was smacked in an empty spot, which had to be Ed's doing. It was then that I noticed how the whole floor was covered in a plushy rug. Not that I knew what color it was, of course. It swooped around the counter island, and continued down a dead-end hallway.

"There you are!" Ed crouched down, placing his big hand on the toddler's shoulder.

"Of course I'm here, Poppa!" The little boy squealed and let go of the wooden car in his fist. It looked like it was a ladybug with wheels, though the wheels were square. Junior brought his arm up to Ed's face, squeezing his nose and patting his eyelids.

It was so strange. Seeing that Ed was a father really threw me. It was like I had jumped forward in time. It was hard to remember a yesterday existed. A yesterday full of youth and exuberance that old age grinded away. I was not old, but standing here, I felt age drape itself around my neck.

"Bruno, meet Ed junior." Ed grinned from ear to ear, patting the rug for me to sit. Mrs. Serrone beckoned Estella, giving her a sweater. I crossed my legs, easing down to be eye level with the boy.

"Bruno, hold out your hand, like this." Ed looked to me, putting his hand out in front of his son. I followed in wonder.

"Junior, this is Poppa's friend, Mr. Bruno." The boy's hand hovered in midair until it bumped mine. His fingers could barely wrap around one of my fingers. With the other hand, he reached up and touched my forehead, poking at my temple. He tapped his palm across the bridge of my nose, down my cheek and ending at the base of my chin.

I didn't move a muscle. It was the strangest process. I studied the young boy's face as he did this. His eyes did not waver. For a toddler, he had very good concentration.

"Well, hello, Junior," I said nicely. The boy lowered his hand. He had sloppy light hair, so light that it resembled worn piano keys. He was a very thin boy, who seemed bold and fearless.

"Good evening, Mr. Bruno," he replied. His voice was loud and bubbly.

"Junior, it's afternoon, son." Ed ruffled his hair, correcting him with the utmost kindness.

"Good afternoon, Mr. Bruno," the little boy said. He easily got distracted, bending down on his knobby knees and pulling at his long socks. "Poppa... where is it?" He patted the rug around himself, circling. "Where'd it go? Poppa! Where is it?" The boy began to wail, pressing his hands to the rug more fervently.

"Sit. Deep breath. And again. Good, very good." Ed's voice was stern and calming. He suddenly grabbed both of Junior's arms and stilled him, watching his chest rise and fall. "I will get it for you. You can show Mr.

Bruno your new toy, okay?" Ed had a soft side that I had never expected to see. But something was strange about Junior. He was an extremely well-mannered kid, but he was different. I stayed with him while Ed went over to the toy basket. He had Ed's exact eyes, but they seemed empty and foggy. It was such an unusual sight. They had a stunning blankness about them... and that's when the realization hit me.

Ed junior was blind.

England

The Violinist

Alice was a nice and nimble person. She had the darkest red hair I'd ever seen. It was like she was fueling a fire on her head. She wore a plaid cotton dress with pockets, and a locket hung at the edge of her white collar. Bruno was sitting with Ed, playing with his son, while Alice chatted with me about different types of tea. Apparently, she had been to India when she was younger, and observed many different kinds of tea leaves that grew there. She claimed that most would get shipped here, to England.

"Here, try this." She placed a chipped cup in front of me. The color was faded, growing darker only at the handle. She poured steaming hot tea into it and offered me sugar, which I politely declined. Then, she poured some for herself in a sterling silver cup. We sat at the kitchen table, watching the boys.

"What's that, Junior, huh? How interesting," Bruno commented, tapping the little golden object in Junior's hands. The boy pulled it away from him.

"It's very, very, very, very special, Mr. Bruno. Poppa give it to me." He smoothed his small hand over the rounded surface, again and again. He seemed hypnotized by the perfect circular shape.

"He's a rascal, that one," Mrs. Serrone sighed, putting her hands on her hips. A tired grin filled her lips. "When we first found out he was blind, my father told me to send him away."

Blind? My brain swelled. The toddler was blind? I watched him play. Only now did I take into consideration his constant stumbling, his unpreventable failure to grab at toys in front of him. His hands were his eyes, navigating his pathway and testing the unsure waters in front of him. And yet, this boy did not know fear. Mrs. Serrone's voice crept into my ears again, cleansing my mind.

"The facility we looked into wasn't right. Edward couldn't stand the thought that somewhere in the world, someday, a man would be walking around with his face, without *him*. It was hard for me to agree."

"Why did *you* want to send him away?"

"I… I thought he'd have a better shot in life. I will never have another child, and I wanted the best for Junior. I thought the best thing for him was for him to be educated, even if it was without us."

"It's very caring of you, to want the best for him. That's very selfless, and respectable, Mrs. Serrone. I agree with you."

"Do you? Well, I didn't succeed. Ed insisted that he be kept here." She lowered her voice. "He… he thinks that he can make Junior's life better than what it could be in one of those schools for the blind. He thinks that he can make him see the world, even if it's not literally."

I couldn't imagine trying to make that decision. Even now, as she sipped the last of her tea, worry wavered about her. Greed was a common treasure found in the eyes of a human, but she housed no greed. She housed no lust, nor nostalgia. Instead, buried deep in her pupils, was an undeniable amount of hope, as if she transformed wishing into an emotion that she dressed herself with every day.

"Maybe I can help you," I blurted out. "I'm sure I could find a suitable place for Junior. My family has all sorts of connections." I sipped my tea slowly, biting my tongue as it burned the inside of my cheek. "If I—"

"No, no. The knot cannot be undone. I can't take my son from my husband. They bring each other such joy. See Junior's new toy?" She jutted her chin in their direction. "Ed got that for him. It makes me smile when I realize how much Junior loves it." The corners of her eyes pulled in as she smiled.

I spotted the particular toy she spoke of. It was round and golden. Junior held it with both hands in his lap. "Leo," I called suddenly. "Let's check if the rain has subdued."

"Sounds like it," he replied, not looking up. "I don't hear it on the roof like before."

"Then come with me to check." He met my eyes across the room in a strange agreement of understanding. I pulled the front door shut soundly behind us, and waited a good few seconds before I spoke.

"Do you know what that child's favorite toy is?" I asked innocently.

"Looks like a compass. Don't worry, it's broken though. He can't do any harm to it."

"*Broken?*" I could feel my eyelashes brush against each other as my lids came together in suspicion. "The compass is broken? And it's *gold?*"

"Yes, it's broken. I can only assume it's gold." He clipped his answer short, finally figuring out where I was going with this whole inquiry. He shot me a dubious glance. "Oh, Estella, you're not thinking—"

"Oh course I am! Tell me, did it have anything written on it?"

"I'm not positive."

"Leo! This is serious! It all makes sense! My grandpoppa claimed he saw a sailor come into his house and steal his compass! You told me that you and Ed worked on that boat together, so he is indeed a sailor or captain!"

"There are hundreds and hundreds of sailors here! You *can't* be serious!"

"But I am! Now, did the compass have anything written on it?" I refused to back down. He wore a plain look of intense denial, but his response contradicted it.

"Yes. Yes, there was some type of writing engraved in the gold," he recalled. His eyes spaced out into nowhere. "But it means noth—"

"I knew it!" I had my hand on the doorknob when Leo pulled me away.

"Are you out of your mind? You're in no position to accuse this family of stealing, Estella." He didn't let go of my arm. I didn't even notice that the rain had stopped until now.

"In no *position?* That compass belongs to my grandpoppa. Just because he's mad, doesn't mean it lessens the value of it. It doesn't make it right for them."

"How could you assume this from nothing? You were the one who *told me* that your grandpoppa is going mad. So how could you go by his account of the story? Even if it was Ed, you'd have to be a wretched person to take the toy from a blind child." He still didn't let go, in fear I'd barge back into their peaceful home.

"It's not my fault he's blind, and the compass isn't a toy! Believe me, I have sympathy for the boy, but it does not cloud my mind. That *toy* is an heirloom, if you must know." My voice came out as a hiss.

"Look, I'll buy you another gold compass. Plate it with diamonds if you want, I don't care. You can't go throwing random accusations at Ed and his family. It belongs to a blind child. A boy who cannot see owns a compass. Can't you see the significance in this?"

"No. Only the lucky coincidence that we stumbled across the Serrones, or else my grandpoppa would never see his precious compass again."

"I'll buy you a compass for your grandpoppa. You're being rash. You can have anything in the world, and yet you choose to remove that *one thing* from the possession of another." As he spoke his voice dwindled lower and lower. His eyes searched the windows nearby for a face. Mine, however, didn't falter. I wanted them to hear me.

"Why don't you understand that it was Grandpoppa's to begin with? You're acting as if I were merely causing all this ruckus for the enjoyment of it. It belongs to my family, Leo. Can't you see I'm trying to act right by them?"

"Ed's an old friend of mine. You can't go ruining him and his name. You have to think of that as well. He's not a bad person. I have to act right by *him*."

"By him and not the law, you mean?" I snipped at him, gaining the upper hand. I wanted him to understand, desperately. Unfortunately, he had no problem with disagreeing.

"You keep forgetting where you come from. You can't be this cruel. I refuse to believe it. I refuse to believe that you would make a false accusation. That you would put Ed's family in jeopardy. Imagine what it might say in the papers? It would publicly and financially ruin Ed's family. Think about it. Where's that average English girl hiding?" He held my wrists firmly, but it didn't hurt. He was intimidating, but not threatening. I could feel his breath on the bridge of my nose. It was warm, like the air around us.

I glared at him and then closed my eyes, remembering. He peeled his fingers from my wrist. I stood there, recalling what it was like to be an average girl, in an average English family again. Learning to love the necessities and cherish the extras.

"Just take it!" The door behind us swung open with an angry force. "I'll give it to you here and now if you promise not to cause an uproar. I should have known you were the Breaker girl." Ed stood rigidly, extending his arm, the compass clutched in his hand. In the background, Junior was crying for it. My whole face flooded red. Not only was he a thief, but an eavesdropper.

"I knew it! Give that to me." I snatched the compass from his hand before he could reconsider.

"Believe it or not, that old man gave it to me. He was sittin' out on his porch, shouting craziness, as usual, when I happened to go by on my cycle. I went over to him and he begged me to take it. Said it was cursed or something," Ed defended, eyeing me sharply. It was like Leo wasn't even there.

A hollow, rude laugh erupted from my throat. "Ha! You expect me to believe that? Who could come up with such a ghastly lie?" I continued to mock him. "Tell Mrs. Serrone thanks for the tea." With that, I took off, down the steps and into the street.

"I knew it!" I muttered over and over. Leo came up behind me.

"In all of your *disrespect*, you almost forgot this." He thrust my violin case at me, which I took with a stiff "Thank you."

"You should have listened to me in the beginning. I knew that—" I tried to continue.

"You didn't know anything, and you still don't. Ed said your grandpoppa *gave* him that compass."

"That's a ridiculous accusation. My grandpoppa loves this thing. And I intend to get it back to him right now."

♪ ♪ ♪

"What's that you've got there, child?" Mrs. Donnel focused on the violin case I held at my hip. I was just getting up to leave. "I didn't even see you come in with it," she added.

"My violin, Mrs. Donnel. I have to go with Leo to practice. He plays piano, you know."

"So you've said. From what you have informed me, Leo seems to be a very talented, kind man. I'd very much like to meet him." She stood and walked me to the door. I had spent most of my afternoon there, having luncheon and chatting with her and Gordon. Gordon had completely changed from when I had last seen him. He was a strong, mature man, with looks that made me want to shrink into a shell, like a turtle. He couldn't keep his eyes off of me. Luckily for me, he had left earlier, so now it was just Mrs. Donnel and me.

"I will bring Leo here soon. Maybe if Momma sees that you like him, she will be easier about me being with a German man." I bit my lip, picturing her horrified face.

"I wouldn't worry, dear. If you like him, your Momma has no choice."

I stopped in the doorway. "I do like him… but he's so *disagreeable*."

"Then treasure it." She kissed my cheek and nudged me out.

When I arrived at Leo's house, I could hear the piano from the walkway. The beach breeze spun the ends of my skirt as I walked. I paused before knocking on the door, simply listening. I did not recognize the tune, which immediately led me to believe that he was making up a song. Although he played many classical pieces, his original pieces did not always sound heavily classical. They were different. It was as if his music spoke. It conveyed his every thought and feeling, like a translator. He had a connection to what he played, like he could breathe it in and have it take him away.

I stood and closed my eyes as a smile spread across my face.

When he stopped, I rapped at the door. Abruptly, my feelings of solace left me. As I waited, I tried to figure out what I was going to say. Maybe he wouldn't answer the door. Maybe he was holding a grudge. The doorknob turned, and I was proved wrong.

"Hello, Estella," came his dull voice. The first thing I noticed was how dark the soft skin around his eyes was. His hair was a bit tousled, as if he had not gone out all day. The sleeves on his buttoned shirt were rolled up to his elbows, and his suspenders were loose. He had a pen tucked behind his ear, which stayed firmly in place. He seemed standoffish to the point where a long pause hung between us. "I… was expecting you a little later," he went on, stepping aside.

"You were? Oh." As I entered, I found papers scattered all over the floor. One crunched under my heel before I realized it.

"Don't mind those. I'll pick them up."

"What are you doing with all of these? Don't you have a desk or a paper bin?" The papers trailed over to the piano, where a bigger mass of them clustered like an audience around the bench. He went down on his knees, picking them up and stuffing them in his arms as fast as possible.

"I was trying to write."

"Oh! More music? Let me see—" I went to pick one up, but he beat me to it.

"No. Not music. I'm trying to write a letter."

"A letter? Seems to me like you have dozens, if only you hadn't crumpled them all up. Who are you writing to, anyway?"

"I... um." The papers crunched in his arms. "My father."

I remembered the last time he had brought up his father. I hadn't heard one positive thing about the man. It made a strange feeling swarm around me, like it was a forbidden subject.

"Leo...." I cleared my throat, twisting at the handle of my case. "Why do you write to him? You could use the telephone in the town, you know."

"I cannot do that."

"Why?"

"I have to write to him."

"Does he not have a telephone?" I questioned.

"I don't know."

He was afraid. It had taken me long enough to realize it. He took the rest of the papers and threw them away, pushing them down with his shoe. I watched him carefully, move for move. Fear was not a regular, noticeable thing lingering about his head. As far as I was concerned, Leo didn't have much fear at all. He had moved here, to England, without a clue, secured a job that he was unfamiliar to him, and had taken a whole new life on by himself. He didn't worry about being alone. He didn't worry about death. He took things as they were thrown at him, and snatched them out of midair. Yet, the rare times he spoke of his father, a certain shaking vulnerability became visible.

"Can I ask you a question?" I suddenly blurted out. He had taken his place at the piano, practicing the same measure five times until he got it right. The tune was now engraved into my ears.

"Hmm?" He stopped, swiveling around on the bench. I couldn't help picturing myself there, too.

"Why did you move here? Five or six years ago, you came to England, right? There had to be a specific reason," I stated.

"We should get to practicing. It's quite a long, complicated story that would bore you," he insisted.

"I want to know, though. What was your main incentive?" I removed my hat, placing it beside me. When I opened my violin case, I noticed that my block of rosin had broken.

"Why do you want to know this all of a sudden? It makes no sense—"

"Did you leave because you hated being a musician? Or because of the war?"

Whispers of the waves stole the silence between us as he tried to come up with a sugar-coated answer. He stared out the window to his right, watching a motion picture scroll in his head. It was a film I wished he would let me see.

"It was mostly that, yes."

"Or was it about your family?" I let the words out softly, hoping to comfort him instead of adding bricks to his wall. Something triggered in his face.

"I hate talking about this. I've already told you." His frustration was not directed at me. It succumbed to his guilt and was carried out through his tone. "I abandoned them. Otto has made that haunt my every thought." He took a long pause, hitting any keys that were in his finger's reach. "When I was younger, it was the best thing, being free and all that. Having my own life was incredible, something I had never considered before. But as days have gone by, I've slowly begun to regret it. I cannot get this... this *grudge* to go away." He placed his hand to his chest. "And I should be damned for it! Those people raised me. But no matter how many times I say the words, they cannot ever bring back the precious time I was supposed to have as a child. No matter how sorry they may feel, they cannot give it back." His face was set in stone, resembling my brother's.

"But that's the past. Of course, you can't change that. You cannot get it back. But wouldn't you want to mend it for the future?"

"I don't know what I *want* to do, or have a clue what I *need* to do. Usually, I try not to think about it. But, ever since my brother visited I can't get it out of my head."

"Get *what* out of your head? What happened that makes you unable to have a vocal conversation? They're your family, you know. They must care about you. You're not the only one in the world who has had this problem, I assure you."

"It's not a singular problem that keeps me from them. It's so many, rolled up and fused into a knot. My father and I rarely got along. Actually, let me give him a *morsel* of credit," he practically sneered. "We got along when I was young. When I was five or six years old. And my mother," he huffed irritably, "she fussed over me all the time. But she is flimsy, and wishy-washy. She—I don't know. She never could stand her own ground. She's afraid of her own thoughts," he scowled as the fire behind his eyes burned a hole in the floor.

"But they *raised* you. They couldn't *hate* you." I had nothing to back up what I was saying, but I knew it was true. "Leo, you *have* to believe it." I bit my lip, weighing out my next words. "You know I am divorced from Roy…." My voice trailed off into nothing. "I thought I hated him for a while. I thought I knew what it was, to hate someone. But I didn't. And he didn't hate me, either. Leo, he divorced me, for my *own sake*. On my own *request*! He was my family! He, Ruby, and myself. But when I was not happy, he stepped to the side, and let me go. This was my husband that we're talking about! You'd be surprised how little you know about hate. You need to simply say what's on your mind, and if they can't forgive you, then they don't deserve a single word you have to say."

"I'll need to think about it." His voice was soft as if the sun streaking through the windows had melted the edges around it.

"I sincerely hope you will. Now, show me this piece you've been working on."

"Piece? No, there are more than one. There are about eight." He handed me a stack of sheet music that had been sitting atop the closed lid of the piano. My eyes swelled from looking at all of the notes.

"You wrote all of these?" My mouth dropped in awe.

"Some I've had for a while, but I edited them so it's just violin and piano."

"I'm… I'm completely amazed," I breathed, picking through them. Butterflies gathered in my stomach as I understood how hard the pieces were. Only a select few could be defined as mediocre. Toward the end of the stack, my eye was snagged by something. "So the accompaniment part right here… is it in bass clef? I think you meant that, but I don't see it written in anywhere." I scanned the paper like I was playing 'I spy.'

"It's there, see? It matches with your part for those two measures." He slid his finger along the page. "And to clarify, the piano is not your *accompaniment*. That's not how I operate, and it's certainly not how I composed these pieces to be. We are either two soloists playing together or a duet. I don't believe in accompaniment," he stated firmly.

A smile smoothed across my face and I lifted my chin. "Then I don't believe in it, either."

♪ ♪ ♪

The Leonardo Leonhardt that I knew vanished when we began practicing. He took the form of a meticulous teacher. The musical theories he tried to explain to me might well have been spoken in Latin. He made me play over and over. The staccatos were never short enough. My accents never had enough of a punch. My vibrato had to be longer and more heartfelt. I felt as if he was tearing away my foundation as a violinist. I wanted to play his songs, but he was becoming obsessive. Whenever I tried to take my own approach, he would explain that it had to be played as he heard it in his head. I attempted to justify for him, putting myself in a composer's shoes, but I could never fully understand.

I increased my violin lessons to three times a week from two. My teacher, Dr. Harbone, was a graduate of Cambridge University, and he could play the violin better than an angel from heaven itself. The change in schedule didn't bother him. He would come to Hampton Court, and I'd have my lessons in the sitting room. Momma no longer minded it.

"Miss Breaker, might I inquire why none of these pieces have titles?" he asked one day. He hoisted his perfectly round eyeglasses to the bridge of his nose. He was a tall, toned man with scruff on his face and grey hair at his temple that he tried to hide. His dirty blonde hair cupped the top of his head.

"I honestly do not know. My friend wrote these, you see. All of them. And that's why I want to learn them."

"You're such a kind, thoughtful person for doing that. I wouldn't imagine any less of you. To take on pieces with such *difficulty* can be hard to work through, but I have not a doubt." I felt a surge of pride well up in me. So they were doable. I didn't care how long it took. I wanted to play them right for Leo, even if it wasn't my version of right.

"Well, thank you, Dr. Harbone. You flatter me too much for my own good," I laughed lightly.

"Not a *bit*. You're my most excelled student, and you continue to surprise me."

"Surprise you with my inability to keep a steady beat?" I gibed.

"Miss, surprises come in all sorts. " He placed his hand on my shoulder, grinning. His eyes were a metallic gray, the kind that makes you wonder how they could have possibly been real. Only expensive dolls had sharp, daunting eyes like his.

"Stell?" The door edged open as though it was too heavy. Dr. Harbone pulled his hand down rather quickly. Charlie poked his head in. "Lemont found a certain... *Mr. Bruno* at the front door... I'm assuming it's for you." His voice was cold and deadpan. I particularly noticed how his clothes appeared to be baggy... almost sloppy looking.

"Tell him to come in. I was just finishing up with Dr. Harbone, anyway," I replied cheerfully. It was certainly unexpected. Charlie knew I had contact with Leo, but not to the full extent. He was oblivious to how fond I was of him. I didn't know if it was for the better or worse.

"Yes, I was just leaving." Dr. Harbone packed up his violin, like it was made of eggshells. Leo entered the room as Dr. Harbone was exiting.

"Two-fifteen on Thursday," he confirmed, kissing my knuckles. I nodded in agreement, as my eyes swooped toward Leo. His presence made my heart flutter. I couldn't stop thinking about that one night. It was probably the most scandalous, unrespectable thing to do, but I didn't regret it. I ached for his hands. He had beautiful hands, but I knew he'd burst out in laughter if I ever said so. The thought made me smirk without realizing.

"You know, Dr. Harbone, I know it's quite coincidental, but oddly enough, this is my composer friend, Mr. Leonhardt. We were just talking about you, Leo."

"Oh. Great minds think alike," Leo replied, coming toward us. One hand rested in his pocket, while the other quietly tapped the side of his leg. Some sort of song had to be bouncing around in his head.

"Leo, this Dr. Harborne, my violin teacher."

"Yes, of course. I remember your name."

"And I *certainly* remember yours." Dr. Harbone didn't seem pleased. "You are that pianist who practically *ran* off the stage! How could I forget *that?*" Dr. Harbone laughed heartily, but Leo did not look amused. "I give you credit for trying to put that one behind you. Whewf! What an embarrassing moment!" Dr. Harbone shook his head, bracing his forehead with his fingers. "I give you my greatest condolences, and best of luck." He was still laughing, and continued to do so, all the way down the hall until his footsteps disappeared.

The tips of Leo's ears glowed red, and did not simmer down. His dislike for Dr. Harbone was branded on his face. I narrowed my eyes at him inquisitively.

"You ran offstage when you were little?"

"*Little?* I was not *little.* I was old enough to know not to, but I was afraid enough to do so. I'm pretty sure I was twenty when it happened." He went over to the piano.

"I personally think it would be harder to run off the stage than stay on it," I replied, really thinking about it. "Anyway, what are you doing here?"

"I can't just show up, unannounced?"

"No. Well, I mean… of course you can. I just wanted to make sure there was nothing wrong." I watched him carefully. He kept moving, pacing around the piano and around the room until he took a seat next to me on the sofa. His defensive wall ebbed away.

"To be honest, I've wanted to make a visit. I wanted to see everyone downstairs again. Does Bentley still work here?"

"Why, of course. You should go down and see him. I'll practice my new part while you're there, and when you come up, I challenge you to a race through the maze." I raised my eyebrows, smiling deviously. "You may be able to outrun me, but you cannot outsmart me."

"We'll see about that." He changed the subject abruptly. "You didn't happen to receive a package in the mail recently, did you?"

"Um. No? Was I supposed to?"

"Never mind. It's nothing to worry about," he assured. Before I could react, he tilted his head and kissed me. Not a short peck like a bird, but one that deemed the seconds slower. He placed his hand on my cheek and caressed my skin until he let his hand drop.

"I've been wanting to do that for a while," he said. My eyes pulled up as he stood, staying pinned to his face. He was so unreadable.

"I'll be back." He grinned, almost as if he was laughing at me. Light danced about his pupils until I saw him no more. He started to whistle as he walked down the hall. The sound grew further and further away, then stopped altogether.

England

The Pianist

"Who?" the tiresome voice called.

"It's me, Bruno, your old valet." I rested my head against his door as our words bashed against the thick wood between us. He said nothing. Instead, I listened to the fluttering of papers. Something thudded to the floor and his dragging footsteps came closer. His shadow slipped under the crack of the door.

"Bruno?" The doorknob twisted and I backed away. Claude looked exactly the same as before. It was as though the five years that I had been gone were mashed into a single day. The dimness of the room made his eyes appear to glow like the bulbs of a cluster of fireflies. He was an alley cat, hidden, afraid, and ready to pounce on anything. "What do you want?"

"I came to say hello. Did you get another valet?"

He looked wary, and still didn't open the door fully. His typical standoff attitude had not weakened in the slightest. "It's actually good that you're here." Suddenly, there was a change in attitude. "I need your knowledge. Either come in, or leave altogether." The door swooped open. It was no longer neat and tidy inside. The whittled wood on the desk could no longer be seen. Papers lay strewn across it, completely obscuring the whole surface. I eased forward, into unknown territory.

His movements were rough and jolted as he attempted to clear a space for me to sit. He tossed piles of paper together, and pushed aside an enormous suitcase in the center of the room. The curtains were drawn; only a sliver of light was allowed to enter. It streamed in with intensity, but got no further than the nightstand at his bed. It was not permitted.

He took his place at his desk, and I was ordered to sit in the armchair in the corner. The cushion was still stiff.

"Bruno, I need you to tell me everything you can about Germany." He swiveled around in his chair and spotted a blank paper on his desk. Then he grabbed his pen and stared at me. Waiting.

"I, I cannot do that now. There are so many things about Germany. Especially now, since the war. I only came to say hello because I must go and find your father, and then I plan on greeting everyone downstairs."

"My father is busy at the moment, and the servants can wait. I need to know."

"Why? What is so urgent?"

"Do they own farms there? What's their form of currency?" he pressed.

"Claude, I need to go. Your sister is waiting for me." I tapped my legs and stood.

"*Please,*" he croaked, closing his eyes as if he was having a hard time sifting through his words. They snagged in his throat. "Sit down," he mustered between clenched teeth. His voice was low and almost pained.

"I don't know how you expect to go on treating me as a servant!" I suddenly lashed out at him, grabbing for the door. It was no wonder that he wasn't well liked. The man took no initiative to be friendly, let alone the least bit cheery.

"Wait! Wait! Just listen to me! God *forbid* anyone else will!"

His words brought me to a temporary halt. I turned around, about to say something, when I bit my tongue. I yanked the door open and collected myself, appearing perfectly calm in the open hallway.

"Bruno!" He was at the door before I was even two yards away. "I need to know what it's like. I have to go to Germany and—"

"Oh, yes, it's a great place," I snorted sarcastically. "It's in depression." Hmph. So Claude and Germany had something in common. They could both wallow in their own sorrow, and flaunt their menacing attitudes.

"You absolute *fool.*" He grabbed my shoulder with his one arm. It easily carried the strength of two. I jolted back in surprise, pushing it away forcefully. "I'm not asking to be bothersome. I'm not asking because I want to hold you up. I'm asking because I *loathe* the thought of the place, and I'm—" He completely stopped, restarting the sentence once again. "I'm terrified of having to go, to be completely honest."

I studied his scattered face. The unknown irked him, a piece of the beyond that could only hover above his fingertips. It stole up the precious space in his head and probably kept him up at night. Germany was a thief that had stolen a part of Claude, and I couldn't possibly grasp why he would ever go there.

"You? Going to *Germany*?"

"I have to go. I got a letter from some high-end literature professor who resides there, in Berlin. He wants to meet with me." His breath trembled.

"Then don't go if you don't want to. I wouldn't blame you. Momentarily, it's a sad, angry country." I put my hand in my pocket, fidgeting anxiously.

"No. I definitely need to go. It's not a matter of choice. It's a matter of me getting a hold of myself, and finding the courage to go. I need to know what I'm going up against. So, I need you to tell me." He was in a battle up against himself now. Germany was no longer the target enemy.

Never had he been so directly sincere. I remembered how much he hated help. How it sawed at his pride, piece by piece. It wouldn't be right to bash him while he was practically on his knees. It wouldn't be fair to him. As much as I wanted to spite this man, and teach him a lesson in kindness, I obliged. Maybe the lesson in kindness would sprout from a pure example of it.

"Fine," I replied shortly, holding my head high. "I'll write to you." It was my final offer before we parted. I did not wish to talk with him any longer.

"Oh, save it, then. If you don't care that much, simply say it." He waved me away, turning to go. His shoulders hunched and he scuffled back to his room door.

"Now you'd better listen to *me*, Claude." I shot back at him with the firmness of an officer. "I give you my word. Words mean more to you because you're a writer, don't they? Well then, you'd best believe mine. They certainly don't derive from the Bible, but they are just as solid, I assure you.

I won't let you go blind with this. I will tell you what I can, and what I remember—just not at the moment. I *really must go.*"

♪ ♪ ♪

"Good Lord! Is that you, Bruno?" Miss G was about to rush by me on the stairs when she abruptly stopped. "I thought I saw you out of the corners of my tired eyes." She hovered for a moment, then continued the trek all the way up the stairs. Her breaths were heavy, as were her steps. She wore the same clip in her hair as I remembered. It impaled the bun in the back of her head and dipped into the rest of her thinned hair.

"Good to see you, Miss G," I yelled up the stairs, watching her disappear above me. She couldn't stand still for too long. I took the rest of the stairs down by twos, excited to see everyone. As soon as I stepped onto the floor, I realized that nothing was really the same.

"Duncan! Duncan Boggs!" I shouted. I saw him pop out of the kitchen doorway and I dashed over. His back was to me, but he turned around at my voice. The man who stood in front of me was *not* Duncan at all. He gave me the strangest look, like I was some sort of lost dog.

"Uhh. Ahem. Who might you be?" He had wiry, bushy eyebrows and stubby eyelashes. His face was round and his cheeks puffed out in his own state of unsureness.

"I—I apologize. I thought you were someone else, from behind. I used to work here, and I was looking for this girl, Pauline, and a couple others. Duncan, Bentley, Mr. Lemont—"

"Mr. Lemont? Oh. He's in his pantry. Go knock on the door." The man pointed toward the wooden door I was so familiar with. There was a tag on it, reading *Mr. Lemont.* I thanked him and did not hesitate to go right over and knock. I rapped on the door half a dozen times before it opened. But the man who came before me was not Mr. Lemont at all.

"*Bentley?*" I stuttered. No, it was not Mr. Lemont. It was his son.

"Actually Bruno, its Mr. Lemont now." He clasped his hands behind his back, as if he were contemplating my sudden appearance. The corners of his judgmental eyes pulled in. "So you decided to come back? No one really knew what happened to you."

"I did something ridiculous in servant standards. I overstepped my place as an employee here. It's no big deal now." I popped his inflated bubble of assumptions. He looked pretty disappointed, like he'd been waiting for some grand story of deception or mystery.

"I came to see you all. I'm sorry it's been this long, actually. Where's Pauline? She's got to be in the scullery, right? I brought her this." I held up a leather-bound notebook, like the one I wrote music in. This one had the letter P burned into the front cover, and it had lines in it instead of music staves.

"Bruno... I'm afraid you're probably four years too late."

"No. Really? She quit?"

"No... she was taken to jail. Miss G went in her room and found a whole box of stolen items. A pile of them! Little things, like pins, toys, even a pair of broken glasses. Nevertheless, they were stolen. Not to mention, she and her sidekick, Wayne, stole food to feed a couple of stray felines that came by occasionally." He nodded to a passing footman, waiting for him to be clear of sight before he continued. "Honestly, a good riddance. I liked Pauline, but I had no idea she was so... so *devious*."

I couldn't believe my ears. Of course, the story appeared to add up. It would explain why she and Wayne were close. Even though it was done and over with, something still bothered me. I looked at the notebook in my hand. She had told me that she never had anything of her own. Those words had been my incentive to buy her the notebook in the first place. I had even written the English and German alphabet in it. She had mentioned how she could barely read, so I figured I could help. Suddenly, her words weighed so much more.

"I liked Pauline. I guess I can't give this to her, then." My grip on the notebook tightened. Before I could think too deeply about it, I made myself speak. "What about Duncan and Wayne?"

"They're both gone. They have moved on. You know, Bruno, these jobs don't pay as much as they used to. They've got little value. So many are getting rid of their servants completely. I feel blessed to even be employed." He had an aura of nostalgia, which made me want to run away. It was like taking a shot of pure guilt; it would start off okay, then the aftertaste would rot your mouth.

"Oh," I replied, staring at my feet. "So you and Miss G are the only ones who stayed?"

"No. Mrs. Hardwick is still in the kitchen. She's losing her hearing, though. I do pity her. And that ladies' maid, Sarah, is still here. Both Breaker women insisted on keeping Sarah."

"Who have I been replaced with?" It spiked my curiosity. I couldn't imagine too many people willing to take on the task of assisting Claude Breaker.

"Finnegan Keldman. Well, call him Keldman. He attends to both Mr. Breaker and Lord Breaker himself. Mr. Breaker does not like Keldman on most days, so he only goes to assist if absolutely necessary." Bentley had gotten more freckles... if that was humanly possible. They even detailed his eyelids.

"Mr. Breaker is hard to accommodate. I'm well aware of *that*."

"Yes, *indeed*," he agreed, nodding his head vigorously. The slightest smirk lifted his cheeks.

"Congratulations on your appointment of butler, then. It seems like a true honor. I'm glad you were able to take over for your father, like you'd always wanted."

"Yes, I feel a sense of completeness. I like this job very much."

"Good, good," I answered. There was a short moment of flashbacks shared between us.

"I should go say hello to Mrs. Hardwick," I concluded, turning my head to look at the kitchen door. Oddly enough, I didn't smell anything cooking yet.

"Yes, I daresay you should. It will do her good to see a new face. She gets irritated rather quickly and she's always complaining about being cooped up in the house. Maybe you will be her breath of fresh air for today," he joked.

"Possibly. I don't want to interrupt you anymore. Thank you, Mr. Lemont." I gave him a slight bow and made my way to the kitchen. It had only been five years, but for some reason, I found myself missing it.

♪ ♪ ♪

"Where have you *been*? I could have written two full *novels* in the time you have been gone! I was about to call the police," Estella exaggerated when I appeared in the sitting room.

"Then why didn't you? I bet your brother could have. He could have written *three*, I bet." I played right along, stirring her up.

"Oh, never mind him." She came over to me with one of the pieces I had written. It was a shorter piece in the key of C flat. "Here. I need you to help me with this part. Line three measure one." She held the third page to my face.

"I can help you afterward. Come on. It's time for me to honor your race challenge." She looked at me as if I was someone else. Soon, the unfamiliarity melted away and she grinned like she was a schoolgirl.

"Where are you *going*? You're going to have to forfeit! The maze is the other way, you clown!" she shouted at me between giggles. I took off in the direction of the wisteria tunnel as soon as we were out the door. A car was pulling up, and a ghastly look stained Flora's face as we raced by. Her nose was pressed to the window of the back seat. We turned toward the side yard. I slowed to make it fair, pumping my legs harder as soon as I caught a glimpse of Estella at my side. She didn't bother looking at me or the car. She strived to keep up with her shoes in her hands.

I made it into the tunnel first, leaning my hands on my knees to catch my breath. She came to a slow behind me, wiping her mouth and tossing her heels on the ground.

"You cheater. This doesn't count!" She swarmed around me like a flustered bee.

"You did better than I thought," I quipped.

"What is that supposed to mean? Hmm?" She rolled her eyes. "I'm not one of *those* girls, Leo. I grew up in the country, remember? I can hold my own." Even though she lost, she relayed it with confidence.

"Ow," I winced suddenly, going down on one knee. "I think I twisted my ankle or something." I put both of my hands around my ankle, putting as much pressure on it as I could. It felt numb.

"You did? Let me see." She came over, crouching down in front of me, but I dismissed it. It wasn't something she could assist with.

England
The Violinist

"No, no. I'll be okay," he insisted again and again. He held his ankle, and wouldn't let go. It was probably swollen. I didn't understand why he wouldn't let me see it. "I remembered these flowers and wanted to pick a bunch of them. You know my neighbor, George? Today is his older sister's birthday. I told him I'd get him wisteria to give to her."

"That's very kind. But let me go get help. I'll find Charlie and we'll help you back—"

"No. I can get back. Hold on a moment. Actually, can you reach those flowers above you?" He looked up over my head, and I followed his gaze, standing.

"I think so." I went up on my toes, staring into the crown of hanging flowers above me. My sky had turned from blue to purple. The flowers were so thick and clustered that nothing could be seen above them. I wrapped my fingers around a few of them.

"Uh, reach your arm a little to the right. More. More. There. Yes, okay, now the left. Nope, your other left," he directed, secretly laughing at me.

"These?" I asked sweetly, trying hard to overlook his exaggerated specifics.

"Yes. Those should be fine," I heard him say. I bunched them into one hand and was handing them off to him when I froze. I could feel my nails dig into the stems.

His hands were outstretched in front of him, reaching out to me. They did not tremble in the slightest. He had the most worried, vulnerable look in his eyes, but his shy smile softened it. In his hands rested a silver ring—with a beautiful peach cream pearl mounted on it.

"Estella Ruth Breaker, would you marry me?"

England

The Pianist

When Mutti first started to teach me English, I was three years old. She'd read to me—the same books, over and over. Then, I'd recite them and we would translate. She read to me all the time in English. The first word I ever said and understood in English was the word yes. A simple three letter word used to answer almost any question, regardless if I understood it or not.

As I went to bed that night, I recalled everything from the afternoon. How I had asked for that same, three-lettered word to be given back to me.

It was.

It was given back without second thought, without an ounce of regret, without pity, envy, jealousy, anger, disappointment, or greed. One single word that took the present second, cut it off, and planted a whole new sleeve of seconds to last a lifetime in its place.

The wedding was planned for the following year. Estella wanted it in the fall and I wanted spring, but I went with her idea.

I visited her as often as I could, between practicing four to five hours each day. Her family seemed leery about me at first, but her father wanted her to be able to choose what she wanted in life. He had granted me the permission in the first place. Her mother, on the other hand… we had some rough edges to sand.

"You know, why don't we move this piano to the ballroom? It would be less distracting to the people in the library, and it probably has much better acoustics," I thought aloud during one of our rehearsal sessions. I came to a halt in the middle of a piece. She set down her violin.

"It doesn't seem like a terrible idea. We could roll it," she suggested. "We've had it placed in there before, after all. It would probably be a good home for it."

"You don't think Charlie would mind too much, right?" I asked unsurely, debating the idea in my head. It would probably be dusty and cold, which wouldn't be too good for the health of the piano, especially one like this.

"Leo, Charlie isn't around enough to mind. He's become like Claude," she jeered. "Both of my brothers are like *bears*! Can you believe it? They hibernate like bears!" She shook her head, and the strands of her waved hair came loose at her ears. Her bangs were beginning to grow out; they briskly brushed against her face.

"If you say so. Then come on. Help me get this piano rolling." I pulled it away from the wall, heaving it toward the open doors of the sitting room. Estella kept the door open, pressing her back against it while I directed it between the furniture. I leaned in, taking slow steps until it passed into the hallway.

She left her violin in the sitting room and sat on the piano, sliding onto it with ease. She was trying not to laugh as she called out "Onward!" We passed one of the servants in the hallway, who looked more confused than when I had called him Duncan.

"I'll find the lights." She jumped off and dashed ahead of me into the sun-dusted room. The hardwood floor was dulled and the chandelier lay in the center of the floor like its time in life had expired. The crystals that dangled from it drooped comfortably. "Uh. Never mind," she realized, staring at the chandelier. "I can call someone up to start a fire if you wish."

"No. That's alright," I grunted, setting the piano in place on the far side of the room. She went over to the windows that were the size of French doors, and threw open the curtains. Light poured in, making the dust glow. Bronze candelabras were attached to the walls, holding candles that looked as old as the piano. The wicks were shriveled and hunched.

"Miss Breaker, this came for you." Bentley, or the new Mr. Lemont, appeared in the doorway and approached Estella. He handed her a package with the word FRAGILE in bold letters on the front. "Be careful with this. It was just delivered." Mr. Lemont turned his head to me. "Good afternoon, Bruno," he acknowledged respectfully.

"Oh. This is so strange! Thank you, Lemont. I shall handle it with the utmost care," she assured, beaming at the package with wonder.

"You're welcome, Miss." He bowed slightly at her, and backed away.

"This is so arbitrary, isn't it? I don't remember ordering anything," she pondered aloud, feeling the package.

"I don't know. I should probably leave, though. We can finish up tomorrow. I told Edward I'd meet him at four—"

"It's not four yet. Please, come help me open this, will you?" She gently placed the package at her feet and began to tear at it. Each piece she tore off, she crumpled in her hands. Out of nowhere, one flew at me and hit me in the stomach.

"Are you not the least bit interested? I never receive anything from the mail," she exclaimed, tossing another piece at me playfully.

"It's for you, though. It's probably none of my business. Let me go get your violin from the sitting room." I started for the door. The package had come at least a whole week late.

"Leo, you're my fiancé. Of course it's your business—" she began, pulling open the flaps of the cardboard and reaching in. Her eyes lit up before she even pulled her gift out. Gently, she lifted it, marveling.

"T—this is from you, isn't it?" she gasped. She couldn't take her eyes off her new violin.

"Yes. It was supposed to come in a long while ago, but it got held up. *Please* say you like it." I bit the inside of my cheek, sitting down on the floor beside her. The violin was specially made. What made it so unique was that it was made of glass. The edges of the body had light golden decals that could only be seen at a certain angle in the light. The bridge was wooden, of course, and the bow itself was also wooden.

"It's stunning!" she breathed. "But it depends on the sound." She held it as if she were afraid to touch it.

"You should try it out. Your other one has had its days. The tuning knobs don't stay put. I've heard it go flat in the middle of rehearsal."

"But you didn't have to get me a whole new violin! You should have said something. I would have brought it somewhere to get it fixed. This violin should be for the top violinist in the world. I'm nowhere *near* deserving this." She was still in awe, plucking the strings and reaching for the bow.

"You are," I stated firmly. I wished I could have taken a picture of her there. She had a welcoming, skeptical smile that gleamed on the glass of her new instrument. Her legs were bent to the side, covered by a simple chiffon dress, and her expression was priceless.

"I can't even—"

"I had someone schedule us for a concert. In two months, we will be playing these duets. And for that, I—I want to thank you." I could feel my voice weaken as I looked at her.

"What?" She sprang to her feet, almost laughing in happiness. She didn't even realize that she had jumped up, in all of her excitement. "Thank me? Leo, I did noth—"

I closed my eyes, and opened them again, finding my words. It was difficult for me. How do you put two parallel lives together in words? My life as a child, and my life now. Somehow, she managed to make them intersect and actually like each other, something I had never thought I wanted. She handed me my talent back, my will, my passion, and told me to take them and keep them. They were my gifts. There wasn't a physical object that I could give her that could ever serve as an equal to that. So many times I was forced to take those gifts. But when she held them to me, I suddenly wanted them back, so I took them. Opa would have been proud of me. He had been the first one to give. I had lost the gifts with Papa, and somehow, Estella had found them and had given them back. Just like with the pearl that she wore so proudly on her finger.

"I can't thank you enough, you know that?" I interrupted before she could say anything else senseless.

She placed the violin delicately in the box and stood in front of me. I lost what I was going to say in the deepest part of her eyes. I tapped her chin—a running joke we now had. She rocked up onto her toes and hugged me so hard I thought she was trying to strangle me. It could have been a bit of both. I could feel her chin poking my shoulder and her fingers on the nape of my neck.

We stood there for a while. Two breaths fused into one. I heard the seconds tick by, and I cringed deep inside. I took their echoes in my head and stretched out the constant ticking. Little by little, I banished the metronome that contained me.

"Leo, you don't have to thank me. Just don't move from this spot." Her soft breath tickled my ear.

England

The Violinist

"Well, look here. You're mentioned in the paper." Claude had unexpectedly joined us for breakfast. Charlie and Momma refused to meet his eyes when he spoke. I leaned toward him, sneaking a peek.

He tapped his finger on my name. It was on the top of the second page, with a picture hovering above it.

"Estella? *You* are in the paper? This is incredulous! What for?" Momma extended her hand toward Claude, waiting for him to pass it, but he did not acknowledge her.

"Oh! It… it was meant to be a surprise," I huffed nervously. "I'm um… I'm having my first concert. I bought all of you tickets for the front row. Leo and I are performing on July ninth." The words spilled from my mouth, uncalled for.

"Well, I cannot attend. I have to be back in Germany in two days, you know that. It seems like my professor has taken a great interest in my novel," Claude remarked.

"You are performing? Oh my heavens—"

"Momma… I know I told you that I would not get too involved with music or performing and all of that, but please don't be—"

"Angry? Is that what you were going to say, Stell? I am not angry in the least. With his impeccable talent, you will bring pride to us. Mind you, I

275

do not like that man in many ways, mainly because he is downright *rude*, but I've heard from Charlie that he is *very* well known." I thought I had gone deaf. I blinked hard, replaying her words in my head. Who was this person? Where was my Momma?

"I—I'd say he is." I stumbled over my sentence. Maybe she was ill.

"Surely you can put two and two together, my daughter. Think of all the money that you will be making! How extraordinary." Of course. That was what mattered. My siblings and I wanted to fall off our seats. So, in Momma's point of view, it was okay to take a job thought to be unrespectable, as long as it paid well. It felt completely backward. Next week, she would develop a whole new opinion, and tell me how disgraceful I was. I by no means found being a musician disrespectable, but not all the world agreed with me.

"Possibly?" I squeaked.

"Stell," Claude whispered hoarsely, "I think you should read this."

"I did. Isn't it wonderful? I am *so* excited." I rubbed the palms of my hands together, smiling widely.

"No. *This.*" His voice was even lower now, and his eyes darted from me to the page uneasily. He shifted in his chair so I could see the bottom half of the page. "Stell, you should take this page to Bruno. I think he'd enjoy seeing it, since he doesn't get the paper all the time. Why don't you bring this to him?" His voice suddenly grew loud, like he felt it important to announce it to everyone.

"But he—"

"No, he says he doesn't get it. Here, take this page and show him. He will surely be pleased." He thrust the page roughly into my hands, eyes scanning across the table. I squinted, stumped by his behavior.

"He... he would like that." I went along with the story, and Claude took a breath of relief. Apparently I had said something right.

He stood, asking to be excused and went up to his room. I folded the page quietly, finishing up my coffee that I didn't like anyway. The war had taught me not to be wasteful.

♪ ♪ ♪

"Please be home. Please be home," I chanted to myself as I approached Leo's house that afternoon. It was unusually warm outside. It was low tide, so the waves barely curled at the edge of the sand. Snails clustered like beads on the nearby rocks.

Before I even knocked at the door, he opened it. "I need to talk to you about something," he uttered. He was wearing a cap, and dirt covered the front of his shirt. I didn't even ask about it.

"Of course, but first, you have to read this! I can't believe someone even wrote this in the paper." I waved the page in front of him.

"Ugh. I *knew* that it would be in the English papers any day now." He closed the door behind him and we took an unsettling walk on the brim of the shore.

"What do you mean? You knew about this?"

"Briefly," he paused. "My father mentioned it."

"Well, let me read it to you," I replied bitterly. "The article is by someone named James Norton." I paused. "'Famous pianist Leonardo Leonhardt once again plans to take the stage, after running away from it six years ago. He plans to perform in England at the City Varieties Music Hall, July ninth at seven o'clock. With him, new to the world of music, will be violinist Estella Breaker. Leonardo, now back in the music industry, has taken to creating and composing his own music, which he will showcase. We turn to ask a few of his fans about the upcoming event:

Norton: As a fan of his from the time he was a boy, what do you say to this, Mrs. Anstillo?

Anstillo: I say it is about time! There's no doubt that boy has talent, but he clearly has no motive and no respect. That day, he ran off the stage like he was seven years old! He needs to choose one thing or another at this point. As for me, I will not be attending. I never got my full ticket refund last time.

Norton: Thank you, Mrs. Anstillo. Mr. Harlend, What do you have to say?

Harlend: He screwed up! Musicians have to take their career seriously. I play the cello, myself, and it takes dedication. He thinks he can come back and be accepted again just because of the value of his name! I also heard rumors that his father disowned him. Good, it's about time he got some instruction.

Norton: We have time for one more. Mr. Genobe?

Genobe: You see, Mr. Norton, when a part of the brain is unusually enhanced, usually another part suffers. Many child prodigies are socially strange individuals. It's a true statement. They strive in nothing other than their chosen pathway. This proves to be true with Leonardo. I give him credit for attempting to come back, but people don't want to be bothered with the drama. They want to hear their music and leave. Unfortunately, I don't think many people will be going to his upcoming concert. That is my hunch.'" I took a breath before breaking into another rant.

"Can you believe this? They *purposely* interviewed people who are against you. How inconsiderate! Those rotten, *shameful swine*," I seethed, crumbling the paper into my hand and tossing it into the lurking waves that grabbed at our feet.

"I was expecting some of that," Leo sighed. His face was extremely pale, and drained of blood. He jammed the toe of his shoe into the sand and dragged it along. "But I was a fool and told myself that the world was a kinder place. Let's talk about something else." He straightened his posture and dusted his hands off. "Have you read your brother's novel?" It was a random comment that shook my mind from the previous conversation, just for a moment.

"Claude's novel? No," I snorted. "He wouldn't dare show me. He rarely lets anyone in his presence—never mind into his head."

He raised his eyebrows. "*Really?*"

"Don't look so surprised," I chortled. "Have you *met* Claude?"

"He gave me a manuscript a month or so back. I just finished it, last Tuesday maybe?"

"Really? What was it like?" I didn't show it, but I was slightly offended that Claude hadn't shown me. "I cannot believe he simply gave it to you. Was there some sort of collateral involved? Did he go into some sad story and make you feel sorry for him?"

"No!" he replied quickly. "He... he wanted me to give an opinion on it."

"Well, I'm glad he thinks your opinion matters. He treats everyone else as if we were scraps in a junkyard." I clenched my teeth, tasting the bitterness in the back of my throat.

"Oh, nonsense!" Leo assured, pointing his finger at me. "He does value his family. You should read his book if you don't believe me."

"I'm sure it's like every other novel on the planet," I countered.

"It's not. It's quite sad, actually. You'd be surprised by what someone can show in their writing."

"Hmm." We turned back toward his house, sinking into the sand with each step. I looped my arm in his without thought, caressing the top of his hand. "Maybe I can get him to show me, though—"

"I doubt it," we said in unison.

England

The Pianist

It was time.

I took the only pocket watch I owned and held it in front of my face. It twirled slowly, like a ballerina in a music box, round and round, dangling right in front of my nose. Then, I pressed it to my ear. The seconds vibrated, sending tremors through my ears, scuttling over my lips and across my chest. They did not stop at my feet. They never stopped, only grabbing at another host like a parasite.

I stood on the polished stage, dressed in a suit I had bought the day before. An old man crouched by the piano, hitting the same key over and over to make sure it was in tune. It was a bit flat. He noticed it as well, and began to adjust it while I looked out to the empty seats.

"Leo!"

I turned and Estella had set foot on the stage. She hurried toward me. She wore a beaded tulle gown that I wished I knew the color of. As she drew closer I could see that the wooden beads and tiny pearls made decals over her middle. She looked as if she wanted to smile, but worry stopped her. Her eyes twinkled like bottomless pools, making the stage light reflect in them. I felt my heart flare, whacking against my chest.

"Oh, I do apologize that I'm late." Her hands were pressed to her cheeks as she shook her head anxiously. "Now we don't have a lot of time to rehearse."

"I practiced before you got here. Then they moved the piano, and I think it's almost tuned. We should try some scales—"

"I'm so afraid that I am not going to remember all of the music. Are you sure I cannot bring a music stand and place it here?"

"You have them all memorized. I'm witness to that." I took her hand in mine and knelt down, pressing my lips to her chilled skin.

"The piano is all set, sir. Give it a try." The old man pointed at the piano and left, carrying his box of tools with him.

"Do you like my dress? Flora altered it for me." She stared down at it, watching as the ends skimmed the floor.

"The dress? Oh, yes. But I was far too busy looking at *you* to take much notice of the dress," I replied smoothly, taking a seat at the piano. The bench matched it perfectly, but it was different than most. It was a bit longer, and wider, more suitable for two people.

I could hear her throw off a small laugh behind me. "I'm going to retrieve my violin."

♪ ♪ ♪

People's voices traveled through the thick velvet curtain. I could barely hear myself think. My leg bounced up and down, and I pretended I was playing, drumming my fingers on my knee. I sat in a little room, all by myself. Estella was going over one of our songs in another room. I listened intently, picking up on how her fingers did not stumble, and how she engaged her dynamics.

My heart began to race, and could not spot the finish line. All over again, I was becoming a nervous wreck. My breathing quickened, my hands trembled. I couldn't stop it. Suddenly, Estella loomed over me. I hadn't even noticed that she had come in. I was too busy being locked in my own head.

"I thought I saw you sneak in here. What are you doing? We're on in two minutes."

"N—nothing. I need a chance to be alone." I was able to keep my voice steady. She patted my shoulders, kissed my forehead, and backed out of the room without another question. I started to count out loud. It was very soft, so no one else would hear me. When I got to sixty, I forced myself to stand up and walk out.

Estella was waiting for me, along with a few backstage operators. She paced in front of the L-shaped stairs that led onto the stage and gripped the neck of her violin until someone announced our names.

My heart was in my throat by now. She watched me carefully. I couldn't understand how she appeared calm. Gently, she reached for my arm and gave me a tug.

"Leo, it's quite alright," she whispered. My stiffened legs started to edge forward. Now we were right at the top of the steps. The only thing separating me from the crowd was a thin curtain.

"And now, please welcome Mr. Leonardo Bruno Leonhardt, pianist, and Mrs. Estella Ruth Leonhardt, violinist!"

"Apparently they have assumed that we are married already," she giggled in a bare whisper as we stepped out from behind the curtain. It would have been funny at any other moment but that one. There were only a few empty chairs in the audience. People clapped as we walked across the stage. I took a side glance to see Estella's reaction.

Her eyes were wide with fear. She had never seen a crowd so big. I felt as if I was holding *her* up at this point, instead of vice versa. She walked wherever I guided her. Her feet didn't stop to think because her head was so preoccupied.

We bowed at the center of the stage, and I took my place at the piano, sitting more toward the left side of the bench. Estella sat down next to me. Her back was to my shoulder because she had to face the crowd directly.

"Leo," she whispered over her shoulder, "I'm terrified." It was as simplistic as that. Her words would have been laid level with that of a child, as if it were the same as being scared of the dark, or scared of a monster under the bed. But being there, right beside her, made the words hit so much harder. It wasn't a flimsy, stupid thing. It was actual fear that was hovering between us. To anyone else, it would seem like nothing. Nothing, or plain nonexistent.

I didn't answer her. Instead, I placed my hands on the piano, and began our first piece. The best method for getting past fear was distraction.

Her arms snapped up like rubber bands as she secured her violin under her chin.

For the first two duets she was hesitant. Hesitant about her entrances, hesitant about her dynamics. I knew that she knew what she was doing, but she had a pit of doubt. Sometimes I'd whisper to her. Something quick like, 'faster,' or 'quiet.' Her tone was impeccable, as usual. It filled my ears, keeping me in time. Confidence bounced between us.

By the time we played the last piece, she had decided to stand up beside the piano. She stayed frozen in place, waiting for me to begin. The duet sounded beautiful at first, like something that could make someone fall asleep, but it became urgent and loud toward the end. It was called 'Crossed Flags.' I had written it sometime after the war. I created it with the image of the war in mind, but it wasn't all pounding on the keys. Some people didn't feel the sorrow of the war as much as others, so I made sure to play it as if I was feeling the loss in Germany, and then celebrating the win in Britain. It had almost disgusting dissonance at parts, but the main melody was stunning.

We locked eyes, and I nodded for her to start. She kind of smiled at me, the type of smile that a doll can give you, making you feel afraid and yet compassionate. Something flashed across her face, and she had an unsteady unpredictability about her. It immediately set me off when I entered. The tempo grew, and *mezzo forte* was pushed into *fortissimo*. She had scattered sixteenth notes, while I threw in arpeggios. It was almost like we were suddenly competing against each other. I glanced at my hands, and right up at her. She was staring me down, not missing a beat. It was then that I understood her game. She was challenging me. A little louder. A little faster. A little more emotion.

The violin screamed, rolling down a scale. It was the only type of scream in the world that could manage to sound beautiful. My left hand flew down to the bass section, while my right danced on the same chord of keys. The melody intensified. I pressed my foot to the pedal, letting my notes ring out. We were in unison now, as my left hand harmonized and then jumped back to the bass.

She swayed to the rhythm, her eyes darting from mine to my hands. The war was breaking out right in front of us, and it was like no one else existed. I was numb to the piercing eyes of the crowd.

It ended abruptly. I wrote it like that on purpose. It certainly wouldn't get an award for being soothing, but the story it told was unlike any other. We cut off at different times, only varying by seconds, but I didn't hold it against myself or her. Everything smeared together from then on, starting with the white keys on the piano as we left the stage. It was like they melded to form a block of solid ivory. Estella's face brought my eyes into focus.

"You were absolutely incredible, Estella." I forced myself to whisper as we took a final bow. She probably didn't hear me over the applause. I was in shock, meeting the eyes of everyone in the crowd. We had shown them.

"What?" She tried to shout, but it did no good.

"You were incredible!" I called louder, grinning from ear to ear. I could see her staring at my lips, trying to read what I was saying. She tilted her head, still unable to hear a word of it.

"*What?* I cannot—" she pointed to her ear.

"You—" I began, but it was useless. I kissed her cheek softly, and we walked off the stage. Echoes of whistles and claps thundered behind us.

♪ ♪ ♪

"Can you *believe* we just did that? Oh, I wish I were home and we could have a glass of Lemont's favorite champagne to celebrate." Estella wouldn't stop smiling. She slumped in her chair, while I sat at the old oak desk that was placed in the corner of the hotel room. It was quite a small room with bare walls and miniature furniture. There was one window that let in a draft, and could not be closed all the way.

"No, not really," I huffed in awe. "I'm just happy that we didn't get tomatoes thrown at us when we first came out. The newspapers had me worried," I chuckled, opening my notebook.

"Tomatoes! Oh, it's a ridiculous thought now. No one would dare throw a tomato at such an *impeccable* performance. I cannot wait to hear what those *idiotic* newspapermen have to say about it tomorrow," she raised her eyebrows, daring to laugh.

I didn't reply. They could always find something if they really wanted to; I was positive about that. It was purely based on whether they felt like being nice. She yawned, which made me yawn. I glanced at my pocket watch, pulling it from its chain and holding it in my palm.

Tick.

Tick.

Tick.

"What do you have there?" She eased up, peering curiously at my hand.

"Nothing, really." I stood up and walked past her, hoisting the window up even farther.

"Leo, what are you *doing?*"

"I hate this thing." I smoothed my fingers over the face and gripped the round edge like I was holding a skipping stone. Endless grass fields rolled out in front of me. I pulled my arm back, and sent it flying through the air. The moonlight cascaded upon the gold, and then it disappeared among the grass beds. I never heard it hit the ground.

"What on earth…? Why did you do that? If you hated it, you could have at least brought it to a pawn shop and gotten money for it. You're being rash." She slapped her hands on the armrests of the chair, scowling at me. Bubbles of confusion floated around her head.

"It's a deeper matter than that. Don't waste your time thinking about it."

"Was that supposed to be a sort of pun?" Her scowl broke into a smirk, softening her whole face. "I will never fully understand you. The only time I came remotely close was tonight. You are much more open when you perform, do you know that?" She crossed her ankles, poking at the decals on her dress.

"I never specifically realized, no." I leaned my arms on the windowsill. "I always feel different, but I can't describe it." I could picture myself sitting there on the bench, having the piano translate my every thought. Having it alter the scenery around me. My sight was removed as the sound created a world around me. I watched that world pass by, and when I stood up and took the final bow, that world disappeared. And here I was.

"That's what makes it so endearing." She stood up and wrapped her fingers around my wrists. I unclenched my hands and watched as she traced her thumb over my knuckles to my fingertips. My veins buzzed with her touch. She kissed my palm, stretched it out a single moment, and then let go of my hand. I was very quiet.

"I will see you in the morning," she affirmed, looking through my eyes.

I really didn't want to go back to my room. Fatigue seemed like a foreign concept. My insides felt electrified, compared to normal days. I couldn't stop thinking about our performance. It brought me to the place where my head soared high above the clouds, and where my thoughts spurred from my heart.

"I will leave if you want me to. But first," I placed my lips on hers, pulling away and exercising my own self-control. I had my hand on the door handle when I turned back to her. "You were incredible tonight. I wish I had half of your courage."

She cast her eyes to the floor, but I could sense her smile. "Thanks." I was pretty much out the door when I heard her call me back. "Leo," she cleared her throat. "One more thing… if you don't mind," she peeped shyly, turning her back toward me. I stayed in place.

"That's not a good idea…." I started, but approached her anyway; my eyes were fixed on the back of her dress. The zipper was gold and almost unnoticeable, but I had spotted it like a landmark when she was seated on the piano bench beside me.

I placed one hand on the curve of her neck, and took the zipper between my fingers, feeling a strong, almost magnetic pull. Her breaths were stifled, as if she were tensed up. I guided the zipper down, rushed and choppy at first, but easing up as it stopped at her lower back. She didn't move. She could feel my eyes, like a deer frozen in a vast field.

My fingertips hovered over her spine for an hours-long second. I didn't want to resist anymore. Didn't want to choose my head over my heart. Didn't want to do any of it, but I had too much respect for her to disregard it. Patience. Patience. Control.

"Goodnight." I pulled my hand up to her shoulder and grazed my lips against her neck. She whispered something in return as I backed out and headed toward my room.

Part IV

Finale

1941

England:
The Violinist

I awaited his letters every day, but I only received one a month. Somewhere in America, a man named Leonardo Leonhardt sat and withered
away in an internment camp, mattering to no one. Over and over I heard
his songs in my head. I knew from the day of our first concert that he had
some sort of eternal grudge against time itself, and now I knew why. I too
held that grudge, and kept it burning in the pit of my heart every time I pictured him throwing that pocket watch out the window. I hadn't seen him in
seven years. Seven. It was a different number when three hundred and sixty
five days was wrapped into each count.

"Estella, how does this look? Stell!" Flora pulled on my shoulder,
wrenching my gaze from the window. Flora had given up her tailoring business, and had taken over a flower shop called Poised Petals. Unfortunately,
the war was crushing it, after all these years in business. Flora was busy arranging Flowers for her daughter's eighteenth birthday. Even the sweet smell
of the lilacs, roses, and daffodils combined couldn't brighten my day. Every
day was dull. Every day shook and trembled like the one before it, making
crumbs of the buildings above our heads. She held up a bouquet of roses and
lilies in front of her face. They were in full bloom, stretching their petals to a
sun they couldn't even see. It was hard to believe she was concerned about
flowers, now.

I admired the clueless innocence of flowers. Hundreds of widows would receive flowers after the war, and yet, they would all perish and mean nothing later on. It was a makeshift happiness.

"Wonderful," I mumbled, fixing my eyes back out the window onto the dead street. A few blocks down, men gathered to pick through the remains of a church. I stared at them.

"Estella, you must come to. Listen to me, I refuse to see you hollow yourself out!" Flora hissed in my ear. "Jackson needs you now more than ever. You need to join the world again, or I will be taking him back to my home to live with me and my children. As of now, you are in no position to take care of—"

"I will not hear of it! Don't you *ever* threaten to take my son!" Hot tears simmered in the corners of my eyes. It was like the burst of a volcano. I could feel something snap inside me. Flora saw it flash across my face, and she retreated.

"I will not be telling you again. I am only trying to do what is good for both of you."

"Good?" I sneered sourly as my lips twisted. I made sure none of the children could hear us arguing. "There is no such thing as *good* in this present."

She completely ignored my comment. "I'm leaving this place to you for a couple of hours. I have to run somewhere quickly before it closes. Do not bargain with anyone. All flowers are set price, and watch out for smugglers. They always go after the seeds." She summoned Arlen, her youngest, and both of them ran out of the shop. "Also," she yelled to me, pulling the door back open. "Trim the stems of the tulips, if you can manage." She smacked the door shut before her comment really attacked me.

"Momma, Momma. Can we go home?" Jackson walked around a barrel full of nutritious soil and grabbed a tiny fistful of my dress. He stared up at me with a sheepish grin, clicking his tongue and simply enjoying the day. He had round cheeks and eyelashes that were so dark they could have been dusted with coal. His cap fell too far down over his head, so I lifted it and bent down to his level.

"Auntie wants us to stay here for a bit, okay?"

"But *why?*" he asked innocently, poking lightly at the freckles on my cheek bones. "Arlen didn't have to stay. Momma, why are your eyes red?" he suddenly asked.

"Momma is allergic to pollen," I replied easily, wiping my eyes with the back of my hand.

"What exactly is allergic? Do your eyes hurt?"

The door opened, making a creaking sound as the bell chimed up above. The footsteps stopped.

"Hello? Anyone here? I need to buy a bouquet of roses, but… I haven't got any money. Please. Someone?" the voice called.

I dreaded standing up to meet the customer. It was probably a homeless man. As bad as I felt, I knew Flora would never get over it if I gave handouts. I rubbed my eyes one last time, and stood, peeping up over a small bed of petunias.

"Sir, I'm *very* sorry but—" I pushed my hair out of my face and froze. I had no recollection of what I said, or had the slightest clue of what I would say next.

"Jack— Jackson. This man is our twentieth customer today. Bring him a yellow rose from over there," my lips jabbered and then fell slack. Jackson sighed and jogged off behind me, returning with the flower. He went around the table full of daisies and held the flower up to the day's special winner. He smiled, urging the man to take it.

"No. Jackson, that's pink. Yellow, darling," my voice barely came out.

"*Momma…*" he grunted, tramping back to the rose section. He pushed his cap up, approaching the customer with another flower. "I'm sorry, mister. Do you have a momma? If you do, you have to know how they are sometimes." He held up his small hand that wrapped around the stem of the rose.

"Jackson, that one is red—"

"No, no. It's perfect." The customer bent down to Jackson, taking the rose. "Do you have trouble with your colors, Jackson?"

"I dunno. Are you a soldier? I want to be a soldier when I grow up." Jackson stepped back and saluted like he had a hinged arm. I approached the two of them. My eyes stayed pinned on the customer.

"A soldier? Not at all. I'm a pianist." His voice was tired and haggard.

"Oh. But... that doesn't sound fun, mister. My Momma is a violinist."

My heart lurched, causing all of my hate to flood away. I stood right behind my son, placing my hand on his shoulder. "Jackson." My voice split. "Jackson, this is your father." It was hard to say those words because I was smiling so hard. I could feel it spread through my whole face and body, like a swell of joy.

Leo stood up, and handed me the rose before crushing me in a hug. He refused to let go. Tears stung my eyes, but it was a good sting. He wore plain, lightly worn clothes, and his skin was streaked with dirt. He smelled like the salt of the ocean and yet the rich soil of the earth at the same time, making the images in my head skip like a broken record.

England

The Pianist

There stood two flags. Two crossed flags, like the title of my duet. The thought nearly knocked me over when I realized it. I had my arms wrapped around her torso, and the pungent odor of flowers stuck my lungs. Though at the moment I couldn't tell which side was winning. Which flag would come out on top? It didn't matter in the slightest. Yes, there was a war going on outside the walls of the tiny flower shop. But inside, a German pianist and an English violinist were perfectly at peace, for one solid minute. And I promised myself then to stop hating the seconds that ticked by. I promised myself and my son and my wife that I would take this solid minute of peace, put a fermata over it, and cast it out into a lifetime.

About the Author

Lindsey Catanzaro's love for writing all started with quotes. Throughout fourth grade, a daily quote would be announced over the loudspeaker at school, and it instantly had an impact on her. This sparked an interest that has grown with her as she enters her junior year of high school. Now sixteen, Lindsey has engaged in various types of writing, but has had her heart set on writing a book. She lives in Rhode Island with her parents and younger brother.

www.ingramcontent.com/pod-product-compliance
Lightning Source LLC
Chambersburg PA
CBHW030645020726
47493CB00006B/1876